MOON UNDERFOOT

MOON UNDERFOOT

BOBBY COLE

THOMAS & MERCER

Published by Thomas & Mercer
P.O. Box 400818
Las Vegas, NV 89140

ISBN-13: 9781612187211
ISBN-10: 1612187218

This book is dedicated to the fine folks of West Point, Mississippi. I'm humbled by their enthusiastic support.

He lifted me out of the slimy pit,

out of the mud and mire;

He set my feet on a rock

and gave me a firm place to stand.

—Psalm 40:2

CHAPTER 1

—— ☾ ——

As darkness enveloped the newly constructed two-story house, the sliver of moon added to the gloom that was a chilly autumn Mississippi evening. Scout was stretched out on the kitchen floor, sound asleep, with her favorite chew toy nearby.

Morgan Crosby had just finished cleaning the kitchen and strongly suspected she had math homework in her immediate future. A quick glance at the wall clock revealed that she was missing *Dancing with the Stars*, but she didn't really care. She was happy. Typically Jake would have had a fire burning in the den by now, but he was at a business dinner and wouldn't be home for at least another hour or so. It was blues night at Anthony's Market, and Jake's bosses loved to schedule business meetings around great food and the Delta's music that flowed there on most nights.

Morgan was thrilled with Jake's renewed interest in his career, but she still didn't like being home without him. Her therapist had promised the anxiety would slowly dissipate. She just needed time. It had been almost two years, and Morgan was doing much better. The recent move to a gated neighborhood had helped tremendously. She finally felt safe. Her face glowed as she placed a hand on her stomach and thought about the surprise she had for Jake tonight. He had no idea she had been to the doctor.

Katy suddenly came crashing down the stairs with her books in hand, ready to conquer her fifth-grade math assignment.

"I'm ready, Mom!" she exclaimed, as if Morgan should drop everything and come running.

"Okay, let me wash up," Morgan replied. "Go ahead and get started."

"Yes ma'am. We started fractions today, and they seem easy," Katy said with confidence.

Morgan dried her hands as she watched Katy enthusiastically dive into her homework. "Just let me know if you need some help."

From across the kitchen, Morgan could hear the friction of Katy's pencil against the paper. Morgan smiled, sat down at the table, and began flipping through the latest issue of *Garden & Gun*. She enjoyed the garden portion. Jake loved the guns.

When Morgan was halfway through the magazine, their normally silent cat grunted a meow, indicating he wanted to go outside. Morgan glanced up from a recipe. As she had done hundreds of times, she walked to the back door and with one hand flipped on the outside light switch. With the other, she unlocked the door and slightly opened it.

The black-and-white cat squeezed through the crack. When the tip of his tail cleared the door, Morgan slowly looked up to see the silhouette of a man less than fifteen yards away, the glow of his cigarette slightly illuminating his sinister face. He looked her dead in the eye before grinning and then stepping backward and disappearing into the darkness of the woods.

Morgan screamed, slammed the door, and quickly locked the dead bolt. Still screaming, she pushed the panic button on the house's alarm, unleashing an immediate high-pitched shrill from the speakers, which were located in the attic. Katy was wild-eyed as she watched her mother race from the touch pad to the cordless telephone and begin dialing.

With remarkable clarity, Morgan Crosby explained to the 911 operator that a prowler was outside of her house and that she needed immediate help. As she ran to the kitchen window in search of the stranger, she quickly verified her name and address. The operator dispatched the police and stayed on the line to comfort Morgan, who was now shaking uncontrollably.

"The West Point police will be there in three minutes, Mrs. Crosby," the young emergency operator said reassuringly.

"I don't know what he was doing! He was just staring, staring in the windows…at me!"

"Can you describe him?" the operator asked calmly and then alertly mouthed to another operator to also inform the sheriff's office.

"I don't know! He was standing in the shadows," Morgan said, shaking her head and realizing there was something faintly familiar about the man's profile. "I need to call my husband!"

"You mean he's not home?" the surprised operator asked.

"No! No, he's not. It's just me and my daughter."

This increased the intensity of the situation. The operator snapped her fingers at a coworker and then mouthed, "She's alone!"

"Listen, ma'am, don't hang up, okay? I need you to stay on the line until the officers get there. Do you have a cell phone handy?"

"Yes! Yes! Right here!"

"Okay, use your cell and keep this line open. The officers are getting close." The operator was trained to keep callers on the line, sometimes improvising to keep the situation under control.

"Please tell them to hurry!"

"They are, ma'am, I promise. I need you to turn on all the outside lights you've got, and then you and your daughter—what's her name?"

"Katy."

"Okay, you and Katy need to get away from the windows. Don't hang up, but run, turn the outside lights on, and come right back. Can you do that for me?"

"Yes."

"Good. Don't hang up."

Morgan wrapped her arms around the now-crying Katy in an attempt to calm her. She told Katy to sit on the kitchen floor and that she'd be right back. Katy started to protest, but Morgan turned around with a stern look and then took off for the front door. After flipping on the light switch, Morgan dashed back into the kitchen, turning off the light as she entered, hoping he couldn't see her inside. The alarm continued to blare. She hugged Katy as she sat down beside her. She picked up the landline and said, "Okay, I'm back."

"Good job. Now call your husband on your cell phone. Don't hang up this phone, though."

"Okay."

Morgan picked up her cell phone and fumbled to dial Jake's number. She started talking the moment the call connected.

"What? Just slow down. I can hardly hear you over the alarm," Jake said. He was shocked to hear her hysterics, but he was already moving in the direction of the restaurant's entrance.

"Some man was just in our backyard, looking in the windows!"

"Have you called the police!" Jake was nearly yelling as he ran toward his truck.

"Yes, I'm on the phone with them now!"

"Good. I'm on my way!"

"Hurry, Jake!" Morgan shrieked, tears of terror running down her cheeks.

"Ma'am, two units just turned into your neighborhood. But stay on the phone and don't go to the front door until I tell you to, okay?" the operator asked.

"Pleeeease tell 'em to hurry," she said frantically.

Morgan tightly squeezed Katy as they cried. The piercing alarm had surely scared off the Peeping Tom, but it was fraying both of their nerves.

CHAPTER 2

———— ☾ ————

J AKE SPED TOWARD HOME, NOT KNOWING WHAT TO EXPECT...
what to think. He'd never heard Morgan so upset; the terror
in her voice was clear.

It had been almost two years since his horrifying all-night
ordeal at the Dummy Line in West Alabama. Not a day went by
when he didn't anxiously remember being in the wrong place
at the worst possible time. His journey through life had hit a
fork in the road on that night. Fortunately, the decisions he had
made were the right ones. Although the event had been physically rough on Jake, Morgan was really having a hard time emo-
tionally. Knowing that she had nearly lost her husband and her
daughter was still taking a significant toll. The event had forced
both Morgan and Jake to reevaluate their priorities and their
relationship. Morgan went to therapy, but Jake just forced it deep
down into his guts—as deep as possible. On some level, he knew
that one day it would surface with a fury, but he didn't have the
luxury of worrying about that now. He had a family to take care
of and to provide for first.

As he sped through the Old Waverly Golf Club, Jake saw blue
lights flashing on at least two police cars in front of his house
and saw another driving through the neighborhood, searching

with a spotlight. The tires squealed as he slammed on the brakes and parked crookedly at the end of his drive. He jumped out and ran toward the house. A young police officer searching the front yard recognized Jake and radioed the other officers that "the husband" had arrived.

Inside the house was chaos. Scout, their aged black Lab, was barking at all the strange men and couldn't hear Morgan's repetitive commands to hush. Several police officers were now in the house, talking excitedly on their handheld radios, coordinating coverage of possible escape routes and asking for additional manpower. Morgan was on the verge of hysterics. Katy's eyes were swollen from crying, but she was watching the police officers with great interest. When Morgan saw Jake, she ran to him, and they embraced for a long moment. Jake looked over her shoulder into an older officer's eyes, trying to read the situation. Nothing in the officer's face or demeanor offered any clues.

"What's going on? What do you know?" Jake frantically asked.

Morgan had her hand over her mouth. The lead officer spoke first, allowing Morgan a chance to compose herself.

"Apparently, Mr. Crosby, at the very least y'all had a Peepin' Tom. Maybe he was gonna rob the house. Maybe worse," he said carefully, knowing they needed to hear the truth. He continued, "But we think when your wife turned on the outside lights, he got spooked and fled the area."

"How did he get in here? How did he get past the security guard?"

"We don't know yet. Since Old Waverly only has two ways to drive in, if he drove, we'll know. We've got backup arriving now to seal off both exits. We'll check every vehicle, stickered or not, and we'll grid search for him in case he's still on foot."

"Has anybody been broken into out here?" Jake asked, assuming the incident to be an interrupted burglary.

"No, sir—not unless it happened tonight and it hasn't been reported yet. This is one of the safest places in the entire state. We've never had *any* incidents out here. Look, we're only ten minutes into this thing, so we really don't know what's going on yet. But we do have most of West Point's officers out there, plus two county deputies, and the local state trooper just radioed in that he's en route. We gotta good chance of catching this guy if he's still in here. He might can hide in the woods along the golf course or around homes that don't have dogs, but he'll be wantin' to get outta here as fast as he can…and that's when we'll catch him," the officer replied confidently.

With his arm still around Morgan, Jake rubbed her back while he looked out the windows. The small town of West Point, Mississippi, seemed to have deployed everybody on this call. He watched the parade of law enforcement officers outside and saw the constable arrive. He realized he didn't even know what a constable was, but there was one in his driveway who apparently wanted to help.

Jake turned to the policeman. "What can I do, Officer?"

"Can we get this dog in a room somewhere and let me ask y'all some more questions?"

"Sure," Jake said as he headed toward Scout. This was the most excitement she'd experienced since retiring from duck hunting a year or so ago.

As Jake returned, an officer opened the front door and stood in the doorway, obviously excited. "I found something!"

Everyone in the room turned to listen.

"Whatcha got?" asked the lead officer.

"There is a big oak tree right there in the corner of their lot. You can see the kitchen clearly and what appears to be the master bathroom. At any rate, there's about twenty-five cigarette butts in a pile behind it, and judging from their appearance, I'd say some are over a week old. Some of 'em are fresh."

Everyone looked at each other.

"Do y'all smoke?" asked the lead officer.

Morgan shook her head and squeezed Katy tighter. Jake shook his head too and then said, "No, sir. None of us do."

"Okay." Turning away from Jake, he said to the other officer, "Let's photograph the cigarette butts and then put 'em in an evidence bag. We might get lucky and find some DNA." He then turned to another officer and said, "Have there been Peeping Toms or anything similar to this going on around town at all?"

"No, sir. Nothing at all," the officer said with certainty. He then turned to Jake and asked, "By the way, Jake, where were you tonight?"

Jake was surprised by the question but appreciated his reasoning. "Working. I...I was at a business dinner at Anthony's."

The police officer nodded. "Okay. Have y'all seen anything or anybody suspicious around here? Anything out of the ordinary?"

Jake and Morgan looked at each other. Both drew blanks. Neither had noticed anything out of the norm; that's why they had moved to Old Waverly in the first place. After the life-altering events at the Dummy Line and the kidnapping of a neighbor, Morgan had insisted they live in a secure neighborhood. Jake understood and agreed. Morgan had been the intended target of the kidnapping—only the bad guys had abducted their next-door neighbor by mistake.

The Old Waverly Golf Club community perfectly fit their needs, although neither Jake nor Morgan golfed. Fortunately, the property had a lot of fishable water that was full of big bass, and there were deer everywhere too, so Jake enjoyed being there. The security at the entrance into the development was adequate. Unless you were a resident, a member, or a registered guest, you weren't getting in...unless, of course, you could bullshit your way past the guard.

"There's never anything out of the ordinary here. That's what we like about it," Jake said with a smile.

While looking out the front window, the officer checked his watch and then said, "Okay. The chief just got here. I need to go bring him up to speed." He paused for a moment, staring outside, and then continued, "Maybe they've spotted the perp's vehicle. I'll let y'all know what I find out." He quickly turned away.

Jake watched him walk out the front door. Turning to Morgan, he finally asked, "Are you okay, honey? Is she okay?" Jake looked at his subdued daughter and then walked over to kiss her on the top of her head.

"Yeah, I think so," Morgan answered as she tightly hugged Katy.

Katy said, "I'm fine, Dad."

"I'm sorry I wasn't home," Jake said, wishing his life could return to normal—before two years ago. Last spring, he hadn't even gotten to turkey hunt. There were no overnight trips that weren't work related. He had been praying this winter and spring would be different, but now he knew better. He also knew he should put Morgan and Katy ahead of his desire to hunt and fish. Jake's mind was racing, when he suddenly remembered something. "Hey, that tree where the guy was smoking—I've got a game camera near it. I've been trying to get pictures of a big deer I saw one morning for Katy. But I haven't checked it in a few weeks."

The officer looked at him curiously. "Will it take pictures at night?"

"Yeah. It's infrared. He'd never know."

"A few weeks? Won't the memory be full?"

"Maybe not. It's digital and can hold about four thousand images."

"Let's go have a look."

CHAPTER 3

———— ☾ ————

T HE THREE OLD MEN BARELY SPOKE AS THEY ANXIOUSLY
sipped coffee and thought of the stolen $116,000 in cash
hidden in four cat-litter boxes upstairs in their rooms. Hot cash
covered in cheap, generic cat litter. No one wanted to look at
cat turds, and since their simple rooms in the retirement center
had few places to conceal anything, these hiding spots were
ideal. Accurately counting the money had been exhausting,
taking almost two hours. Stealing it had been easy and the most
exhilarating activity anyone in the group had ever experienced.
They hadn't felt that alive in years…if ever. Thievery had been
the geezers' equivalent of meth; they were hooked after trying
it only once.

For the past six weeks, the retirees had intricately planned to
rip off the Kroger in Columbus, Mississippi. Most importantly,
they had executed it to near perfection. Now, a little more than
forty-eight hours after the crime, they were struggling to act normal and maintain their pre-felony daily routines. They were all
full of pride in a well-planned, well-executed venture and their
future plans for the money. Each knew the ramifications of loose
lips, but they found not talking about it extraordinarily difficult.
It's human nature to brag, but the basis of this desire was foreign

and seductive. After lifetimes of never breaking the law, other than a few speeding tickets, the three felt they had just stepped into the big leagues, and they were flying high.

The gray-haired gangsters were sitting at a table in the Henry Clay Retirement Community's restaurant, the Point, in downtown West Point and drinking a pot of black coffee, just as they had almost every day for the last few years. Ordinarily the scene would have been best described as monotonous, but not today. The tension at the table was palpable. No one could sit still. Fingers drummed the tabletop, and toes tapped on the tile floors. No one spoke about inane topics now that they had a taste for something more. Their former "everydayness" was now boring.

The retirement years had not been so golden for them. In fact, they all were concerned that they would outlive their money. Arriving within a few months of each other at the old four-story historic hotel that had been renovated and repurposed into a retirement community, they had become fast friends, spending most of their days together discussing politics and talking about the good old days but mostly worrying about the future.

At sixty-eight, Walter Severson was the youngest of the three. He worked as a greeter and a grocery bagger a few days each week at the targeted Kroger. It was at the Kroger that he had formulated the plan. Walter was the inside man. He had retired from managing a chain of Minnesota ice-skating rinks that eventually went bankrupt. He was shocked to learn that the parent company had mismanaged his 401(k). His dream of a cabin on Leech Lake wasn't going to happen. After a massive garage sale, Walter loaded his wife and what was left of their belongings into a rented orange truck and headed south to live out their lives in a rented modular home near Fairhope, Alabama. They never made it. While Walter was driving though Mississippi, just south of Tupelo, his wife died peacefully in her sleep. The good people of Mississippi were so nice to him during that difficult time that he just decided to stay.

"Nothing in the Columbus or West Point newspapers." Bernard Jefferson cracked a smile as he cocked his head down to peer over the top of his bifocals. "And not even a mention in that small weekly paper—the one that prints all the arrests. I like looking at all those mug shots."

"You'd have a better chance to make it in there if you beat someone with a baseball bat," Sebastian Snead stated.

"Guys, we don't *want* to be in the paper. No news is a good thing," Walter said, shaking his head.

Bernard nodded and then said, "Did y'all know that back in the 1920s West Point, Mississippi, was the smallest city in the world with a daily newspaper?"

"I reckon I didn't know that," Sebastian said, "and I've lived here all my life."

Walter was ignoring the trivia discussion. He was the only one who seemed nervous.

"Be sure you double-check to make sure you don't miss a small article," Walter directed.

Bernard didn't answer except to take an annoyingly loud slurp of coffee. The arrival of the newspapers was highly anticipated at the retirement community and a source of much discussion, since newspapers were all rapidly going digital. After the heist, Bernard had been tasked with scouring the papers and the Internet for information. So far, it had been just as Walter expected. There was no mention of the robbery—nothing.

Because they hadn't stolen all of the cash, the theft was not as obvious, and Walter hoped, therefore, that it might take Kroger a week to establish with concrete certainty that money was missing. Every employee and the management trusted Walter, and he moved throughout the store without raising any concerns. Most importantly, he knew of one lazy store manager who was more interested in a certain curvaceous young cashier than in the daily business operations. The way Walter designed the crime, that store manager would likely lose his job. The group decided this was an acceptable consequence, since the guy was cheating on his pregnant wife.

Missing from the table was their fourth partner in crime and the only woman, Lucille Garrett. At sixty-eight, she looked like your average grandmother and could blend seamlessly into a crowd, which they determined could be an asset at some point. The men also loved being around a woman they trusted and respected.

"Tonight, when Lucille gets back with the MRI, we'll go eat and discuss it. Y'all in?" Walter asked. He chuckled to himself, surprised at how quickly he had picked up the word *y'all*.

"MRI?" Sebastian asked.

"Most recent information," answered Walter.

"Oh. Gotcha."

"I thought if everybody agreed, we'd take a couple hundred dollars, have the first meeting of our new organization, and eat some really good food. Kinda celebrate a bit."

"That's an excellent idea," Sebastian said.

"What time are you gonna go see that lady lawyer?" Bernard asked, with obvious interest. "I'd *really* like to go with you."

Bernard Jefferson had been a traveling salesman for a chainsaw manufacturer and had been married and divorced more times than he could count. He still claimed to have girlfriends scattered across three states. He loved the ladies, though the many divorces had cost him everything.

He was a source of humor at the retirement center for the females, who complained that he bathed in Old Spice. Always dressed in a starched JCPenney-brand dress shirt, he prowled the halls of the retirement center like a college boy at a sorority house. He imagined himself one day marrying a rich widow or divorcée. Bernard was often overheard saying, "Every man's gotta have a dream; might as well be a big'un." None of the best

Internet dating websites could find him a match…except one, and judging from the photo, "her" gender was questionable. She was a middle-aged French Canadian lumberjack from Nova Scotia. Bernard had immediately closed the account, losing a great deal of hope for the future.

"The lawyer's not your type," Walter explained as he poured another cup of coffee. "For one, she doesn't know *anything* about chain saws…and she doesn't appear to have a whole lot of money."

Bernard grunted. The group chuckled and nodded their agreement.

"Have you decided yet?" Sebastian asked. "You know, whether or not to tell her?"

Sebastian Snead had been at the Henry Clay Retirement Community longer than his two buddies and most of the other thirty or so inmates, as he called them. He had been a gunsmith by trade. He was a widower with a married son who was currently deployed in Afghanistan, and he had recently lost a daughter in a car accident. Sebastian was full of grief but still retained a zest for life. He also had prostate cancer but wouldn't do anything about it, and he hadn't told anyone. Sebastian was about a hundred pounds overweight, but, all things considered, he was extremely agile. He constantly surprised everyone with his strength. No one suspected he was sick. He'd watched his wife die from breast cancer years before, and he wanted no part of chemo or radiation. When the time came, he planned to fly to Alaska, walk out into the wilderness, and disappear. He didn't want to burden anyone. Unfortunately, he didn't understand modern medicine like he did firearms.

"I'm gonna lay all the cards on the table and tell her about our proposed foundation. She'll be stunned, but she'll be bound by attorney-client privilege. I really like what I know about her. She's not your typical lawyer. She's perfect for us. She's been through some tough winters. She knows that the legal system fails good and right people too often, but she hasn't given up her ideals. She still thinks she can save the world one client at a time," Walter explained

"Sounds good," Bernard offered.

"Her true passion, though, is trying to save the endangered Florida panthers," Walter added.

"Panthers?" Bernard asked.

"Yeah, they're down around the Everglades; big long-tailed cats that look like small mountain lions. There are supposedly less than a hundred alive in the wild, and she's really into protecting them and preserving their habitat," Walter continued.

"So what does that tell you about her?" Sebastian inquired.

"She's capable of caring about a cause, something way bigger and way more important than just her own needs. Something she can't even see or probably even win, but she tries. I like that level of commitment," Walter said, watching the guys as they considered his analysis of the attorney. He continued, "It's been my experience that very few people and even fewer lawyers have her attitude. I don't know if it's nature or nurture. Maybe it's genetic? She's got something that causes or allows her to care about something she doesn't directly benefit from."

Sebastian's cynical side came out. "Anybody can write a check."

"She does more than send money. She gives her time. And we all know how lawyers value their time."

"No they don't. Lawyers *overvalue* their time," Sebastian said with a huff.

They all grunted their agreement.

Walter's charisma and ability to effortlessly elicit trust naturally made him the group's leader. All of it—the robbery, their future plans for the money, everything—had been his idea. He had brought excitement into their otherwise uninspired lives. He had demonstrated (or possibly conned them into believing) that he was brilliant, and he could quickly and accurately determine what really made people tick shortly after meeting them just once.

One day they were drinking coffee, discussing the weather; the next, there they were, planning to rob the local Kroger grocery store.

The group got quiet as they watched a few residents meander in to order breakfast. Sebastian and Walter thought about the money and what it represented. Bernard looked around at the women in the room and wondered how and when he was going to meet and marry his future retirement fund; it was pretty much always on his mind.

It was Bernard who broke the silence. "Come on, Walter, let me go. I'll buy lunch, wherever you want."

Walter turned to look at him and then shifted his gaze to Sebastian, who nodded slightly. "Okay, but don't try to flirt with her. You're old enough to be her grandfather."

"I won't…I'll just ask about panthers."

Walter rolled his eyes.

Sebastian said sincerely, "Oh, she'll love that."

CHAPTER 4

———— ☾ ————

S AMANTHA OWENS REGRETTED SIGNING A ONE-YEAR LEASE
on the small office in downtown Columbus. Apparently the
previous tenant, a new-age marriage counselor of some sort,
had offered more services to her male clientele than just marital
advice. Since Sam had moved into the office two months earlier,
hardly a day had passed without some guy walking in to request
an appointment…for counseling. Their enthusiasm and desire
for "counseling" peaked when they saw Sam.

She was a thirty-five-year-old recent divorcée who was trying
to put her life back together, and thanks to her mama's genes, she
didn't look a day over twenty-five. Sam had moved to Columbus,
Mississippi, from Tupelo in hopes of a clean start. Her ex-husband
had made the last eight years of her life miserable. She had been
a victim of abuse from a scheming, well-connected, old-moneyed
bastard who had orchestrated every advantage available to hide
assets and influence the judge so that, after ten years of marriage,
she was left with little more than her car. Sam was glad simply
to get out, but she was upset that her husband had walked away
financially unscathed due to questionable legal maneuvers and
quite possibly judicial manipulation. All she had wanted was an
equitable settlement. What she got was shafted.

With her law degree from the University of Mississippi and recent admittance to the bar, she was anxious to get to work. As one of the oldest in her class, she considered her age an advantage— more life experience and such. After the bad marriage, her success in law school had helped her regain most of her self-esteem and self-reliance. Sam was now hell-bent on helping others, and although she might not admit it, she wanted a little payback on her ex-husband.

Taking the vacated office space of a high-dollar call girl posing as a marriage counselor wasn't in her plan, but she didn't have the cash to break the lease and move. Apparently the local married-male population *really* appreciated marriage counseling, and word had not spread successfully that their favorite counselor had been run out of town by a pack of angry wives. Sam and the secretary, whom she could barely afford, finally found the humor in the situation and began handing out business cards to the men with instructions to give the cards to their spouses. Confused looks followed.

Sam needed clients, and each time the door opened, her hopes rose. More often than not, she was disappointed. She joined the local Rotary Club to network, but they met only once a month. Yesterday she'd had one appointment, and although she was giving this one client world-class treatment, the project wasn't going to generate many billable hours. Ole Miss Law had taught her to understand and apply the law but not how to generate clients. Last month she had scraped together enough cash to buy commercials on a local cable-television channel. Freshly filmed and quickly edited, the commercials had been running for almost three weeks, with very limited trackable results. She could afford one more week.

Samantha Owens said a silent prayer that her efforts would translate into business.

CHAPTER 5

———— ☾ ————

JAKE AND MORGAN HAD SPENT SEVERAL ANXIOUS DAYS AND sleepless nights since the man had been spotted in their backyard.

The police, along with assistance from the sheriff's department, finally had determined that the Peeping Tom had not driven himself into the neighborhood or been dropped off. Law enforcement had carefully followed his tracks and determined that the perp had boated Tibbee Creek, which ran near the back of the golf course, and then walked in. This really perplexed everyone. To do this took an enormous amount of effort and a tough thousand-yard hike through dense woods and thick undergrowth. "Not typical of a burglar," said one deputy. "They're usually lazy. Opportunistic."

Security was heightened. All the community's residents were on edge. Security alarms that had had never been used were suddenly being activated and monitoring contracts signed. The sheriff's department had an undercover team working, as hunters patrolled the large creek, which in some states would have been considered a river. Law enforcement of both West Point and Clay County were doing their best to protect their citizens.

Jake's motion-sensitive game camera had several profile images of an unidentifiable man from seven different nights. The photos confirmed Morgan's account of the man, but they didn't establish his identity. All that the police knew about the man was that he was white and probably thin, but winter clothing made it difficult to be certain. He was obviously knowledgeable in nighttime navigation of both woods and waters. He also smoked Marlboro Lights.

Morgan's initial response was that the family should move again, but they couldn't afford it. "How and to where?" Jake asked.

They'd sunk everything they had into this house after they had taken a bath on the one they had just sold to move quickly. The housing market was now almost another two years in the tank, not to mention that no one would buy a house with a recent history of a stalker in the backyard.

Jake and Morgan owned a small cabin on the Tombigbee River that they could sell if absolutely necessary. It had been in Jake's family for decades, so he wasn't too keen on that idea.

A frustrated Jake Crosby had met with law enforcement officials to discuss the possibility of the stalker being connected to what had happened in West Alabama about eighteen months earlier. Departments collaborated and files were studied, but nothing had been decided yet.

During the night of the Dummy Line incident, an Alabama deputy sheriff had encountered a suspicious male at Johnny Lee Grover's trailer—one Ethan "Moon Pie" Daniels, who had disappeared after evading the deputy's attempt to follow him. Moon Pie had flown under the radar for most of his adult life, but he had basically dropped off the grid since that awful spring evening in Alabama. Since his involvement in that night's crimes could not be established, law enforcement from both Alabama and Mississippi were content to let Moon Pie and the matter quietly fade away.

Another Dummy Line suspect was Tommy Tidwell, commonly known as Tiny. He too was thought to have been in the area of the crimes and was a known associate of the gang. He was located several months after the killings, but the police could never get him to talk about that night. Since Jake could not positively identify him in a lineup, the local district attorney had been forced to close the case, knowing that three very bad guys had been killed that night and two more may have been involved.

Tiny had a solid alibi for the recent events in West Point, and he didn't match the physical appearance of the suspect's outline that had been captured in the game camera photographs. Tiny weighed 365 pounds without bulky cold-weather clothing. Additionally, for the last year, he had worked the day shift at a fish hatchery in Montgomery, Alabama, and nights as a maintenance man at an Indian casino. He hadn't missed any work in over a year. The law enforcement officers were left wondering when he had time to sleep. His live-in girlfriend mildly complained of the same, but somebody had to work to pay the bills, and it obviously wasn't going to be her.

CHAPTER 6

———— ☾ ————

"WHOA. HANG ON. OKAY—LET ME GET THIS STRAIGHT," Samantha said, holding up a hand and then flipping to a clean sheet of paper.

She leaned forward, staring at the two old men, and then asked, "The two of you robbed the Kroger. We're talking about that giant grocery store?"

"That's the store. But we didn't exactly rob it. We sorta embezzled the weekend deposit," Walter said with a sly grin. "And we had two more people helping. It was an inside job, and we didn't use guns—just brains."

"We doubt they've even figured it out yet," added Bernard Jefferson with a sense of confidence.

"And you want me to help you start a legitimate foundation with this stolen money to help older people who don't have any money." She stared back at them and noticed a distinct twinkle in Bernard's eyes.

"That's a bit of oversimplification. We want to start a foundation to help older people who worked all their lives and don't have anything to show for it...like us—to do one final, life-changing act for their families. Help them get a break, a leg up, so to speak," Walter explained calmly.

Sam, in obvious disbelief, took off her glasses and rubbed the bridge of her nose.

Walter allowed his comments to sink in for a moment and then continued, "For instance, we have a guy in our group with a grandson who's going to medical school and having to work two jobs just to pay the bills. He doesn't even have time to study. Imagine not being able to study properly at medical school because you're worried about paying the rent, buying gas and books…and eating. He's a great kid who's trying really hard. Imagine what twenty-five thousand dollars would mean to him. Imagine his granddad being able to give it to him. The kid could study properly, be competitive with the other students, and perform at his best. People like him deserve some help."

"You're serious."

"You betcha! You see, we help him, and in return, he pledges to help someone else when he can," Walter added with an unvarnished Minnesotan accent and a broad smile.

"So that's how it perpetuates," Sam remarked.

"Absolutely. But we can't help everybody. We know that. We want to be selective. We need requirements and a means to help us decide who really qualifies and to spot the freeloaders. Whether it's school tuition, helping start a business, paying for a surgery, whatever…there's a lot of need out there, and there are a lot of people like us who want to help but can't. We need a lawyer to set up the foundation and then to monitor, administrate, and help it continue," Walter explained and then glanced over at Bernard, who was excited to add, "That's why we hired you."

"You haven't hired me yet," she shot back.

Sam's mind was racing. She could count her clients on one hand and still have a couple of extra fingers. That did not translate into a healthy practice. Now these crazy old men waltz in, lay down an envelope full of much-needed cash, and then casually admit to stealing the money to help those in need. Her ethical compass was spinning wildly.

"I haven't seen anything in the news about the robbery," she said with certainty. Sam watched the local news each night while thinking about exercising.

"It wasn't robbery, and we're good guys."

"How much money are we talking about here?"

"One hundred and sixteen thousand dollars. There's five grand in that envelope to retain your services," Walter replied as he gestured toward her desk.

"We saw your commercial on TV," Bernard contributed confidently.

"Actually, I did a pretty thorough background check on you," Walter said with a smile.

"On me?"

"Walter Googled you," Bernard interjected enthusiastically.

Before Walter could clarify, Bernard added, "We know about the panthers."

Sam looked at him with a furrowed brow.

"It's important to have the right person help us," Walter explained.

"Well, gentlemen, I'm not sure I'm buying your story, and even if I did, that's not enough money to start a foundation like what you've described. You could start it, I suppose, but you just couldn't help many people."

"Oh, we're gonna get a lot more money. I have a plan for that," Walter explained.

Sam blinked. She had to ask, "How? More Krogers?"

"No, ma'am. I can't tell you. I don't feel comfortable explaining crimes we're considering."

"But you told me about the Kroger felony."

With steely resolve, Walter stated, "What we've done is done…and you're our lawyer, so you can't betray us."

"I'm not your lawyer, yet."

"I told you because you need to know that we're being totally honest."

"Nobody's gonna get hurt," Bernard promised.

"Look, gentlemen, y'all seem sweet, and I've enjoyed talking with y'all. The foundation concept is worthwhile, but your funding methods don't make sense. Doing something bad to do something good? If everything you've said is true, this creates an ethical, if not legal, dilemma for me." Sam leaned back and stared at the cash on her desk. *Five thousand dollars sure could go a long way around here*, she thought.

"We aren't asking you to break the law. Just execute our wishes. We'll pay your hourly rate and allow you to be the administrator—for a fee, of course. It's our legacy, and we are very serious about it," Walter explained as he leaned in for emphasis.

Walter let a long moment pass and then sat back to study her office. From the looks of things, it appeared she needed the retainer. Need was everywhere. Everybody needs something.

Sam glanced down at her watch and then at the two old men smiling at her. She could hear her receptionist explaining to a confused walk-in that the therapist was gone. Sam sighed and wondered just how much of their story was true. At least they could pay.

"Okay, here's my proposal: we go to lunch, you buy, and I bill you for a minimum of one hour and pro rata every fifteen minutes beyond the first hour, including travel time. You tell me everything, and I'll decide if I'm going to be your attorney."

"Deal," the old men said in stereo.

Walter smiled; after a few more heartfelt stories about helping others, he would have the lawyer he wanted. He would bide his time before explaining to her what he really wanted the foundation to accomplish.

CHAPTER 7

———— ☾ ————

E VERYONE WORRIED ABOUT KATY. SHE HAD BEEN ONLY NINE years old when she and Jake endured an unimaginable night of terror. Jake and Morgan took her to the best counselors in Mississippi. She talked, they listened, and everybody felt like Katy was improving. Initially, the counselors all said she simply didn't know how to process the information. They also spoke about her compartmentalizing the issues. Talking seemed to help Katy. To Jake, it seemed all the counselors did was listen and ask, "How did that make you feel?" But, since he was worried about his tiny daughter, he participated, and he would have sold a kidney to get her the best help. Their insurance soon quit picking up the tab, forcing him to sell a few old guns to help Morgan balance the budget at home.

Katy was remarkable in her ability to process all that had occurred. The professionals—the counselors and educators— ultimately attributed her resiliency to her knowledge of the fact that she was loved and also that her father would do whatever was necessary to protect her. The community helped by reaching out to the Crosbys, particularly Katy. Local churches and Sunday-school classes regularly placed the family on their prayer lists.

Jake and Morgan were extremely concerned about the long-term effects of what Katy had seen and heard. No one—especially a nine-year-old—should ever be that close to such evil. It wasn't until three weeks after that harrowing night that Katy had started to fear being alone, and she would cry when her dad left the house. She had a few really bad nightmares, and once Jake had to pick her up from an overnight party at 2:00 a.m. Morgan and Jake grieved for the pain of their only child. Morgan never openly blamed Jake, but when Katy got really upset, he knew she was thinking it.

Morgan had spent countless hours searching the Internet, looking for the best therapists and treatments for Katy.

Jake vowed to do whatever the experts suggested. He worried about Katy, about Morgan, about everything…all the time. He was concerned about his marriage, and he was apprehensive about how he was going to pay for it all, since his income was falling along with the economy. Working as a stockbroker in a small town during a recession was proving to be brutal. Jake and Morgan both prayed. They didn't know what else could be done.

On top of everything, this peeper had come along and threatened to erode every inch of their collective healing progress.

CHAPTER 8

———— ☾ ————

E IGHTEEN MONTHS EARLIER, IN THE PREDAWN DARKNESS OF a spring Alabama morning, Ethan "Moon Pie" Daniels had to make a critical decision: abandon his drug-running buddy, Reese Davis, or stick around to face the real risk of being busted for several serious crimes.

A deeply suspicious sheriff's deputy had attempted to interrogate Moon Pie while he was awaiting instructions on what to do with a woman he had kidnapped earlier, following the shooting death of his criminal gang's leader. Subsequently, that same deputy had unsuccessfully attempted to tail Moon Pie's vehicle. And when Moon Pie couldn't contact Reese on the push-to-talk radiophone at their prearranged rendezvous point, his blood pressure had escalated. Then, at the instant his high beams illuminated Jake and Katy and the rescue party, looking like survivors of a suicide bombing, being escorted from the swamp by a uniformed deputy, his flight reflex kicked into overdrive.

Moon Pie had tried to contact Reese numerous times as he quickly drove away from the group that was congregating in the middle of that rural roadway. Each unanswered call intensified his bad feelings. Realizing that he had to run, he began implementing his preplanned disappearance into the Ozark

Mountains of southern Missouri. He took quick inventory of his readily available assets, cash, weapons, and illegal drugs that he could convert to cash later.

Moon Pie had feared this day would come, and he had a plan. He had always assumed, however, that he would be fleeing a drug task force, not a felony kidnapping charge, and Lord knew what else he'd be implicated in by his association with his redneck, drug-dealing buddies. He had only a few hours to get fuel and additional supplies with credit cards before law enforcement would be using them to track him, and since that nosy Alabama deputy had his tag number, he knew he had to get the hell out of Dodge. He set the cruise control at a safe sixty-five mph and headed north on Highway 45. Mindful that an APB would be out for him and his vehicle, when he spied a broken-down car on the side of the road, he considered it providential and stole its tag.

His time hiding out in Missouri had been frustrating. The local competition for selling drugs was intense. The Ozarks were ground zero for meth production, and he found the customer base to be even car-struck-dog crazier than he expected. He lasted only a month before giving up and moving to the Cotton Belt railroad town of Jonesboro, Arkansas, with a brilliant idea for a colossal scam. Jonesboro was only about eighty square miles, but it drew hunters from all over the state, as well as southern Missouri, western Tennessee, and northwest Mississippi.

He quietly assumed a new identity, paying for quality forged documents, and placed a cheap option on a vacant Kmart building. After a few months of advertising a new state-of-the-art indoor rifle and pistol range, he soon had over five hundred future members who paid him a thousand-dollar membership fee. He bailed on the real-estate option and radio-station ad debts, leaving Arkansas in the middle of the night with a pile of cash.

Moon Pie had changed his hair color, put on a few pounds, and grown a goatee when he moved back to Mississippi. He settled in Columbus, where he promptly opened a cash-for-gold business called the Gold Mine—his front to launder cash from dealing drugs. He ran drugs on the Tombigbee Waterway, a 250-mile river system channelized in the 1970s by the United States Army Corp of Engineers to connect the Ohio Valley with the Gulf of Mexico. Columbus was close enough to his old base of operations in Tupelo to easily recruit some trusted criminal support, yet far enough away for him to feel somewhat comfortable with his new look and identity. The old river town was a perfect place to set up shop. It also allowed him to be near his old stomping grounds, where he could participate in his favorite pastime—poaching whitetail deer.

CHAPTER 9

————— ☾ —————

WALTER AND HIS CREW CELEBRATED THEIR SUCCESS WITH fine food, wine, and a few cocktails at Café Ritz in downtown West Point. On their limited budgets prior to the robbery, they had rarely dined at a place like the Ritz, although it was only two doors down from their hotel home.

Walter made a point of explaining that this would not be a frequent event but that once a month they would have a foundation meeting, which would involve breaking bread. The foundation would cover the expenses, of course. "Might as well be fine food," he added with a sly grin. That news excited everyone.

"I think we have our attorney," Walter advised as he sampled a crab cake appetizer. "Should know tomorrow."

"What's our next step?" Bernard asked, shifting his weight and wishing he'd brought his hemorrhoid cushion.

Walter looked around the dining area to make certain no one could hear them and then answered, "Basically, we'll have a little over a hundred grand after we pay the retainer to Sam."

Everybody smiled, and Walter rubbed his forehead. "It's a really good start, but we need more to help more folks if we want it to be self-perpetuating one day."

After a moment's pause to look at one of several old movie posters decorating the wall above Walter, Sebastian asked, "How much do you think we need?" He then took a loud sip of red wine.

"About six hundred and fifty thousand more," Walter said emphatically.

Everybody grunted at once. That was a hell of a lot of money. More than any of them had ever seen...or could collectively imagine.

"That's more than you originally thought. Almost twice as much," Sebastian said with some concern.

"I know. But after talking with Sam, it's clear to me that being well funded is the key to the foundation's success. We need three-quarters of a million dollars," Walter said in a low voice. "And we can't do it robbing Krogers. It won't work again. I have something in mind, though." Walter had initially believed it would take them at least two years to raise the additional seed money. Now, he had a new plan—one that could net them about half the entire amount in one fell swoop.

Not fully understanding what was in his future, Bernard was relieved. The stress of the responsibilities to pull off the initial heist still had lingering effects. It was way more pressure than the average senior citizen needed.

The group had discussed splitting the hundred grand among themselves and helping their own families, but they had unanimously decided to pursue Walter's original vision to create the foundation first. They all wanted to be a part of something bigger than themselves. They wanted to learn more, but they were nervous about what might be required of them.

Sebastian knew that kind of money wouldn't come without a price, and he wondered whether an old chain-saw salesman, a gunsmith, and a skating-rink manager could actually pay the tab. He watched Walter and thought about all his charismatic talk of money and the foundation. Then it occurred to him that it was odd for someone with his persuasive skills to be so broke. He hadn't considered this before. Something didn't make sense, but he didn't want to derail the group's discussion. *I'll just do some research on my own*, he thought.

They were all enjoying the most exciting thing that had ever happened to them; most importantly, they had a goal, a purpose in life. They had called this their project. Now they were going to be able to help people. They considered themselves good guys, and the idea made their eyes twinkle.

"So, what's the new plan?" Bernard asked excitedly.

Sebastian placed his wineglass down to focus.

Walter looked around the room like he was expecting someone to be eavesdropping. "Lucille's granddaughter works at this place in Columbus called the Gold Mine. It's one of those cash-for-gold places. Her boss is a real sleazeball, and according to Lucille, he keeps a pile of cash in a safe."

"How much cash?"

"We don't really know for sure how much money. She says it's got to be over three hundred thousand. Boot boxes full of hundreds and twenties."

"Hot damn!" Bernard exclaimed.

"He keeps trying to impress her by showing her inside the safe. He's done it several times," Walter said.

"Combination safe?" Sebastian wondered.

"Yes."

"Can she get it?" Bernard asked.

"She's trying. She thinks she knows two of the three numbers."

Everyone squirmed a bit as they excitedly absorbed the new information.

"So, two things here," Walter said, as he looked again to make sure they were not being spied on. "Lucille's granddaughter, Bailey, is in trouble. Her boyfriend's beating her. She says he's into drugs. And this guy at work is harassing her, hard. Basically she's fallen in with a bad crowd. She knows it but says she can't afford to get out 'cause her boyfriend will find her and just beat the crap out of her."

Walter paused when the waiter brought their food. He took a sip of wine, glanced around the room when the waiter left, and continued, "So, Lucille told Bailey about our foundation... against my expressed wishes, by the way. At any rate, apparently this girl has her heart in the right place, and she immediately volunteers up this money...says she only wants twenty thousand dollars to start over somewhere. Her dream is to design clothes. She's a really good girl, from what Lucille says, and she's talented. I've seen some of her designs; they're good, I guess. Bailey wants us to have the rest of the money for the foundation. That's the kind of person we need to help. She's practical. She's willing to go to school and build a life for herself the right way. She just needs a little help up, not a handout."

Sebastian took a big sip of his drink and let out a deep breath in obvious disgust. "For the record, after she's someplace safe, I'm gonna castrate the boyfriend. He won't even look twice at another woman when I'm done with him."

Walter and Bernard stared at Sebastian. Walter went from stone-faced to a sly grin. He liked Sebastian. "He sounds like Earl."

"Earl?" Sebastian asked.

"The Dixie Chicks," Walter answers.

Sebastian said, "Oh yeah, and Earl had to die!"

Sebastian and Walter chuckled.

"Suppose the safe doesn't have that much money. Why don't we go to a casino and bet it all on a roulette wheel? We could double our money with one spin!" Bernard said.

"Or lose it all!" Walter said in disgust.

"Hey, that's not a bad idea," Sebastian offered.

"What?" Walter asked.

"Doubling our money...but let's do it in the stock market. Let's invest it. I hear about companies' stocks exploding all the time on those money shows on cable TV."

"It's almost as dangerous as roulette."

"Come on, Walter. You're a smart guy. You out of all of us should appreciate the idea. This is the twenty-first century. Let's modernize," Sebastian said encouragingly.

Walter sat quiet, deep in thought. *The foundation needs an attorney for all things legal. A savvy investment manager could certainly earn his keep.* He was warming quickly to the idea, but for reasons of his own, he didn't want to seem too enthusiastic.

"Makes sense to me," Bernard offered.

"I know a stockbroker. Lives here in town. Good guy…I put a recoil reducer on a .243 rifle for him a couple of years ago."

"Is he any good at investing money?"

"I don't really know about that. He's a nice guy, though."

"Is he rich?"

"Well, he paid me four hundred dollars to make a rifle that barely kicks anyway not kick at all just so his daughter could shoot it…he's got some extra money."

Walter nodded his agreement. "I'll Google him. If he passes that initial vetting, you can call him and set up a meeting."

The three gray-haired men smiled as they looked at each other. Just like that, their adrenaline was pumping again.

Walter discreetly pulled out three rum-flavored cigars and handed them out like prizes. "Looks like we gotta lot of work to do, you guys."

CHAPTER 10

———— ☾ ————

F OR JAKE, THE PAST EIGHTEEN MONTHS HAD BEEN DIF-
ficult, to say the least. He kept his worries, fears, and
anxieties bottled up. He never shared any of it with anyone—
not the multitude of counselors, therapists, and doctors—not
even Morgan. It was ten hours of hell. Jake had tried to avoid
a confrontation, but when cornered, he had killed a man to
start a night of terror and then killed another to finish it.
Jake had done what was necessary to survive and to protect
the lives of Katy and Elizabeth Beasley, a young woman who
also happened to be in the wrong place at the worst possible
time.

The night's aftermath could have easily broken Jake and
Morgan's already strained marriage; however, their relationship
became noticeably stronger. The episode served to bring them
together and make each appreciate the other more.

Jake maintained to Morgan, and to anyone else who asked,
that he was doing fine and suffering no ill effects. But he was
slowly deteriorating from boredom. Every day he went to work,
watched computer screens, and held the hands of his clients, who
expected him to see into the future. He was in the rat race, chasing cheese, and he cared nothing about it.

The events of that night in an Alabama swamp—being stalked, lying in wait to kill a man, running for his life in the inky darkness, and being responsible for other lives—had purged Jake of normalcy. He now needed more from his life and out of it; but at forty, with a huge mortgage, two car payments, and private-school tuition, a career change was not in the cards. He had no financial reserves or assets to sustain any deviation from his current path.

He missed the rush he experienced in those deadly encounters, and he had begun dreaming that he worked as a federal game warden, tasting the adrenaline.

For the past eighteen months, almost every morning before work, he had eaten breakfast with a group of older men—in their seventies and eighties—all veterans, at a gas station diner. They noticed the change in Jake but didn't discuss it in front of him. Jake could sense that they knew, and he felt at peace in their company. The only thing that appeared to matter to the old men was their newfound respect for him—for his character and what he had been willing to do when faced with evil. Jake was beginning to feel as though they now considered him a peer.

He poured himself into a career that he didn't love and strove to be a better husband. He paid more attention to Morgan, he began teaching a young-adult Sunday-school class, and he went to a Southern Baptist couples' retreat where he badly wanted to fish in the scenic mountain lake but didn't, which killed him; he knew it had to be the most underfished lake on the entire North American continent.

CHAPTER 11

———— ☾ ————

IT WAS A DREARY, RAINY DAY ABOUT FIFTEEN MINUTES before noon when Morgan and Jake walked through the front door of the Old Waverly Clubhouse. The Sunday buffet, loaded with quintessential Southern cooking, was a family favorite, and they rarely missed it. With Katy at her grandparents' house in Columbus, the couple was alone. Morgan requested a table near the grand piano.

The stately dining room was about half-full of mostly Baptists, since their church let out earlier than those of the Methodists, Episcopalians, and Catholics. The only other folks eating were golfing guests. Jake spent most of the meal daydreaming of slipping off to deer hunt that afternoon, but he didn't know how Morgan would react, since the police hadn't caught the Peeping Tom and didn't have any leads. He knew deep down he probably shouldn't go.

"That was delicious," Jake said as he leaned back.

"As usual," Morgan replied with a smirk.

"I ate too much macaroni and cheese."

"As usual."

"I love it." He sighed as he tossed his napkin on the table.

"It's on the kids' buffet," Morgan observed, smiling.

"So?"

"I'm just saying. It's on the kids' buffet; not all adults share your passion for mac and cheese."

"It's easier when Katy's here. Folks just think I'm fixing her a plate," Jake said, indicating he had thought this through.

Morgan was enjoying the moment. The dining room was elegant and the music enjoyable. "What if I told you that it was going to be easier to get in the future?"

"They're moving it to the main buffet?"

"No. Not exactly."

"You got the recipe?"

"No…yes…I do, but you know mine's not as good."

Morgan and her close friends weren't known to be women of the kitchen. In fact, one of her best friends joked that her family ate out so much, when she announced, "Supper's ready," her kids would run to the car. Morgan had set off the kitchen's smoke alarm more than once.

Before Jake could answer, a young waitress asked if they would like coffee. Morgan always enjoyed a cup, especially when it was cold outside. Today she politely declined.

"You don't want any coffee?" Jake asked.

"No. I can't have the caffeine," she said, thinking he might connect the dots.

"Planning a power nap?"

"Jake?"

"Yeah?"

"I'm pregnant."

Jake was shocked. He stared straight at her and began smiling.

"We're gonna have a baby," she explained, glowing.

CHAPTER 12

———— ☽ ————

S AMANTHA WAS LISTENING TO SARA EVANS AS SHE WRESTLED with the ethical issues involving her new clients. Occasionally she explained her thoughts to her cat. The cat pretended to care, but soon his eyes grew heavy to Sara's smooth, sentimental voice. The cat stretched out asleep, and Sam was beginning to feel better about the situation with the old men.

After graduating, Samantha had moved into her late aunt's antebellum home that had been in the family since the 1850s. It had sat vacant for the last two years, and someone had stolen all of the period furnishings and paintings. Sam was certain it was a local antique dealer who had constantly pestered her to sell him the home's contents. It pissed her off every time she thought about it. The Columbus tourism bureau had been begging her to restore the unique house and include it in the annual historic-homes tour. Sam knew she eventually would, but first she wanted to track down the authentic furniture. The giant old house was depressing with no furniture.

Sam had decided she could act as attorney for the old men because if they had actually robbed the Kroger, any crimes they may have committed occurred prior to their meeting. She would be comfortable representing them as long as they didn't discuss future crimes or ask her to cover up any criminal activity. Tomorrow she would deposit the cash retainer and pay some bills.

As she finished the last sip of coffee, she turned off the music, clicked on the TV, and tuned in to the local news. The cat rolled over when she gently rubbed his head. Tom the cat was the only male in her life, and that was fine by her. Since her divorce almost two years earlier, dating had not figured into her lifestyle just yet.

"So, Tom," she said to the motionless cat.

"We agree on our new clients?" Sam asked as she watched the anchor struggle through a news story. The teleprompter obviously wasn't working correctly. It reminded her of the president. She chuckled.

"I know it's weird, but the old guys seem sweet and excited about helping others. I like that."

Samantha watched the cat ignore her.

"Bottom line, I'm an attorney, and they need a good one."

Sam hoped to see her commercial run during the last newscast, but she never did.

CHAPTER 13

──────── ☾ ────────

E THAN "MOON PIE" DANIELS HAD NO FORMAL EDUCATION but a lot of street smarts. His savvy business instincts had created enough success to allow him to pursue his obsession of poaching big whitetail deer. Some people scuba dive; others play golf. Moon Pie loved to sneak onto someone else's property and poach the biggest deer on the place. He loved the rush of getting away with it more than anything. He also sold the antlers to a taxidermist, who in turn sold them to interior decorators via the Internet.

His daddy had introduced him to poaching as a way of putting meat on the table, just like he taught him to grow marijuana as a cash crop to supplement the family's meager legitimate income. His daddy had worked on a soybean farm, but he was also the best old-school poacher around northeast Mississippi and northwest Alabama. He taught his son well.

As an adult, even though money wasn't an issue for Moon Pie, he continued to hunt but upped the excitement by poaching. With more landowners spending large sums of money to grow big, healthy deer, Moon Pie's poaching grounds became more specific and more of a challenge. He would target a specific individual's place and make it personal. He watched outdoors shows and read hunting magazines, looking for the prime spots within driving distance. Fortified with cash from his criminal activities, Moon Pie took poaching to a whole new level.

Since moving back to the area, Moon Pie paid cash to rent a single-wide trailer close to the Columbus Air Force Base. It was cheap, since it was next to the busiest air base in the country, averaging 269 daily takeoffs and landings. The base ranked second only to Atlanta's airport in terms of air traffic. The constant noise didn't bother him. The trailer was a temporary accommodation that perfectly fit his needs.

Moon Pie also owned a customized thirty-six-foot houseboat he had named *Mud Cat*. He had used her for years to move drugs up and down the river. She had ample hidden storage and a huge diesel engine that could burn almost any mix of diesel fuel available and move her at surprising speeds. She looked a bit worn and was in dire need of a bottom job, but mechanically, she was in great shape. He rented her out between his runs, so the marine police and the Army Corps of Engineers lockmasters were used to seeing the old vessel all over the river system.

The Columbus Marina was home base for *Mud Cat*. She was making him a lot of money and didn't appear to be attracting unwanted attention, which made him more brazen daily. The people supplying Moon Pie were pleased with his transportation and dependability. It might have taken a few more days to get the goods to their destination than the interstate system, but nobody ever questioned him. The state highway patrol was always a threat to make a random stop of a suspicious vehicle or driver, or for any type of traffic violation, real or fabricated. Since the suppliers were from the Gulf Coast, they were familiar with boats, and they appreciated Moon Pie's resourcefulness in using one this far inland.

These suppliers now had a chance to move a sizable load of cocaine to a Tennessee distributor, who had just made a recent connection serving several larger cities in the Northeast, doubling demand, which was serious market growth for the coast suppliers.

In two days, Moon Pie would receive a down payment of $900,000 in cash to pass to his suppliers. He could sense that the money was about to really begin to roll in. With the cash-for-gold business, originally envisioned to be only a front, being surprisingly profitable, and this new distribution deal he was about to make, he would soon become wealthy. *In a year, I'll have enough cash to burn a wet mule*, he thought.

After years of being a small-time criminal, struggling to survive, Moon Pie had finally positioned himself for success, but he still had one nagging issue—one unfinished piece of business he thought about every day: killing Jake Crosby. Moon Pie had followed the story on the Internet of what had happened at the Dummy Line that night. He still had unanswered questions, but he did know that Jake had killed Johnny Lee Grover and Reese Turner. Those guys were like family to him. He had made a vow to Reese on that fateful night, and he planned to keep that promise.

Over the years, Moon Pie had developed patience—a trait that had helped him successfully evade conviction for his multitude of crimes. He knew that if something immediately happened to Jake, he would be the principal suspect. He also knew that by lying low, with each passing week, everyone would return to their normal behavioral patterns. All he had to do was wait for the right time and place. He could be very, very patient. In fact, he enjoyed the thought of Jake's anxiety at not knowing if or when he and his family were going to be terrorized again. And now that Morgan had seen him watching their house, they would all be on an emotional roller coaster that he alone controlled. Moon Pie smiled.

Moon Pie had seen Jake at his office and at home, and he had even let Jake walk within ten yards of him in the woods one Saturday morning while Jake was plowing a food plot. Jake had gotten off of his small tractor to take a leak, and Moon Pie had planned to kill him and run over him with the tractor to make it look like a farming accident; however, two other guys had driven up, and Jake had immediately left with them. The anticipation of what was to come for Jake was becoming more and more enjoyable to Moon Pie.

Over time, Moon Pie decided to make Jake's death look like a hunting accident, since those were rarely investigated as rigorously as other deaths. He'd never be linked to it. And with Jake gone, there wouldn't be anyone to protect his hot wife and little girl. Another sinister smile crossed Moon Pie's lips.

CHAPTER 14

W ALTER SEVERSON SPENT THE MORNING GOOGLING THE name Sebastian had given him. He didn't learn anything about Jake Crosby's stock-picking abilities, but he spent a solid hour reading about Jake, his daughter, and a young couple being victimized in a series of violent crimes about two years earlier. Three cups of coffee later, he was convinced that he wanted to talk to Jake, so he called the brokerage office to set up a meeting for early afternoon because Walter had to work the late shift at Kroger that day.

Walter was sitting on the deck of Proffitt's Porch, a remote "lakeside restaurant" between West Point and Columbus. He shook Tabasco on his gumbo before he even tasted it. He'd become addicted to the hot sauce since moving to Mississippi. He loved that it was on nearly every Southern table. He wished he had discovered it earlier in life. Each time a red drop splashed onto his food, he cussed the bland Northern cooking he had grown up eating.

He checked his watch, knowing Jake would be arriving soon. He scanned the parking lot for BMWs and Mercedeses—something appropriate for a stockbroker. Nothing fit the bill. Halfway through his cup of gumbo, he noticed a dirty Chevrolet four-wheel-drive pickup roll into the gravel parking lot. He watched a fortysomething-year-old guy wearing khaki pants and a dark-green button-down shirt get out and climb the eatery's steps. He carried a camo fleece jacket in his left hand.

"Mr. Severson?"

Walter accepted that this was the man he was scheduled to meet. He had expected more, however, someone who looked a bit more like he actually worked in a financial institution. This guy's demeanor, coupled with his dress and vehicle choice, was fitting for a sporting-goods-store manager, not a money manager.

"Yes, that's me. Nice to meet you, young man," Walter said as he stood and extended his hand.

"Jake Crosby. Pleasure to meet you, sir."

"I really appreciate you coming on such short notice."

"Not a problem. I had to move a few things around, but I got it done," Jake lied. He didn't want anyone to know he was starved for clients and that if he didn't add a few soon, he'd be fired.

"Do you mind if we eat outside?" Walter didn't want anyone overhearing their conversation.

"No, sir. I actually prefer that. I came prepared…just in case," Jake said, holding up his jacket.

Walter chuckled to himself as his potential financial manager slipped on camouflage at a restaurant. Then he remembered that Mossy Oak Camo was based in West Point; consequently, practically the whole community wore camo as fashion.

"You're not from around here, are you?" Jake asked with a smile, seeing the smile in Walter's eyes as he watched him pull on the jacket.

"No, I'm not. I'm from Minnesota, but I retired to the area recently. Is that a bad thing?"

"No, sir," Jake said with a grin. "After a while, you'll have a new accent."

Walter smiled. He liked Jake. He said, "I've become quite the fan of the hospitality and Southern idiosyncrasies." He held up a bottle of Tabasco and said, "And this stuff. Can't seem to get enough of it."

A college-aged waitress arrived to take their orders. The two men exchanged pleasantries for a while. Jake was hoping to land a client, and Walter was hoping Jake would give him an opening so he could ask him about when he had killed the rednecks.

"Well, Mr. Severson, what specifically can I help you with?" Jake finally asked.

"Please call me Walter."

"Okay, Mr. Walter. What can I help you with?" Jake's Southern upbringing wouldn't allow him to call him simply Walter just yet.

Walter smiled at the politeness. "Basically, I'm starting a foundation and have cash I'd like to invest for fast growth. I'm looking for a good broker, someone who can make me some money while protecting the principal."

This was sounding like an account Jake needed. On Monday morning, he had endured a scathing lecture from his boss about growing his client base. Walter's foundation may be an answer to his prayers. Jake wanted to know how much money he had but didn't want to sound too eager, so he just said, "That's what I do. I would love to help you. Our firm is one of the most trusted brokerage houses in the country. I must say—and I'm sure you already know this—that the market right now is not as...vibrant as it's been in the recent past, so we need to discuss your expectations."

"Growth is important."

"We can grow it as much as anybody. I don't mean to scare you, but the market's just tougher these days. We have to work even harder and sometimes take more risks, but our offices have access to the best analysts in the world, and, well...basically, we have our finger on the pulse of global finance and trends." Jake laid on the last line a little thick, but he had heard his boss use it successfully.

"I see." Walter looked down. He really didn't know what to ask.

"Tell me about the foundation," Jake asked, and then he took a bite of the sandwich the waitress had placed before him a few moments earlier.

Walter glanced around and then gave Jake his prepared speech. He could tell that Jake was honestly impressed. Everyone who heard about it loved it. There was something appealing about grandparents assisting their grandkids. It felt good. The foundation would actually benefit two people at once; the old folks felt good about helping, and the younger folks got a needed boost in life.

"So how much capital do you need to fund it?"

"Right now we have about a hundred grand, but in the next few weeks, I expect it to be significantly more."

Jake was disappointed but didn't show it. The words *significantly more* sounded promising, though.

"Mr. Walter, I need this as much as *you* need this to grow. I promise I'll bust my tail for you. We can talk every day if you like," Jake said honestly.

Walter appreciated Jake's openness. He liked Jake, and he especially liked his willingness to work hard at growing the investment. Walter knew the others would agree with his decision, but he wanted to know more about the young man, so he said, "To be honest with you, Jake, I Googled you to see what was out there, and it seems as though you had a rough go of it a few years back."

"Yes, sir. That was a tough night," Jake said, looking down at the table.

"I know it's none of my business, but does it bother you now?"

Jake was accustomed to people asking questions about that night. It had been a living nightmare, and people were naturally curious.

"No, not really. My daughter and wife still have some side effects."

"It doesn't haunt you to have killed two people?"

"No, sir. Not in the least. I knew those men were gonna kill us—me, my daughter, and this teenage girl that we found. What does haunt me is that there are still two members of that gang out there somewhere." Jake pointed, looked around indiscriminately, and then continued, "I really worried the first few months about some type of retaliation, but now I feel like I gotta get back to normal...wherever that is."

"I'm sorry, son. I had to ask. I needed to know for the foundation."

"I understand. That night...I...I just did what I had to do—what most anybody would've done." Jake was growing a bit uncomfortable.

Walter sensed Jake's change in demeanor. "Okay, Jake. So what do I do? Just bring the money to your office tomorrow?"

Jake's disposition lifted. "Sure. You can come in today or tomorrow, if you like, to fill out the paperwork, and your bank can wire the money or you can bring by a cashier's check."

Walter said, "Um," as he rubbed his face and looked around. "The money's in cash."

Jake was stunned, his eyes wide. "We can't accept cash, Mr. Walter. Can't you just write a check on the foundation's account?"

"We don't have an account just yet. We will soon, though."

Jake was trying to think fast. *Surely there's a way to make this thing work.*

"I just hired a lawyer named Samantha Owens in Columbus to set everything up," Walter added, hoping to calm Jake's obvious concerns.

"Oh, I see. So this is just being formed?" Jake was trying to think if he knew Samantha Owens. The name did not ring any bells.

"You betcha. Brand-new."

"Well, you can't just walk into the bank and deposit a hundred grand without having to fill out serious paperwork. Banks are now required to report any cash deposits over ten thousand dollars. They call it suspicious-activity reports. It's just the government's way of making sure they get their cut if someone's not reporting income or if it's from illegal activities."

"I didn't realize that."

"I mean, you're legitimate, so there's no worries, but the bank and even our offices would face hefty penalties, including jail time, if we didn't file the reports. But I'm sure your lawyer will know what to do." Jake paused for a brief moment, hoping to keep this deal alive, and said enthusiastically, "How about I call her to work on the details?"

Walter nodded and began looking through his notebook for Sam's telephone number.

Jake took a deep breath and glanced out across the big lake at the foot of the restaurant and noticed something interesting.

"Mr. Walter, ever seen a bald eagle?"

"Sure," Walter said, looking at Jake, who was pointing out over the lake. "But it's been a while." He followed Jake's gaze to see a majestic bald eagle floating a few feet above the water's surface and said, "Oh, wow!"

"There's a huge nest at the back of the lake. That's the male hunting for fish. We might get lucky and see him catch something."

"I had no idea there were nesting eagles here."

"There used to be a lot more, but apparently use of DDT in the sixties and seventies really took a toll on the population. It's building back now, and federal protection really helps."

"Sounds like something that interests you," Walter said, noting that Jake seemed more enthusiastic when talking about the eagles than investments.

"Oh yes, sir. I love wildlife. My wife and I eat here regularly, just hoping to see the eagles."

"That's remarkable," Walter said reverently as he watched the big bird. "Your wife likes eagles?"

"She likes salads," Jake said.

Walter quietly chuckled. Jake sensed a tiny connection with Mr. Walter Severson falling into place. So far, he actually liked him, which was more than he could say for over half of his clients.

"I'll talk with your lawyer to see if we can't work out how to quietly handle the funding issues. How does that sound?" Jake figured the lawyer surely had a plan.

"That sounds good. I'll let her know today to expect your call and to discuss specifics with you in confidence."

Jake was relieved to get the lawyer's contact information, since his career depended on this working out. He appreciatively shook Walter's hand and then glanced to Walter's right as the eagle landed in a giant pine tree.

CHAPTER 15

———— ☾ ————

M ORGAN CLEARED THE SUPPER TABLE AS JAKE SLOWLY rubbed his forehead, thinking of ways to increase their income. They had just discussed the upcoming pregnancy expenses. Morgan had already created a new family budget forecasting the next two years. It looked dismal. All she could really focus on, however, was turning their guest bedroom into a nursery.

"Why can't you just ask for a raise?" she asked while loading the dishwasher. "I can't remember the last time you got one."

"It's not that simple. I'm a commissioned broker. Their position is that I can improve my income by signing more clients."

"Well?"

"Well, it's not easy, Morgan," Jake said defensively. "The economy is in the shitter, and nobody wants to get into the market or move any money. Plus, West Point's lost a lot of jobs these last few years. It's tough out there."

"Our family is growing. Our expenses are growing. What are we going to do? What are *you* gonna do?"

"I don't know. I'll think of something." Jake ran his hands through his hair.

"Jake, you always say that, and this time it's not good enough. We both agreed that I should be a stay-at-home mom, but do I need to get a job?"

Jake sat motionless. He wanted what was best for his family. He clearly saw the benefits of Morgan staying home to take care of Katy and knew it would be the same with the new baby. It was worth the sacrifice.

"No."

Morgan exhaled deeply and looked over Jake's head.

"If we have to, we could sell the river camp." Morgan knew this solution would not be well received.

Jake grunted. As a young man, Jake's grandfather had built the camp house. It wasn't much, but it had been in his family for years. It was an old-growth cypress A-frame on pylons overlooking the old river channel. Jake had grown up there fishing, tubing, boat riding, and just hanging out with friends and family. He had to find a way to keep it.

"I know."

Morgan sat down at the table and looked straight at Jake. "Look, I know you don't want to sell it...I get that. But we gotta keep all our options open. This baby is going to be expensive, and it won't be long before Katy's driving and then going off to college. But we don't have to do it tomorrow."

"Just give me a little while to work this out. I swear I'll think of something."

"Maybe I could start selling Arbonne. I hear some women in town are doing really well selling cosmetics and accessories."

"You'll *love* the pink Cadillac," Jake said with a hint of sarcasm.

"They drive Mercedeses."

"Really?"

Jake looked around at his home. He could hear Katy taking a shower upstairs. In a few years she'd be driving. Morgan had that expectant-mother glow, with a baby due in seven months or so. He was beginning to feel like he was failing as a provider. Morgan wanted more. His boss wanted more. Somewhere he had to find the more that everyone demanded. His thoughts turned to the cash that Walter Severson had stashed somewhere.

CHAPTER 16

————— ☾ —————

M OON PIE HEARD THE LOCKS CLICK IN PLACE ON THE front door as the last customer left. It had been a good day at the Gold Mine. He studied the newest shiny gold pieces while the two employees quickly straightened up and prepared to leave. His employees never worked a moment longer than they had to. Today's haul included a dozen rings, bracelets, chains, medallions, and four gold teeth. He weighed the items collectively and instantly knew he had netted more than $5,000 today. *Not bad. The economy's not shitty for everybody*, he thought.

The Gold Mine was notorious for paying less than the other gold business in town, but most of the customers were desperate and didn't consider comparing prices. They typically needed quick cash, and Moon Pie was happy to exploit their desperation. He knew that once someone walked in, he or she was ready to sell, and some money was better than nothing. But not all were down on their luck. Many wealthy wives cashed in jewelry for mad money, and divorces always created a general abandonment of sentimentality.

Through the one-way mirror built into his office wall, Moon Pie watched his favorite employee, Bailey, walk toward his door. She wasn't the most productive, but she was the best looking. Moon Pie had his sights set on her the day she applied. Bailey was twenty-four years old and had been forced to drop out of college to take care of her sick mother, who had just recently passed away. A three-year battle against leukemia with no health or life insurance had left Bailey broke. Moon Pie had tempted Bailey with all sorts of side offers for financial assistance, but she never took the bait. Her redneck boyfriend was jealous of anyone who looked at her, and he had threatened Moon Pie early on. That wasn't smart, and the boyfriend soon realized it.

Bailey didn't know everything Moon Pie was into, but she knew he was of no account. She planned to leave the first chance she got. She had applications out all over town, but things just weren't happening for her. She felt like she was stuck in the mud and couldn't get out.

"Do you need anything else?" Bailey asked as she stuck her head inside his office door.

"Wanna go to dinner tonight?" he asked as he bagged the gold jewelry.

"You know I can't."

"I'm thinking sushi," he said, ignoring her rebuff. He squirted antibacterial spray on his left palm and then vigorously rubbed together both hands. Moon Pie left the gold teeth on his desk. They gave him the willies, so he decided to see how other people would react. He arranged them into a smile.

Bailey was hungry, and ramen noodles were most likely on her menu.

"Sounds good, but you know I can't. I'm leaving, if there's nothin' else for me to do."

"I got sump'n for you to do."

"Ethan, please." Bailey used his real name to emphasize her displeasure.

"When you gonna dump that piece-a-shit loser and go out with a real man—someone who knows how to treat a lady?"

Bailey wanted to say, "I've already broken up with him, but I can't get rid of his sorry ass," but she knew it would be harder to explain than that. He had promised her severe pain if she didn't come back to him.

"Look, babe, I'm going to North Alabama in a few days to pick somethin' up. I may need you to drive me so I can work on the way. Strictly business, and it's important," Moon Pie said.

"What about Levi? Can't he go?" she asked.

Levi Jenkins was Moon Pie's half brother from another mother. His desire was to be Moon Pie's right hand, but he hadn't proven himself capable so far.

"That peckerhead got arrested yesterday in Tuscaloosa. I don't know how quick I can get his sorry ass out...or even if I really wanna get him out," he said with a glint of anger in his voice. It was just a quick glimpse of his well-known two-foot-wide mean streak, but it was unmistakable.

Bailey knew she had to get out of this toxic environment. She regretted having borrowed money from Moon Pie to pay her mother's funeral expenses, but she'd had nowhere else to turn. She exhaled deeply. The only thing she liked about the Gold Mine was Levi. He treated her with respect, and he made her laugh.

"I'll pay you double," Moon Pie said, leaning back in his chair.

Bailey desperately needed the money, but she absolutely did not want to go on a road trip with Moon Pie. She did, however, want him to leave town so she could get to the cash in the safe. She thought she knew two of the three sets of numbers to the combination, but she wasn't certain. Her mind started racing. *Maybe if I go on this trip I can get the other set out of him and steal the cash later.*

"Can I let you know tomorrow?" Bailey asked, stalling.

Moon Pie started to grin and then caught himself. "Sure."

Bailey forced a smile, waved good-bye, and for good measure added a little extra swing in her hips.

Moon Pie quietly laughed as he watched her walk out the door. After he heard it shut, he spun his chair around to place the gold inside his safe. He had configured the interior of the Browning safe to serve his needs. Inside on the top shelf, he had six loaded semiautomatic pistols with extra loaded magazines; underneath on the left side stood three different-caliber hunting rifles he used when poaching, depending on the terrain, and two customized fully automatic black rifles he used for protection. On the right side were shelves for his purchased gold, and underneath were boxes of money.

At the moment, he had $200,000 in cash packed inside three Tony Lama boot boxes. He calculated that he'd have enough room in the safe for the duffel bag of cash he would pick up in a few days. All he had to do was take delivery, store it overnight, and then hand it off. It might be in his possession for only thirty-six to forty-eight hours. The Gold Mine's security was adequate, and the heavy safe was against an internal wall, secured to the concrete slab with four five-inch-long wedge anchors.

Moon Pie had no worries. In front of him was a simple pickup and delivery of cash that would net him 20 percent, a great football game on ESPN on Saturday night, and a new place to poach Monday morning, when the landowner was back at work. *Life's good and gettin' better…particularly if Bailey decides to go with me to Alabama.* He leaned back in his chair, put his feet on his desk, lit a Marlboro Light, and smiled.

CHAPTER 17

———— ☾ ————

L EVI JENKINS SAT IN A TUSCALOOSA, ALABAMA, JAIL WEARING
an orange jumpsuit with the sleeves rolled up to showcase
the barbed-wire tattoos on his lanky arms. He was craving a dip of
Skoal. He cussed under his breath for getting caught transporting
the precursors for manufacturing crystal methamphetamine.
He was especially disgusted at his situation because he had the
biggest drug run of his career brewing, and he didn't need this
attention. Arguing his innocence had proven useless. No one
was buying the story that his church was purchasing a case of
Sudafed to deliver to the needy in Haiti.

The twenty-seven-year-old neophyte drug dealer knew that
his boss and half brother, Moon Pie, wouldn't help, so he called
their cousin in Tupelo, who had finally passed the bar exam on
his fourth attempt. He was a classic ambulance-chasing plain-
tiffs' lawyer but with a gift for being hired by clients who couldn't
pay or who were seldom offered settlements, much less awarded
judgments. After two minutes of cussing and ranting about
issues of jurisdiction and licensing, the lawyer finally promised
to see what he could do.

Back in his cell, Levi bragged about the big stick his lawyer would wave. Levi assured his cellmates that he would be

out within twenty-four hours. What Levi didn't know was that officials within the Mississippi Drug Task Force had already put the wheels in motion to spring Levi. All that was left was the final paperwork. The rail-thin drug runner was a well-connected small fish they hoped would lead them to a large fish—a fish significantly large enough to make their careers. The Alabama counterparts just had to make it appear that Levi's less-than-competent cousin was responsible for his release.

Jenkins was known as Levi by everybody, but his momma insisted on calling him by his full name, Leviticus. He was from a wide spot in the road in Monroe County, Mississippi, called Becker Bottom. He perpetrated his illegal activities only on the unsuspecting folks in the surrounding counties—never in his own. It was one of a few codes that he followed. Levi was a two-bit hustler whose initial crimes were mostly scams. His most successful con to date was selling hot tubs and television satellite systems to folks who lived far out in the country. He convinced his unsophisticated victims to make deposits either in cash or by check written to him personally. No spa or dish deliveries were ever made. He had not graduated to violent crime just yet, but he was heading down that path with the allure of drug money—which his half brother, Moon Pie, was blazing.

Like many small-time criminals, he loved to talk about his conquests, embellishing the stories when the truth sounded just as good, maybe even better. Levi Jenkins told so many lies that he could hardly remember the truth.

When the jailers moved Levi into the main population, a huge guy accosted him—the common-law husband to a girl Levi had once dated. The mountain of a man had endured years of being compared to Levi's two redeeming qualities: he was a big spender, and he was otherwise well gifted. Levi would spend his last cent to impress a date with expensive dinners, movies, concerts, gifts, and flowers. He would also listen to every story and small detail his date wanted to discuss. This and his other "characteristics" were endearing.

When Levi's ex-girlfriend's huge husband saw Levi, all he wanted to do was punch him in the mouth. Levi sensed the danger, but there was no way to retreat. After a few minutes of increasing tension between the two of them with each unanswered threat, Levi finally had to fight. The promise of violence fueled the other prisoners' enthusiasm as they cheered and jeered from their cells. In short order, Levi had his ass handed to him. He had a bloody nose and a cut under his left eye, and was nearly unconscious from a relentless chokehold before the guards rushed in to stop the one-sided fight.

The guards aggressively and effectively subdued Levi and his huge foe, making sure neither one had any more fight left in him. When Levi tried to stand without permission, an older guard kneed him in the groin, even though it was immediately obvious to everyone that Levi wasn't going to cause any more problems. Levi's enormous assailant loved the outcome. While Levi rolled on the nasty jail floor, two suddenly sober University of Alabama fraternity brothers huddled in a corner vowed to never drink again.

The sheriff shouted obscenities at the top of his lungs as he hurriedly entered the jail block, angry that his men had momentarily lost control of the prisoners. When he saw the situation, he knew any lawyer could successfully challenge the guards' reaction to the fight. He loathed lawyers. His day had just gotten complicated, and the handling of what he assumed to be an irrelevant prisoner had just become a nightmare.

Writhing in intense pain, Levi swore to himself to never be incarcerated again. Grimacing, he obeyed the deputies who pulled him to his feet.

CHAPTER 18

—— ☾ ——

J AKE SAT AT HIS CUBICLE AND ALLOWED THE INTERNET to answer a few questions about Samantha Owens. He felt sneaky doing it, but no one in Jake's circle of office friends knew her. There wasn't much information available. She had gone to college at the W in Columbus. She had earned her law degree at Ole Miss and just recently had passed the bar. Her Facebook page was blocked. There really wasn't much more information available. She wasn't listed as a member of any law firms in Columbus. That seemed odd.

Jake got his morning started by checking a waterfowl-migration map online and a few select stocks that were anticipating bad news while he waited for eight fifteen to arrive so he could make the call.

"Law office," a cheery voiced answered after four rings.

"Samantha Owens, please," Jake stated.

"May I tell her who's calling?" the cheery voice responded.

"Jake Crosby. I'm a broker with Morgan Keegan."

"Hold, please."

Jake refreshed the satellite image page that followed a radio-collared mallard drake that was currently just north of Memphis, heading south.

"This is Samantha Owens," a similarly cheery voice said, very businesslike. She sounded younger than he was, but it was hard to tell.

Jake paused as he smiled and wondered if she was answering her own phone calls, "Ms. Owens, I'm Jake Crosby. How are you today?"

"I'm well, thank you."

"Good. I must admit you're a new name around here."

"I just moved back to the area," she responded, careful not to tell too much. She didn't trust men. "What can I do for you, Mr. Crosby?"

"Yesterday I met with Walter Severson about me helping manage his excess cash reserves and…well, he gave me your name and said his foundation was just getting established and that you could help me."

"That is correct. He hired me to start a foundation, but it's not operational yet."

"I see. He indicated that he had the money but it was all cash. Since we can't take cash deposits here, I was hoping you could give me an estimated time that you think the foundation would be active."

"Mr. Crosby— "

"Please call me Jake," he interrupted.

"And you can call me Sam. Jake, it is going to be at least a week before the foundation's legally on its feet. We still have a lot to do. Mr. Severson and his friends are retired gentlemen with a lot of free time to dream and wish and hope, but they're gonna have to let the paperwork catch up to them."

"I understand. Well, as soon as you can cut checks, I'd appreciate a call so we can get his brokerage account set up."

"I'll do that…and…if you know anybody needing an attorney, please remember me," she shamelessly pleaded. Sam was also relieved to have somebody participating in the foundation who sounded somewhat normal.

"Yes, ma'am," Jake responded politely. "Somebody around here always needs a good lawyer...and besides, you have such a nice-sounding receptionist."

Sam blushed and moved the phone to her other ear. "Could you tell?"

"I had an idea."

Sam laughed at herself and her attempt to impress. "We're pretty new around here. My actual secretary is a single mom, and there's a big play at her daughter's school today."

"No need to explain or be embarrassed."

"Thank you. It's been difficult getting established. Oh, one thing you mentioned—something about cash being a problem."

"That's right. We can't take cash to open an account. As I'm sure you're aware, financial transactions are no longer private, since banks and brokerage firms now have to comply with what's called suspicious-activity reports, which basically obligate banks and brokers like me to report transactions that could be considered suspicious or over ten thousand dollars, but for the most part, all financial businesses, even precious-metal dealers, report every transaction over five thousand. It's a nightmare, and if I don't report it, I'm the one who gets in serious trouble. Big Brother is watching. At any rate, the tax issues are probably going to be the worst part of it, though."

"I hadn't fully considered all that."

"You need to find a good community banker and tax attorney. They can help."

"Thank you, Jake. I'll be in touch."

"Sure. Just have your secretary call my secretary," he quipped and heard her laugh.

CHAPTER 19

————— ☾ —————

WALTER WASN'T AN HOUR INTO HIS SECOND SHIFT SINCE the heist when he knew something was amiss. The store associates' attitudes were notably different. A cashier carefully whispered that the manager had been in meetings all day, and she had heard a rumor that he was going to be fired. Everyone was on their best work behavior. The young, big-breasted, tattooed cashier who the manager had been lusting over was visibly upset. She'd been crying. Walter thought the store hadn't operated this efficiently since he began working there. *Hell, I might have even done Kroger a favor,* he rationalized.

Walter did feel bad for what he had done to Kroger, even though their business insurance would likely cover the loss. Most people didn't realize how philanthropic the company was within their respective communities and that they were the number-two retailer in the country. Walter figured that given the right setting, pitched to the right Kroger executive, they probably would donate to his foundation as much as he had stolen, provided the foundation was legit. Right now, however, he didn't have the time or the life expectancy for legit. If the foundation ever got cash flush, he'd pay back the grocery giant. Kroger had a secret IOU with his foundation. That thought made him smile.

During Walter's shift, as he helped customers find the correct aisles for products they needed and straightened the blue buggies, he marveled at how his group of old-timers had pulled off the theft. Their plan to steal no more than two-thirds of the cash from the weekend bank deposit had worked for two reasons. First, the deposit initially appeared to be intact, and it would take some time to determine exactly what was missing; and second, the manager had created the perfect opportunity by concentrating on the stripper giving him lap dances in the back office—the private hump and grind necessitating the temporary disabling of the office's security cameras.

Walter had studied the store's timing. He knew when and where the money moved, when the dances occurred, and, most importantly, when the security system went down.

As a trusted associate and because of his age, Walter was almost invisible to the other employees. His most valuable attribute was that he was trusted. He could go anywhere without question. Early in his tenure, Walter had ingratiated himself to management by always running errands for the manager and assistant manager and doing odd jobs away from work; consequently, it was not uncommon for him to be around when receipts were tallied.

That busy weekend's sales receipts, including cash, were piled on the manager's desk, to be organized and counted, and then picked up by armored truck on Monday. Sunday evenings were prime lap-dance times, since the manager's wife would be at church. After the stripper slipped out the rear door and the manager went to the restroom, Walter simply walked into the office carrying an empty barbecue-grill box and hurriedly filled it with most of the cash. He carried the box to a concealed space behind several pallets of merchandise, and with a big yellow label, he identified the box as being customer pickup to ensure that no one would attempt to put it back into stock. He then placed the box in the appropriate spot in the hold bin and returned to bagging groceries.

Earlier that morning, Lucille had purchased the last matching grill with cash and then returned it late that night, complaining that it was missing the bottom grate and the handle. As if they had read the script, customer service paged Walter to exchange it, which he did with the one stashed in the back. When he returned to the customer-service counter, Sebastian was pitching a fit about some incomprehensible injustice that completely overwhelmed the manager and the customer-service staff. When the customer-service representative saw that the grill boxes were the same, with Walter holding the receipt, she waved the old woman through without a second glance. The automatic doors opened, and the cash went out.

Walter had almost headed straight to the back to take a blood pressure pill. He could feel his pulse in his ears, which had begun to ring. That didn't bother him; he hadn't felt so alive in years, maybe ever. He certainly hadn't felt this alive since his daughter's murder.

CHAPTER 20

———— ☾ ————

MOON PIE WAITED IMPATIENTLY FOR LEVI TO ARRIVE AT THE Gold Mine. He passed the time by looking at pictures in the *Commercial Dispatch*—the Columbus newspaper that covered almost everything that happened in the Golden Triangle, the area formed by Columbus, Starkville, and West Point. Moon Pie loved to see the published photos of everyone who had been arrested recently. Their mug shots and criminal charges were right there for all to see. Moon Pie rarely read an article, but he savored perusing the pictures.

Mustard dripped from his gas station sausage biscuit as he flipped the pages and glanced up to check the time. When he heard Levi's truck pull up near the back door, he finished the sausage and tossed the biscuit into the trash. Moon Pie was pissed, and he took a deep breath to calm himself.

The moment Levi stepped through the back door, Moon Pie punched him in the stomach. Levi buckled over and then dropped to his knees, gasping for breath.

"That's for being stupid," Moon Pie barked, his fists clenched by his side.

"I deserve that," Levi said under his breath but loud enough for Moon Pie to hear. Those simple words of repentance kept him from getting a further ass kicking.

Moon Pie flopped back down in his desk chair and stared at his half brother sitting on the floor, catching his breath.

"Just what in the hell were you thinkin'?"

"Man, I was just tryin' to make some extra cash, bro."

"Don't I pay you enough?"

Levi slowly stood, walked to an armchair, and sat down. "I just wanted to make some extra foldin' money, you know. I'm really sorry, Moon."

Moon Pie glared at him. He didn't like incompetence. "You've developed a bad habit of doing things without tellin' me or askin' me, and some bad shit always happens."

"I know. I know."

"And I get a call from our cousin at midnight saying you've been arrested? Just how in the hell did you get outta jail so fast, anyway?"

"I don't know...maybe he's learnin how the system works."

"I don't know why we even use him."

"He's family, and he's cheap."

"He's an ambulance chaser!" Moon Pie said in a louder-than-normal voice. "We can't go to the next level with him watchin' our back."

"Well, I'm out. He got me out. And fast too."

"Yeah, I guess." Moon Pie lit a Marlboro and aggressively exhaled the smoke. He was suspicious of Levi's quick release. After another long drag from the cigarette, he made up his mind.

"Take your shirt off."

"What?"

"I said take your shirt off."

"You don't think that I would—" Levi asked in an astonished tone.

"Take it off, or I'll rip it off!"

Levi stared at him in disbelief. He was hurt more than angry. After a few tense moments, he unzipped his jacket and pulled a long-sleeved T-shirt over his head, revealing his bare chest."

"Satisfied?"

"Pants too."

"Shit, Moon, I'm your brother!"

"Half brother, and you proved yesterday that you ain't got shit for brains."

Levi unbuckled his jeans. With a quick downward motion, he dropped them to the floor and stood there in dingy tighty-whities, completely humiliated and praying that Bailey didn't walk in on them.

Moon Pie started laughing. It was apparent Levi wasn't wired.

"Okay, pull 'em up. In this bidness, paranoia's healthy. That's your school-of-hard-knocks lesson today."

"You ain't paranoid, you're psycho."

"Careful with your mouth. You better show me some respect or I'll give you another black eye. I can't be too careful. Tomorrow we're gonna pick up a pile of cash, and a lot could go wrong. I need your mind in the game."

"Where we goin'?" Levi asked curiously.

"They wanted someplace remote. I suggested we meet their moneyman at the Coon Dog Cemetery near Muscle Shoals, Alabama. It's about halfway, and it's extremely isolated."

"I always wanted to see that place."

"It'll bring a tear to your eye, my li'l half brother. Now get your shit together. Go home, shower, and for God's sake, put on some clean clothes," Moon Pie ordered. "We're gonna make a delivery tonight."

CHAPTER 21

———— ☾ ————

THE ANTIQUE GANG ASSEMBLED IN THE LIBRARY OF THE Henry Clay Retirement Community. It was dark outside, unseasonably cold, and misting rain. Most of the residents were already in their rooms for the night, so the group had the area to themselves. Two Pizza Inn boxes sat in front of them. Everyone grazed at their leisure, happy that Walter now fed them at every meeting.

Walter sat nervously bouncing his right leg as he made notes on a legal pad. He was visibly anxious. Kroger's home-office security team had interviewed him earlier in the day. They were pushing hard for answers. The team had reviewed every frame of the surveillance tape and had a lot of questions for him. It had been an intense meeting. They had homed in on him faster than he expected, but it was obvious they didn't have enough facts to have him arrested. Walter knew it wasn't over. They had made that obvious.

Bailey had been invited to join the group after her grandmother Lucille's casual mention of the foundation as a response to Bailey's comment to her about the safe full of cash at the Gold Mine. Knowing two of the three pairs of numbers was the tipping point for Walter's acceptance.

Bailey excitedly explained to the group, "My boss will be out of town in two days, and that might make the robbery safer."

Walter and company listened intently, and their eyes darted nervously as they considered what she was saying.

"He's always armed to the teeth, and even on the two times a year when he goes to church with his momma, he carries two pistols. Nobody else in the store will be armed, though," she finished, as if that should be the deciding factor.

"Easter and Mother's Day?" Bernard asked, already knowing.

"Yes, sir."

"Bailey, we aren't going to bust in there and stick the place up like a bank robbery," Walter explained.

Bailey looked puzzled, but the other members of the group looked relieved.

"Somebody could get hurt, and frankly I doubt that our hearts could take the stress."

"I just assumed...that's the way—"

"No. We're going to break in after-hours and steal the contents of the safe," Walter explained, cutting her off. The gang members smiled. Burglary sat better with them than armed robbery.

"But the place has an alarm system that Moon Pie arms every night," Bailey said, concerned.

"We'll need to know specifics about it, but when I looked around a few days ago, I didn't see any motion sensors in the main room."

"The windows and doors are wired for sure. I've heard the alarm go off by accident; it's really loud. He sets it sometimes when we're counting money. He's paranoid."

"He couldn't move around if it had motion detectors, unless he has a high-tech system that can be set to different modes and zones."

"It looks pretty basic to me, but I don't really know," Bailey said.

"I think I have a solution for the alarm, but we still gotta get in the safe. I've been researching it. It takes a six-digit security code. If you don't get it in three or four tries, it shuts down for, like, thirty minutes," Walter explained as he placed on the table the printed camera-phone pictures of Moon Pie's office, alarm keypad, and safe. "Bailey took these. They've been extremely helpful."

Bailey smiled. It had been a long time since anyone other than her grandmother had praised her, and everyone could sense her appreciation.

Walter said, "Okay, gang—here's my idea."

Everyone inched a bit closer as their heart rates escalated. They all felt so incredibly alive. The collective energy was palpable. Tomorrow, when and if their sons and daughters called to check on them, casually asking, "What's new? Anything exciting going on?" each would smile and say, "Nothin'. Not much." In fact, however, they all would have spent hours the evening before planning a burglary expected to net them $300,000, and it was, in fact, their second major crime within a month.

Walter continued, "Tomorrow I'll order several balloons to be delivered to Bailey at work. Bailey, you'll need to place them near a vent—in the office would be great—and then forget them when you leave work. We'll find out pretty quickly if the place has motion sensors when everyone's gone for the day and the heater turns on. Bernard, get two flat, very thin magnets, and paint one white and one off-white. And get a bottle of Krazy Glue. Then the day before we break in, Bailey will glue the correct-colored magnet over the magnetic sensor in the top of the doorframe. It looks like a little black dot. That should trick the system into thinking the door's closed when they set it, and it won't go off when we open it."

"How do we do that?" Sebastian asked.

"Bailey's gotta get us a copy of the key—somehow. Think of something."

"Yes sir."

"What about the rest of the safe combination?" Lucille questioned.

"I'm working on it. People generally use passwords and numbers that involve birthdays, hobbies, interests, important dates, and things they like. The combinations are endless, and I'm trying to nail down the obvious first. We know he is a football fan and more specifically a Manning fan. He has framed pictures of Eli, Archie, and Peyton displayed in his office."

Bailey nodded her head excitedly. "He talks about 'em all the time, especially Peyton, and if either Eli or Peyton's playin' on TV, he's watching."

"I'm betting the last number in the code is ten, sixteen, or eighteen."

"Their jersey numbers?" Bernard offered.

"You betcha," Walter said in his nasal Minnesotan accent.

"There's at least six combinations of those numbers, if Bailey's numbers don't work. And we don't know how often he changes the combination. Bailey's numbers could be good today but not tomorrow," Bernard stated after he quickly computed the possibilities.

"True, so we'll need to get his birthday too," Walter said to Bailey, who nodded her understanding.

"He's a big hunter too. But I don't know what numbers work with huntin'," Bernard noted. He had studied the photos Bailey had secretly taken of everything in Moon Pie's office and the store, and of his truck tag.

"Bailey, while he's gone out of town, I'll give you some number sequences to try. If you can start trying the combinations, it would be helpful. I'll print them out so you can mark them off. I'm hoping it's something simple. Without the combination, we're dead in the water."

"I'll do it," Bailey responded positively.

"Good girl. That way if one of those doesn't work, Lucille and Sebastian can work on another set of combinations. Birthdays, important dates, phone-number prefixes."

"I may can trick his half brother, Levi, into telling me…he's kinda sweet on me," Bailey said.

"He's a cutie pie," Lucille instantly replied, and Bailey blushed, although no one noticed except Lucille.

"No, I don't like that idea. He'll be suspicious after the money vanishes. You don't need anything pointin' back at you," Walter explained.

"Let's just get a blowtorch and cut it open," Sebastian suggested excitedly.

"Not there. That would set off the smoke alarm," Walter responded quickly. He didn't want Sebastian losing focus at the thought of getting to break out the power tools.

Sensing what was going on, Lucille jumped in excitedly to change the subject. "When do you think we'll try?"

"This Saturday night might be good. It's opening weekend of deer season, and any hunter worth his salt will be at his camp, or at the very least going to bed early. It's a tradition that's played out from here to Minnesota, and I'm willing to bet Mr. Daniels will be somewhere other than at work, so we'll have time to do what we need to do."

"That's pretty soon," Bernard said, as if he had plans for Saturday night.

"We ain't gettin' any younger," Walter shot back.

"That's true," Bernard responded, nodding his head.

"Besides, what else were you doing Saturday night?"

"Nothing—except now, I guess I'm committin' a felony."

"We're all in, then," Lucille said emphatically, with a big smile.

CHAPTER 22

——— ☾ ———

MOON PIE WAS DRIVING AS HE AND LEVI HEADED SOUTH from Columbus. They were listening to a CD of Hank Williams Jr.'s greatest hits.

Levi knew something was going to happen tonight. Moon Pie always used Hank to get himself worked up for a job, like an athlete pumping up before a game. Levi searched for something to talk about. He saw an envelope on the dash and grabbed it.

"See that FedEx logo?" Levi asked.

"Yeah, I'm not blind."

"But do you see the arrow in the logo?"

"The what?"

Levi held up the envelope so Moon Pie could see it better, "In the second *E*. The arrow that's pointing to the right?"

"Huh? Yeah, I see it."

"Pretty creative, ain't it?"

"You notice some weird shit, man."

Levi wanted to ask where they were meeting the drug drop but decided to keep quiet for a while. He was just happy to be around Moon Pie and even happier to be out of jail. Full of nervous energy, he checked the glove box and console for pistols. He found several and worked the actions of the different semiautomatics, admiring their precision. One had laser grips, which fascinated him. When he held it in firing position, the red laser turned on, reflecting off the windshield.

"Those are sweet, huh?" Moon Pie offered as more of a comment than a question.

"Hell yeah. I'm guessin' that anybody that's got that red dot on their chest gets an immediate attitude adjustment."

"If they're looking at you, they immediately know the deal. But if you're at a distance and it's daylight and they don't know you're there…they may not see the dot. That's frustrating," Moon Pie stated flatly, with firsthand knowledge.

"If you ever saw it, though, it'd scare the shit outta ya!"

"That's what I thought. Once while I was hid in the woods where the guy that killed Reese lives, I saw him messing around with some duck decoys in the back of his truck. Anyway, I was about seventy-five yards out, and I lasered him in the chest, hoping he'd see it and freak out…but he never did."

"Maybe he's color-blind?"

"Could be. I think he just didn't notice it. I wanna kill him bad, but I gotta wait. I've been screwin' with him off and on for a while, but some things I think he notices and others I don't know."

"Like what?"

"Just subtle shit that would mess with his mind. I've rubbed streaks of blood on his truck windows a couple times."

"He had to see that."

"Ya'd think. I mailed him an article about that night from the newspaper, and I burned the edges."

"Is it gettin' to be time to keep your promise to Reese?"

"Maybe. Patience pays, Grasshoppar. Besides, I want that sumbitch to suffer—mentally, you know?" Moon Pie's eyes were fixed on the road ahead. "I'm not in a rush. I haven't decided just how I'm gonna do it. Kill him…kill his wife…take the kid…kill him and the kid and then take his hot wife for a while? I ain't done anything just yet because I know I'll be the first on the cops' short list of suspects. I ain't as stupid as *you* look."

"Low under the radar's good," Levi commented as he watched some headlights behind them. They'd been back there for a while, and paranoia was creeping in. They were driving on a desolate two-lane road that went down the west side of the Tombigbee River toward Aliceville, Alabama.

"We got company," Moon Pie said. "Don't turn around. Use the side mirror. They've been followin' us since Columbus."

Moon Pie's heavily modified black Toyota FJ Cruiser had every accessory Toyota offered, plus a Warn winch, KC HiLites, and Buckshot radial mudders. It was quiet, almost impossible to get stuck in the mud, and very easy to maneuver—an outlaw's dream machine. In the rear, hanging under the trailer hitch, was a set of red Truck Nutz that looked like giant bull testicles. Moon Pie smiled every time he saw them.

"Who you think it is?" Levi asked.

"That's a stupid question. It's the law. Gotta be. We don't need 'em—not tonight with this drop and especially not tomorrow."

"Whatcha gonna do?"

"Text Smitty and tell him tonight's meet's off. Tell him we got company."

Levi's thumbs went into action. He could text faster than he could talk.

"We'll head to Aliceville and figure out if it's the law actually followin' us."

"Then what?"

Moon Pie was growing aggravated with the questions. "That'll depend on them," Moon Pie said, jerking his thumb toward the car behind them.

CHAPTER 23

———— ☾ ————

WHEN THE TELEPHONE RANG, JAKE, COMPLETELY STAR-
tled, sat up in bed. His thoughts were murky as he
looked at the alarm clock. It glowed 3:55. The phone rang again
and snapped him out of it.

"Hello?"

"Mr. Jake Crosby?"

Jake cleared his throat and answered, "Yes, yes it is."

Morgan rolled over to listen.

"This is Rosco Blue with the Pickens County Sheriff's
Department."

"Yes, sir?" Jake sat up in the bed.

"I'm sorry to call you so early, but I got some bad news."

"What? What is it?" Jake asked, now wide-awake.

"Yo' camp house down here on Pumpkin Creek has burned down."

"What!"

"I just left there. It's a total loss. The volunteer fire department couldn't do much. It went off like fat wood."

"Burned? I...what happened?" Jake was trying to get his
mind around what he was hearing.

"What's wrong?" Morgan asked with a feeling of déjà vu.
Jake held up his hand.

"We got a call 'bout midnight from a tugboat captain, and by the time we got a fire truck down there, the structure was totally consumed. I'm sorry."

"Good grief," Jake said in disbelief.

"At least no one was injured."

"How'd it start?"

"We don't know. It's been drizzlin' rain here all night."

"Lightnin' maybe?" Jake offered, trying to make sense of the news.

"I doubt it, but NOAA weather can let us know if there was any strikes associated with that band of rain. I'm really sorry to call so early, but I figured that iffin it was mine, I'd want to know." Sheriff Blue tried to sound empathic, but his true motivation was to establish if Jake was home at the time of the fire and to gauge his reaction to the news. He suspected arson, but he didn't want to mention this just yet. He continued, "We'll check into it later this mornin'. The fire marshal will look it over. It's all standard procedure."

Jake was still stunned. "I don't know what to say. What do I...what do you need me to do?"

"Can you come down this mornin' and fill out some paperwork?"

"Yeah, sure. Absolutely."

"You're in West Point, right?"

"Yes, sir."

"Well, don't leave now. Just be down here midmornin' if you can. My office is in downtown Aliceville. Just ask anybody. I'm the sheriff."

"Yes, sir. Okay, I'll be there." Jake didn't know whether to thank him or just hang up. He hung up the telephone, and Morgan rapid-fired questions at him. He stared straight ahead. After a moment, Jake said, "That was the Pickens County sheriff. The camp house caught fire and burned down tonight. The sheriff said it's a total loss."

Morgan rubbed the sleep out of her eyes and started fresh with more unanswerable questions. Jake finally held up his hand and asked her to stop so he could ask one very important question.

"Please tell me you paid the insurance on the camp house."

CHAPTER 24

———— ☾ ————

THE GERIATRIC GANGSTERS WERE EATING BREAKFAST AT the local Mennonite bakery, and no one was counting calories. Now that the group had access to other people's money, they were eating out at every opportunity. They weren't spending big bucks, but they weren't eating canned soup and oatmeal as regularly as before. Today they were all a bit jumpy in anticipation of the Gold Mine burglary.

"Bailey just called and said the magnets need to be off-white," Walter remarked to Bernard.

"I'm on it," Bernard replied.

"She also said that she's gonna be able to get a copy of the key today."

"Now we just gotta find out the rest of the safe combination," Sebastian said confidently.

"That's easier said than done," Lucille remarked.

Walter glanced around to make certain no one was eavesdropping. "Guys, I'm starting to get some heat. I got a call early this morning requesting I come down to the store at ten so corporate security can ask me some more questions. They're very good. I'm not sure where we messed up to allow them to connect the dots to me. I really thought they would snoop around, fire that piece-of-shit manager, and move on. It's been almost two weeks, and they haven't let up a bit…I was wrong. I'm sorry."

"What can we do?" Lucille asked.

"I don't know. I swear, I'll never give you guys up if something happens."

"And us either; it goes both ways," Sebastian said immediately.

They all nodded as they looked around the table at each other.

"There's no *I* in team. We're a team," Sebastian said.

Walter smiled. He really liked Sebastian. He had a level head, and he loved to fight for the underdog.

"I'll know more later today, but to be honest, I'm nervous."

"Just keep quiet and play dumb, and we'll all back you up," Sebastian calmly instructed.

"Act like you got Alzheimer's," Bernard said with a chuckle.

Walter appreciated their spirit and knew he could trust them. He hated that his plan had potentially gotten everyone into trouble. They didn't deserve the humiliation that would follow the public scrutiny. He had to devise a means of deflecting the attention. Walter had an awful lot on his mind.

"Guys, I think we should slow down the formation of the foundation for a bit. If Kroger's security brings in the police and they find out we started a foundation shortly after the money went missing, it could lead to more questions that we don't want to answer."

"He's right," Sebastian said as he sipped his coffee.

"So, are we going to"—Lucille looked around the room nervously—"you know, rob the Gold Mine?"

Walter was drinking a Code Red Mountain Dew for its maximum caffeine effect. "I think so. It's too good an opportunity to pass up."

They all nodded their agreement, and Lucille began to tear up, thinking of how this was going to help Bailey.

Through sniffles, Lucille said, "Walter...what if we get in the Gold Mine safe and there's two hundred and fifty thousand dollars in there? Why can't we give Kroger back their money? We'd be back to square one. Even Steven. All Bailey needs is enough to disappear and get her business started; twenty thousand would do it."

Everyone agreed that it seemed like a good, workable idea.

Walter slowly looked around the group. He knew it was a good idea and nodded his agreement. How to return the money was going to take some thought.

"Walter, you've had some great ideas, and I agree that we should delay the foundation until things settle down with Kroger," Lucille pleaded. "Have our attorney hold up the paperwork and give us a month at least."

"Yeah, and since we've paid her a retainer, have her go with you to the meeting at Kroger today," Sebastian added.

"Yeah, lawyer up, like they do on tee vee," Bernard added.

CHAPTER 25

———— ☾ ————

M OON PIE SAT AT HIS DESK, WORKING ON HIS EVER-
expanding to-do list. He imagined that he organized his
day as would the CEO of a Fortune 500 company. He went to
the Gold Mine early, read several newspapers, and surfed online
for market trends and opportunities while eating gas station
grits, eggs, and sausage that he picked up every day on the way
in. Moon Pie wanted to watch YouTube videos and order all his
high-tech gadgets from Amazon while he was on the go. *What I
really need is an iPad*, he thought.

Moon Pie lived in a twenty-year-old single-wide trailer
that he rented for two hundred a month, but he had a fifty-inch
plasma TV and every satellite and cable channel available. He
had wireless Internet and an iPhone, with a long list of apps.
All this technology cost twice his rent. That's how he liked
to live…mostly low-key but surrounded with state-of-the-art
technology. He had high-tech dishes and antennas along with
worn-out tires on his rusty roof. What he didn't have was a
woman. He was gun-shy, and now that he was accumulating
some wealth, he was becoming more cautious about getting
involved again. Yet he really liked Bailey and thought she was
different—trustworthy.

Today was going to be a red-letter day for Ethan "Moon Pie" Daniels and his growing, always-flexible criminal business. He and Levi were scheduled to pick up almost a million dollars that they would then pass to their connections on the Gulf Coast, netting Moon Pie a healthy percentage for being the mule. If they did these monthly transactions as anticipated, he would be raking in some serious coin.

Moon Pie wanted to move to the past—the old South, complete with the stars and bars—and become Colonel Reb. With his cash, he was going to buy an old antebellum home and restore it to its glory. That was his dream.

Lately he had grown more concerned about security. Last night he thought he had been followed, so he had postponed his drop. After a quick loop through Aliceville, he had finally realized they hadn't been tailed. He laughed at his paranoia and explained to Levi that it came with the territory.

Moon Pie was so relieved that they torched Jake Crosby's camp house as an afterthought. He enjoyed knowing that he was torturing Crosby. After stealing the only items of value in the camp, he and Levi had dripped a mixture of diesel fuel and gasoline through the small cabin and dropped a match.

Jake had two deer-head mounts, a big ten and a heavy eleven-point that would both score over 160 inches, and a couple of nice-size bass. Moon Pie figured the deer heads were worth about five grand each. He'd wholesale them to his taxidermy buddy, which would net him about half. The financial score alone had made the night worthwhile.

When Bailey walked through the back door of the Gold Mine the next morning, she saw the two deer mounts on the floor and didn't think anything of them. There was always some kind of critter lying on the back-room floor—mostly antlers of a fresh kill or something already mounted, ready to hang. Currently in the back room there was a full-bodied African lion she knew Moon Pie had stolen from a doctor's camp. She had overheard a telephone conversation about how Moon Pie was waiting on a buyer from Texas to come get it.

The last several years of Bailey's life had been challenging. Her mother's prolonged illness and eventual passing had forced her to grow up fast, and she had missed out on most of her teen years. She'd been left with no choice, but she was not bitter or resentful. She loved and respected her mom for everything she had done alone. When Bailey was four, in the middle of the night, her father abandoned his only child and her mother, leaving them $40,000 in debt. Bailey's mother didn't say anything bad about him or the situation; she just found a second job and worked six days a week for twelve years. She never took a penny of government money.

After her mother became ill, Bailey tried for a semester to manage a college workload while taking care of her, but as the leukemia progressed, so did her mother's need for constant care. Bailey dropped out of school. Medicaid helped with expenses, but the associated costs, coupled with the loss of her mother's income, quickly drained their meager savings. Bailey was forced to sell her mother's car, all of the family heirlooms, such as they were, and then their small, modest home. By the end, Bailey had managed to pay down the medical bills to a balance of ninety-five hundred dollars. She was steadily chipping away at the debt, making monthly payments while dodging other creditors.

When Bailey discovered that her boyfriend had been stealing from her, she began thinking about how that money in Moon Pie's safe could solve her problems. It got to the point where it was all she could think about. She had never stolen anything in her life. She wasn't a criminal—yet. But knowing there were stacks of cash just lying around was very tempting, almost overwhelming. The pressure of collection agencies and a desire to get away from her abusive, addict boyfriend had begun to help her justify stealing the money. *All I gotta do is figure out that safe combination.*

Fighting back her anxiety, Bailey took a deep breath as she tried to settle the nauseous feeling in her stomach. She placed her lunch inside the mini-fridge and then knocked on Moon Pie's office door.

"Yeah?" Moon Pie hollered.

Bailey slowly entered the cluttered office. "Hey, Moon, do you still need me to drive for your trip?"

"Damn, you look good!"

"Be serious."

"I am."

"Then be realistic."

"No, I don't. Levi got out…but I do need you to pick me up an iPad this morning." Bailey already knew Levi was out because they had traded text messages earlier.

"An iPad?"

"I gotta be connected and workin' when I'm travelin'."

"Okay, I'd be glad to," she said, relieved, and then she realized that she had a rare opportunity. "Can I take your truck? My car's actin' up. I think it's my battery."

Moon Pie never questioned her motives. "Yeah, sure. Here's the keys, and fill it up while you're out."

Moon Pie gave her a sleazy smile as he openly appraised her from head to toe. She was wearing jeans, Ugg boots, and a Drake jacket he was sure belonged to Levi that concealed what he considered her best assets.

"Here, let me get you some money," he said, turning around in his chair toward the safe. She strained to see the numbers, but his shoulders blocked her view. She distinctly heard six beeps as numbers were punched, just as Walter had explained. After the final beep, the safe's lock clicked. Moon Pie turned the handle and then swung open the door. He reached inside for a stack of bills and then started counting.

"Here's a grand. I gotta have it by one o'clock today. I'll learn about the iPad while Levi's drivin'."

"Okay, I can handle that."

"Thanks, babe." He noticed her scanning the safe but didn't say anything about it. "Try not to wreck it."

"No problem."

"Hey, what's the matter? Need some money?"

"Nothing. Nope. I'm good," she replied. She took the cash from his hand and quickly walked out of the office.

CHAPTER 26

———— ☾ ————

SAMANTHA WAS NERVOUS ABOUT HER MEETING WITH WALTER and the Kroger security team. Her appearance on behalf of Walter would be a complete surprise to them, but the advantage was theirs because effectively everything discussed would be new to her. Although Walter had briefed her, she really didn't know what she was walking into, and she didn't have time to prepare. She asked Walter as many questions as she could and grabbed her coat. Since he now really needed a lawyer, she didn't have any qualms about keeping the retainer. This was why she had gone to law school. She wanted to help those who couldn't help themselves. As she drove to the Kroger, she prepared by pushing the knowledge of her clients robbing the store to the back of her mind.

Walter parked his car next to a distant light pole in the Kroger parking lot, exactly as Sam had directed. She watched and then pulled her green Volkswagen Bug over next to him.

"Cute car," Walter said as he opened Sam's door for her.

"One more time, I need to know what you've told them."

"I haven't said shit...excuse me...I-I'm just nervous. I've just answered their questions about that night, what I did, what I saw."

"Okay, good. I understand. I'm nervous too," she said in a moment of anxious honesty and immediately wished she hadn't. She quickly added forcefully, "I'm going to find out the tenor of this meeting and decide my next move. This may not last long at all."

"These guys don't show any emotion. They're impossible to read. They make me nervous."

"You're nervous because you're guilty," she said, bending over to check her makeup in her car's side mirror.

"Yeah, okay, so why are *you* nervous?"

"Because you're guilty...and this is my first real case. Okay?" she said as she reached inside her car and grabbed her briefcase and a scarf, which she wrapped around her neck as she headed for the store.

"Your first case?"

"Yep. They say you always win your first. Don't you feel lucky?" She smiled to hide her tension.

"Not especially."

Sam glanced up at the giant building and saw security cameras pointed downward, presumably recording everyone and everything. "Actually, neither do I. But what's the worst that could happen?"

"I could go to prison."

CHAPTER 27

―――――― ↄ ――――――

J AKE PARKED HIS TRUCK IN FRONT OF THE PICKENS COUNTY
Sheriff's Office and surveyed what he could see from his truck.
Aliceville, Alabama, like much of the rural South, particularly
in the Black Belt, had endured a rough couple of decades, maybe
longer. Times had obviously been better, but people still held fast
to small-town life and tried to maintain it. A shrinking tax base,
however, made it all the more difficult.

Jake remembered his dad telling him that in the 1940s during World War II, Aliceville had one of the largest prison camps
of German and Italian prisoners of war. At one time, the prison
had hosted nearly six thousand POWs, some from the infamous
Afrika Korps who fought under General Rommel. It was a significant part of Aliceville's history that easily could be forgotten,
since the prison camp had long been gone, except for one huge
stone chimney.

Jake had already been to see his camp house, or what was
left of it. Everything was gone except for the chimney. *Just like
the prison camp*, Jake thought. The pile of ashes that had been his
family retreat was still smoldering. Nothing of value had survived
the hot, consuming fire, and yet less than forty yards away was a
huge river of cold water. A number of family antiques that weren't

really worth much were gone, along with dozens of family photos. All Jake could think about was arson. *It had to be arson.*

Jake pushed open the sheriff's office front door and announced, "I'm Jake Crosby. I'm here to see the sheriff."

"Yes, sir. I'll get him for you," an older black lady in a deputy's uniform offered.

Jake glanced around and thought about his time in the Sumter County Sheriff's Office. *Not much difference. Probably had the same interior decorator,* he thought.

Jake saw an office door open, and a huge, uniformed man with a very friendly face and demeanor waved him on back.

"Jake Crosby?"

"Yes, sir."

"I'm Rosco Blue. Pleased to meet you. Just hate that it's under these circumstances." Rosco's giant hand swallowed Jake's, but his warm smile kept his enormous presence from being too intimidating. He motioned for Jake to sit.

"I just left out there…it's a complete loss," Jake said as he sat in a chair facing the sheriff's desk.

"Yeah, it is. Most of the time these fish camps like yours and hunting camps scattered across the county…when they catch fire, about all the volunteer firefighters can do is keep the surrounding woods from goin' up. They can't ever save the structures…but by golly, they give it their best."

"I'm sure they did," Jake replied.

"You ever see 'em respondin' to a call?" Rosco loved to hear himself talk.

"Uh…no, sir, I haven't."

"It's pretty amazin'. It doesn't matter whether it's rural Michigan or backwoods Alabama. Volunteer firefighters are a gung-ho bunch of folks. They live for that call, and they drop whatever they are doin' and race to the fire. Hell, I've seen 'em race each other. I'm sure last night was no different," the aging sheriff explained.

Jake guessed Sheriff Rosco was about sixty years old and close to retiring. He'd probably been in law enforcement his entire adult life. Except for the few extra pounds he was carrying around his waist, this guy could have been Bo Jackson's twin brother.

"Yes, sir. I really appreciate them tryin'."

"When I was a state trooper, stayin' over in Elmore County, we gotta call one afternoon that a car had flipped into a ditch near the top of this really steep hill, right there in the toenails of the Blue Ridge Mountains. At any rate, the responders started comin' from every direction, and they parked on the side of the road on both sides...and then this ambulance arrived and pulled to the side of the road and opened its side doors out into the middle of the road. Well, as soon as I got outta my cruiser, I could hear a fire truck coming up the hill on the other side, siren blaring and the engine straining. I checked on the guy in the ditch, and he was okay; he was just stuck upside down, and his seat belt wouldn't release. By now there were twenty or more responders, all in full fire gear, tryin' to get this poor bastard outta his car, when the fire truck topped the hill at full speed."

Jake sat still, wondering why Rosco was telling this long story.

"That old fire truck was haulin' about six thousand pounds of water alone, and when it topped that hill and the driver seen all those vehicles blockin' the road, he stood on the brakes. That big old truck went to swayin', and you could see the fear on the faces of the men. There wasn't nothin' to do but get the hell outta the way. We all took off running. The truck sideswiped every vehicle except mine and took the ambulance doors smooth off. They finally got the fire truck stopped about a half mile down the hill. I learned a valuable lesson that day: you don't wanna get between the enthusiasm of volunteer firefighters and their jobs. They got some enthusiasm."

"That's an interesting story," Jake said as he looked around the office at the old pictures.

"Awww, I get to tellin' stories sometimes and forget what I'm doin'. Sorry 'bout that."

"No problem."

"Look, Mr. Crosby, you got any idea how that fire started?" Sheriff Blue asked, trying to catch Jake off guard.

"Please call me Jake, and no. I was about to ask you the same thing. I haven't been out there in over a month. Could the wiring have gone bad? It's pretty old."

"How old?"

"Well, when I was just a kid, my dad rewired it himself, so about thirty years, I guess. It's been added on to over the years. It wasn't anything fancy."

"Who's yo' daddy?"

"Robert Crosby. He worked as a production supervisor at Bryan Foods in West Point. Worked there about forty years."

"Lots of folks worked there at one time or another."

"Yes, sir."

Sheriff Rosco Blue leaned back in his wooden chair and placed an unlit cigar in the corner of his mouth. "It's kinda peculiar that it suddenly catches fire and burns to the ground. Got insurance on the place?"

"Yes, sir."

"Uh-hunh."

"I agree that it's strange, Sheriff. I know I said somethin' about the wiring, but I can't help but think it might be arson."

"Well, we got us a real good fire marshal here, and he'll figure it out."

"Does insurance pay if it's arson?"

"I don't think so," the sheriff said, watching Jake closely.

Jake dropped his head into his hands

The sheriff said, "Look here, son, it'd save us both lots of time and trouble if you know somethin' about this. You need to go on and tell me. You got somethin' you need to get off your chest?"

"No, sir…but do you remember almost two years ago…during spring turkey season, over in Sumter County, where two rednecks got killed one night chasing a man and his daughter and another girl through the woods?"

"Yeah, of course."

"That was me. I'm the one they were chasing—me and my daughter and this high school girl. The police never caught at least two other guys from that gang. I've been worried that someday they'd come after me and my family."

"So you think the ones that got away set your fish camp on fire?"

"Maybe. I killed two of 'em, and from what I understand, they were a real tight bunch. It wouldn't surprise me."

"I remember Johnny Lee and Reese. Those assholes kept us busy up here at times, and quite frankly, they both needed killin'."

"I'd never even heard of 'em until that night."

"Well, I'll be damned," the sheriff remarked. He carefully considered the gang torching Jake's fish camp, but he knew their style of payback would be murder, not arson. An eye for an eye would be their response.

Sheriff Blue leaned back again and tried to analyze Jake Crosby's body language. He was aware that it was very common for young couples to get way over their heads in debt and need immediate cash. The reasons were too numerous to count. Insurance fires were often a quick fix. That's what this smelled like, and the man sitting in front of him sure looked stressed.

"Jake, those rednecks' payback would be painful. Burning your camp ain't vengeful enough." The sheriff suspected that Jake was trying to throw him off the real trail.

Jake rubbed his face and looked uneasily out the window. After a moment, he said, "It's the only answer I got, Sheriff."

CHAPTER 28

———— ☾ ————

T HE TWO-MAN KROGER SECURITY TEAM WAS VISIBLY surprised to see Samantha Owens representing Walter Severson. They politely invited Walter and Sam to the rear of the store, where they commandeered the employee lounge. On the way back, Walter waved to the friends he had made at the store. He was confident with Sam by his side. The lounge was small and cluttered. Sam and Walter seated themselves on the far side. Sam immediately placed a tape recorder on the table and turned it on with a click. Everyone stopped talking and stared at it for a few seconds. After a long moment, Sam casually glanced up and asked if the men minded. They looked at each other and shook their heads. Sam smiled.

In her best slow, sweet Southern drawl, Sam asked, "Are y'all charging my client with anything?"

"No, ma'am. We're just trying to get some answers. We hope Mr. Severson knows something that will be helpful to us."

"My client is very distraught about this and your threats to fire him. This job and his reputation are important to him."

"He offered to resign of his own free will."

"He doesn't feel welcome anymore, and he feels intimidated."

The men were silent. They had been suspicious of Walter's sudden offer of resignation. They were under serious pressure to quietly solve the case and recoup the stolen funds. Corporate didn't want to involve the police unless they didn't have a choice. The ease of the crime was not something they wanted to become public. Each day that passed meant the money would be harder to trace and recover; it would be burning a hole in someone's pocket.

With a lawyer present, the men were more cordial to Walter than before.

"Mr. Severson, we have a few follow-up questions about Sunday the fourth of November."

"Gosh, I've slept a bunch since then. That's been over two weeks ago," Walter responded as he glanced toward Sam. "By the way, where's Ed…you know, the manager?"

"He's been temporarily reassigned."

Samantha was scribbling something on a legal pad.

"Can you confirm that you worked that day?" one of the security specialists asked, reading from a prepared list.

"I got a full week's pay, so yes, I guess I worked that day."

"Can you confirm your shift was from two to ten p.m.?"

"I always work weekends so others can be with their families."

"Did you see anything strange or out of the ordinary during that shift?"

"I see strange things every day I work here, young man."

"Did you see anything out of the ordinary or strange happening in the back area of the store while you were on your shift that day?"

"Would *you* call it strange or out of the ordinary for someone to get a lap dance by a stripper moonlighting as a cashier?" Walter turned the question around while maintaining a straight face.

Sam betrayed no emotion.

"Yes. What can you tell us about that?"

"It happened a lot. Mostly on Sunday nights. She and Ed had a thing going on. I heard that she was a stripper and worked here for the medical benefits and Ed's wife is pregnant. I don't know for sure. You know how rumors are."

"Did you actually see it?"

"What?"

"The lap dance."

"No—not with my own eyes. I'da liked to…she's a looker… but…she's too young for me."

The men made notes and studied their sheets of paper.

"She didn't really talk to me. I guess I'm not her type."

"Mr. Severson, we're missing some money. A significant amount."

Sam was extremely attentive now and ready to jump into the conversation.

"I don't think she stole it."

"Why not?"

"Well, I saw her yesterday, and she was driving a beat-up, old four-door Nissan. I think that a girl like her…if she'd got her hands on significant money, she'd be driving a Ford Shelby Mustang the next day."

"Did you study psychology?"

"No, I'm just old. I've seen a lot. If you pay attention, people's behavior is fairly predictable."

"What do you think happened to the money, then?"

"Somebody probably…miscounted."

"Not a chance. We have all of the register receipts. Do you know who stole the money or anything about it? Anything?"

With that line of questioning, Sam jumped in, holding up a hand to Walter to stop him from saying anything. "Whoa. Stop right there. It sounds like you're insinuating that my client is involved somehow or complicit."

"No, we are not. As I explained earlier, we're just trying to get answers."

"I'm not going to allow him to answer any more questions."

"Why not?"

"Let's just say…hypothetically that this missing money was in fact stolen. If he states something that implicates anyone, he could be opening himself up to a civil suit for slander."

"I don't think so."

"Are you licensed to practice law in Mississippi?" Sam glared at the guy, who was shaking his head. "I didn't think so; besides, what's in it for my client to get involved?"

"A chance to do the right thing?"

"I wish it were that simple."

"It is that simple."

"Gentlemen, if you want my client's cooperation, come back to us with an offer. If you want to ask any more questions, you'll have to come to my office. Here's my card."

"We don't make offers."

"My client is a fine, upstanding citizen, with no previous criminal record or work history that gives you any reasonable grounds to suspect his knowledge or involvement with this missing money, which may or may not be stolen." Sam stood, placing her hand on Walter's shoulder. "And if you question other employees with the intent of implicating my client or otherwise disparaging him or his reputation in any way, we'll know within moments, and then you two will be answering *my* questions."

The two security experts leaned back, trying to put distance between them and the fireball attorney.

The senior agent picked up her card and looked it over. "We'll be in touch, Mrs. Owens."

"That's Miss Owens, thank you very much."

CHAPTER 29

———— ☾ ————

W ALTER HUDDLED WITH HIS TEAM IN THE LIBRARY OF the historic hotel. He paced while they settled in their seats and then shut the door. His emotions were all over the place, and anxiety flooded him, just as it had eleven years ago in the Minnesota police station. He fought to suppress the memories and keep his mind on track. Fortunately, the meeting with the security team had been much less intense than he expected. Samantha's presence had totally changed the dynamic. When he was alone with them a few days earlier, he had been certain they were onto him and about to call the police. *Maybe they were just fishing*, he thought.

Glancing at his watch, Walter exhaled deeply. Bernard, Sebastian, and Lucille all awaited Walter's update.

"Samantha was a big help this morning. That was a great suggestion, Sebastian," Walter said.

"Balloons are ordered," Bernard blurted. "Sebastian and I are taking her a special cut magnet and glue when we get outta here. It was a refrigerator magnet from Rose Drugs that I spray-painted."

"Perfect. I'll need you to park across the street when they close and monitor to see if the alarm goes off. It could take a few hours."

"Lucille…we need small flashlights, two handheld radios, a small tool kit, and gloves for all of us," Walter explained.

"Is that all?" she asked as she jotted down the list.

"Some Clorox wipes, unscented if you can find them, a small tote bag to carry it all, and a larger bag for the cash."

"Anything else?"

"How 'bout black coveralls with black stockin' caps?" Bernard offered excitedly.

"I think we're better off looking like a bunch of old guys working than a bunch of old, white, crippled ninjas."

"I'm definitely not the covert-spy type," Sebastian said matter-of-factly. "I'm more of the 'just walk up and shoot 'em in the head with a forty-five' type."

Bernard imagined the three of them in all black, pumping gas and getting strange looks or having to explain to the police what they were doing. "Lucille, since you're goin' out, I'm gonna need some Zantac. All this stress has got me so wound up you couldn't pull a greased string outta my butt with a tractor. My heartburn's killin' me."

Everyone chuckled except Bernard.

Walter looked at each of them and then placed the cigar he had been chewing into the corner of his mouth and smiled. They weren't exactly the A-Team, but he liked their spirits. *They have heart…and probably heart disease*, he thought.

CHAPTER 30

———— ☾ ————

A WILLIE NELSON CD WAS PLAYING AS LEVI DROVE AND Moon Pie fooled around with his new iPad. They were excited about the meeting and the prospects of making a significant amount of money through this new venture.

Moon Pie constantly checked the mirror for tails. About a half hour into the trip, he had Levi turn around and backtrack a few miles. Their vehicle was loaded with all manner of weapons, loaded spare magazines, and several hundred rounds of ammunition, all of which would be difficult to explain to the police if they were pulled over.

"I like Willie," Levi said for no particular reason other than to break the silence.

"He's a classic," Moon Pie replied without looking up from his iPad.

"I like John Denver too. Great lyrics."

Moon Pie made a snorting sound, expressing his total lack of agreement.

Levi adjusted the steering wheel and squirmed in the seat. He tried to think of anything to start a conversation. "Did you know that during the Michael Jackson song 'Beat It' you can hear somebody knocking on the studio door?"

Moon Pie looked up. "What?"

"Yeah, at about the two forty-five mark you can hear a knockin' sound. It's a tech who was tryin' to get in the studio."

"You're full of shit."

"I'm serious."

"Where did you hear this?"

"On a radio program."

"One of those shows that asks listeners if they prefer Ginger or Mary Ann?"

"Yeah, exactly. I like those discussions," Levi said.

"Mary Ann for me. Give me a country girl. Ginger would have been way too high maintenance."

"I liked Ginger. But see, that's why they do it...nobody agrees, everybody calls, and it's interesting."

"I don't call."

Levi gave the rearview a quick glance. "I do sometimes. It gets pretty borin' sometimes makin' river runs. Thank goodness for satellite radio."

"You are so lame, listening to that shit."

Moon Pie turned back to his new iPad to search the Internet for a free version of "Beat It."

Levi was aggravated with Moon Pie, but at least they were talking. He'd been trying his best to develop a better relationship with Moon Pie so that he would give him more responsibilities within the business.

"I hate that Bailey's at the shop without one of us there."

"She's fine. She knows how to buy. I left her five grand to work with and told her to close up if she bought more than that."

"I'm sure that'll cover it."

"It'll have to. I sure ain't givin' her the code to the safe."

"I think you can trust her with that much cash or gold."

"I ain't got much choice on this one. But no, I don't trust anyone with my money. Money's got a way of changin' folks. You'll see firsthand one day. Hey, don't forget to watch the rearview for a tail." Moon Pie never looked up as he tried unsuccessfully to play the song he had illegally downloaded.

"We're clean. I've been watching."

"Good. The cemetery's 'bout ten more miles. Don't stop when you get there. Drive by so we can check it out first."

"I've heard the name Coon Dog Cemetery but don't really know nothin' 'bout it," Levi lied to engage Moon Pie.

Moon Pie slid his iPad into its sleeve and sat up straight. "Well, years ago—like, in the thirties, maybe—this local guy had a coon hound called Troop that was legendary. He was the best anybody had ever seen, and trust me, coon huntin' used to be a big deal back before the deer and turkeys made a comeback. Back then, most everybody coon hunted, but not everybody had a dog, especially a good one like Troop. Anyways, a bunch of local coon hunters all used this hilltop as a meetin' spot on nights they hunted. When old Troop died, his owner wanted to do something special, so he decided to bury Troop there and even carved him a monument. Then other hunters started buryin' their coon dogs there, and before you know it, it's the coon dog cemetery. There's only one in the world."

"Man's best friend."

"A good huntin' dog's like a soul mate."

"Unconditional love and an undyin' desire to please," Levi said with a smile.

"Exactly right. Now, I'm done talkin' 'bout it. It's makin' me want a puppy, and I ain't got time to raise *you* and a dog."

Levi smiled at Moon Pie's comments.

"Slow down, here it is. But don't stop. We're lookin' for a black van."

"Like, minivan?" Levi asked as he spotted a family-looking minivan parked in the far corner.

Before Moon Pie saw the vehicle, he responded, "No, fool." Then he recanted with, "Well, maybe," when he too saw the minivan.

CHAPTER 31

———— ☾ ————

MORGAN'S NERVES WERE FRAYED SINCE JAKE HAD CALLED to explain that the camp house was in fact a total loss and that arson was suspected. She wasn't too concerned about the fish camp. Her only real worry was that Peeping Tom and that awful smile on his face. It had happened so fast that she wondered if she had imagined it, but now somebody had deliberately burned down the camp. She worried what was next. The West Point city police were doing around-the-clock drive-bys of the house, and the Old Waverly security guards were doing their part by actually looking in the backseats and trunks of every vehicle that came into the development—to the point that the members began complaining. Everyone was watching for something. They just didn't know what. Morgan began to fear the worst, and she was especially worried about Katy.

It was almost two that afternoon when Morgan decided to explain the situation to the headmaster at Katy's school and then check her out for the rest of the day. Morgan wanted to know exactly where her daughter was at all times. She was met with understanding and comfort from the school's staff. They all remembered Jake and Katy's ordeal and appreciated Morgan's concerns, given these recent developments. The headmaster promised to convene a teachers' meeting to put everyone on alert. He reminded Morgan that, since Columbine, Oak Hill Academy had actively rehearsed lockdown drills and that every teacher and staff member knew how to set it into motion. Morgan felt much better about Katy's safety. *They don't think I'm crazy, and they really do care*, she thought.

Katy begged her mom to stay in school. She wanted to attend the pep rally during last period for a big basketball game. Katy's eyes filled with tears as she pleaded over and over until Morgan relented.

"Okay, okay. But you gotta come straight to the car when you get out. I'll be by the flagpole."

"Yes, ma'am. I will. Thanks, Mom," Katy yelled as she ran back to her class.

As Morgan walked toward her Lexus, she called Jake to tell him what happened.

Jake's computer screens were a maze of stock-tracking charts when his direct line rang. He instantly recognized the number.

"Hey, babe, what's up?"

"Can you talk a minute?"

"Sure." Jake was happy to take a break from watching the computer screens for the last hour. He was trying to determine if he had missed any market opportunities by going to Aliceville.

"I'm worried someone's stalkin' us."

Jake exhaled. He felt the same but didn't want to alarm her. She was a worrier, and she would get worse if any of her fears were confirmed.

"I just went to the school to talk to the headmaster and the office staff…and asked them to keep their eyes open. I thought it was better to be safe than sorry," she said, almost as if she were asking forgiveness.

"I'm glad you did. I'm concerned too."

"Wadda we do?" she asked, pulling out of the parking lot.

"Do you remember me tellin' you about R. C. Smithson? You know, the deputy from Sumter County?"

"Yeah, of course. The guy who rescued y'all."

"Right. Well, I called him earlier today to ask his opinion on what's going on. Turns out he's now a private investigator in Meridian."

"Really?" she asked, wondering why.

"Yeah. He really didn't go into why he changed jobs. At any rate, he agreed to drive up and talk to me tomorrow. He also said he'd look into the loose ends from that night at the Dummy Line for any connections."

"Do you trust him?"

"I don't have any reason not to. Katy really liked him, and he was a big help before. Maybe he can help again. He and Sheriff Ollie understand about that night, and they know those redneck thugs better than anybody."

"Well, then, what about gettin' Ollie involved?"

"He's outta town till next week."

"Okay. Let's see what R.C. thinks."

Jake could tell from Morgan's voice that she liked the idea. He looked back at one of his monitors and said, "Babe, I gotta go. I love you. Bye." Jake hung up.

Morgan rubbed her baby bump, feeling slightly apprehensive about the future. Her mind then returned to the image of the smiling man disappearing into the darkness of her backyard. Morgan reached into her Coach purse for the comfort of the cold steel of her Smith & Wesson LadySmith.

CHAPTER 32

———— ☾ ————

S EBASTIAN AND BERNARD CASUALLY WALKED INTO THE
Gold Mine. They knew of the security cameras and assumed
they were active. Their goal of quietly checking out the place was
shattered when Bailey bounded from behind the counter and
hugged them both. *So much for being inconspicuous*, Sebastian
thought.

As Bernard chatted with Bailey, he discreetly slipped
her a small envelope that contained the magnet and glue.
Sebastian adjusted his reading glasses to study the posters
explaining what happens to the purchased gold. The material was a confusing attempt to demonstrate the high overhead costs associated with reclaiming jewelry. He was not
impressed.

For show, Sebastian handed Bailey a small gold chain. She
weighed it and offered him thirteen dollars, according to Moon
Pie's chart. It was exactly 50 percent less than most other dealers
would have paid. Sebastian said that he would keep his necklace
and thanked Bailey.

"Can you attach the magnet?" Bernard asked quietly. When
he heard the front door, he turned to see a filthy college-aged
guy enter.

"Yes, sir. I'm positive," Bailey replied. When she glanced at the new customer, she sighed loudly enough for Bernard to hear.

"Woody, you know you shouldn't be here," she said with frustration.

"Anything wrong, miss?" Sebastian asked from across the room.

"No, sir, I can handle this."

"I just came to see you. You ain't been returnin' my calls," the young guy responded, but he was looking at Sebastian, trying to determine why he would get involved in a private matter.

"You know Moon Pie doesn't like you comin' in here."

"I ain't scared of him."

"What's a Moon Pie?" Sebastian asked Bailey.

"The owner. It's a nickname."

Sebastian and Bernard had heard the owner's actual name but not his nickname. If they had, they would have remembered. Bernard chuckled.

The young guy's clothes were covered in grease and some metallic dust. He appeared to work as a mechanic or in some type of shop, maybe as a welder.

"You can't keep avoidin' me."

"I've been busy. If Moon Pie sees that you've been here, it ain't gonna be easy on me. So, go. Please leave, Woody," she said as she motioned with her head toward the cameras.

"You need a new job," Woody said hastily as he glanced at the old men. "Are these old farts botherin' you?"

"Please leave. I'm askin' nicely."

"One of my buds said he seen you and Levi together the other day."

"It was business. He works here too, you know."

"He sees you more than me. That's gotta change...and soon."

"Woody! Please!"

"If you don't do somethin', I'm gonna."

Sebastian turned to face the loudmouth. His own face was red with anger. "Son, if—"

Bailey cut him off by placing her hand on his arm and saying, "It's okay. Woody, please leave. I'll call you later."

"Who *are* these old farts? They in here sellin' gold teeth from their dead ol' ladies?"

"Why, you!" Sebastian lunged toward Woody, but Bailey still had his arm, stopping him. He glared at Woody.

"Come on, ol'-timer. I'll kick your ass so hard, you'll taste shit for days."

As Bernard moved in, he quickly looked at Sebastian, who was just about to explode. It wasn't good that Bailey was standing between him and Woody.

She wheeled to face Woody and screamed, "Go or I'll call the cops!"

Woody had a wild look in his eye. After a tense moment, he snarled at Bailey, "I'm goin', but this ain't over…for any of y'all!" Woody kept his eyes on the group as he made his way out the front door.

Sebastian badly wanted to punch Woody in the eye. It suddenly became his new life's mission. "You gotta stay away from that boy. He's nothin' but white-trash trouble."

"I know, I know. That's the guy y'all heard about—the one I can't get away from. We used to date. He was different back then."

After several moments of silence, Bailey recovered her composure and changed the subject, saying, "I'm gonna try more codes later. I've been trying 'em between customers, and after four wrong ones, it locks me out for about twenty minutes. I gotta be careful not to go in there too often, 'cause Moon Pie will notice if he watches the security tapes."

"I knew it wouldn't be as simple as Walter thought. We'll be outside when you close to see if the balloons set off the alarm," Bernard said.

"Bailey, honey, you gotta get away from that loser."

Bailey looked up at Sebastian and said, "You're right. I'm trying. He just won't leave me alone. He's very possessive."

Sebastian gently grabbed her shoulders and looked her straight in the eye. "I can help. And he won't feel a thing—that is…unless you want him to."

CHAPTER 33

——— ☾ ———

I T WAS JUST PAST DUSK WHEN THE HALF BROTHERS PULLED into the cemetery. The shadows were disappearing into the night. Darkness hid secrets, and criminals loved the obscurity it offered.

"Yep, it's a minivan. That's real smart. Doesn't attract attention," Moon Pie said excitedly when he saw his contact.

"Or women."

Moon Pie grunted and asked, "Is that all you think about?"

Joe Walsh's song "Life's Been Good" began playing on the car radio. Levi started keeping the beat, singing, "My minivan does one eighty-five. I lost my license, now I don't drive."

Moon Pie almost yelled, "Shut the hell up, and pull over there and wait for them to signal us. They'll wanna make sure nobody's followed us."

"We're clean. I've been watchin'."

"You keep sayin' that, but they don't know it. These dudes are pros. They're gonna be real careful."

"Why don't you just call 'em or text 'em?" Levi asked.

"I swear. Just shut the hell up!"

Moon Pie nervously watched the minivan. Suddenly his phone rang. He recognized the number as he answered, "Yeah.

It's me in the Toyota." Levi turned the radio down and strained to hear the other voice. Moon Pie continued, "Yeah, we were careful. We're clean. Let's do this. Okay." Moon Pie ended the call and then dropped the phone into the console.

"Pull up next to 'em. Keep your eyes peeled. This won't take long."

Moon Pie was obviously anxious, which Levi had never seen. Normally Moon Pie had ice water running through his veins. One time they had poached a giant buck in the middle of a bean field and had sunk an old Bronco in the mud trying to get it out as the game warden was walking toward them. Moon Pie never showed the slightest bit of concern. Levi assumed that Moon Pie was nervous about making a good impression on the Tennessee connection.

Levi eased the FJ Cruiser next to the minivan. When he stopped, the van's doors electronically opened slowly. Moon Pie got out and initiated a fist bump gesture to the other guy, who ignored it. *Awkward*, Levi thought.

The passenger of the minivan was a very well-dressed Hispanic—maybe Cuban; Levi wasn't sure. But he knew that the jeans the other man was wearing cost over $1,000, and the shirt and jacket were incredibly expensive too. Inside the van, Levi could see a beefy driver, who constantly looked around for danger signs. It occurred to Levi they all were just like animals at a water hole. Their senses were heightened because they knew predators were lurking somewhere. Watering holes were death traps. These particular animals knew that law enforcement could explode from the shadows and catch them at any moment. They were vulnerable. An added risk with this herd was that you could never trust others—ever. Levi tried to keep an eye on Moon Pie while scouting for signs of an ambush.

The well-dressed Latino looked Moon Pie over slowly and then bent down and looked inside the FJ. Levi gave him a thumbs-up, while Moon Pie tried to act cool with his hands on his hips, looking like a cross between a Western gunfighter and an East LA gangster.

"Y'all have a good trip down?" Moon Pie asked and immediately wished he hadn't.

The well-dressed man ignored the question and continued to look around. He spoke softly in broken Spanish-flavored English, "A *perro cementerio*. Good meet place. Yes."

A third, smaller man, who had gone unnoticed, jumped out of the van holding a metal-detecting wand.

Moon Pie knew the drill, turned around, and assumed the position against his SUV.

After a thorough search, the small guy nodded to the well-dressed man, who stepped to the back of the SUV, where Levi couldn't hear the conversation. "I have the money. The product is good? *¿Sí?*"

"Yes. Only the finest. The folks I represent are excited about doin' business with you."

"We need supply. Steady source."

Moon Pie knew that their source from southern Florida had been shut down in a high-profile bust. Their front was a top-tier accounting firm that specialized in the citrus and sugar business. Some missteps on the supporting documentation on tax returns caused the IRS to delve deeply enough to uncover suspicious reporting, which ultimately led to over $85 million in various assets being seized and several arrests, effectively taking down the domestic side of the cartel.

"You'll be pleased."

"Good. That's real good." The well-dressed man reached into the van and retrieved a blue duffel-type bag and held it up. "Nine hundred thousand US dollars."

"Don't mind if I count it, do ya?" Moon Pie asked rhetorically and then motioned for his counterpart to follow as he walked to the rear of his FJ Cruiser. He opened the tailgate, but the dome light did not come on. He sat the bag down inside the cargo compartment, unzipped it, and took out the first of ninety stacks of hundred-dollar bills. He broke the band and dropped the bills into the hopper of a bank-grade currency counter that was plugged into an inverter hooked up to the SUV's electrical system. It began whirling.

"This won't take but a couple minutes," Moon Pie said, not looking up. He continued the process of counting every bill, just as his boss had requested. When each batch of ten thousand dollars came out, he grabbed the wad and quickly wrapped a rubber band around it and then placed it back inside the duffel bag. When Moon Pie finished, he zipped the bag shut, made sure that all of the broken paper bands were not near the door, and closed it. He turned to the well-dressed man, smiled, and lit a cigarette.

Moon Pie was energized by the sight and smell of so much money.

"I want my *cocaína* in *cinco días*," the Latino man said firmly, holding up his hand, fingers spread.

Moon Pie took a long drag as he translated and then nodded and said, "You'll get it by then, I'm sure. We need about that long to provide a secure drop-off."

The well-dressed man reached into his pocket and withdrew something. He held it up to Moon Pie's face and then bent down and pulled up Moon Pie's pant leg so he could attach the GPS ankle monitor. "It stays on *tobillo* until I have *cocaína*."

Moon Pie nodded. He wasn't really surprised. These guys were serious. He could learn a lot, and if he delivered as promised, he could make more money than he had ever dreamed. And if he continued to impress them—and he could tell from their expressions the bill-counting machine had—opportunities could abound. If he failed, he knew that they would kill him.

Moon Pie looked at the ankle monitor and then with false bravado said, "You'll get your *cocaína*, *hombre*."

The man smiled wickedly and with a quiet chuckle said, "I will...or...I will have your head, Señor Pie."

CHAPTER 34

———— ☾ ————

TWO EXHAUSTED OFFICERS FROM THE MISSISSIPPI DRUG Task Force sat in their hotel room, worrying about the next few days. Their most reliable confidential informants were certain a significant deal was about to go down. The two officers had been trying for longer than either cared to admit to break the supply chain of narcotics moving from the Gulf Coast into northeast Mississippi. Every time they got close, a small thread would unravel, ultimately exposing their efforts. It was as though the bad guys had a sixth sense or perhaps someone inside local law enforcement tipping them off. A leak was their worst fear. That meant all of their efforts were wasted. Information of this kind was invaluable to drug dealers, and they were capable of corrupting almost anyone with their seemingly unlimited cash.

They didn't know whom they could trust, so this time they hadn't told anyone what was going on. The pressure from their superiors in Jackson and from the governor himself—who personally told them to "tighten up" after a friend's son overdosed—was weighing heavily and added significantly to their stress levels.

Spread out and taped to the wall of their hotel room was a puzzle of information they had accumulated on Moon Pie,

Levi Jenkins, and six others. Their number-one target was Tam Nguyen, the Mississippi Gulf Coast's drug king. He operated from Biloxi to Mobile but never came out of the shadows. They had a few old pictures of him, but that's it. Basically, they were chasing a ghost. They sensed they were closer than ever as they studied the wall and sipped stale coffee. They had surveillance photos and mug shots of all the other suspects and their known associates, and they knew that both Moon Pie and Levi were traveling to some type of meeting, but they had given up trying to follow them. The officers had been quietly planning a sting operation for weeks. They had confirmed intelligence that Tam's future wife, Alexa, was an extremely enthusiastic fan of the band Rascal Flatts and had attended every concert event within a six-hour drive of her home.

Having exhausted every other avenue to flush the drug king from hiding, they decided to try something out of the box. They contacted Rascal Flatts's management, carefully explaining their situation and plans. The manager explained that Rascal Flatts loved to support the military, law enforcement, and especially programs protecting kids. After detailed discussions confirming that neither the band nor the crew would actually be near the undercover operation, the manager said they would gladly help. The task force officers thanked him and said this was a perfect fit for a sting. Law enforcement already had Alexa's e-mail address. They just needed an official e-mail from the band to be sent to her.

The officers had found her on Facebook under the alias Alexa. Her real name was Donna, but apparently she found Alexa to be more interesting. She was an aspiring swimsuit model, and by the volume of posted photographs, she obviously loved to have her picture taken. They carefully studied all three hundred–plus images. One candid shot provided them with a current photograph of the elusive Tam.

The plan was to invite Alexa and a guest to a private meet and greet with the band before the concert. The officers were confident that she couldn't resist the invitation and would drag Tam along. Since the concert was several hours' drive from Tam's home, hopefully his guard would be down. In an effort to tighten the trap and have fewer bystanders around, the actual takedown would be not at the concert hall but next door, inside the Hilton Garden Inn. Only recordings of the band members talking and singing would be played in a darkened hospitality suite. The best part—Tam would be expecting security at the event to protect the band.

This project had taken several weeks to coordinate, and only those who absolutely had a need to know were read in and then only to the limited extent of what was absolutely necessary for their specific role.

Fewer than five individuals knew the big picture—they hoped.

CHAPTER 35

——— ☾ ———

BAILEY LOCKED THE GOLD MINE'S FRONT DOOR AT STRAIGHT-up six o'clock. Her red balloons were swaying under the current of the heater vent. She would be able to try only four codes before she would have to leave. Moon Pie and Levi would return at any moment. She knew Moon Pie would review the surveillance tapes after the money was discovered missing, and she could not justify going into the office too many times. Securing the gold and cash inside the office desk drawer took only a few minutes, allowing her time to try a round of codes. A security camera was focused on the office door but could not see inside. However, the video time stamps would reveal how long she was in the office. She didn't want to be the focus of Moon Pie's rage after the theft. Walter was crystal clear that she had to appear to be above reproach so she could start a new life without fear of retribution. Not knowing exactly when Moon Pie would be back added to Bailey's anxiety. He seemed to have been purposely vague about where they were going and when they would return.

The back room was dimly lit, requiring Bailey to take extra care as she stepped around the full-body lion mount and the deer heads lying on the floor. When she opened the office door and flipped on the light, her mind raced as she stared at the safe.

Inside that refrigerator-size hunk of metal was a small fortune, more than enough to get her out of trouble, out of town, and far away from Woody. She hurriedly secured the day's gold purchases inside Moon Pie's desk drawer and then stood for a moment in front of the safe with the cheat sheet of codes Sebastian had given her. She took a deep breath and punched in the next code on her list: 18, 16, 10, pound. Each time she typed a digit, an electronic beep chirped, giving her hope until she pressed the pound sign and nothing happened.

"Okay. Do you like sixteen, ten, eighteen, pound?" she quietly said aloud. "Awww. Well, okay, how 'bout ten, sixteen, eighteen, pound? Shit!"

There was a warning beep after this attempt, and when Bailey tried to press the fourth combination, the lock was frozen, stopping any more attempts for thirty minutes. She gathered her composure and flipped off the lights as she walked out of the office.

Bailey pulled her jacket tight and reached into her purse for her car keys. When she opened the back door, she could see clearly by the streetlight illuminating the parking lot. Glancing up at the doorframe, she saw where she would place the magnet tomorrow. The paint job matched perfectly, and she knew it wouldn't be noticed. She didn't know how it worked, but she trusted Mr. Walter. She punched the arming code into the alarm keypad—1-9-6-4 and then "exit." It was the only code Moon Pie had shared with her. The alarm chirped twice, and then the tiny light turned red. She had sixty seconds to shut and lock the door.

As she drove out of the parking lot, she quickly looked at Sebastian and Bernard sitting across the street in an old Ford truck. She gave them a slight, inconspicuous nod as she went by. Thirty seconds later, a car that had been sitting about two buildings down pulled away from the curb and followed Bailey.

"Woody?" Bernard asked as the car went past.

"Gotta be," Sebastian said between clenched teeth. He glanced at his watch—6:13. "Call Lucille and find out Bailey's home address and her cell phone number."

"This wasn't in the plan," Bernard said as he put on his bifocals and prepared to dial.

"Don't blame me; it's Woody's fault."

CHAPTER 36

———— ☾ ————

MOON PIE CLIMBED INTO THE PASSENGER SEAT, SHUT THE door, and let out a deep sigh of relief.

"Go," he instructed Levi as he sank back against the leather.

"Those guys didn't seem like they were normal…like us," Levi said as he pulled the FJ onto the county road, headed south.

"They ain't."

"Them dudes don't play. That one spic makes me real nervous."

"I noticed. Don't worry, I ain't gonna be friendin' him on Facebook. Regardless of how scary these dudes are, they can put us on the map…my partial brother," Moon Pie said as he watched them drive away in the side mirror. He was slipping back into his typical cocky attitude. "Drive the speed limit, and stop at the first squat-n-gobble. I need some caffeine."

"What's up with that monitor on your ankle? Our new partners aren't very trusting."

"It ain't a thing. I've taken 'em off before. Besides, Pedro back there just wants to make sure we don't walk with his money."

"A healthy choice, my friend."

Moon Pie grabbed his iPhone and said, "I need to call the boss."

Levi turned his attention to the road and set the cruise control at four miles per hour over the speed limit.

"Hey, boss. It's done." Moon Pie chose his words carefully in case the phones were tapped. "They're expecting us to flip it pretty quick. Clock's ticking."

Moon Pie listened to his boss give him directions in code and then said, "Got it. Perfect. I'll holler at ya later." Moon Pie ended the connection and then turned off the phone.

Levi asked, "What's the plan?"

"They're gonna come here Saturday. He's takin' his squeeze to the Rascal Flatts concert in Tupelo."

"Tupelo?" Levi asked.

"Yeah. Apparently their concert on the coast got canceled, so they're comin' up here. I didn't ask details. You know how he is."

Levi scrolled through the satellite-radio channels and stopped on ESPN. "We oughta go to the concert too."

"Dude, it's huntin' season. I need my rest."

"It'd be fun."

"I ain't gonna be your date."

Moon Pie was almost back to his normal self. He was feeling much better and was thrilled that both the goods and his boss were coming to him. He might even be able to hunt this weekend. He forgot about the ankle bracelet as he started coming down from the adrenaline high.

"Hey, let me ask you a question. Whaddaya think of me changin' my name? I'm tired of Moon Pie."

"Whatcha thinkin'?"

"I got it narrowed down to two."

Levi realized he had given this some thought. He was curious now. "Hit me."

"Colonel."

"Colonel?"

"Yeah. Like in the old-South days...distinguished men were called Colonel."

"But you're not distinguished."

"No, but it'll fit me perfect when I get my old plantation house one day."

"What's the other?"

"Memphis."

Levi looked at his half brother and smiled. "Memphis. I like it. I really do."

"I'm just thinkin' about it…ya know. I'm gettin' older, and I need to work on my image."

"You can be Memphis, the drug runner formerly known as Moon Pie," Levi said sarcastically.

"Just shut the hell up and drive."

"Really. Consider Memphis. It's classy."

CHAPTER 37

———— ⌒ ————

WALTER PULLED THE MONEY OUT OF THE CAT LITTER, spread it out on the bed, and admired the cash. It was more than he had ever been able to accumulate during his career. As he slowly studied it, he thought of his wife and wished they had vacationed in Hawaii like she always wanted. He was suddenly filled with regrets for never taking time to enjoy time with his family. He had worked nonstop out of fear of not being able to provide for his family. He was born in the waning years of the Great Depression and clearly remembered its effect on his parents and others. He slowly stacked the cash and rewrapped it in a black garbage bag. The knock on his door caused his heart to race, even though he expected the visitor was a friend.

"Just a minute," he yelled as he returned the money to the litter box. His knees popped as he stood to open the door. He peered through the peephole to see Lucille standing impatiently.

Opening the door, Walter said, "Come on in. Sorry it took so long."

"We got a problem," she said as she placed a plastic bag of recently purchased burglary accessories on the counter.

"What?"

"None of the codes for the safe worked. She was able to try sixteen versions from your list."

"Damn," Walter said as he toyed with the cigar between his index finger and thumb.

"We still have twenty-two versions to try."

"What if one of them isn't it?"

"I don't know. If it's not bolted down, we might could rent a hand truck that's used to move refrigerators and just take the whole safe...that would give us more time to try more codes."

"Where would we hide it?"

"We could rent a storage unit."

"Yeah, I suppose so," Lucille replied as her cell phone rang, surprising her.

"Hello?" she answered.

"Hey, it's Bernard. What's Bailey's home address?"

"Why?"

"We need to go check on her. Woody followed her when she left the store."

"Oh dear. She lives in those apartments by the hospital. Building G, apartment four. Downstairs on the right."

"Okay, don't worry. Sebastian says to tell Walter there aren't any motion detectors, and he has an idea for the code. He'll explain when we get back."

Lucille stared at Walter, growing concerned. "Please let me know about Bailey. That boy's got serious anger issues."

"Sebastian said for you to call her and warn her."

Lucille stood staring at the phone and looked up at Walter. "Yes, okay, I will. Right now!"

Walter flashed back to Minnesota, where ten years ago on a cold night much like this one, his own daughter had been physically abused by her husband.

CHAPTER 38

S EBASTIAN AND BERNARD ARRIVED AT THE APARTMENT complex after only two missed turns. They parked facing Bailey's apartment, and even looking through overgrown azalea bushes, they could tell someone was inside. Sebastian switched off the key, and they sat in silence. The truck windows began fogging as soon as the engine died.

"You see that punk's car."

"No, but he's gotta be in there," Bernard answered.

"Stay here, and if you see him approach, honk the horn," Sebastian said, opening his door.

"What are you gonna do?"

"I don't know for sure. But I have to check on her."

Sebastian pulled a large stainless-steel revolver from under his seat and stuck it inside his waistband at the front.

Bernard watched, nodded his assent, and said, "You be careful."

"I will," Sebastian replied, and then shut the truck door.

The parking area was illuminated well, but Sebastian could not see Woody. He sensed that Woody was close. As Sebastian slowly approached Bailey's apartment, he could hear raised voices that he recognized. In the center breezeway, he could see

Bailey's door was slightly ajar. As he approached, the upstairs neighbor opened his door and made eye contact with Sebastian, who indicated through a hand gesture that he had this under control.

As he stood beside the door listening, he could hear Woody yelling, demanding money. Bailey was holding her own but losing ground fast to Woody's increasing anger. Sebastian waved at Bernard to come join him. As he stepped through the entrance, he could see splinters on the floor from where Woody had kicked in the door.

Woody had Bailey cornered in the small kitchen, and he didn't hear Sebastian step in. He was slinging her around the kitchen by her ponytail and was just about to hit her again when Sebastian caught his arm and forcefully threw Woody headfirst against the refrigerator. Woody was momentarily stunned and fell to the floor. Sebastian thumb-cocked his stainless Smith & Wesson model 686 .357 Magnum and touched the cold barrel to Woody's forehead. As his vision cleared, Woody could see copper-clad, hollow-point cartridges in the two visible cylinders on each side of the barrel. There was no doubt the gun was loaded.

"Bailey, call the police," Sebastian calmly stated as Bernard came in the front door. "Whether it's a domestic disturbance or a justifiable homicide is entirely up to this piece of trash.

"Son, if you move even one inch, I'm gonna shoot you… and I'll enjoy it. You hear me? I got absolutely nutten to lose." Sebastian stood with all his weight on Woody's left hand.

Woody was obviously angry, but the gun barrel in his face had served to temporarily subdue him.

Bailey was crying. She had been through this time and again. She couldn't break free of Woody. She needed a restraining order, but she knew it wouldn't work. She had endured all of the Woody tirades that she could take. There was no more defending him. She didn't care what happened to him anymore.

She tried to dial 911 on her cell, but her hands were shaking too badly.

"Let me make sure you understand: you ain't ever going to hit another woman. I don't even want to hear about you beatin' a dog. You listenin' to me?"

Woody nodded his head. His eyes darted between the pistol, Bailey, and Sebastian's wild, crazed eyes.

"Who are you?"

"I'm your worst nightmare," he said as he squeezed the trigger and then caught the hammer with his thumb.

Woody tried to sit up straighter but couldn't. "I've never, I've never seen you before today."

"We're her guardian angels."

Bailey stood up slowly. She still hadn't dialed 911 yet. Bernard was watching Sebastian and quickly went to help Bailey. He could tell she was going to have a black eye.

"What makes you hit a woman?" Bernard asked.

Woody didn't respond; he just looked at the floor.

Sebastian studied Woody's face and eyes, and he saw no emotion and no feelings. He was simply sorry he had gotten caught. But Sebastian realized they could use Woody. He might be very helpful to them in the next few days. He needed to talk it through with Walter. Bernard was about to dial the police, and Sebastian motioned for him to wait. On the floor was a can of Copenhagen with a customized silver lid that only the most refined rednecks possessed. Sebastian realized it had dislodged from Woody's belt holder when he fell. He repositioned a foot and slowly pushed it between the refrigerator and the base cabinet.

Woody groaned in pain, and Sebastian asked calmly, "Where do you live?"

"Out on Military Road," he said with a grunt as he straightened up and ran his hand through his hair.

Sebastian was very familiar with Military Road, as were most of Golden Triangle's residents. Andrew Jackson had built it after the War of 1812 to connect Nashville with New Orleans, and it ran right through the river town of Columbus. Sebastian bent down and looked him dead in the eyes. "Where exactly?"

Woody told him.

"You gotta job?"

"I'm a freelance gynecologist," he answered, smirking.

Bam! Sebastian slammed his fist into Woody's face. Blood instantly began to flow from his right nostril.

Sebastian gritted his teeth as he watched Woody grimace in pain. "Let's try this again real slow, you little prick. Do. You. Have. A. Job?"

Woody quickly nodded as he wiped blood from his face. "I work at the new steel mill. Out by the airport."

Sebastian glanced at Bailey's injuries and was furious. He then looked back at Woody. He knew he had the perfect punishment, if necessary.

"Look, I'm gonna cut you a break. If you swear on all that's sacred to you that you won't ever come back here again, we won't call the police," Sebastian said in a monotone voice. He was struggling to keep from killing Woody on the spot.

Woody was silent. He slowly raised his head to look at Bailey. "Is that what you want?"

Bailey paused and bit her lip. "Yes," she finally answered.

Sebastian was relieved. He knew women sometimes defended the person who abused them.

Woody looked off. For a second, Sebastian thought he saw tears in his eyes. He realized he must have cared for Bailey at some level. He just lost control of his feelings and anger took over. *Gotta be on drugs now*, Sebastian thought. He had heard that meth drastically changed people. Woody had that meth-head look in his eyes.

Sebastian leaned down to Woody's ear and then whispered through gritted teeth, "Swear to God that you'll leave her alone, and I won't cut your nuts off and shove 'em so far down your throat that it kills ya!"

CHAPTER 39

———— ☾ ————

MOON PIE AND LEVI TOOK THEIR TIME DRIVING BACK TO Columbus. They stopped in Amory, Mississippi, and ate supper at one of the ubiquitous Mexican restaurants now scattered all over the South. They ordered steak fajitas after their cheese dip. Levi commented that they were probably the only diners in the state who had nearly a million dollars in cash stashed in their automobile at that moment. Moon Pie agreed with a loud laugh.

Levi was amazed at how the excitement of future earnings combined with the margaritas made Moon Pie talk. He yammered about their shared daddy and how he had taught him to poach, fish, and live off the land. They talked about the *Swamp People* show on the History Channel, and while he knew Levi wanted to be on *The Bachelorette*, Moon Pie wanted to try alligator hunting in the bayous of Louisiana. He had already poached a few gators in Tibbee Creek, near West Point, and he had his eye on a ten-footer in the Noxubee Refuge. He liked the challenge.

Moon Pie talked to Levi more than he ever had before, and he even opened up about that night in Sumter County that made him go on the run. Levi listened intently while Moon Pie drove.

"I blame all that shit on Johnny Lee," Moon Pie said. "He never planned anything in his life. He just jumped on whatever opportunities came his way. I read what was in the papers about that night and compared it to bits and pieces that Reese told me over the two-way phone. They should have never been out there. There was no real money. It was just something for their drunk asses to do on a Friday night. When it got ugly and Johnny Lee got shot, they weren't near prepared to deal with how much that guy wanted to survive and protect his little girl. Remember that… when folks are fightin' for family, it's all different. If I put a pistol in somebody's face and ask for their wallet, they'll give it to me… but if I try and hurt their kid, that changes everythin', even if you got that pistol stuck in their ear. That's love, man, and that's some very powerful shit."

"So how in the hell did you not get charged with anything?" Levi asked.

"I was really lucky. Really lucky. The chick I grabbed couldn't or wouldn't ID me…did you know they moved to Atlanta? Yeah, sure did; I think I freaked her out. Although the sheriff knew I had been to Johnny Lee's trailer that night, that's all they had on me. It still pisses me off that Reese is dead. He was my partna'. I liked him a lot. Johnny Lee, on the other hand, was a real pain in the ass most times. But the good news is, I got all that river-runnin' business. I guess things work out…sometimes."

"So? Reese just called you up and said go grab this dude's wife and without askin' any questions, you just up and done it?" Levi asked in amazement.

"Yeah, man…that's how it works…plus, I was tryin' to make a name for myself and they were the big dogs, and their ox was in the ditch. I was gonna help push or pull. Whatever was needed."

Levi shook his head.

"I'd expect you to do the same shit for me. You would, right?" Moon Pie asked.

"Of course...I mean, hell yeah...of course I would," Levi answered, although he wasn't as positive as he tried to sound.

"Yeah, well, you don't seem real sure. I get that. Reese asked a lot of me that night. He paid a heavy price...and hell, I did too. I'm still payin'. Those freakin' deputies are still watching me. I see 'em. I just gotta be extra careful, that's all. But that's the difference in me and Johnny Lee. He'd do some off-the-wall, crazy shit, man. I think things through, and I've always got a backup plan," Moon Pie explained as he parked the FJ Cruiser behind the Gold Mine.

The digital dash clock glowed 9:02 when Moon Pie turned off the ignition. He and Levi looked around for anything suspicious.

Moon Pie pulled a small semiauto pistol from the glove box and stuck it into the pocket of his fleece jacket and then looked at Levi. "You let me get the back door open, and then you bring the bag in. If someone drives up, stay in the truck."

"Gotcha."

Moon Pie keyed open the back door, then flipped on the light switch. After a quick glance around inside, he waved at Levi.

Struggling with the weight of the bag, Levi awkwardly hurried inside. Moon Pie slammed the door behind him and immediately threw the dead bolt. He calmly punched the alarm code, and the keypad turned a soft shade of green. Only he and Levi knew the entrance code. Moon Pie then went to the safe and punched in his six-digit code. Swinging the heavy door back, he pulled out two guns to make room for the cash. He handed them to Levi.

"We may need these this weekend anyway."

"I love deer season."

"It does make life easier when the season's in...I don't mean the huntin', I mean the not gettin' caught."

"I hear ya," Levi said as he grabbed the two rifles. One was a Steyr Mannlicher .270 with expensive night-vision optics, and the other was an old Sako .264 bull barrel with a high-powered scope. Both were covered in Mossy Oak camo tape, and Moon Pie bragged that if you laid them down in the woods, they'd disappear. These were Moon Pie's favorite guns, and he could remember exactly where he'd stolen them. Even with factory loads, they both shot dime-size groups at a hundred yards. Levi leaned each gently in the corner of the office behind the door.

"Hand me that bag," Moon Pie demanded.

After some pushing and shuffling, the bag was in place. Moon Pie replaced one gun, leaving the other out for his opening-morning hunt. He slowly shut the safe door and locked it.

"You should tell me the code. What if you're gone and I need something? How am I gonna get in there?"

"I'll tell you then. That's why we got cell phones."

"Dude, you can trust me. I'm your brother."

"Half brother, and there's over a million dollars cash in there right now. I can't trust nobody. Maybe Momma. Maybe. But she ain't gettin' the code either."

"It would show how much you trust me."

"Like I just said, I don't trust nobody."

"Not even me?" Levi asked as he looked down.

Moon Pie could tell Levi's feelings were hurt. Deep down, he wanted to trust Levi. He rode Levi's ass hard all the time, but that came with the territory. Moon Pie actually needed and wanted somebody he could trust with everything. He stared at his half brother and knew he shouldn't tell anyone the code.

"That bag of money ain't mine. If it doesn't get in the right hands in a few days—you see this thing on my leg—I'm dead."

"That's exactly why we need to take it up a notch. Help each other. I got your back."

"You got my back?"

"Yeah, I do, brother."

Moon Pie wanted to change the subject. "I'll think about it."

"Come on."

"I said, I'll think about it. Don't push it!"

Levi looked at him with a slightly cocked head.

Moon Pie smiled. "Come on. Let's go get a beer. I'm thirsty."

CHAPTER 40

———— ☾ ————

S EBASTIAN CALLED WALTER ON HIS CELL PHONE, INSISTING that they meet that night. It was almost ten, and Walter could hear the intensity in his voice. Something either really good or really bad was about to happen.

Lucille sat in Walter's recliner, occasionally glancing at *Law & Order* while trying to guess what Sebastian was so worked up about. She was concerned about her granddaughter and berated Walter for not asking Sebastian any questions. His explanation that cell-phone communications were not secure and shouldn't be trusted didn't do much to mollify her. Only the fact that she had talked to Bailey just a few minutes prior and knew she was driving back to spend the night reduced her stress level somewhat.

When the knock came at the door, Walter immediately looked out his peephole and then opened the door. Sebastian allowed Bailey to enter first, and Bernard followed her.

"Got any coffee?" Sebastian asked.

"Sure," Walter answered as he shuffled toward the kitchen. "So, what's up?"

"Oh, we just had a little run-in with Bailey's *ex*-boyfriend Woody," Sebastian replied as he watched her hugging Lucille. "We thought it best if she stayed here for a while."

Walter poured coffee and asked, "Then I'm guessing he's still alive?"

"He's breathin'."

Walter looked at Sebastian and Bernard and then at Bailey, who was standing by a small suitcase that looked thirty years old and a grocery bag full of something.

"Okay. What happened?" he finally asked, since no one was volunteering information.

"We watched him follow her from the store after work, so we discreetly tailed him."

"We got lost twice," Bernard offered, holding up two fingers for emphasis.

Sebastian sighed. "We couldn't keep up, but I figured I knew where they were going."

"He drives like Grandma Moses," Bernard added with a grin.

"Anyway, as I was saying, by the time we got there, he had kicked in the door and had knocked her around some."

Everyone turned to look at Bailey. Lucille made her stand by the floor lamp, and they could see that she was going to have a black eye. Aged tempers rose.

"I had a good *talk* with the little shit, and since we couldn't lock up Bailey's apartment, I insisted that she come and stay here. I knew that's what Lucille would want."

"I'm glad you did," Lucille said, and she stroked Bailey's hair as only a grandmother can do.

Walter unwrapped a cigar and stuck it in the corner of his mouth while he thought. "Anything else? What about the store?"

"The owner was there when we drove back by a little while ago," Bernard said.

"Is that normal, Bailey?" Walter asked.

"No sir. I don't think so. But they coulda just been gettin' back from their trip."

Walter sucked on his cigar and looked around at the group. Sebastian gulped his coffee, and Bernard was scrounging for cookies. Bailey looked shell-shocked, and Lucille looked concerned.

"We still goin' in tomorrow night?" Sebastian asked.

"It's pointless until we know the code to the safe," Walter said, staring out a window at the red flashing light on the town's only microwave tower.

"Anything else?"

"Nope." Sebastian didn't want to discuss his idea in front of Bailey.

"What took y'all so long to get here? The store closes at six."

"Oh, we took her out to eat, to cheer her up," Bernard said.

Walter realized everybody was spending the stolen money like drunken sailors on leave and sighed deeply.

"We used some of our emergency-expense-account money you gave us," Bernard added quickly.

"Well, if that's it, I'm taking this baby to my room for a good night's sleep. Walter, you see? She needs our help."

"I do." Walter was unfortunately aware that most abuse cases start with a few punches to the gut and then slowly escalate. But when a man hits a woman in the face, it's real rage, and the severity of the abuse progresses quickly. That's what had happened to his daughter, and he had failed to recognize the signs. It haunted him daily.

Lucille and Bailey walked for the door. Sebastian opened it for them.

"Y'all call us if you need anything during the night. Anything at all," Walter said. The other men voiced like sentiments.

"Oh, Bailey—you work tomorrow, right?"

"Yes, sir. Levi and I almost always work Saturdays."

"I need to see you before you go in. It's important. I'll explain to everybody in the morning. Seven thirty."

When the door shut, Sebastian set his coffee cup down and pulled off his overcoat. He rubbed his hands and stood up like a Baptist minister about to preach in front of his own momma.

Walter was a bit taken aback.

"I got an idea."

"Yeah, I figured something was up. What is it?" Walter asked.

"Look, I know we all wanna kill the little prick, but he ain't worth goin' to prison over," Sebastian said.

"Yeah, so what are you thinkin'?" Walter prodded impatiently.

"When we steal the money from the gold store, we frame that little peckerhead for it."

Walter let a smile creep across his lips. He picked up his cigar and pointed it at Sebastian and Bernard. "Gentlemen, that's a damn fine idea."

"I'm bettin' Moon Pie will get to him, and presto, he's outta her hair," Sebastian said. Then he added, "And hopefully the gene pool."

"Bailey said that he and the owner guy don't get along anyway," Bernard said, wanting to contribute.

"It's just brilliant," Walter said.

"But how do we frame him, specifically?" Bernard asked.

Sebastian laughed, and all eyes turned to him. He carefully retrieved something from his handkerchief. "With this?" He proudly held up the smokeless-tobacco can, making sure he didn't add his fingerprints to it.

"A lot of people dip, dude," Bernard said sarcastically.

Walter looked at the can in Sebastian's hand, studying the unusual top. "What's this jerk's name again?"

"Woody Walker," Sebastian said with a chuckle.

Walter said excitedly, "Bernard, my friend, lots of folks indulge in the pleasures of smokeless tobacco or, as you refer to it, dip, but how many have a sterling-silver lid with a gold-plated *W*?"

"I thought you'd like that," Sebastian said, watching Walter's eyes and seeing his mind race.

"Well, I'll be damned," Bernard said to no one in particular.

"Does he know you have it?" Walter asked excitedly.

"Nope, and by now, he's probably missing it. But he doesn't have a clue that I've got it."

"It's just perfect! This just might work. Good thinkin'," Walter said as he patted Sebastian on the back.

CHAPTER 41

————— ☾ —————

J AKE HAD LONG SINCE KISSED KATY GOOD NIGHT. NOW HE
lay on the bed with his arms crossed behind his head while
Morgan washed her face and prepared for bed. It had been a long
day and an even longer week. Katy had sensed that her parents
were on edge and had asked some questions about their safety.
Hearing Katy's concern made Jake realize how important it was
for him to take the primary responsibility for the protection of
his family.

The police periodically drove by the house, the Old Waverly
security was heightened at the guard's gate, Morgan had alerted
the school officials, and in general, the entire town of West Point
was looking out for them. It was comforting to know folks genu-
inely cared—but it wasn't going to be enough.

Jake wondered if he or his family were being stalked, if
someone had deliberately burned down the camp house, and if
any or all of this could be related to the events of the Dummy
Line. *Maybe it was just a Peeping Tom spying on Morgan. She's
hot and parades around the house all the time in a tank top
with no bra and skintight yoga pants or shorts. It's hard not to
look. And the camp was old and the wiring was probably shot.
Or maybe a bunch of drunk kids did it for kicks; it happens. If*

somebody was lookin' for revenge, they'd have done it by now. Hell, that night was front-page news for days, and it stayed in the papers for weeks.

"Do you still have your pistol in your car?" Jake yelled to Morgan.

"Nope. I keep it in my purse now."

"Good. But you gotta get your concealed-carry permit."

"What's that?" she asked, brushing her hair hard enough that Jake thought it should hurt.

"You have to have a permit if you're gonna carry a pistol around with you."

"Do you have one?"

"Well, no, but I don't carry mine around with me everywhere either. It's in my truck, though."

"Maybe you should."

"Yeah, I was just lyin' here thinkin' that."

"I hate that we're havin' to think about this, Jake."

"Me too. It's not anybody's fault. It just happened."

Morgan came and sat down on the bed next to him. "I'm not blamin' you, babe."

"I know. I didn't mean to imply that you were. Tomorrow R.C. will be here, and he'll be able to help us think through this. He's pretty street-smart."

"I'm glad you called him," she said, walking back into the bathroom.

"I think I'll teach Katy how to shoot your LadySmith this weekend. Just so she knows."

"Jake, she's only twelve. She's kinda young, don't you think?"

"Not at all. I can't believe I haven't taught her already. I don't want her to be afraid of handguns, just to respect them like she does her rifle and shotgun. And, I want her to understand that gun control is about bein' able to hit what you aim at."

CHAPTER 42

——— (———

D AWN BROKE CLEAR, COOL, AND CRISP AT 6:33 A.M. WALTER had been up for an hour. He knew that one of the largest armed forces in the South was positioned all across Mississippi to take part in a tradition as serious as Thanksgiving—opening day of deer season. Tomorrow, hundreds, if not thousands, of smiling young girls and boys, holding their trophy deer, would have their pictures in small-town newspapers across the state.

Hunting's economic impact is staggering. Hunters not only pay for their privilege to enjoy their natural rights to the outdoors, but also purchase food, gas, equipment, clothing, and the list goes on and on and on. Walter wished he were out there. Sebastian had offered to take him hunting on some land along the river that the Corps of Engineers made available for public. Walter promised himself that he would enjoy a hunt sometime soon, but for now, he had a crime to plan. He remembered what his favorite major league baseball player, Roger Maris, said: "You hit home runs not by chance but by preparation."

Not having the codes continued to bother him, and he had devised a new approach that hopefully would solve the problem. Yesterday he'd purchased an expensive motion-sensitive and voice-activated video camera that he planned to have Bailey set up in the office to capture the code being entered. It was a waste of time and too risky to attempt breaking in without knowing the code. It wasn't realistic that they could guess the combination, and the safe was too heavy for four old farts and a girl to move...even if it weren't bolted to the slab. The surveillance camera was their best bet, and hiding it seemed plausible because of all the junk in the office. To maximize their chances for success, Walter was willing to wait—as long as it took—until the camera captured the code.

Walter started thinking about his recent conversations with Jake Crosby while he waited on the rest of the crew to make their way downstairs. There was no means of getting the cash into a bank account without raising suspicion, except by making small deposits over an extended period. *Shit, we're all too freakin' old to even consider doin' much of anything that extends any distance into the future.* Walter chuckled at the thought.

He could tell Jake was disappointed and knew he wasn't willing to risk breaking any laws, and his brokerage wouldn't allow it anyway. Jake had wished him the best and hoped he could help Walter in the near future.

Walter took a long sip of coffee and then changed mental gears to Samantha's phone call yesterday telling him that Kroger had requested a meeting for Monday and that they had disclosed that they would have attorneys present. She was nervous—he could hear it in her voice—and that, in turn, made him anxious.

At about seven thirty, Lucille and Bailey came down for breakfast. Lucille had toast with homemade blackberry jelly. Bailey drank a Mountain Dew. Her eye didn't look as bad as Walter had expected.

After a few more minutes, Walter tired of waiting for Sebastian and Bernard and pulled out the camera. "Bailey, this is what I want you to do. It's real simple. This is a motion-sensitive video camera that makes no noise. I need you to position it so it can film Moon Pie entering the safe's combination. If we can get that, we're home free."

"How do I turn it on? Do I have to focus it?" she asked, a bit intimidated.

"It automatically focuses, and all you have to do is turn it on by pushing this switch. Point it at the lock, and make sure it's hidden. Make sure it's at an angle so the person punching in the code doesn't block the camera. You may have to experiment a few times. Here's how you review it." Walter demonstrated by filming Lucille.

"Okay. I get it."

"From looking at your cell phone pictures, I seem to recall that there is a shelf with magazines and some other junk on the right-hand wall. Somewhere on that shelf would be perfect. You'll just need a few minutes to set it up. Can you handle that?"

"Sure. Levi always leaves to get us breakfast after he opens up. It takes him about twenty minutes."

"Be careful."

"This is a *great* idea," Bailey said enthusiastically as she looked at the camera.

"It should work," Walter said confidently.

"Now, if he'll just show up and unlock the safe today," Bailey said thoughtfully.

"Bailey, honey, we're really not in a hurry," Walter said. Then he added, "Does your ex-boyfriend know that your grandmother lives here?"

"Yes. Yes sir. He does," she said, shifting her gaze to Lucille.

CHAPTER 43

———— ☾ ————

MOON PIE OVERSLEPT AND WOKE UP PISSED OFF AT THE world. He had a narrow thirty-acre property that he loved to hunt the first day of the season. It was basically a place to park his truck, but it bordered a nine-hundred-acre private farm in Noxubee County that was intensively managed for trophy whitetails. Every opening morning for the last three years he had killed a nice buck by being in the woods before the doctor who owned the fine place put out all his hunting buddies. The doctor's friends typically made so much noise that nearly every deer on the place got spooked, and Moon Pie knew their primary escape routes. If the wind was calm or out of the northwest, he would be in great shape.

He jumped into his hunting clothes, grabbed his rifle, and dashed to the woods as daylight was breaking. He needed to kill a buck on opening day because it tied directly to his sense of self-worth—saying to whoever saw it that he was such an accomplished hunter that he could take a wall hanger in the first few hours of the season opening.

Moon Pie and Levi rarely missed a day of hunting during the season, and if they did, they went during that night. Levi also had two horses they occasionally rode on large, open properties.

Horse tracks weren't obvious signs of poachers and were often dismissed as merely signs of a neighboring landowner rounding up lost cattle. They also road-hunted the beautiful Natchez Trace, a 444-mile, ancient, wooded road that sliced through prime whitetail habitat between Nashville and Natchez.

In all of Moon Pie's illegal activities, he was as slick as a greasy BB. While law enforcement agencies were aware of his nefarious ways, Moon Pie had paid off so many locals with meat and drugs that they watched his back, making him that much harder to catch.

By nine o'clock that morning, Moon Pie was already pissed at himself for oversleeping. He'd stayed up late watching a *Swamp People* marathon and the doctor's friends had beaten him into the woods by at least thirty minutes. As a result, he had missed an excellent chance to poach one of the doc's big deer. After hearing someone shoot three times, Moon Pie slithered down from his perch atop a blown-down white oak and headed back to his truck. There were too many hunters on the doctor's place for him to slip across the property line today, and since he didn't know exactly when Tam would be arriving to exchange the drugs for the cash, he felt an urgency to leave the woods.

Tam Nguyen made Moon Pie extremely nervous. The late Johnny Lee had introduced them about four years ago, which was yet another reason Moon Pie felt compelled to avenge Johnny Lee's death. Tam had been searching for trustworthy drug runners and compensated proven dependability through a unique profit-sharing program, and with greater reliability came greater base pay. In the Vietnamese criminal culture along Mississippi's Gulf Coast, trustworthiness was frequently challenged and constantly had to be proven.

Historically, the Dixie Mafia, as it was known along the coast, had been run exclusively by good ol' boys—white boys. Recently, however, a few Vietnamese—and Tam Nguyen specifically—had proven they not only were excellent shrimpers but also possessed other talents, and they had staked a significant claim to a piece of the Gulf Coast drug trade.

Tam's vision was to expand northward. To do so, he had to improve his distribution network. He would use Biloxi as a base, which worked especially well, since there was no port authority and any vessel could simply enter the bay and dock unchecked. Biloxi's proximity to Interstate 10, a major drug route that went from Florida to California, and several interstates heading north, made Biloxi and the surrounding area ideal for drug trafficking.

Moon Pie had met face-to-face with Tam only a few times. Tam lurked in the shadows as much as possible. His trusted lieutenants did the heavy lifting. Because of Tam's notoriety, he had to work and sleep in a different location every day, all the while maintaining a powerful and growing criminal empire. Rumors were that he had numerous bay houses and houses on the intracoastal canals. When Moon Pie needed to talk with Tam, he called a prepaid cell phone, which was rarely operational for more than two weeks.

Moon Pie had heard stories of unfortunate souls crossing Tam. The tales ranged from more than one person being drowned in a shrimp net to another guy being hog-tied and partially fed to alligators; there was just enough of him hanging out of reach to be identifiable. One story circulated about a college kid on spring break who had been relentlessly hitting on Tam's girlfriend. He went missing and was found three days later naked, frozen solid in a flash freezer at a seafood company. One of his shoes was stuck down his throat, and the other was up his rectum. The stories had the desired chilling effect—no one ever considered crossing Tam, ever. Moon Pie was one of the scores of true believers.

When Moon Pie got back to his truck, he retrieved the key from behind the driver's-side front tire. The hair on the back of his neck stood. He felt that he was being watched. He tried to act casual as he peeled off a layer of clothes and glanced around surreptitiously. Not knowing who was out there was killing him. *That damn doctor probably tipped off the game warden,* he thought.

Moon Pie had resented the doctor since the day he had purchased the land. Moon Pie had hunted the place years before the doctor started raking in the big bucks from Jackson socialites' boob jobs and face-lifts. *Maybe it's a damn good thing that I didn't kill one today! With Tam coming up here and all, I don't need any more hassles than I already got.*

Moon Pie climbed into the truck and backed out, and, not seeing anyone or any vehicles, he slung gravel as he stomped the gas. As he neared the doctor's gate, he slowed and laughed as he tossed out a double handful of roofing nails in front of the fancy entrance.

CHAPTER 44

———— ☾ ————

T HE TENNESSEE MEXICAN CRIMINALS HAD THEIR REGULAR Saturday-morning staff meeting in the back room of Shoney's. They conducted their illicit business in almost the same manner as any legitimate growing commercial concern. The ringleader read off a list of projects and asked his staff for updates. By all appearances, this was a typical business meeting for the development of a new software program, not criminal activities. However, the sixth discussion item was the money given to Moon Pie for the *cocaína*.

"We have every reason to believe that this venture is on track, Jefe."

"When will the first transaction be concluded?"

"By the end of business on Monday. We are electronically monitoring the money and Mr. Pie. We know exactly where both are."

"*Excelente. Siga supervisando*," the ringleader said before taking a sip of water. Then he added, "Tell me as soon as the money moves."

"*Sí, señor.*"

To the group, el Jefe said, "Sources tell me that his organization can supply us well. We need them to *crezca grande*."

With those comments about monitoring the money and growing their business, they moved on to the next item on the agenda—killing a known informant.

CHAPTER 45

B AILEY ARRIVED AT WORK WORRIED THAT WOODY WAS
going to show up and cause a major scene. She wanted so
badly to break away from him. She dreaded what was ahead of
her if she didn't. With the money they were going to steal, she
would be able to get out of town—start over.

Once the store was open for business, as if he had read the
script, Levi offered to go get breakfast.

"You want cheese in your grits?" he asked, walking out the
door.

"Yes, please," she replied, anxious for him to leave.

When the door shut, she went straight to her purse to get the
camera. As soon as she laid her hands on it, the back door sprung
open, and Levi was standing there with a goofy smile on his face.

"I was just curious...what's your favorite movie?"

"Uh...what?"

"I just realized that I don't know what you favorite movie is.
That really says a lot about someone."

Bailey was flustered and couldn't think of anything else to
say, so she asked, "I don't know. What's your's?"

"It's hard to say. This chick that cuts my hair, she's always
talkin' about movies and lines from movies. It made me realize

that I might enjoy a movie, but the ones that I really remember are the ones with great lines."

Bailey wanted him to leave, but she nodded her head as though she actually cared about what he was saying.

"Hell, I like so many, it's tough to choose one. *A Christmas Story* is probably my all-time favorite, and that movie has got some great lines. I watch it every year when they play the marathon at Christmas. 'You'll shoot your eye out, kid!'"

"I've seen that. I love it when the kid sticks his tongue to the light pole," she said with a giggle.

"Sometimes I kinda think me and Moon Pie are like Ralphie and his little brother."

Bailey laughed. "I don't think so. Y'all might be those two boys that are always picking on him, though."

"I even drink Ovaltine sometimes."

"Well, you certainly take your movies seriously, and I'd love to talk some more about 'em, but I really gotta get to work."

"Tell me a movie you like, and I'll let you go."

Bailey sighed and thought. "I did rent a movie recently called *Double Jeopardy.*"

Levi was leaning on the doorjamb, intently watching her. He offered, "Ashley Judd. I love her."

"I watched it twice. I kinda identified with her character, and I loved it when she said, 'Hello, Nick.'"

"Oh yeah! That was really good. See…I learned somethin' about you. Okay, be right back."

Levi was gone for ten seconds, and then he suddenly burst back through the door, scaring the crap out of her again.

"Did you know Michelle Pfeiffer was the first choice to play Clarice Starling in *Silence of the Lambs*? She turned it down 'cuz it was way too scary."

"Really?" Bailey replied.

"Yep. I love movies."

"I do too."

Levi smiled at her. "Great. Okay, now I'm gone to get break-fast. Be right back."

Bailey walked to the back door and peeked outside to make certain that Levi had indeed left. When she saw him drive off, she grabbed the camera and began looking for an optimum location. She figured that she had twenty minutes to set the camera and place the magnet inside the doorframe, all the while being mind-ful of Moon Pie's static cameras.

After setting up the spy camera, she stood on a chair and affixed the magnet to the inside of the metallic backdoor frame. She quickly shut the door and replaced the chair in the back room.

When she heard the back door slam, she playfully called out, "Hello, Nick."

She could hear footfalls and assumed it was Levi as she turned to leave the office.

"Who the hell's Nick?" Moon Pie asked as he appeared.

"Nobody. Levi and I were just talkin' about something, that's all," Bailey said, hoping to hide her surprise at seeing Moon Pie.

"Uh-huh. Where'd he go?"

"He went to get us breakfast. It's always slow Saturday morn-ings."

Moon Pie walked into the office and looked around suspi-ciously. "So, who's Nick?"

"He's from a movie that Nick—I mean Levi—and I were talkin' about before he left."

"You never talk about movies with me."

"I really don't ever really talk movies with anybody. Levi just asked me what I liked."

"He's so gay," Moon Pie said, sitting down in his desk chair.

"No he's not."

"So tell me, does Woodrow know about Nick?" Moon Pie asked with a sly smile.

Bailey rolled her eyes and, with a sigh, hurriedly walked toward the front of the store. The best thing about today was that Moon Pie would most certainly open the safe, revealing the code and putting her that much closer to freedom. She planned to call Walter with an update at her first break, when she could go outside for some privacy.

CHAPTER 46

————— ☾ —————

T AM NGUYEN AND HIS FIANCÉE, ALEXA, SAT IN THE BACK-
seat of his black Mercedes-Benz S600 sedan, heading
toward Tupelo, Mississippi. They were three hours late because
Alexa had had to shop for new clothes for the meet and greet.

When she had received the e-mail inviting her, she had
almost fainted. Tam really didn't want to attend, but she had
pleaded and begged. She finally resorted to insisting that, since it
was their anniversary weekend of their first date, it was the only
thing she wanted as a gift. He was more of a Black Eyed Peas fan,
but since he could conduct business too, the long trip would be
worthwhile—even justified.

Following behind Tam's Benz was a black Ram truck with
a matching camper shell. In the bed was nearly $1.7 million of
cocaine at wholesale value. The huge Mercedes and its blacked-
out windows attracted a lot of attention; however, the Ram truck
looked like one of the thousands of other pickup trucks that
Mississippians loved to drive. The two drivers communicated via
handheld CB radios and cell phones, but they were never out of
sight from each other.

Tam glanced at his watch and exhaled deeply. Alexa would
have a screaming fit if they were late to the event. It was going to

be close, but he couldn't risk either vehicle being pulled over for speeding.

Tam preferred military-like precision and was having to learn to be more flexible with Alexa around. She sometimes would take thirty minutes to simply put her hair up in a ponytail. That was hard for Tam Nguyen. Tight controls kept him unincarcerated, ahead of his competition, and alive.

He decided that for the peace of his relationship with Alexa, he would have to make the exchange with Moon Pie the next morning. He studied Alexa as she slept. He knew that his wealth attracted women, but he still couldn't believe she was his fiancée. She had been working as a swimsuit and fitness model after having been a Hooters calendar girl. Two years earlier, she had dropped out of Tulane University to pursue modeling full-time. *How many guys can say they are engaged to a professional fitness model?*

Alexa was also good for his image. He made a mental note to check into leasing or fractional ownership of a private airplane like the King Airs hangared at the local airport. That not only would save him time but also would impress Alexa and his clients. On second thought, he realized that Alexa would insist on flying to Dallas and Atlanta just to shop or attend concerts. It could end up costing him a fortune.

The six men Tam had killed with his own hands would have been surprised to learn that he even considered what others thought or felt. His reputation was one of brutal violence. He intimidated the competition, and rarely, if ever, did he blink at using force first. Somehow Alexa could look past his tough facade to see a caring person. She understood his lifestyle and seemed to enjoy the dichotomy of it. Tam believed that all people, at some point during their lives, would meet someone who appreciated their true being. Alexa was that person for him.

Tam palmed his cell phone and searched for Moon Pie's number. He typed a text message: "No time 2nite. 2morrow 4 sure. B ready." Then he hit send.

He laid the phone on the tan leather seat, made himself more comfortable, and pulled out a small notebook to review his coded financials.

CHAPTER 47

———— ☾ ————

T HE TWO NORTHEAST MISSISSIPPI DRUG TASK FORCE OFFIC-
ers were working overtime preparing for the meet and
sting, as they now referred to it. They discussed it only with
those who absolutely needed to know. One of the officers had an
old high school buddy who was a police officer in Tupelo, so he
had called him in to help put together an undercover squad who
could pretend to be concert attendees.

The plan was to use the Hilton Garden Inn, which was adja-
cent to the BancorpSouth Arena, the concert venue. The task
force had reserved the Hilton banquet room and paid an outside
caterer and party planner to make the setting seem authentic.
An undercover police officer acted as DJ, spinning Rascal Flatts's
hits to set the tone. Officers from several agencies played various roles, from road manager to groupies. Wearing an Ohio State
ball cap, one sheriff's deputy actually looked like Gary LeVox, the
lead singer. They couldn't find an officer thin enough, however,
to portray Joe Don, so the play was that the other band members
had yet to arrive. The meet and sting appeared to be authentic.
Everybody had been briefed extensively on the target. Hopefully
by the time Tam walked into the room and discovered the festiv-
ities were a fake, the trap would be sprung. The deception was on.

Inside the BancorpSouth Arena, a legitimate meet and greet was under way behind the stage. The genuine members of Rascal Flatts were there, safe. The band had beefed up their security as a precautionary measure. The state and local police had also increased their covert presence and added additional video surveillance. Coupled with the seventy-five stagehands, there was no shortage of testosterone.

For the task force, this sting had a different feel. They knew something good was going to happen when they read a Tweet on Alexa's Twitter account saying: "Headed 2 meet Rascal Flatts w/ my sweetie ☺!" They had taken the bait.

Finally, after two relentless years, they would get to cuff the drug kingpin of the Mississippi Gulf Coast. Both men worried, however, that they were understaffed because they couldn't risk divulging the scope of the operation, since they were confident that they had a leak within the department. They were mitigating their typical staffing levels because they assumed that Tam wouldn't have his typical security contingent, since they were several hundred miles away from home and this was Alexa's deal. The cops expected two, possibly three, in Tam's security detail. The two officers went over the plans, trying to think of any base left uncovered. Thirty minutes earlier they had slipped on their bulletproof vests and radioed the team to get into position. Music blared, and the lights were dimmed. They had all listened to "Life Is a Highway" so many times they were sick of it.

"And Oprah likes these guys? Over," one officer commented into the mic hidden inside his shirt collar.

"She loves 'em. You don't? Over."

"Stand by. I see a big-ass black Mercedes pulling up. This could be them."

"Places...everyone! Game time!"

"I can't see the plates, but the driver's checking the place out. Hang on."

Sixty seconds crawled by while the music played and two female undercover officers acted as if they had just seen Elvis—the young, hip-swinging version—live and in person.

"What are they doing now!"

"They just pulled off...headed toward the concert hall. Must not have been them."

"Damn!"

CHAPTER 48

—— ☾ ——

MOON PIE HATED DOING ANYTHING BUT HUNTING ON Sunday. He loved Chick-fil-A's corporate policy, since 1946, of being closed for business on Sundays. This recipe for success had made such an impression on him that he had decided the Gold Mine would close on Sundays as well.

When he received the text from Tam, he knew he didn't have a choice but to work that Sunday. *At least I can watch the game Saturday without anyone bothering me,* he thought.

Moon Pie had become a Tennessee Volunteer fan when he lived in Chattanooga with his grandparents. That was also where he picked up the nickname Moon Pie. His grandfather worked in the original Moon Pie bakery, and at a young age, Ethan was never seen without one of the snacks in his hands—thus the moniker.

At halftime Moon Pie called Levi to update him and talk about what he expected to happen on Sunday. He realized he wasn't hanging around his trailer, as was his custom. "Where the hell are you?" Moon Pie asked, and then spit into a plastic bottle.

"I'm eatin'." Levi had been expecting Moon Pie's call.

"I hear lots of voices," Moon Pie said as he logged on to Facebook with his new iPad.

"I'm downtown."

"You with a girl?"

"Kinda," Levi said as he smiled at his date.

"Who is she?"

"I ain't tellin'."

"White girl?"

"You're funny, Moon. Do you need me?"

"No, we ain't gonna make the exchange tonight. It'll be tomorrow. You wanna go shinin' tonight?"

"Nah, man," Levi said, "I'm busy."

"All right, then. Be ready in the mornin'. I don't know what time yet, so be expectin' my call."

"Where you thinkin' of doing the deal?"

"Shit!" Moon Pie said out loud. "I never have any friend requests."

"What?"

"Facebook's broke."

"It ain't broke, you just need a better picture. That photo looks like some perv's mug shot, dude."

"Commercial's over. I gotta get back to the game," Moon Pie said and then started to hang up.

"Whoa, wait! Where we meetin' at?"

"Probably at one of the boat ramps. They'll be pretty quiet till duck season opens. I'll call you in the mornin'," Moon Pie said authoritatively. Then he spat loudly and broke the connection.

Levi looked at his cell phone. He was glad he wasn't at Moon Pie's trailer watching ESPN. More than once, Moon Pie had thrown a beer bottle at his television when Tennessee lost. He smiled at the reprieve from Moon, looked at his date, and then asked, "How'd you like to go to the Rascal Flatts concert tonight?"

"You have tickets?" she asked enthusiastically.

"Nope, but I can get us some."

"Yes! Yes! I'd loooove too! I loooove those guys! I know all their songs!"

"Great! Okay. Let's get goin', then." Levi thrived on spontaneity.

CHAPTER 49

———— ☾ ————

D ARKNESS FELL. WALTER AND HIS TEAM WERE DRINKING coffee in the Henry Clay Hotel library. They were studying the video from the camera Bailey had brought back. The combination appeared to be 36, 24, 36, pound.

Walter laughed out loud when he realized what the code represented. He knew that no one would have tried that particular combination of numbers. Sebastian had spent countless hours studying relevant numbers in Moon Pie's life, and something so off the wall as a woman's measurements—it was just too much for him.

Sebastian grunted at the genius of the code.

Lucille blinked in disgust.

Bernard smiled, knowing that he would have chosen that exact sequence; it would have been so easy to remember.

Now the gang had to decide when to do it.

Bernard and Lucille wanted to strike right away—tonight. Walter wanted to plan for a few more days, study the layout more. Sebastian didn't really care but was very anxious to see Woody get what was coming to him.

"Tonight's a good night. Everybody's watching football on ESPN," Bernard pointed out. "What else do we gotta do?"

"I'm not sure. I'm just worried about gettin' in and gettin' out without bein' caught by our boy or the police," Walter said with a worrisome tone.

"What? Lucille and I'll be watchin' from across the street. We've talked about this."

"What's the matter, Walter?" Sebastian asked.

"Nothing. I-I-I...I mean, we just had the Kroger job planned so well, and I know they suspect me...but with this...we really haven't considered all the angles—in the same detail—so it could go to hell in a hurry. I don't want any of us getting into trouble."

"It could also go off without a hitch," Bernard said. "All we gotta do is get in and get out. It's pretty simple, really. And easier than the last one. There won't be any people around."

Sebastian stood up and then made sure that no one was outside in the hall who could hear him.

"Look, Walter Severson. Listen to me! I've been here for almost three years, basically sittin' 'round with nothin' to do, nowhere to go, and nothin' keepin' my mind engaged other than readin' the paper. I had a good life, but I ain't got shit to show for it now. My wife died years ago. She tried to be healthy, but it wasn't in her genes. I lost my daughter in a car wreck, and my son's overseas, fightin' in the war in Afghanistan. Hell...he'd understand.

"I ain't told y'all...but I've got cancer, and it don't look good. I won't go into that—but my point is...until you came along, Walter, with this idea to help others, I was just wastin' away. Waitin' to die. Just goin' through the daily motions. Now I've got a reason to hang in there. Yeah, I don't really agree with robbin' folks, but these guys are criminals and...and we're gonna do good with the money. I believe in this. None of us has got material wealth, but we all have big hearts, and we wanna help other people. If we do get caught, I'll tell 'em that it was my idea and that y'all didn't know shit about what was goin' on. I'll take whatever punishment they lay out. What you don't know, Walter, is that you done me a favor and I owe you...big-time."

Walter tried to swallow the lump in his throat. He looked around the room. Lucille had tears in her eyes. Bernard wiped his nose.

"This whole foundation makes sense to me, and it would to a lot of people if we explained it to 'em. One thing I do know—there are way more people who need a little assistance than we can actually help. Way more. But we gotta try. So when you worry about something happening to us…I don't want you to, 'cause if anything does, I've made up my mind; I'm gonna take the fall. I'm gonna tell the police that I'm just a blind hog that found an acorn. That way you and Lucille and Bernard and whoever else you get can keep this foundation alive."

Bernard put down his coffee cup. "I feel the same way. The exact same way. I'm settin' my alarm clock now. You know, I used to just sleep till whenever. Now I don't want to miss a thing. You've given us life…purpose."

Lucille was sitting next to Walter and took his hand in her hands. "Walter, I raised two kids by myself, and wasn't any of it easy. I had about lost faith in the male of our species," she chuckled and wiped her nose, "until you came along. I don't have anything to leave my kids and grandkids. I'm okay with that, and so are they. Oh, I have some silver and a few pieces of jewelry, but that's it. What you offered to do to help Bailey is a dream come true for me. You don't have any grandkids, so maybe you don't know how it is for us." She indicated the others with a wave of her hand. "We wanna help them, and it's sad when we can't." She leaned over and kissed Walter on the cheek. "Thank you."

Walter was moved by his friends' heartfelt words. He didn't quite know what to say, since he hadn't been open about his motivation for starting the foundation. The gamut of emotions was swirling through him. For a long moment, all he could do was stare out the big windows into the dark street. He eventually looked at his watch, shook his head, and smiled.

"We pull this off, you gotta go see an oncologist," Walter said to Sebastian.

Sebastian, a big, burly man, didn't like being told what to do. He looked at his friends and saw true concern. Bernard and Lucille both nodded their heads.

"That's a deal."

"Well, we better get started if we're gonna rob the place and get back in time to go to bed at a decent hour."

CHAPTER 50

———— ☾ ————

J AKE HAD HAD A BUSY DAY. HE HAD TAKEN KATY DEER HUNT-
ing, and just getting her out of bed before daylight had been
a chore. Inside the shooting house, Katy had texted on her cell
phone more than she watched for deer. He'd allowed her to do
what she was enjoying, but when a nice buck trotted across a
power line and she couldn't get ready fast enough, his frustration
boiled over. He said some things that he immediately regretted
and spent the rest of the morning apologizing.

Jake kept reminding himself that the purpose of their hunting was about spending time together and not about killing something. He was relieved that being in a shooting house didn't seem
to bother Katy or bring up any painful memories from their ordeal
on the Dummy Line. In fact, she didn't seem troubled by it at all.
Jake thought about it enough for both of them. He wondered if
texting was a diversion. Then he finally realized that for a typical
preteen, texting occurs about every waking minute. She was fine.

Morgan was spending the day shopping in Jackson at the
Junior League's Mistletoe Marketplace and wouldn't return until
late that night. Katy had a birthday party to attend that afternoon, and R. C. Smithson was coming to town to talk with Jake
about the family's security.

R.C. hadn't changed much. He may have put on ten pounds, and he'd grown a scruffy beard. He dressed professionally for his new job as a private detective, but Jake kept picturing him in his muddy, wet deputy's uniform. Sitting in Jake's den, they caught up on the last eighteen months. They had not met before that fateful night, and now there was a bond between them. Jake knew firsthand that R.C. was a good guy, and Katy really took a shine to him.

R.C. pulled out a notepad and asked Jake to explain everything that had happened recently. Jake walked over to the fireplace, looked into the flames, gathering his thoughts, and then sat down on the hearth and started talking in as much detail as he could recount about the Peeping Tom, the camp house, the mysterious cars that drove by, the time he had seen a strange car parked down from his house, and the cryptic letters he had received in the mail that he hadn't even mentioned to Morgan. He described moving into the gated golf-course community and the expensive security system, which necessitated a bank loan. He explained that the local police had increased their patrolling of the neighborhood and that both he and Morgan were carrying pistols now and how he thought he was becoming paranoid.

R.C. took detailed notes, and when Jake finally paused, he said, "I've done some diggin' since you called. Spoke to Sheriff Ollie. He said to tell you and Katy hello, by the way. Bottom line is that they've got concerns also. You may not know this, but several law enforcement agencies have been keepin' an eye on you."

"What? Really?"

"Yep—here's the deal. They suspect that there was one more key player on the other team that night—this piece of shit named Ethan Daniels. His buddies call him Moon Pie or Moon. He's an opportunistic criminal entrepreneur. He's into anything that can make him money. He disappeared after the events of that night and stayed gone awhile. Everybody thinks he was next in line to be the top drug-running dog in northeast Mississippi after

Johnny Lee and Reese checked out early and that he's back and has taken over most of their activities, only he's taken it up a notch."

"Why don't they just arrest him?"

"It ain't that easy."

"Why not?"

"First, they haven't been able to catch him in the act, and second, they really want who's supplyin' him. The bigger fish. So they've been lettin' ol' Moon Pie have some rope to see where he'll take 'em. They suspect he's being supplied drugs by this Asian dude from the coast. He's the big fish. That's who they really wanna take down."

"That doesn't make me feel any better about my family's safety," Jake said, punching a log on the fire with the poker.

"Trash like Moon Pie live for revenge. They live in the moment and don't even think about tomorrow or consequences. If he was gonna avenge his buddies' deaths, he'da done it already. Trust me, I know about these things."

Jake stared at the fire and tried to work it all through his mind. After a moment, he asked, "Isn't revenge more satisfying when it's unexpected?"

"That's not how these redneck criminals think. They're programmed different. They are all about payback—an eye for an eye...and if that's what he's after, he woulda already done it."

Jake turned to face R.C. "Then tell me, why are the police watchin' my family?"

R.C. put a fresh dip in his bottom lip and thought for a long moment. Then he said, "Well, 'cause they got a different mindset, if you will. They're givin' ol' Moon Pie more credit than I do. They think that since he slipped away from us, he's smarter than the average dope dealer. They may be right. Also, I do know that, since y'all are kinda celebrities, and since Moon Pie's got lots of patience—he's a hell of a poacher, after all—that it's worth it to them to make sure y'all are safe. Also, I think that they really wanna catch him doing something worth federal time. It's like killin' two birds with one shot—protectin' y'all and keepin' an eye on Moon Pie at the same time. At any rate, law enforcement from West Point, Columbus, and even Tupelo—both city and county—are watchin' and waitin'. Some of those drive-bys and odd vehicles you've noticed are probably unmarked cops, just checkin' on y'all."

Jake shook his head.

"They didn't want you to know and have you worried all the time."

Jake let out a nervous laugh. "So where were they when this Peeping Tom scared the crap outta Morgan and Katy, and what about my camp house burnin' down?"

"I can't explain that. All I do know is that whenever Moon Pie goes missing, somebody's checkin' in on y'all. As far as the camp, I was a deputy along that river for years, and at least one old camp house catches fire every year for no reason. It just happens."

"Well, my insurance company claims it was arson. They aren't gonna pay for it."

"I hadn't heard that. If you'll give me the adjuster's name and number, I'll call to see if I can find out anything. Maybe I can help."

"So are the police watchin' this guy right now?"

"Maybe not every minute. Twenty-four-seven surveillance costs too much…but they are keeping an eye on him for sure."

"Do you know where he lives?"

R.C. flipped back several pages in his notebook. "His mom lives in Tupelo. He has a trailer over by the Columbus Air Force Base, and they believe that he has a houseboat docked at the Columbus Marina. It's not registered in his name, though. He's actually pretty clever. At any rate, he runs a business on the old side of Columbus called the Gold Mine. He buys and sells gold. That's his front. He's also a suspected poacher."

Jake stood. "R.C., that's too damn close. I can't believe nobody ever told me that he lives just twenty minutes down the road! This is unbelievable! What should I do?"

"Nothing. From what I've seen around here and what you've told me, you're doin' all you can to protect your family, and I promise you're being watched. Just let the pros do their job."

"Man oh man. If that guy was actually runnin' with those rednecks, he's bad news too. They were pure evil."

"I agree…but the police think Moon Pie can lead them to a dude that's even worse. They'll get 'em both. I've gotta ask you somethin'. You got anything to eat?"

Jake exhaled. "Yeah, sure. Whatcha hungry for?"

"You got any sardines and crackers?"

"Uh, no sardines. We probably have some crackers, though."

"Crunchy peanut butter and white bread?"

"I think so."

"I'll just make a sandwich," R.C. said, following Jake into the kitchen.

"What would you like to drink?"

"I'll take a Tab."

Jake took a hard look at him to gauge his seriousness. "We don't have Tab. How about a Diet Coke?"

"That'll work. What about a banana?"

This exchange reminded Jake that R.C. marched to a different beat and was totally clueless that he was different from most folks. As Jake searched for the peanut butter, he said, "Tell me how you got into the private-detective business."

"Remember the BP oil spill?"

"Of course."

"Well, I got hired by BP to provide security for their executives when they were on the coast. They also paid me real well to hang out with the locals to find out what regular folks were thinkin' and doin'. But to be honest, I really miss law enforcement."

"You seemed like a natural cop—like you really enjoyed your work," Jake said with a twinge of envy.

"Yeah, I really do miss it," R.C. replied, almost in a whisper.

Jake looked at him. "R.C., what do you think I oughta do?"

"Nothin'. Don't do anything." R.C. smeared peanut butter on white bread.

"That's gonna be real hard, knowin' that he's so close."

"I'm tellin' you, it's the best thing. Let the law handle it. They want him as badly as you do."

R.C. took a long, hard look straight into Jake's eyes, stressing his point. Then quickly, as if he had just remembered something important, he clapped his hands and said, "Man, I almost forgot. I've got four tickets to the Rascal Flatts concert tonight. My girl-friends can't go. Long story. You want 'em?"

"Are you kiddin'? Absolutely! Whoa, wait a sec. Did you say *girlfriends*?"

"Like I said, it's a long story."

CHAPTER 51

————— ☾ —————

SAM WANTED TO EAT OUT MOST NIGHTS BUT COULDN'T AFFORD it. As a new lawyer, she hadn't generated much income, and each month when her bills came, she was reminded of just how sorry her ex-husband was. She still couldn't believe he had cheated on her and yet she had ended up with nothing. But she appreciated that being broke and happy with cereal for supper was infinitely better than married and miserable with fine dining.

She giggled at the memory of the six bottles of skunk scent she had strategically hidden in the attic of her former home. Little glass time bombs. That winter, they would freeze and break. Eventually the scent would thaw and begin stinking to high heaven. It was her only act of retaliation, and it gave her great pleasure.

Sam and Tom the cat were celebrating her liberation by painting the foyer of her childhood home. The red-and-green-stained-glass transom above the front door was well over 140 years old. Frequently she would touch the hole in the doorframe where a bullet intended for her grandfather had lodged and was preserved. He had been a respected doctor in the community, but during the strife of the 1960s, he had treated an injured Negro teenager who had been beaten while walking home after a civil-rights rally. The young man was the son of their much-loved maid. Sam's grandfather was carrying the boy up the porch steps when a car drove by, and someone fired several shots. Fortunately, no one was injured.

As she painted, she began to worry about Walter Severson. She had a gut feeling that the Kroger security team was going to have him arrested soon. They had been building a case, and she sensed where it was heading. Anticipating their next move, she began planning hers. It was a high-stakes chess match and her first time to sit at the game table.

CHAPTER 52

————— ☾ —————

TAM'S DRIVER PULLED UP TO THE SIDE OF THE BANCORP-South Arena in Tupelo and then lowered his window to ask a guy wearing a staff jacket where to park for the meet and greet. He glanced at the black Mercedes and pointed to the convoy of buses and eighteen-wheelers parked inside a ten-foot fence. "It's usually back there. You gotta go around to the gate. There will be somebody to give you directions."

As soon as they pulled up to the back gate, a man dressed in a heavy coat and holding a clipboard put up a hand to stop them.

Alexa rolled down her window and waved the printed e-mail invitation at the man, who appeared predisposed not to talk. She yelled, "We're here to meet the band!"

The man took Alexa's letter, looked at her, and then bent down to look inside. He stood and read the invite. A chill ran down his spine when he realized from the local police's briefing that this was the man destined for the sting. He kept his composure and did not look directly at Tam.

"Okay, here's what ya gotta do. The party's been moved to that hotel right over there. The Hilton Garden Inn. That's it right there. The band will be along in a few minutes. Hope y'all have fun."

"Why did they move it?" Tam asked, always suspicious.

The man acted as if he didn't hear the question.

The driver knew Tam would want an answer and didn't pull away.

"I asked you, why did they move to the hotel? Is that normal?"

The man bent back down and said the first thing that came to mind: "The heat went out backstage is all I know. Apparently it's as cold in there as it is out here. Your lady there would freeze to death." He leered at her in her skimpy clothing.

Tam looked at him and then at the big building for a few seconds. Finally satisfied, he directed the driver, "Just go." Alexa clapped her hands and squealed in delight.

The man flipped a page back on his clipboard, found the number he was looking for, and immediately dialed it on his cell phone.

"Your bad guy is on the way," he said with relief.

"You identified him?"

"Yes. They just left the back gate, headed to the hotel. Good luck. He's a mean-looking dude."

"Thanks," the voice replied appreciatively yet sarcastically.

The lead drug-force officer went to the sound system and turned down the volume. "The hay's on its way to the barn, people. Look alive!" he said and immediately turned the music back up. He winked at the guy controlling the music. Instinctively, he felt his weapon, and it comforted him. Several men wearing staff jackets acted busy just outside the conference room, and two officers carried trays of hors d'oeuvres around to appear as if they were setting up for the party. Everything and every person appeared legit.

The black Mercedes pulled under the portico at the Hilton Garden Inn. Alexa and Tam were arguing. Tam didn't want to go in. It was a gut feeling, but he didn't tell her that. Alexa refused to go in by herself, and they locked horns. The driver had heard it all before. He sat quietly, glancing around and assessing the situation for potential threats. It was what he was paid to do.

Alexa was growing increasingly aggravated and began to question if her fiancé was paranoid or just incapable of enjoying the simple pleasures in life. She knew he earned a living illegally, and she very much enjoyed the fruits; however, she also wanted a taste of normalcy and pledged to drag him along kicking and screaming if she had to. *What's the good in havin' money and power if I can't make my friends jealous?* she thought.

"Go in. I'll be there in a minute. I have some business to deal with," he said.

"There's only one invitation," she said, making a case for both of them to walk in together.

"Then watch for me."

"Tam, we're five hours from the coast. Nobody knows you up here in the boondocks," she pleaded.

Tam recognized her naïveté—a dangerous, usually fatal, trait in his line of work, but one of her attractive qualities.

"Look, baby, do me this favor…go on inside, and when you see everything's okay, text me and I'll come in. Okay?"

Alexa looked him in the eyes, saw concern, and then sighed deeply. "Okay. I'll text you."

She grabbed her Louis Vuitton purse and opened her door before the driver could get out. She stood there in a tiny, tight, stylish dress and cowboy boots. She was going to attract a lot of attention. She slammed the car door and then headed to the hotel entrance.

"What ya thinkin', boss?" the driver asked, looking in the rearview mirror.

"I don't know. Just being cautious," he said confidently. "I don't really give a shit about meeting these guys anyway. It's all just to make her happy."

The task force quickly zeroed in on Alexa and knew Tam was still in the car.

Into his lapel mic, the lead investigator said, "Once she's in the room, keep her busy! If she's acting too suspicious, make sure she doesn't call him. Unit Two, prepare to block the driveway; they may get spooked and drive off. He can't leave here. I don't need her without him. We want Tam. But I don't want his body-guard making this violent. Let him drive off. Copy?"

"Unit Two. Roger that."

"Unit Three. Prepare to block the rear of the vehicle, in case he reverses."

"Unit Three. Affirmative. We got his ass-end covered."

All of the law enforcement officers were concerned that if the takedown happened outside, there would be civilians caught in the middle. They shut down the elevators, and several plain-clothes officers were stationed at each floor to block anyone from coming down the stairs. An officer posing as a maintenance worker also secured the first-floor passageway to guest rooms. The hotel was in lockdown. The only people milling about had hidden badges and firearms.

Alexa strolled into the lobby, looking like she had just stepped out of a Texas fashion magazine targeting the rich, size-zero demographic. The music drew her to the main room as planned, except she wasn't dragging Tam along. The officers' tensions were high.

Tam eyed his drug truck across the parking lot, which was idling just as instructed. He and his driver scanned faces for signs of nervousness and body shapes for bulges in clothing along waists and ankles. Due to the cold, however, most folks were wearing bulky jackets. Tam noted that no other vehicles had pulled up behind them to either check in or attend the meet and greet.

As Alexa approached the room, a lady who appeared to be the hostess welcomed her and asked to see her invitation while checking for her name on the list. The music and noise coming from the room increased Alexa's anxiousness. She was visibly relieved when the woman read aloud her name and motioned to a man inside to allow her entry.

Alexa smiled and said thank you as she strutted through the door of the dark room. Everyone wore official backstage badges around their necks, and Alexa immediately wanted one. There weren't as many people as she expected. She glanced around and thought she recognized one of the band members, but, upon taking a closer look, she determined that he wasn't. She knew the Rascal Flatts guys; she'd seen them in concert several times.

"Excuse me," she asked a staff member, "when will the band be here?"

"They're almost ready. They'll be on their way real soon," he replied with a broad smile.

Alexa was extremely excited that the meet and greet was much more intimate than she had expected and quickly pulled out her phone and texted Tam.

The nervous undercover team watched, prepared to grab her at any second. But since Alexa was obviously excited about being there and not demonstrating any suspicious behavior, they held their ground and maintained the charade.

She quickly thumbed: "Hurry up. I'll meet you at the door ☺."

Tam's phone beeped the receipt of the message. He read it and grunted.

"Wadda ya want me to do, boss?"

"I'm going in…park close. Check on the truck."

Tam allowed his driver to open his door. As Tam stood, they both suspiciously looked around. Tam adjusted his coat collar and stepped toward the hotel. The motion-sensitive doors opened, and country music spilled out. Tam sighed, started across the lobby, and then stopped. Either paranoia or a sixth sense had him on edge. He stood very vulnerable in the atrium of the hotel, and, upon seeing a happy Alexa at the end of the hall, he finally moved forward.

Halfway down the hallway, somebody asked if he knew the score of the Ole Miss game. When he turned to the voice, all hell broke loose. Four officers immediately had weapons drawn.

"Hands in the air! Now!" the lead officer screamed.

Officers flooded the area. Tam began cursing in Vietnamese and was coiled like a snake ready to strike. His head was cocked, and he was defiantly ignoring everyone's instructions, weighing his options.

"Put your freakin' hands in the air or your brains are gonna be on that wall!"

When he slowly began raising his hands, an officer tackled him from his blind side. Four officers pulled each limb out and began a group frisk of his body, uncovering two weapons.

Had the driver lingered ten more seconds, he would have seen what had happened to Tam. Once Tam was inside, out of sight, the driver pulled away, hoping to grab a bite to eat. As he drove, a Tupelo officer in an unmarked car contemplated following him but knew that the already slim crew needed manpower to secure the location. He watched the Mercedes and jotted down the tag number.

Alexa heard the commotion out in the hall, and when she turned to go look, a female officer twisted her thin arm behind her as she pushed Alexa into a wall.

"Oh shit!" Alexa screamed at the top of her lungs as she fought hard, cursing nonstop. A burly male state trooper wearing a staff jacket jumped in to assist.

Law enforcement had finally apprehended the notorious Tam Nguyen. Every person was amped up on adrenaline. Each officer double-checked gear, weapons, handcuffs, and procedures. One officer Mirandized Tam while another videoed everything for evidence and to establish that protocols were properly followed. A few high fives were exchanged. When the two lead drug-force officers made eye contact, they both knew they had done it— finally. After two years pursuing Tam, they had him in custody.

With the mound of evidence they had built through the years, he wasn't going to see the outside of prison for a long time. A huge sense of relief washed over them.

Out in the parking lot, a pickup truck casually drove off as law enforcement vehicles from several state and federal agencies poured onto the hotel property.

CHAPTER 53

———— (————

A S JAKE AND CREW PULLED INTO THE LINE FOR CONCERT
parking, they could see blue lights flashing all around the
Hilton Garden Inn. Jake and Morgan wondered aloud about
what could possibly be happening. The spectacle stalled traffic to
a crawl as everybody slowed to rubberneck. Katy and her buddy
didn't seem to notice because they were busy texting their friends
and probably each other.

During the drive north from West Point, Jake had contemplated everything that R.C. had explained to him and shared
most of it with Morgan. He had held back the part about Moon
Pie living just across the river. He knew that would freak her out
completely.

The BancorpSouth Arena was packed with country-music
fans from all walks of life. The Crosbys' seats were to the side
of the main stage. Jake and Morgan enjoyed watching Katy and
her girlfriend dance and sing. Once the concert had started, Jake
and Morgan momentarily forgot all of their problems and thoroughly enjoyed the show. Morgan sang along, looking Jake in the
eyes at just the right times. It was just what they needed.

Levi and his date sat lower in the arena than he preferred, but
her company caused him to forget the cost of the seats. On one

of several trips to buy cold beer, he recognized Jake Crosby. Levi had seen his picture on numerous occasions and had been with Moon Pie on several drive-bys of Jake's office. He was positive it was Crosby and texted Moon Pie to tell him the situation.

Moon Pie, however, was as drunk as Cooter Brown, as his momma used to say, and pissed off at the weather. Ole Miss was finally ahead of LSU, which made him somewhat excited, but it was raining too hard to go shinin'. Deer just wouldn't be moving in such bad weather. It didn't matter that he had already killed six before the season opened; he hadn't gotten one that day, and it was eating at him.

When Moon Pie received the text, he laughed out loud and thought hard about what he could do. He strongly considered trashing the Crosbys' house, but he knew firsthand that it was under surveillance and had an alarm system. Ever since he had been spotted in their backyard, the Old Waverly community had really tightened up their security. Killing their dog was an option that he strongly considered until he opened the front door of the trailer to check the weather. He decided to stay put and drink another beer.

"How?" Levi texted back.

Levi nodded at the next text from Moon Pie and smiled at the thought of impressing his half brother. He also wanted to get back to his hot date. He had priorities. Following Moon Pie's instructions, he borrowed a pen from a security officer. He wrote a simple message on a napkin, read it several times, and then decided to rewrite it. He handed back the pen, shook his head, acknowledging the meanness of the note, and carefully folded the paper and slid it into the pocket of his down vest as he hurried back to his date.

"What took you so long?" she yelled as she continued to dance.

"Long lines," he responded.

Levi eyed Jake, who stood straight while everyone around him was dancing or swaying to the music, but he was clearly having a good time.

After about twenty minutes, Levi checked the current radar on his iPhone and saw a band of rain covering Tupelo. Anticipating the end of the concert, he bent down to his date, and in an attempt to sell an early exit he said, "Let's beat the crowd. It's raining now, and it'll be crazy."

"Okay," she replied, following him toward the stairs.

When they got there, Levi allowed her to lead. As they approached the row Jake Crosby was on, he paused, letting his date to turn down the tunnel and disappear. Jake and his wife were facing away from him, watching the stage. Levi pulled out the folded napkin and grabbed the shoulder of the man on the end of the row.

"Excuse me, would you pass this note to my buddy down there?" he hollered as he pointed at Jake. The guy took it and nodded his understanding. Levi patted him on the back, hopped down two steps, and disappeared. His date was standing there waiting, hands on hips. He put his arm around her and apologized, saying that he had seen an old friend.

Jake Crosby jumped when his shoulder was tapped. He turned and took the note from a stranger's outstretched hand, trying to understand what was going on.

"Your friend said to give this to you," the man yelled and then walked off.

Confused, Jake yelled, "Thanks," as he slowly unfolded the napkin. It read, "Your wife looks good tonight. But she looks so much better through the bathroom window."

Jake quickly wheeled around and frantically grabbed the stranger. "Who gave you this?"

"I don't know. He said he was your buddy," the guy responded and pointed down the tunnel. "He went down there."

"Jake? Jake? What is it?" Morgan asked as she watched her husband looking worriedly into a sea of unfamiliar faces.

CHAPTER 54

———— ☾ ————

T HE OLD GUYS SAT INSIDE WALTER'S RECENTLY RENTED minivan, the windshield wipers keeping rhythm with a Neil Diamond song playing on the radio. No one had said anything for several minutes. The tension was thick. They all stared at the dark front of the Gold Mine. During the chorus of "Sweet Caroline," Bernard leaned to one side and farted loudly.

"Dammit, Bernard!" Walter said as he rolled his window down.

"Sorry. Dinner made me gassy."

"We don't wanna hear about it...or smell it," Sebastian chimed in.

Walter rubbed his nose in disgust. "Sebastian, whatever you do, do not lick your lips...or smile. It'll stain your teeth!" He laughed as he dropped the minivan into drive and pulled out of the parking lot with all the windows down. After a moment, Walter said, "Okay, guys, back to business. Wadda y'all think?"

"Tonight's the night. We're ready. We'll be in and out in seven and a half minutes," Sebastian explained. "That's the maximum exposure we can afford."

"He's right. Tonight's the night. Plus, the storm and the football game being televised on ESPN makes it even better," Bernard added.

Walter pulled into an all-night convenience store, and the three guys filed out to pee and get coffee. Nobody said a word. Walter paid cash for everything. When he saw Bernard eyeing a pickled egg in a giant jar, he emphatically said, "No way in hell are you eatin' one of those!"

Everyone laughed, including the store clerk. The levity seemed to ease everybody's tension as they exited the store, chuckling to themselves.

Before they got back inside the van, Walter looked around at each of the guys and exhaled. "Okay. Let's do this. Bernard, you're driving." Bernard clapped his hands and briskly rubbed them together. Sebastian smiled.

Bernard drove past their target. Nothing appeared to have changed. After a second pass, he pulled directly behind the store and cut the engine.

"Radio us if something happens."

"No problem."

"Bernard."

"Yeah?"

"Please pay attention."

"I will."

Walter looked at his watch and said, "Someone call it."

"I've got nine forty-five" Sebastian said.

"Okay, boys, synchronize. Let's do this," Walter said as he exited the vehicle.

Sebastian and Walter eased their doors shut and walked quickly to the rear entrance. Sebastian slid the new key into the stainless door handle, and they grinned at each other as the lock accepted it and turned.

"One down," Walter whispered as they opened the door and rushed inside.

Walter used a small flashlight to illuminate the room. Sebastian used a clip-on light attached to the bill of his ball cap. After shutting the door, Walter went straight for the keypad. It was right where Bailey's diagram had indicated. He stood in front of it, and it glowed red, indicating it was still armed and the magnet had kept the connection complete. Walter looked at Sebastian, and both men laughed as Sebastian patted Walter on the back.

"Two down," Sebastian said just above a whisper as he looked at a ceiling-mounted camera pointing into the room. He knew it was too dark for the camera to reveal more than their outlines.

When Walter turned toward the office door, his light illuminated the full-body lion mount, causing him to jump back from shock. "Holy shit!"

Sebastian almost knocked Walter down when he saw the mount. "Dammit...I'm guessing Bailey didn't tell you about that," he nearly yelled.

"Not a word."

Walter shined the light toward the office door. Sebastian's gloved hand grabbed the knob. He tried to twist it, and it didn't budge.

"Locked," Sebastian said excitedly.

"What!"

"It's locked!" Sebastian snapped as he turned to look Walter in the eyes.

"You're blinding me!"

"Sorry," he said as he clicked off the light.

"She also never said anything about this door bein' locked!" Walter almost screamed in frustration.

"Well, it is, and we gotta deal with it."

Walter tried the knob himself, and when it held tight, he exhaled. "Shit fire. Should we call her?"

Sebastian dropped to his knees and clicked on his flashlight. "No. Give me a minute."

"Can you pick it?"

"Maybe," Sebastian said as he studied how the lock's mechanism pushed into the doorframe.

Walter stood still and held the light on the lock as Sebastian studied it. He couldn't believe it was locked. From inside his jacket pocket, Bernard's voice cracked over the radio, "Hey, guys!"

"Go ahead."

"A black-and-white just went by."

"The police? Shit. Did they stop?"

"No. They just drove by kinda slow, but they didn't stop. Y'all hurry up."

"We're trying. We've encountered a slight problem."

"What problem?" Bernard asked.

"Hang on," Walter said. He was beginning to feel the pressure of the mission.

With a surgeon's steady hand, Sebastian carefully slid his AARP card between the door and the jamb. When the card didn't release the lock, he pulled out a thin-bladed pocketknife and inserted the blade in the same fashion.

"Is that gonna work?" Walter asked anxiously as he looked around the room.

"Just hush so I can concentrate!" Sebastian fired back. "You're makin' me nervous."

The radio cracked again. "Fellas? What's the problem?"

"Shut up, Bernard! We are workin' on it," Walter said and instantly regretted his tone. He knew Bernard was just trying to help. Everybody was wound too tightly at the moment.

"Damn! I almost had it," Sebastian exclaimed. He took in a deep breath and continued working. His knife bit into the latch bolt, between the face place and the strike plate, and just as it was about to move, he released it suddenly and leaned back as if he had been shocked. He stared straight ahead at the knob and said, "Walter! What if this door is wired to the alarm? We didn't plan for this."

Walter cussed under his breath and then said, "I don't know…you're right. I don't know what to tell you."

Sebastian stood and calmly ran his fingers over the top of the door frame. "Nothing. You'd think he'd have some tight security," he said.

"Sebastian, we're just two old men who have never burglarized anything before in our lives, and we got inside this place with a magnet from a drugstore."

"So, what are you sayin'?"

"This ain't Fort Knox."

"You may be right."

"Just open the damn door. If the alarm goes off, we'll just run like hell."

Sebastian exhaled and leaned forward. "Promise me one thing."

"What's that?"

"Before you start runnin', you gotta help me stand up."

CHAPTER 55

———— ◡ ————

T AM'S DRIVERS WERE TOTALLY FREAKED OUT. NOTHING like this had ever happened, and they didn't have a contingency in place, let alone a succession plan. His guys did only what they were told, which was not much. Tam didn't employ freethinkers. He made all the decisions, and those decisions were final.

As discreetly as possible, the driver of the truck slowly exited the hotel parking lot. His partner tried to call Alexa, but it went straight to voice mail. At the first major gas station south of town, they pulled over to refuel and make a plan. After several minutes of discussion, they decided to alert the crew back home with a quick call to sit tight, wait for further instructions, and, most importantly, not breathe a word about the situation to anyone outside the organization. They broke the connection and then called Moon Pie, whom they had met on past drops, to give him a heads-up.

Moon Pie was deep in cold beer when his cell phone rang. He assumed it was Levi, but when he saw the area code, he knew it was Tam.

"Yeah, man," he answered, hitting the mute button on the remote.

"Moon Pie?"

"Yeah?"

"Can you talk?"

"Yeah, sure. Who the hell is this?"

"Mike. I work for our mutual friend…we've met a few times."

"I remember you. What's up, man?"

"We got a big problem."

"Talk to me."

"He got busted tonight."

"You're shittin' me. Where 'bouts?"

"Tupelo."

"This ain't good." Moon Pie was more concerned about the deal at the moment than about Tam's arrest.

"Yeah, they got him and his girlfriend."

"Why did they get her?"

"She was just in the wrong place at the wrong time."

"Have you talked to him?"

"No, we split with the product and headed south. We just pulled over to call you."

"Sounds like y'all were lucky. What are you driving?"

"A black pickup with a camper shell."

"Okay, let me think." Moon Pie's mind raced, trying to devise a way to benefit from this. After a long silence, he asked, "Where y'all at?"

"'Bout fifteen or twenty miles south of Tupelo."

"Okay, here's what you do for right now. Remember coming through West Point?"

"Yeah."

"Good. There's a new hotel right in front of that big Mossy Oak store. Get a room and let me do some more thinkin', and I'll get back to you in the mornin' or sooner. You're only about thirty minutes away from there now. I gotta relative that's a lawyer up in Tupelo, and he might can find out what's going on and at least get Tam's girlfriend out, and y'all will be close enough to go get her."

"That makes sense."

"We also gotta make the trade tomorrow or I'm dead."

"We're still good to go. Call us if you learn somethin' from that lawyer."

"Don't worry. I'm on it," Moon Pie said and hit the end button.

Moon Pie had the money, and he knew where the drugs were going to be parked. This was a unique situation that might prove particularly lucrative. He just didn't want the Tennessee Mexicans and the Gulf Coast Vietnamese hunting him down like a dog. He punched in the speed-dial number for Levi as he walked to the refrigerator for another beer.

CHAPTER 56

J AKE WAS IN THE TUPELO POLICE STATION PACING BACK AND
forth after explaining his situation to the desk sergeant, who
was now on the phone with the West Point Police Department.
Listening to one side of the conversation and trying to gauge what
was being said on the other end was driving him crazy. Through
the glass front doors, he could see Morgan talking on her cell
phone. Katy and her friend had their heads lowered, texting, he
assumed. *Even if you're as innocent as Job, police stations make
me uncomfortable*, Jake thought.

The desk sergeant wrapped up his call and leaned back in his
desk chair, looking down at the menacing words on the napkin.
Jake turned to face him.

"Well, you've got a pretty interestin' past, Mr. Crosby."

"I'm more concerned about the future. I didn't ask for any
of this."

"I understand completely."

"So, are there cameras in the arena that we could use to try
to find him?"

"I'm afraid not."

"What about askin' some of the folks that were sittin' around
us to see if they saw him?"

"It'll take us days to determine who was sitting where and actually contact them. And most people watch the band. I just don't think we'll find out much."

Jake sighed and looked around the office, his mind racing, trying to think of some way to get the upper hand, but he wasn't coming up with anything, "So what can we do?"

"I don't think there is anything we can do tonight, to be honest. You should take your family and go home."

"There's gotta be something. I just can't believe he was that close to me and I didn't see him," Jake said, starting to pace again.

"Look, we all know who Moon Pie Daniels is. We've arrested that punk several times over the years. Last time I saw him, he had gotten the shit beat out of him by some guys from the air force base. He said somethin' very unpatriotic 'bout someone's mama, and they didn't appreciate it. Kinda tells you either how dumb he is...or how much he likes pokin' hornets' nests. I know you're worried, and you got good reason to be... he's obviously trouble. He's big trouble 'cause he'll do anything and he's fearless, and that makes him that much more dangerous."

"Believe me, I've heard."

"Do you have a self-defense weapon?"

"Yeah. A pistol."

"You know how to use it?"

"Oh yeah, that's one thing I know I can do."

"Good," he said, acting sympathetic as an awkward silence fell across the room.

"Mr. Crosby, we are gonna have a unit follow you to the county line, and a state trooper will pick you up there and escort you all the way to West Point. Once you're there, the West Point PD will follow y'all home and then check out your house."

"You think that's necessary?"

"Probably not, but we're gonna do it anyway. Just to be safe."

"Thanks" was the only thing Jake could think to say.

"Look, tomorrow I'll work some of our contacts and see what I can find out about old Moon Pie," the desk sergeant said, holding up the napkin by a corner. "We haven't seen or heard of him in a while, but since he's around, we can put some pressure on him and see what happens."

The desk sergeant looked out at Morgan talking on her cell phone and said, "I suppose your wife's freaked out about all this?"

"That would be an understatement."

The sergeant rose from behind his desk and walked around to Jake. He gently grabbed Jake by the elbow, guiding him toward the door. "Well, let's get you and your family home safely. You'll all feel better then."

CHAPTER 57

———— ૮ ————

I T HAD BEEN A WHILE SINCE TAM NGUYEN HAD BEEN BEHIND
bars, and he was livid. Incarceration was something he
couldn't handle. He never could appreciate that he would eventually get out. From the moment he was arrested, he started looking for an opportunity to escape. He physically submitted to the
overwhelming show of authority, but not mentally. Tam, a caged
animal, was preparing to attack, waiting for any opportunity.

The task force officers knew Tam's reputation and had seen
what he was capable of doing. They locked him down as quickly
as possible. The Tupelo police had all heard the stories about
Tam, but as they peered through protective glass and heavy bars
at the small man, they wondered if he was as capable and cruel a
criminal as they had been led to believe. In his striped jumpsuit,
he looked like a small, tanned shrimper from the Gulf Coast—no
different from what they had seen on family vacations. He didn't
fit their idea of the stereotypical drug kingpin.

Alexa had not been the primary target. She was more or less
an unknowing victim of the sting. Her love of the band had led
her and Tam straight into the trap. They would have let her walk
except for her temper. When she saw Tam being arrested, she
bitch-slapped the female undercover officer who had initially

tried to restrain her. An hour later, the handprint was still visible on the face of the police chief's only daughter. As Alexa was introduced to the most heinous outfit of her life, she recognized clearly that her lavish lifestyle was in jeopardy.

Tam was arrested on current and outstanding warrants relating to several drug charges and other crimes, including the deaths of three rival dealers found buried up to their heads on the beach after the tide had receded. The officers vigilantly and thoroughly processed his booking paperwork and fingerprinting. He was then placed in an initial holding cell with four others—two black guys, one of whom had robbed a convenience store and one who had stolen a new car off the dealer's lot; a skinny white meth head who had stolen his father's hunting rifles to buy prescription cough syrup; and another Asian, about Tam's same height and build, who had been caught stealing copper from a construction site.

Before the steel door shut, Tam began assessing everyone for potential usefulness under the circumstances. He slowly made his way to the far corner, spread his legs a bit, and squatted down on his heels, surveying the room for weaknesses, both human and structural.

CHAPTER 58

———— ☾ ————

WALTER WATCHED SEBASTIAN CAREFULLY TRYING TO tease the lock open with his pocketknife.

The radio in his pocket cracked again. "You guys okay? We need to hurry up."

"Yes, Bernard. Just relax."

Sebastian grunted at Bernard's impatience. "What's the matter with him?"

"I think as a kid he used to chase the mosquito truck down the street, and that probably melted some of his brain cells."

"I remember those days," Sebastian commented with a chuckle as he worked. "We drank water from a garden hose, not a plastic bottle, and we didn't have a care in the world."

"And we ate what we wanted."

Walter laughed. "You know, when I was newly married, sometimes I'd tell a white lie about where I was or what I was doing. Nothing serious. My late wife, rest her soul, didn't like me playin' poker. Then when I got older, hell, I had to lie about what I ate for lunch just to keep her off my back. She thought I ate a great many grilled-chicken-breast sandwiches and salads."

Sebastian was enjoying the distraction as he worked. "I know exactly what you're talking about. Now we're old, worn out, and facing Obamacare…but at least we can eat whatever the hell we want."

"You get that door open and the future's gonna look a lot brighter."

"I think I got it…hang on and get ready to run," he said as the lock slid back. He slowly pulled the door open.

They both stared at each other for a few seconds as they listened for an alarm, and then wide smiles broke over their faces.

"Walter? Just to be sure, go check the keypad; it'll probably be flashing if it's sending a silent alarm." Sebastian slowly raised himself from the floor.

Standing right in front of the keypad, Walter pulled on his bifocals to read all the buttons. "I think we're good to go."

"Thank you, Lord. Now, let's get busy. We've been in here over eight minutes already," Sebastian said as he walked into the office.

"Gold's over seventeen hundred bucks an ounce. We should grab all the gold he's got and sell it somewhere else," Sebastian said as he stared at the big gun safe.

"First, let's get the safe open. I'll let you have the honors," Walter said with a twinkle in his eye. He glanced around the dark room and saw framed Manning jerseys. *Those numbers woulda been my choice for a code*, he thought.

"Thirty-six, twenty-four, thirty-six, pound," Sebastian said as he punched the keypad, listening to each high-pitched beep.

When the lock released, Sebastian turned the five-spoke handle to the right and pulled open the safe door. They focused their flashlights on the inside.

"There are the boot boxes! Just like Bailey said!"

Walter reached inside and started taking out the boxes. They weren't too heavy. He opened the top of one and saw cash stacked haphazardly.

"How much you think's in there?" Sebastian asked with schoolboy excitement.

"I don't know...maybe a hundred thousand?"

"It's gotta be more than that; she said it was sometimes as much as three hundred grand!" Sebastian said.

"It's hard to say. It's a pile of money, though. Help me fit 'em in this bag. We gotta get outta here! We'll count it later. See anything else in there?" Walter asked as he placed the boxes in his duffel bag.

Sebastian peered inside like he was looking in the stomach of a whale.

"Hell yeah!"

"What is it?"

"I can't believe this."

"What the hell is it?" Walter asked as he slung the duffel on his shoulder.

"It's my old huntin' rifle that got stolen years ago!"

"Are you serious?" Walter had what he wanted, but if Sebastian could get his old rifle back, that was fine by him.

"Yep, it's my old Steyr. I know it. I loved this old rifle. I'm taking it!"

"That's fine with me, but let's get the hell outta here."

Sebastian looked at his watch and realized they'd been inside twice as long as they had anticipated.

Walter stepped toward the door and grabbed his radio. "We're ready to come out."

"Clear as the coast," Bernard reported back. Walter shook his head.

"Hey, you feelin' guilty about this?" Walter asked Sebastian.

"The Kroger deal, yeah...but this guy's a two-bit dirtbag, and no," he said with a serious look. "You?"

Walter had already given this plenty of thought. He had grown up in a household of strong values and tried to live as an adult by the same standard. Until Kroger came along, he had never stepped out of line. What he had promised his wife somehow justified the path he was now on. Walter looked at the rifle in Sebastian's hands and said, "This redneck had your rifle. It's just payback."

"Man, am I glad to get her back," Sebastian remarked, holding the gun with the same care as he would a newborn baby.

"Okay, we need to wipe everything you've touched since you took your gloves off," Walter said, trying to cover their tracks. "I'm gonna place this can of dip where it can't be missed."

Walter placed the silver-topped can on the desk next to the safe, as if it had been forgotten in a moment's haste. He walked out of the office and from the shadows looked out the front window. Rain gently fell. A few cars passed. His heart began to race as he thought about how close they were to pulling off this heist. He knew that once they got into the van and hit Highway 45 heading north, they were home free. He couldn't wait to count the money. He started to unwrap a cigar, when he heard Velcro being ripped apart and wondered what Sebastian was doing.

"Walter," Sebastian said in a strange tone.

"Yeah?"

"You need to get back in here and look at this."

CHAPTER 59

———— ☾ ————

A MUTED CELL PHONE HAD BEEN SILENTLY RINGING FOR twenty minutes in Levi's pocket while he explained in great detail to his date that the most bacteria-infested place on a man was his wallet. She had been fascinated with his trivia knowledge but didn't like hearing how bacteria colonies were formed in a guy's sweaty wallet and were being passed around through the exchange of currency.

"What's wrong?" he asked, glancing over at her as he drove south through the rainy night.

"Let's talk about something else, anything...please."

"Sure. Wadda ya wanna talk about?"

Levi's date unbuckled her seat belt and sat Indian-style facing him. "What's next?"

"Wadda ya mean?"

"What do you want to do with the rest of your life?" she asked. "This gold rush probably won't last forever."

"I dunno," he said sheepishly.

"You haven't thought about it?"

"Oh, I have, but you'll laugh if I tell ya."

"No I won't."

"I love trees."

"Trees?"

"Yeah. I've been takin' some online courses from Mississippi State...and I'd like to be a guy who travels around saving old trees."

"Really?"

"Yeah...think about it. There are trees that have been around since the American Revolution. They can live a long time, and they've experienced a lot of history. There are trees around here that were alive when the Union and Confederate forces marched through back in the 1860s. But every year, I notice one dyin' somewhere...in a neighborhood or a pasture. I wanna save trees."

"I hadn't ever thought about that. Can you make any money doin' it?"

"I don't really know, but it's what I really wanna do. I figure if I save up enough money to bankroll me for about a year, then, if I'm any good, maybe I'll make a decent living, and at least I'll be happy."

Levi's date appreciated his honesty and smiled at him as she brushed her hair behind her ear. "So, what's a tree savior called?"

"An arborist, but some folks call 'em tree surgeons."

"Oooh...I like that. I always wanted to tell my friends I was datin' a doctor, but a surgeon would work!"

"So...we're dating?"

"Well...you're not a surgeon yet."

Levi smiled and turned up the volume to the CD he had bought at the concert and sang "Bless the Broken Road" to his date. It had been an enjoyable night. He'd had a good meal and seen a great concert, he had luckily crossed paths with Moon Pie's nemesis, and now he was telling a beautiful woman his dream and she wasn't laughing at it or him.

Levi had been on a direct course for incarceration, particularly over these last few years. His half brother was the worst influence imaginable. However, given the proper inspiration and influence, Levi had the basic values to be a productive citizen. He just needed the proper motivation.

Meanwhile, in his pocket, Levi's cell showed seven missed calls and two unread text messages from his quickly angering half brother. The last text read, "Call me asap u stupid shit!!!"

CHAPTER 60

B ERNARD DESPERATELY WANTED TO TURN AROUND TO SEE the money Walter and Sebastian were excitedly talking about, but he had to concentrate on driving. They couldn't get stopped by the police. Judging by Walter and Sebastian's comments, they had stolen a hell of a lot more money than they had anticipated.

Sebastian was trying to rough-count the cash. "I'm telling y'all, there's a million bucks here…just in this bag!"

"It's gonna take us all night to count."

"You got something better to do?" Bernard asked.

"Nope. Just get us back home safe," Walter replied. Then to Sebastian he said, "You did really good tonight. Crackin' that door lock was impressive."

"Thanks. It felt good."

"What door are y'all talkin' about?" Bernard asked.

"The door to the office was locked, and our man here picked it."

"Years of gunsmithing finally pay off."

"I'll say it's paid off," Walter remarked, slapping the side of the money bag.

Bernard held up a silver key. "Bailey gave this to me this yesterday. She said it's the key to the office and that we might need it. Sorry, I forgot."

Walter placed his cigar in the corner of his mouth, leaned forward, and took the key from Bernard. "This certainly would have made things easier."

"I'm sorry," Bernard said as he watched Walter's eyes in his rearview mirror.

"Don't worry about it. Thanks to Sebastian, we went over that hurdle."

"Did y'all leave the evidence?"

"We sure did," Walter stated as he pointed with his cigar.

"Woody's not gonna have time to bother Bailey anymore," Sebastian added.

"Perfect!"

"And thanks to Bailey's insight and direction, our little foundation just received a huge donation," Walter said.

"Is there really a million dollars back there?" Bernard asked as he turned his head to look.

"I'm thinkin' there is…this bag's is full of big bills. They'll add up to a huge number quick."

Following a moment of clarity, Walter said, "Guys, listen to me. This is serious shit. We gotta be really careful. We can't tell anyone or draw any attention to ourselves. Somebody's gonna get killed for this."

"Yeah, like Woody," Sebastian chuckled.

"Seriously. It could be Bailey or us if we aren't careful. That's a lot of money, and somebody's gonna be really pissed."

"Are you thinkin' that we shouldn't have framed Woody?" Sebastian asked.

"Maybe."

"You serious?"

"Somebody's gonna completely freak out about this money! Woody's an abuser, and that's about as low as it gets in my book, but we shouldn't be playing judge and jury."

"But what we're doing is to help others," Bernard said.

"We just stole a shit pot full of money…and now you're feelin' guilty?" Sebastian asked.

Walter's guilt was that he had convinced the others to believe in him and his ideas. They now believed that some wrongs were right, if they were done to benefit another. How did one determine what was right and what was wrong? And who gets to make that determination? He had convinced them to alter their core beliefs. The allure of money was powerful. It motivated people to make excuses for their actions rather than taking responsibility for their choices.

"Let's just get back to the Henry Clay. We are all jacked up on adrenaline and coffee. I don't mean to suddenly change and sound like a television evangelist after we've done all this."

"You think we oughta go back and get the can of dip?" Bernard asked.

"I don't know…maybe? The fact that there was all this additional cash makes me think something really big was about to go down and that we got real lucky."

"We can go back if you think we should. I trust your judgment," Sebastian said. Then he added, "But I gotta say, I think we'd really be pushin' that luck."

CHAPTER 61

ᴄ

J AKE FOLLOWED A MISSISSIPPI STATE TROOPER ALL THE WAY
to the north side of West Point and then followed a local
black-and-white to the house in Old Waverly. At first Katy and
her friend thought it was "so cool" to follow a police car, but they
had both fallen asleep after about fifteen minutes. Morgan hadn't
said much, and Jake could tell she was angry—not necessarily at
him, but he was the handiest target. He wondered what more he
could have done.

Two West Point police officers walked around the outside
of Jake's house and shined flashlights in potential hiding spots.
Everyone assumed the inside was safe, since the alarm had been
set. Jake shook each officer's hand and thanked them. He noticed
that it had quit raining and the temperature had dropped several
degrees since they left for the concert.

"You sure you don't want us to look around inside? We don't
mind," one of the officers politely offered.

"No, it's not necessary. Y'all have done plenty, and the house
alarm was set. I really appreciate the offer, though."

As the police cruiser pulled away, Katy's friend's parents
pulled up. It didn't surprise Jake that they would want to take her
home. He'd do the same thing. He'd even offered to drop her off

on the way home, but they insisted on coming to his house. He assumed that they didn't want him anywhere near their home.

Morgan met them at the front door with a very sleepy twelve-year-old girl. She was clutching her concert souvenirs, including a curled, airbrushed cowboy hat with pink feathers that seemed like a good idea at the time but would never be worn again.

Not knowing what to say about everything that had happened, Morgan said to the mom, "I think she had a great time. The concert was really good."

"Thanks for taking her. She texted me that she had fun," she said as she stroked her daughter's hair.

Jake quickly added, trying to assuage her fears, "Don't worry; she was with Morgan and me the whole time."

"Are y'all gonna be okay?" the father asked.

Morgan looked at Jake and then back at the dad and said, "Oh yes. A whole bunch of cops are lookin' for this guy."

As the parents were heading for the car, the mom said, "Call us if you need anything or if Katy needs a place to stay. Oh, and congratulations! I heard you're expecting!"

"We will, and thank you," Morgan said with a slight wave. She folded her arms tightly as the parents hurriedly drove off.

Jake looked at her and sighed. "I'm sorry."

"It's not your fault, Jake."

"I sure feel like it is."

"Come on, let's get inside. I'm cold, and I wanna lock the doors and turn on the alarm."

"Go 'head. I'll be in shortly. I need to make a phone call first."

"Who are you going to call at this hour?"

"R.C."

"It's almost two."

"Knowin' him, he's probably watching *Law and Order* reruns."

"Okay. Please be sure and set the alarm when you come in."

Jake nodded and then watched Morgan walk into the house and close the door. *She doesn't need all this stress, particularly bein' pregnant.* They had finally gotten their lives and marriage back on track since the Dummy Line.

Jake knew that he had to do something; everything was in jeopardy yet again. He had plenty of firepower, and if he had the element of surprise, he could take out Moon Pie. He'd kill him Pie if it came down to it.

Jake looked back through the leaded glass of the front door, thinking that others were depending on him, just like at the Dummy Line. He needed a plan. He couldn't go off half-cocked. Success, and most likely his life, would depend on it.

He glanced at the dark sky, wondering where the moon was, and realized he had to talk to R.C. He dialed the number. When it went to voice mail, Jake said, "R.C., this is Jake Crosby. We had an incident at the concert tonight. Moon Pie saw us there and passed a note to me. By the time I read it, he was gone. At any rate, I'm sick and tired of this bullshit. Monday mornin' I'm goin' to his gold shop and confront him. I was hopin' you might join me. You've got my number. Please give me a call."

Jake slid the phone into his pocket and opened his front door.

A distraught Morgan met him. "I can't find Scout!"

CHAPTER 62

———— ☾ ————

MOON PIE SAT IN THE DARK, CHAIN-SMOKING CIGA-rettes, waiting for Levi. By 2:10 a.m., he had been through every scenario he could imagine, trying to determine a way to at least keep the cash and possibly even Tam's drugs. Each scenario, however, involved him eventually losing his life in a manner that would make a sadomasochist flinch. Moon Pie finally settled on making the drop as planned, demonstrating to Tam that he was more than capable of handling the business in Tam's absence.

When Levi finally dragged in, Moon Pie snuffed out his ciga-rette and cussed him for not responding to his calls or texts. The only way Levi finally got him to settle down was by telling him the story about seeing Jake Crosby at the concert. Moon Pie loved the message that he had passed to Jake and laughed hard about it.

"You know, truth be told, Crosby did me a favor." Moon Pie lit another cigarette.

Levi's eyes were closed. All he wanted to do was to go to sleep. "How so?"

"I've told ya, I wouldn't be the main runner in the area if Johnny Lee was alive and kickin'."

"Yeah, but he was your friend."

214

"He was an asshole. Always wantin' to fight. He had a plate put in his head after he fell off a four-wheeler and was just plain mean after that."

"What about Reese?" Levi asked without much interest.

"He shoulda never even called me that night. They shoulda handled it themselves insteada draggin' my sorry ass into it and then makin' me promise I'd avenge Johnny Lee's murder."

Levi hovered somewhere between sleep and boredom while he listened to Moon Pie rant. In between nodding his agreement, Levi kept thinking about trees and out-of-state colleges. He knew that he needed to get away from his half brother's bad influence and make his own life—one that didn't include looking over his shoulder for the police or a rival runner. All he needed was the ability to pay the bills while he focused on school. *About fifty grand is all I need.*

"Okay, in the morning I'll get them to meet us at the Barton Ferry boat ramp," Moon Pie said as he stood to go to bed.

"Bad idea; there may be duck hunters scoutin' the river. The first three-day season comes in next week," Levi explained.

"You gotta better idea?" Moon Pie said as he turned off the television.

"What about the abandoned bomb-makin' plant in Prairie? It's a huge place, and nobody's ever there. It's easy to hide and defend. Plus, it ain't that far."

"The reason nobody's ever there is cuz it's haunted, dumb ass. Don't you remember that TV show filming up there and that good-lookin' reporter gettin' attacked?"

"I didn't see it," Levi said as he tried to close his eyes again.

Moon Pie tossed his iPad onto Levi's lap, making him jump, and then sat back down in his recliner. "Google *Prairie, Mississippi, bomb plant* and you'll find it. I don't do ghosts."

"Hell, Moon, half these big-ass old houses 'round here are haunted. And I thought you said you want to live in an antebellum mansion."

"They're cool, but I don't want a haunted one."

"Good luck with that. Even that fancy old Waverley mansion has that little-girl ghost in it."

"I might could handle a little-girl ghost. But unh-uh, this thing at Prairie...that grabbed that reporter. I don't wanna get grabbed," Moon Pie said as he sucked the bottom out of his beer.

"Come on, we won't even go in the building. We'll just meet around back. It's a safe place."

"You got a point there," Moon Pie said in a rare agreement.

"It's a great place to do the exchange. You know it."

"All right, but you gotta watch that video first."

"Man, you're such a badass and you spend all night out in the woods by yourself poachin'...and you're scared of ghosts?" Levi asked, astonished.

"I don't want no dead Confederate touchin' me. That place is built on a mass grave of Confederate soldiers. That shit creeps me out, man."

"Have you ever seen a ghost?"

"Once," Moon Pie said as he leaned forward.

"Where?"

"In Clay County about four years ago. I got dropped off after dark at those rich folks' huntin' club on the west side of the Chuquatonchee Creek. I was watching a whole pile a deer in the moonlight in this bare bean field when an old man in a Confederate uniform and a top hat came out the woods across the field like he was going to a meetin'. I ain't never been back... and that was one helluva good place to deer hunt too."

"I think you musta been smokin' that night."

"Nope. I wasn't stoned; I was in serious stealth mode. That old dude just about freaked me out. I've heard 'bout others seein' him too. I ain't the only one. He looked just like the pictures of Robert E. Lee. It was some crazy shit, man."

"You seen Robert E. Lee walkin' in the woods?"

"No, dipshit. I said he *looked* like Robert E. Lee. You know, that old-guy-with-a-beard look."

"It was dark. How the hell could you see details?" Levi asked.

"The moon was real bright. I could see fine through that big scope I got. And you know I got cat eyes."

"Okay. Fine. Whatever—just call them boys and tell 'em we'll meet up tomorrow."

"You found that video clip yet?" Moon Pie asked as he stood and started toward his bedroom.

"Almost," Levi responded as he Googled the words *arbori culture degree.*

"Just watch it and you'll see that the place is haunted," Moon Pie said as he shut his bedroom door.

CHAPTER 63

—— ☾ ——

SEBASTIAN TRIED COUNTING THE MONEY WHILE THEY DROVE, but the amount was so overwhelming that he couldn't do it. He finally just laughed and then showed Bernard his long-lost rifle. Walter gazed at the bag, knowing they had hit the mother lode and that there would be repercussions beyond anyone's wildest imagination. He knew it, but he was still thrilled at what they had pulled off. Three old men, with the help of a girl, a magnet, a stolen key, a surveillance camera, and a pocketknife, had managed to steal an absolutely absurd amount of cold, hard cash.

As Bernard parked the rented minivan in front of the Henry Clay, Walter told everyone to sit still. He could see a West Point police officer on a Segway patrolling on the sidewalk, making sure businesses' front doors were closed. He was heading in their direction, and Walter didn't want to be unloading the bags when he came by.

Bernard started breathing heavy. Walter had to place his hand on his shoulder and tell him to calm down.

"Oh shit, here he comes," Sebastian said under his breath. "Act normal."

"What's normal about having a million dollars at your feet?" Bernard said without moving his lips.

When the officer saw the men, he rolled over to them and stopped, balancing on the Segway's two wheels. The men had seen the Segway before, but it still seemed like the policeman was some futuristic supercop, and he certainly seemed out of place in a small, rural Mississippi downtown at night.

Sebastian, who was sitting in the passenger seat, opened his door, and the dome light came on, revealing the interior. Walter cringed but didn't move.

"Evenin', Officer," Sebastian greeted.

"Y'all are out mighty late," the officer replied, bending over to look inside at everyone.

"It's been a long night. We had to go to a funeral visitation down near Jackson, and we're just now gettin' back," Sebastian said respectfully.

"That's why I'm wearing black," Bernard offered.

The officer nodded his understanding as he watched a brightly painted lime-green Chevrolet Impala with spinning rims roll by. Everyone could feel the bass thumping from the music inside the car.

"How can that be enjoyable? It's so loud," Sebastian added, seizing the opportunity to change the topic.

"That will definitely cause hearin' loss. There was a party goin' on at Chocolate City, and now they're startin' to leave," the officer said, irritated. "We'll get some DUIs tonight."

"That's where we shoulda gone," Walter said, moving toward the door to get out. "Probably woulda had more fun."

"Or gotten shot," Sebastian said, as if he knew something Walter didn't.

"Y'all live here?" the officer asked, motioning to the old, historic hotel.

"We do. Yes, sir."

"Okay, good. Then y'all are home."

"Home sweet home," Bernard gushed.

"Sorry one of your buddies died," the officer said, clearly not in a hurry to leave. He seemed to relish conversation.

"At our ages, we attend lots of funerals. But it's much better to be in the audience than it is to be the center of attention."

"Yes, sir. That's a good way to look at it. Hey, do y'all need any help carryin' those bags in?"

"No, thanks. We're just gonna leave them. It's just some of our friend's old stuff, and we're gonna sort through it tomorrow," Walter said, hoping the officer would leave so they could haul the bounty upstairs. He had no intention of leaving it in the van. West Point was safe but not safe enough to risk a million dollars.

"I wouldn't. Just between us, we've had some vehicle burglaries that haven't been reported to the paper just yet. Let me help y'all," the officer said, stepping off the Segway.

Walter tried to stay calm as the big sliding door slung open. Bernard accidentally hit the horn as he was exiting the car.

Sebastian was near panic too but had noticed a shopping cart in the hotel lobby and had an idea. He quickly said, "Just help us get the big bag into that shopping cart, and we can roll it inside and use the elevator."

Sebastian rolled the cart to the curb as Walter slid the big bag to the edge of the vehicle for the officer to pick up. They all held their breath.

"This thing's pretty heavy. What's in it?" the officer asked as he dropped it into the basket.

"You a hunter?"

"No, sir. Never had time."

Sebastian pulled his recovered stolen rifle out from under the seat. "Our friend collected huntin' magazines. That's what's in there."

The officer barely looked at the gun since it wasn't unusual to see hunting rifles in Mississippi at this time of the year. All he said was, "Well, y'all sure got enough to read for a while." He dropped the smaller bag on top. The officer climbed back on the

Segway as Sebastian and Walter started pushing the cart away. "That's a nice bag—that big black one. Where did ya get it?"

Walter stared at the bag and scratched his head. Bernard and Sebastian waited.

"Do you mean where did he buy it?" Walter asked.

"Yes, sir."

"I don't know. But I tell you what—after we get it unloaded, you're welcome to it."

"No, I couldn't do that."

"Seriously, we don't need it, and if you want it, I can bring it by the station later in the week for you," Walter said as he looked at the officer's name badge.

"No, I couldn't let you do that."

"Seriously, it's not a problem. We don't need it."

"I'll be honest—I sure could use a bag like that to store my SWAT gear in."

"Give me a couple of days and it'll be yours," Walter said, smiling broadly.

"That's awful generous. I'd really appreciate it. Thanks," the officer said as he admired the bag one last time, waved at the old men, and then quietly rolled down the street on the side of Rose Drugs.

The old men stood on the sidewalk, watching him ease away. After he rounded the corner, they all let out deep breaths and at least one quiet "Oh shit!"

Walter turned to Sebastian. "If he'd been a hunter, you know he woulda wanted to see the magazines, don't you?"

"Then I'da said they were *Playgirls*. I doubt he would've wanted to see those! You see, I was thinkin'."

All three doubled over laughing, slapping their legs.

Walter finally said, "That'd start one hell of a rumor—three old dudes at the Henry Clay were caught smugglin' in big bags of *Playgirl* magazines."

"Thank God it didn't come to that. My image woulda been ruined," Bernard said with a smile.

They all heard another car's bass, thumping louder than the first one's. "Good grief! Let's get inside before we get robbed," Walter said, clearly annoyed.

CHAPTER 64

❧

THE TENNESSEE MEXICANS NOT ONLY WERE PROFESSION-
ally organized but also had talent—not just muscle. They
had players with sophisticated computer skills. The techni-
cal guy spent hours each day tracking their various money
exchanges and drug shipments thanks to tiny, state-of-the-art
GPS chips.

This Sunday morning he logged on to check the status of five
different packages. He immediately noticed that the Mississippi
money had moved overnight. Following protocol, he alerted his
boss via prepaid cell phone.

"The Mississippi money has moved."

"Where is it right now?" he asked, and then took a sip of a
Starbucks canned coffee.

"It's moved west about seventeen miles. It's still there
right now."

"¿Dónde está?"

"Commerce Street. West Point, Mississippi. I can get exact
if you want."

"No. They probably made the exchange last night. Keep an
eye on it. We're to settle the deal *un pequeño número de días.*
Until then, I want to know where the money goes. Also, el Jefe

wants to know everything we can provide about this organization. I want to cut Moon Pie completely out."

"*¡Sí, por supuesto!*"

"*¡Gracias!*"

CHAPTER 65

———— ☾ ————

JAKE—A TYPICAL BAPTIST—SAT ON THE BACK PEW, STARING past the music minister at the choir, which was singing "Blessed Assurance." Next to him, Morgan wrote a check for their tithe and then placed it into a small envelope. On Jake's other side, Katy had gotten comfortable and was almost asleep. Jake resisted the urge to elbow her like his momma would have done to him. But he knew she was exhausted, because he was too.

Jake had spent over an hour last night and then again this morning looking for Scout. She sometimes got confused, but it wasn't like the old Lab to just wander off. He couldn't help but think that she had been stolen.

As he looked around the congregation, Jake considered that no one knew of his problems. He was alone in a tough situation. He thought about the words on the napkin and imagined how cold and calculated the note appeared. A chill went up his spine when he thought about how close to his family Moon Pie had actually been.

As the lights dimmed and the preacher stepped into the pulpit, Jake whispered to Morgan, asking if he could borrow a pen. Briefly, she thought that he was going to take notes about the sermon, but then she realized he was going to make a to-do list.

As she opened her purse wide in search of the pen, Jake saw her pistol resting in a side pocket. He pointed at it, and when they made eye contact, she shrugged her shoulders. Jake was surprised she had brought a weapon into church.

He scribbled a note on the back of the bulletin: "Did you bring it on purpose?"

She took the pen from his hand and wrote, "Yes."

Jake took the pen and looked up at the preacher, who seemed to be looking straight at him. When the preacher finally looked away, Jake pulled up his right pant leg above his boots so Morgan could see the handle of his pistol. "Me too."

Morgan then wrote: "Good! Listen to the sermon. You need to set an example for Katy." She underlined *you* and *example*.

Jake sighed and looked down at Katy, who was sound asleep, and then up at the preacher, who was hitting his ministerial stride. Jake folded his arms and crossed his legs in an effort to get comfortable.

When Jake realized that the sermon was about vengeance, he decided to pay attention.

CHAPTER 66

———— ☾ ————

A S DAWN CRACKED THAT SUNDAY MORNING, MOON PIE WAS leaning against a giant oak along the Tombigbee River in Monroe County, Mississippi. The property owner was a Columbus ER doctor who Moon Pie knew, through a paid source, was working that morning. Moon Pie intended to capitalize on the deer movement he knew would follow the storm front that had blown through that area the previous night. Everything in the woods was dark from the all-night soaking rain, allowing Moon Pie to walk silently on the wet leaves. He plumed his breath in front of him to check the wind and then pulled down a face mask and set off to walk a wooded ridge bordered by the river on one side and an oxbow lake on the other. This was prime ground, intensively managed, and nothing less than a 150 buck would excite him. *I only have about two hours before I gotta leave to meet those Gulf Coast gooks to make the trade.*

Moon Pie eased through the hardwoods, always careful to not walk on bare areas that could leave tracks. It was taking him fifteen minutes to stalk a hundred yards. He had seen several does and a couple of small bucks when a group of mallards flushed at the far end of the oxbow and flew right over him. He instinctively dropped, knowing that something had spooked them. He positioned himself behind a cypress knee and patiently waited.

Within a few minutes, he noticed a hunter wearing an orange cap moving on the far side of the oxbow. Moon Pie found him in his scope and tried to determine who it was. The hunter's face was partially obscured by a neck gaiter. Moon Pie then tried to study him with binoculars, but they weren't as clear as his scope. When the hunter moved deeper into a thicket, Moon Pie leaned back against a cypress tree. Since he had a moment, he decided to check his phone. He saw an hour-old text from his informant, a janitor at the hospital: "Dr just left ER swapped shifts said he was going hunting U o me $50 or some backstrap."

Moon Pie swore to himself. He appreciated the heads-up but was pissed at himself for not checking his messages earlier. He was caught up in the beautiful morning and ideal conditions. Moon Pie spotted the hunter again and cranked up his scope to twenty power. He was pretty sure it was the doctor—the same guy who had almost caught him poaching last year.

The doctor couldn't have been hunting. He was walking at a steady pace. It was as though he were looking for something or somebody. Moon Pie realized that he was being hunted, and he loved it. He cautiously glanced around and knew he was trapped. The doctor had rounded the edge of the oxbow and would be on top of him soon. If he stood, he'd be seen, and the doctor probably had a radio like last time. He envisioned that the doctor was trying to drive him like hunters sometimes push deer—trying to force him in the direction of a waiting game warden. *They'll never catch me.*

The doctor—with a high-powered rifle slung over one shoulder—was only 125 yards away and was walking in Moon Pie's general direction. He was coming down the center of the ridge, completely silhouetted, while Moon Pie was hidden on the edge where the undergrowth was thick. Moon Pie scrunched up, making himself as small as possible, and pushed back against a tree.

Moon Pie knew he could take the doctor in a fistfight. The guy was well over fifty and obviously out of shape. With his right thumb, Moon Pie silently slid off the safety, just in case. He hated rich doctors and businessmen who bought up the land he had freely hunted since he was a kid. They didn't even know how to hunt. Most of them just sat in heated shooting houses on the edge of food plots or power lines and shot whatever walked out.

When the doctor was at thirty yards, Moon Pie made a fist with his camouflage-gloved hand. He was covered head to toe in camo and coiled like a cottonmouth ready to strike as the doctor approached. At ten yards, he watched the doctor's eyes. He seemed to be looking everywhere but directly at Moon Pie. Moon Pie was low but positioned to leap to his feet. If the doctor stayed his course, he would walk within five feet of Moon Pie.

The doctor suddenly ducked under a large vine hanging at an odd slant. It was just enough to alter his course, which would now carry him close but not as close as before. Moon Pie held his breath. The doctor looked right through him as he walked within ten feet. Relief washed over Moon Pie as he watched the doctor walk down the ridge. Moon Pie knew he would not see any of his tracks, particularly when the doctor was looking off in the distance instead of paying attention to close details. Moon Pie mentally laughed at the doctor's lack of woodsman's skills.

When the doctor stepped off the ridge and into a depression about ninety yards away, Moon Pie began a silent escape pace that took him in the opposite direction. Within moments, Moon Pie was clear of the doctor's sight and hurried back toward his truck, which he had parked in a public hunting area. He carefully picked his cover and was soon off the doctor's place. At that point, he squatted down and pulled on an orange vest and cap. He then stepped out onto a gravel road and walked casually but briskly to his truck. He looked at his watch. He had been pinned down for almost forty-five minutes. It was nearly time to make the trade. Feeling completely bulletproof, he called Levi to tell him that he was on the way and that he had a story to share.

Moon Pie had driven less than half a mile when he saw the game warden's dark-green pickup parked on the side of the road. It had been just as he suspected. His daddy had taught him well and emphasized one thing: never get caught on another man's land. His daddy's words rang in his ears: "You can hide or you can run, but don't ever get caught." He was taught to understand the woods and recognize nature's alarms. Some were audible, but most times they were silent. But that was all before cell phones, handheld radios, surveillance cameras, high-dollar hunting clubs, and good deer-ground leasing for more than farming rights. It was much tougher being a successful poacher today, and so far Moon Pie had kept his promise to his dying daddy that he would never get caught.

His satellite radio beeped an alert that his favorite song was coming on the country-outlaw channel. He clicked over and listened to Charlie Daniels sing "Uneasy Rider," telling a story about a fight in Jackson, Mississippi, on a Saturday night. Moon Pie knew every word and sang along.

CHAPTER 67

c

A FTER ABOUT FOUR HOURS OF BEING COUNTED AND RE-counted on Sunday morning, all of the money was stacked neatly on Lucille's kitchen table. They had chosen her place because no matter how small the risk, they didn't want to be at Walter's if the police happened to drop by to question him about Kroger, and the policeman last night had seen only three old guys. Lucille was totally off the radar.

There had been exactly $900,000 in the large black bag, and the boot boxes held a total of $332,876. With bleary eyes from little to no sleep the night before and the tedium of counting tens of thousands of bills multiple times, Walter and crew stared at the stacks of cash. It was more than any of them had ever seen or imagined they would ever see. Bailey, in her own world, quietly sat on her grandmother's couch, intently listening and watching.

Walter announced with satisfaction, "Okay, kids, it's official: one million, two hundred thirty-two thousand, eight hundred and seventy-six dollars!"

"I never thought I'd ever see a million dollars," Bernard said in amazement.

"Everybody wash your hands. That money's nasty," Lucille said, prompting everyone to look at their hands.

Bernard's hands looked like he had just changed a flat tire. "Now I know what they're talking about on TV when they say-*launderin' money*."

Walter shook his head and looked at Bernard. "What?"

"The reason for laundering money. I know why now. 'Cause it's dirty."

Walter couldn't stand it. "Bernard, they're referring to unaccounted money, like drug money, and the need to run it through a legitimate business, thereby making it clean so it can be deposited into a bank and used for whatever they want after that. Since the dirty money is now clean, it's considered to have been laundered."

"That's what I mean; they're cleaning it."

"Bernard, it's a turn of phrase. It's not literal." Walter shook his head and then threw his hands up. Frustrated, he looked at Sebastian and Lucille for help.

"I wonder if they put it in a washing machine," he said as he washed his hands.

"Probably," Sebastian said sarcastically.

After all had washed their hands and gotten something to drink, they stared like zombies at the stacks of money, as if it were magical. Just a few days ago none of them had had any extra cash, and they had slept like babies. Now they had serious cash, and not one of them had slept last night. They were so nervous they doubted they ever would again.

"Wadda we do now?" Lucille asked.

"Maybe we need to hire a security guard."

"We can't keep this in our litter boxes," Sebastian reminded them.

"Where do you suggest we keep it?"

"I don't know. I'm thinking maybe a climate-controlled storage unit," Walter said.

"Who'll keep the key?" Lucille asked quickly.

Walter looked at everyone slowly and noticed their eyes flashing with distrust for each other. He realized that he too was having the same feelings toward them. Overnight this amount of money had changed the dynamics of their group.

"Okay, let's all calm down and talk this through. What do you guys think we should do?" he asked.

"We should put it in the bank, in a safety-deposit box," Sebastian said.

"Again, who gets the key?" Lucille quickly asked. "And I think it's too much to put in a safety-deposit box. They say you can't put cash in 'em, although I don't know how they would know."

"We could divide it four ways, and each person guards a fourth," Bernard added.

Bailey had a calculator on her phone and quickly did the math. "That's $308,219 each."

"Is that what you guys want to do?" Walter asked, but nobody responded. "What's happened to us? We're acting like we don't even trust each other anymore." He continued, "Sebastian, do you trust me?"

"Of course I trust you."

"It's me he doesn't trust," Lucille said.

"I didn't say that."

"You didn't have to."

"Okay, stop it." Walter sighed and stared at the cash. "We started off wanting to do good. Help people. Start something positive. We can't let a windfall like this turn us against each other."

"Walter, the good we can actually do is only a drop in a bucket compared to the needs. We can't help that many people. There are just too many in need." Lucille sighed and then hung her head.

"So what are you saying?"

"Maybe we should split it…pay back Kroger so you don't get in trouble and just split the rest. Each of us could do our own thing."

"Yeah, we definitely don't want to get you in trouble," Bernard added quickly.

They alternated between looking at each other, their hands, and the money. They had known each other for only a few years, but during that time, they had learned each one's true self. They knew each other's fears, weaknesses, strengths, and talents. They knew each other's idiosyncrasies. They knew each other's values. They knew about sons and daughters who didn't visit. They knew who couldn't afford to eat at restaurants. But most importantly, they knew that each of their hearts was filled with compassion and a desire to help others. That was the principal reason they had chosen each other as friends. Prior to this million-dollar acquisition, these were people who made the right decisions and cared about doing the right things. After a long while, they each began to come to terms with their departure from their core value system, and the resulting shame.

Sebastian broke the silence. "Look, I really don't care anymore. I just want Bailey to get away from that monster."

Lucille's eyes began to tear. Bailey smiled at him. "Thank you, Sebastian. And I want you to go to the best oncologist there is, wherever you need to go to get the best treatment."

Bernard tossed his hand towel into the sink. "I'll do whatever y'all wanna do. All I ever wanted outta this deal was to fund a scholarship in my daddy's name at my high school."

This was the first time that Bernard had spoken about his desires, so everyone listened intently. When he noticed, he continued, "I was the youngest of five brothers and sisters, and my momma died givin' birth to me. My daddy, he never remarried. He'd only made it through the eighth grade. He worked two jobs so we all could go to college if we wanted. We all did. He put all five of us through college. The only time he ever saw a college was when he came to watch us graduate. He never took a vacation or a day off. He worked at the lumber mill and a dry cleaners, and he took care of us at home. The man worked seven days a week.

Christmas Day was the only day he ever got off work, and that was because both the mill and the cleaners were closed at the same time."

"You must really be proud of your dad," Walter said.

Bernard covered his face. A tear fell to the floor through his fingers. The group looked at each other, confused. They had never seen him like this. Walter and Sebastian both put their hands on his shoulders in an effort to comfort him.

"What's wrong, big guy? Tell us."

"By the time I graduated from college, my daddy was all broken down from working so much. He was just pretty much worn down and give out. After graduation, there was this big shindig. All my class had their families there, and everybody was dressed up. It was all real fancy and everything. At that stage of my life, money, or the appearance of money, was way too important. I was ashamed of my dad, and I didn't invite him to the party. I've always regretted that. I can't believe I did that. He died a few days later…it was almost like he worked to get us all educated and out into the world better off than he was, and once he accomplished that, he was finished. He just collapsed."

Bernard took a deep breath. The guys nodded, heads down. Lucille blotted her eyes with a napkin. Bailey cried too.

After a long moment of silence, Lucille said, "It sounds to me like your dad really accomplished a great deal. He must have been a really fine man."

"He was. He really was, and all he cared about was us kids gettin' an education. That's why I…I've always wanted to do a scholarship at my high school for a student that otherwise might not be able to afford to go to college and name it the Willie Washington Jefferson Memorial Scholarship."

Walter looked at everyone and saw the nods of agreement. "Bernard, consider it done. Only let's do two. We'll do two annually—one in your daddy's name and one in your name."

Bernard looked around at the nodding heads and said, "Are y'all serious?"

"Absolutely!" exclaimed Sebastian.

"We'll get Samantha on it tomorrow. She'll know how to set it up. Where did you go to high school?"

"Macon, Mississippi."

"Well, two young 'uns in Macon, Mississippi, don't know it yet, but their road to a higher education just got a lot easier."

Bernard smiled, and the members of the group felt better about themselves.

"Thank y'all so much. This means the world to me."

Sebastian poured himself another cup of coffee and then looked at Walter. "What about you, Walter? Besides wantin' to keep the *Prairie Home Companion* radio show on the air, wadda you wanna do? I haven't ever heard you say specifically."

Walter swallowed hard as he held up his cup, indicating that he needed more coffee. He thought about what to say. He knew he hadn't been perfectly honest with them, and his true motivation had been buried—completely hidden. "My wife and I had a daughter. She was our life. We adored her. She married this guy right out of college, and looking back now, we weren't crazy about him, but she loved him and her happiness was all that really mattered. They lived nearby and came over a coupla times a week, and we were close. She taught kindergarten. He was computer nerd and worked for a software company that designed games, and he didn't make squat but got stock options. After about two years of us havin' to feed 'em twice a week and slipping her money to help make ends meet, the company he worked for went public, and shit, suddenly he's rich."

The group was hanging on Walter's every word.

"That's when things started gettin' weird. They bought a big house on the other side of town and started havin' lots of excuses why they couldn't come and see us. She wanted to have a kid and he didn't, and that got ugly. Then he didn't want her comin' to see us. She wanted to start a family, put down roots, and he was suddenly interested in nothing but being around other people that had lots of money. He was designin' these really violent video games, and I think it started having an effect on him.

"Anyway, the company's stock went sky-high, and he was selling it every chance he got. He quit working and started day trading and I think probably doin' drugs too. He also made my daughter quit working, but he got so that he wouldn't let her outta the house. She became like a slave to him. When we tried to go over, he'd just lock us out. He cut us out of their lives. We could tell she was miserable. She'd slip away and call us, but we really couldn't do anything. I talked to the police, and there just wasn't anything we could do. They even advised that we stay out of it. Their house had a huge fence and was gated, so we couldn't just show up and see her. It was killing us. We knew something was wrong.

"After a while, when we'd see her, she wouldn't take off her sunglasses. We didn't know how bad things actually were. Then one night, my wife got a call from a friend of hers that's a nurse, saying that our daughter was in the ER. She'd been beaten up bad—I mean really bad—and was in a coma. She stayed that way for about four weeks, and the bastard never once came to see her. His parents came to the hospital, and when he found out, he threatened them. They were scared to death of him. My little girl died from that beating. My wife and I were both there when she passed. You should never have to watch your kid die. That's as tough as it gets."

"Oh my God! That's so sad," Lucille said as she rubbed her arms and looked at Bailey, who was crying.

"Is he still alive?" Sebastian asked.

"Hang on, Sebastian, let me finish. So I went to his house with a baseball bat and climbed the gate, and I busted out a door with windows, but before I could find him, the police arrived and I got into all kinds of trouble. Restraining orders and you name it, court-ordered counseling. I couldn't get within five hundred feet of him or I'd go to jail. Hell, I had a wife to take care of, and believe me, she was a mess by now."

"What about him? Was he arrested?" Bernard asked.

"Yes, the police were all over him, and he confessed to the beating. He said she refused to have sex with him and she got what she deserved. But at the trial, because of some damn legal technicality, he got off scot-free. It was a nightmare. The judge knew he was guilty, but they couldn't violate his civil rights. Both the judge and the prosecutor resigned. They said they couldn't continue to enforce laws after such a travesty. So, he's free as you and me today.

"The police begged me not to do anything. They were worried that I'd do something crazy, and believe me, I wanted to. Irene had a nervous breakdown, so I had to take care of her. I had to focus all of my hate and desire for revenge into love and compassion for my wife. We went through all of our savings pretty quick, and our quality of life tanked. That son of a bitch now lives down in Tampa, Florida. I keep up with him as best I can, and I've been biding my time. One day, soon, I'm gonna kill him. That's the real reason why I wanted the money. I wanted to make sure I could kill him, have a solid alibi, and get away with it."

Silence once again filled the room. Coffees had gone cold. Everyone was wide-eyed. Walter bared the palms of his hands as if to say, "That's my story."

"I'll help you do it," Sebastian said with complete sincerity. "It would be my absolute pleasure."

"That's how come you know so much about spousal abuse," Lucille stated with an understanding nod. "Is that where you were headin' when your wife died?"

"Not exactly, but we were getting closer. It's a long way from Minnesota to Florida. But Fairhope, Alabama, is within a day's drive of the Tampa suburb where he lives."

Lucille studied Walter's face. "You've been holding a lot of hurt in your heart."

"Yes, I suppose. I guess I have, and a lot of anger too."

"I like your plan. I like how you've been patient and lulled him into feelin' like he got away with it," Sebastian said.

"It ain't been easy. You don't know how many times I wanted to just go down there and just shoot him between the eyes. I've talked to several preachers and I've read all about revenge in the Bible, and I get it. God will deal with him. But I just feel like I need my pound of flesh. An eye for an eye. My blood revenge. I'd also like to help others in similar situations. It happens—these technicalities get these freaks off, and there they go, back into society. They move off, start fresh, and reinvent themselves, and they are almost always worse the next time around. They don't stop. I've studied it."

Lucille said, "Look, we got each other. We gotta trust each other. We've committed crimes here—crimes that could put us all in prison. I don't think we really did it to benefit ourselves as much as to somehow help others. I guess I'm tryin' to justify it, and there really ain't any justifyin'. What we done is wrong, plain wrong, and we gotta deal with that in our own way. Let's take a few days and get our thoughts together, get some rest, and we'll decide what we're gonna do."

Everyone nodded agreement. They all seemed closer to one another now as bonds formed through fire.

"I suggest we go get some luggage with wheels and pack it all full of money, and we'll just store it here in Lucille's apartment. She has the biggest one. The Kroger tapes have us three guys on them, and they could wanna talk to us and look around. I think it's the safest thing to leave it all here," Walter suggested.

"That makes sense. I can live with that."

"I'm not going anywhere," Lucille said.

Bailey sat on the bed with tears in her eyes. She had more love and admiration for these men than ever before. She wished she had known her dad and that he had loved her like Walter loved his daughter. Her heart ached when she thought of the pain he was enduring.

The old guys stood and stretched. They had much good to do and so many reasons to look forward to tomorrow.

"Let's take a nap and then go eat lunch at the Ritz," Walter suggested, and everybody cheered.

"Hey, Walter. How 'bout we invite everybody from the Henry Clay? Surprise 'em!" Bernard said excitedly.

Walter looked at him and shook his head. He knew that the new money was already burning a hole in his pocket.

CHAPTER 68

————— ◡ —————

A FTER HANGING UP WITH LEVI, MOON PIE STARTED TO wonder how the doctor had known he would be there. In order to keep a property fresh, he rarely poached on the same piece more than a couple of times a year. The most plausible explanation was that the law had placed a tracking device on his truck. *That's the only way they coulda known where I was this mornin'. I know Levi didn't tell 'em, and I doubt that my janitor buddy at the hospital ratted me out, cuz he knows that I'd kill him.*

Moon Pie quickly entered the Gold Mine through the back door, stopped, and looked around. Something felt wrong. He pulled a pistol from its holster inside the waistband of his jeans. He realized that the alarm wasn't chirping. He went to the keypad and saw that the system was activated. He typed in his code, and the lights flashed to green and the LED screen changed to "UNARMED."

"That's really freakin' weird," Moon Pie said aloud and re-holstered his pistol. His mind went through the mechanics of the alarm, but nothing added up. *Maybe the rain shorted something out.*

As he stood in the dark thinking, he heard Levi's truck drive up. He relaxed a bit and walked into his office. As soon as he sat at his desk, he saw the tobacco can with the shiny silver lid. He reached out to touch it. *What the hell!* he thought.

Levi busted in the office door, full throttle as usual. "You ready, dude?"

"Almost. I just got here." Moon Pie started to tell Levi about the alarm but decided against it.

Levi had brought biscuits from the gas station and dropped one with sausage and mustard on Moon Pie's desk.

"You know whose this is?" Moon Pie asked Levi, tossing him the can of Copenhagen. "It was on my desk. Who do we know whose name begins with a *W*?"

Levi looked at the lid and turned it in his hands. "That's not a *W*; it's an *M*."

Moon Pie took a bite of his biscuit. "Well, genius, who do we know whose name begins with an *M*?"

"Mom."

"That dips Copenhagen?"

"Mom."

"My mom or your mom?"

"Mine."

"You sure come from trash."

"Like your ass is any better."

"*My* momma don't dip Copenhagen! Is that *your* mom's can?" Moon Pie asked, exasperated.

"Nope. I don't know whose it is. Maybe it was brought in to get some cash for it. The *M*'s gold-plated."

"Yeah, you're right. Bailey probably didn't know what to do with it and laid it on my desk till Monday."

Levi leaned against the doorframe, slowly eating his fried-bologna biscuit. "So the doc knew you were there?"

"I think so."

"That's weird."

"How could he know that? Lucky guess, you think?"

"I doubt it. Maybe. But I doubt it."

"It's the first weekend. It stands to reason that he could be thinkin' he might have poachers."

"What about that device on your ankle?"

"It ain't like they're gonna be sharin' info with the law."

"Yeah, you're right 'bout that."

"I gotta have a trackin' device planted on my truck."

"Damn…we should check it out. We need to use a lift to look underneath. That's where it would be."

"You think they could track my cell phone?" Moon Pie asked as he looked at it.

"Hell yes! I've heard how they can triangulate off cell towers and figure out real close where folks are at."

"Now that I think about it, they don't even gotta do that. I got this app that lets me find my phone wherever it is. They can get the carrier to do it for them. Damn phone companies. All big businesses are hooked into the government and politicians and vice versa, and we're the ones gettin' screwed cuz of it!"

"That's gotta be it."

"We should go back to prepaid cells. They're almost impossible to trace and track. We'll check out my truck after we meet. We'll use your truck today to be safe."

"Dang it. I *love* my BlackBerry. I hate to give it up."

"You can keep it; just don't carry it when we're workin'."

"Good. Okay. Thanks."

"Let's get the dough and hit the road. Go look out the back door and make sure it's clear," Moon Pie said as he stood to open the safe.

Touching the coded keypad, Moon Pie thought about his phone betraying him. He had never considered that before. The last code beeped, and the lock released. He turned the handle, swung open the door, and almost immediately started screaming a string of cuss words that would make a crab fisherman blush.

CHAPTER 69

———— ☾ ————

TAM AND HIS VIETNAMESE CELLMATE TALKED FOR SEVERAL hours. The man knew of Tam and held him in high regard. They squatted and bounced slightly on their heels as they discussed the situation and potential solutions. Tam learned that his new friend was to be released at 8:00 a.m. the following morning and that the jail didn't have any biometric screening. They stood to compare their heights and weights, and then Tam made him one hell of an offer.

After the others in the cell were asleep, the two Vietnamese men swapped jumpsuits. Tam's had green stripes, denoting felony charges, and his buddy's was solid orange, representing a misdemeanor offense. They spoke Vietnamese so no one would understand the plan, which depended on Sunday morning's new shift of officers—who wouldn't know the specific circumstances surrounding those being held there temporarily.

Tam shook his new best friend's hand and again pledged that he and his family would be protected and well taken care of financially. He nodded; then the two embraced. This man didn't know what might be ahead of him, but he was confident the American judicial system would eventually determine that he wasn't Tam Nguyen and he would be freed. What he didn't appreciate was that he had just agreed to commit numerous federal offenses that actually would send him to prison for the next several years, if not decades.

At 7:30 a.m., a young police officer walked into the holding area and unlocked the door. He looked at the two Vietnamese men and then focused on the orange jumpsuit. He said, "Let's go, Lan. Time's up. You're free," and then yawned.

The other prisoners watched as one of their cellmates left for freedom. A few yelled racial obscenities. All were jealous.

Without hesitation, Tam stood up and walked toward the officer, who looked at the discharge papers and then down at the real Lan and shook his head. *Hell, they all look alike to me*, he thought.

CHAPTER 70

———— ☾ ————

MOON PIE AND LEVI WERE BOTH IN SHOCK AS LEVI DROVE his truck to the abandoned bomb factory. They left both of their phones at the Gold Mine. Moon Pie was freaking out and kept staring at the ankle bracelet, knowing that he had to get it off soon. He had been ranting, making no sense for the last twenty minutes.

"I'm a dead man," Moon Pie said as he reclined in the seat. "The sumbitches got the Mexicans' money and mine. Shit! Shit! Shit!"

"Look, we can figure this out. Okay? Think. Who knew the money was in there?"

"Just you!" Moon Pie gave his half brother an evil look.

"Don't go there; you know me better than that."

"That's it. You did it."

"You know I don't know the safe's combination. Plus, I was at the concert and then at the trailer. Now, both Tam and the Mexicans knew you had the money."

"Why would they steal their own money?"

"To save your percentage. To cut you outta the deal. To get the other side to kill ya. There's a ton of reasons, and they're criminals!"

"My percentage ain't shit to Tam, but I ain't considered the Mexicans."

"That locator shows them where you're at, where you went after you got the money. They know it all."

"But why would they steal it back? They'd know I couldn't get the drugs!"

"No, but you'd owe them. You'd owe them big-time. They might be tryin' to leverage you."

Levi could see the old factory's tall brick chimney rising out of the prairie soil, and it caused him to started thinking about the place. In the 1940s it had been a bustling bomb-manufacturing plant that employed thousands of workers and stored bombs in hidden underground bunkers all over the area. Now it was just a few old buildings and remnants of the past.

"But why?" Moon Pie asked.

"Maybe it's some kind of corporate-takeover shit. Maybe they want to take over Tam's operation and need an inside man. What better way to get your attention...do this for us or die?"

"I don't know. Turn right here. Go behind those buildings there."

Levi's old Bronco turned on the gravel road. "Dude, they put a locator on your ankle. How weird's that? They did it. I guarantee it!"

Levi was making sense to Moon Pie. His mind started really racing as he saw the black truck parked right where it was supposed to be. *What if Tam and the Tennessee Mexicans are in on this together and setting me up? What would they gain?*

Moon Pie was quickly moving into paranoia. He sat up and took a deep breath. He was in a real mess. The Mexicans were gonna hunt him down unless he came up with the money. Tam would just take his drugs and leave and probably never do business with him again, or, in the best case, slow down deals until Tam's confidence was built back.

"Flash your lights."

Levi did as he was told.

"There. They know it's us."

Levi pulled the Bronco right up next to the truck with two men in it. Moon Pie recognized Mike's face. Both men visibly relaxed a little.

"Just you guys?"

"Yep."

"This is my half brother." Levi waved. "Ya seen anybody?" Moon Pie asked.

"Nope."

"Besides being haunted, this is a pretty secure place."

Mike laughed nervously as he looked toward the building as if he expected to see a ghost in a window.

"Heard from Tam?"

"Not a word."

Mike didn't respond. He just smiled and said, "You ready?"

"Mike, we got a problem," Moon Pie said in the most appealing tone he could muster.

Mike didn't like problems, and the last twelve hours had been nothing but one big problem. He didn't respond.

Moon Pie continued, "I got robbed last night, and I ain't got the money."

"That's not good." Mike suddenly wanted away from Moon Pie. This trip seemed doomed.

"I know. I know. I just found out, and I'm workin' on it, tryin' to find out what happened. But I…I wanted to come and tell ya face-to-face. I can't trust my cell phones anymore."

Mike didn't respond. He just stared out the window and then at his partner, knowing Tam would be pissed.

Moon Pie pressed, "I don't suppose you could just go ahead and let me take the cargo and I get y'all the money later? I'm just thinkin' of a way to keep the customer happy." Moon Pie gave a little nervous laugh.

"No. That ain't gonna work. Tam would never agree to that."

"Yeah, that's what I figured. Tell Tam what happened and that I'll be in touch to explain everything."

Mike cranked the diesel truck. He was ready to go. "I'll do it."

"Hey, can you tell me what happened last night?"

"I don't know yet. Sounds like a setup. I'm wonderin' now if it's not related to your missing money."

Levi and Moon Pie looked at each other. Everything was getting more and more complicated by the minute. Moon Pie said, "Hell, I don't know. I gotta get it figured out. I don't know what the hell's goin' on!" Moon Pie shook his head.

All criminals hated the notion of a setup, mainly because they were all susceptible. Greed or egos or both usually brought them down.

Moon Pie gave Mike a quick salute, saying, "Keep it real, Mike. There's some crazy, weird shit goin' on."

Moon Pie turned to Levi and growled, "Get us the hell outta here."

CHAPTER 71

———— ☾ ————

A FTER A LONG NIGHT OF SWAPPING TAM STORIES AND CEL-
ebrating his capture, the two Mississippi Drug Task Force
officers rose from their beds at the Hilton early and started back-
filling the story to their superiors. It was a glorious event in their
careers, and both men were appreciative of everyone who had
helped, especially the guys from Rascal Flatts. The last several
months had been a strain on the officers' lives and marriages.
Many family events had been missed in an effort to put cuffs on
one of Mississippi's largest drug importers. They justified their
extended stays from their families by knowing they were making
Mississippi safer. It was a thankless job.

They walked out to their black sedan after a free continental
breakfast and were due to meet an official transport van to haul
Tam to Jackson at 11:00 a.m. sharp. They were nervous about the
transport and had decided to have a decoy van also. Tam's gang
was notorious, and they would do anything to free their leader.

"You sleep good?"

"Not really. My son lost his retainer for the third time, and
my wife was pitching a fit."

"I bet he'll find it."

"I sure hope so. My wife was pretty upset. Hell, she's been upset...mainly because I wasn't there to help with the parentin'," he said as he put the key in the ignition.

"At least we got Tam. That's got to be a career-makin' night for us."

"And Alexa. Maybe we can learn something from her."

As they pulled onto the road, the senior officer's cell phone rang. He didn't recognize the number but could tell it was local by the area code.

"This is John Wesley. Yes. What!"

The other officer strained to hear what was being said but couldn't.

"How in the hell did that happen? Have you put out an APB? We'll be there in ten minutes," he said in disgust and ended the call.

"What is it?" the driver asked.

"They mistakenly let Tam go. They had another Vietnamese man about the same age, height, and build. Apparently they swapped clothes, and nobody could tell the difference."

"That Mercedes that he was in last night—we need to put out an urgent APB on it."

The officer searched through his notes for the tag number.

"Dammit. We should have picked up the driver too, when we had the chance."

"What about Alexa?"

"I didn't think to ask. Let's just get to the police station. Shit! I can't freakin' believe this!"

CHAPTER 72

───── ☾ ─────

S AMANTHA HAD PLANNED ON SPENDING SUNDAY MORNING
cleaning out closets, but she got distracted reading cherished
old newspaper clippings about Friendship Cemetery, which dates
back to the mid-1800s. Columbus was a hospital town for the
Battle of Shiloh during the War Between the States, and an untold
number of injured soldiers from both sides were brought there.
Many of these soldiers were buried in Friendship Cemetery. In
the spring of 1866, a group of Columbus women placed flowers on the graves of *both* Confederate and Union soldiers in an
attempt to heal the nation. That act of kindness is credited with
becoming our modern Memorial Day. Sam's great-great-grand-
mother was one of those women.

Sam was deep in thought when her cell phone rang. Since it
rarely rang on Sunday, she expected it to be important. She got
up and sat on a small couch that was almost a hundred years old.
Tom the cat climbed into her lap and quickly went to sleep.

"Hello," she answered.

"Sam, it's Walter. I hope I'm not interrupting something
important."

"I hope you're not in jail."

"No, I'm right here at the Henry Clay. Listen, I'd like to come see you tomorrow about a coupla things, if you have time."

She didn't want to tell Walter that she didn't have any other meetings planned and he was free to come whenever, but she had learned to play the game. "I've got a full morning until ten thirty. You could come then."

"I'll do that, and maybe afterward I can buy you lunch."

"Perfect. Can you clue me in?"

"We wanna start a college scholarship at a school, and I wanna discuss givin' the Kroger money back," Walter said.

"I think that's a fine idea, Walter. We'll talk about how to play our hand so no one is incriminated."

"That's why we want you to handle it. Maybe there'll be a reward. If there is, you're welcome to it."

"Thank you, Walter."

"You're welcome."

"Walter? Are you all right? You sound tired."

"I haven't been sleepin' good. Turns out, stolen money can weigh heavily on you."

"We'll take care of it. This might help you rest: I have a friend who goes to church with the store manager who was having that fling. He and his wife have been going to counseling, and it looks like they're going to make it. He's broken, and he realizes what he almost lost. There are still some trust issues, obviously, but apparently, he really manned up and is committed to doing everything he can to save his marriage. He's even gone back to church."

"So, you're saying something good came outta all this."

"In a very roundabout way, yes."

CHAPTER 73

———— ☾ ————

L EVI AND MOON PIE HAD SPENT ALL AFTERNOON DRINKING
Old Charter and trying to determine who had stolen the
money. Each theory sounded more preposterous than the previous one. Only one scenario made sense to them, sober or
drunk: the Tennessee Mexicans had stolen the money. They
could not, however, agree on what could have been their motive.
The Copenhagen lid was the deciding factor in settling on the
Mexicans. They brilliantly determined that the gold *M* stood for
Mexico.

At around noon, Tam had called Moon Pie, asking to borrow
his FJ Cruiser for his trip home. Tam would leave his Mercedes,
as collateral, behind the Gold Mine. Tam promised to either wire
Moon Pie money for a new vehicle or have someone return it.
Moon Pie agreed and told him how to quickly get into Alabama
and then a southern route to avoid any roadblocks. Tam was
highly agitated and concerned about Moon Pie's money, but he
was more anxious about maintaining his freedom. He promised
to contact Moon Pie later.

On the ride home from the bomb plant, Moon Pie had carefully cut off the ankle monitor. When they stopped at a convenience store in Aberdeen, Mississippi, Moon Pie—being the

sorry-ass white trash that he was—hid the monitor under the front seat of a bright-purple 1986 Cadillac Deville with gold twenty-twos. That was the only time he smiled all day.

By dark, Moon Pie began to sober up and take the imminent threat and his options seriously. He stumbled through his trailer and found seven thousand dollars in cash that he had hidden, while Levi texted his latest girlfriend.

"How much cash you got?" Moon Pie asked Levi.

"I dunno—couple grand, easy."

"We need to talk about making a run for it."

"You're serious, aren't you?"

"Dude, these Mexican sumbitches ain't gonna play. That was a lot of money."

"What are you thinkin'?"

"I'm thinking about running up into either northern Missouri or Iowa. I can make some money killing big deer this time of year. You wanna go?"

"You know I hate cold weather," Levi said.

"How can you be my brother?"

"Half brother, and the half my momma gave me don't enjoy freezing my nuts off. Could I stay here and run the Mine?"

"They're gonna want blood—especially after I skip town. That'll be the first place they come lookin'. I'll give you some money if you wanna go south for six months and find you somethin' to do. You can take the houseboat."

Levi nodded at the thought of floating down the river and docking near Mobile.

"We gotta do something. I expect they knew the minute that ankle monitor got cut. Those things got sensors."

"You could tell the cops that we were robbed. You ain't gotta tell them how much they took. They might catch somebody that we could toss to the Mexicans."

"I can't. Not everything at the Gold Mine is legit. Look, I'm gonna load up my stuff, clean out the store, and I'll be gone before it gets dark tomorrow. I don't mind running. I made a small fortune last time on that gun-range scheme. We'll stay in touch on Facebook; just don't say where you're at. We also got these prepaid cells."

Levi looked around the trailer. He really didn't want to leave.

Moon Pie looked closely at Levi. "Look, bro, it's all rented, this trailer and the store, so we aren't really attached to anything. That's a good lesson for you to remember."

"All right. I'm goin' south. You think there's still any oil-spill work left down there?"

"I doubt it, but you can always claim that you're a sea turtle researcher or some shit like that, make up a fat résumé, and you'll probably get rich."

"I like those big old live-oak trees that grow near the coast."

"Listen to me, tree nerd, we have a couple of days to get organized and then we gotta get lost. You understand?"

"Yeah, I got it."

"Look, here's two grand. That gives you four and the houseboat to get started. I got five. After things cool down, we'll hook back up."

They hadn't been honest with each other. They both had more cash hidden.

CHAPTER 74

T HE MISSISSIPPI DRUG TASK FORCE HAD REACHED OUT TO every state and federal agency to find Tam. They made a special plea to the state troopers along the major arteries leading to the Gulf Coast. They were running low on hope when the Columbus Police Department called to inform them that they had located Tam's Mercedes parked behind the Gold Mine. The task force officers asked the Columbus PD to surround the building and wait for their arrival.

Traveling at over ninety miles per hour, the adrenaline-infused officers discussed how Tam's hiding made sense and how the slightest mistake could result in a criminal's capture when he was on the run. They also talked about how this was a deadly time for law enforcement and the public because desperate criminals routinely take desperate measures to stay free. Alexa had been no help, since she realized it was her fault Tam had been lured into the trap, and her lawyer had advised her not to talk unless he was present. They knew Alexa feared Tam's rage and figured that she had seen it many times. Her lawyer would no doubt have her released inside the next twenty-four hours, and she was probably thinking through the next steps in her life that would more than likely be without Tam, assuming he didn't kill her.

As the officers approached Columbus, they were given the Gold Mine's street address, which was programmed into the dash-mounted GPS. When they arrived, all the other units turned on their blue lights, and they lit up the city block with rapid-fire, intense light. The Columbus PD had a canine officer at the scene, and the sudden light show caused him to bark once at all of the activity. His handler was surprised at the dog's uncharacteristic breach but understood his excitement.

As they strapped on ballistic vests, the officers were briefed on the layout of the building and possible scenarios. A captain from the Columbus Police Department explained that they had monitored the building from a distance, and no one had come or gone. No inside lights were on, and the Mercedes's hood was cold.

"You think he's still in there?" he asked.

"He very well could be, and this little dude is dangerous when cornered."

"I suggest we send the dog in first and tell your men to expect that the suspect is armed and violent as hell and to act accordingly."

"Roger that," the captain replied. Then he walked a few feet away, talking on his shoulder-mounted microphone.

"You ready, John Wesley?" his partner asked.

"Sure."

"Let's do this."

A group of six officers and a well-trained German shepherd rushed to the front door and crouched outside. One officer in a full protective suit and helmet punched the lock with a lock gun, and in less than ten seconds, the front door swung open.

The police officers all looked to the task force guys. John Wesley nodded, and the dog handler pulled the dog close to him, whispered something, stroked his head, and sent him inside.

Everyone took a deep breath. They all had the utmost respect for the dog and the handler.

John Wesley looked at his partner. They knew they were thinking the same thing: *I sure hope our dog doesn't get shot.* They had witnessed it before. When a canine officer got killed, his partner always took it really hard.

For thirty seconds, there wasn't a sound. Each person imagined the dog checking every corner of the dark building. Suddenly they heard a loud yelp, and the handler cracked open the door. The dog flew out and sat next to his handler, shaking and whimpering.

All the officers stared in disbelief. What could have scared a fearless police dog and made him retreat! Radios cracked with questions from the police brass who were watching through binoculars. No one could answer. The handler had never seen his dog back down from anything.

"Captain, something really bad is inside. We need reinforcements, lights, and thermal imaging!" John Wesley requested on the dog handler's radio. "And tell the guys at the back door to be ready!"

"Ten-four. Give me a minute. We have all that gear here in the SWAT van."

Within two minutes, twelve more officers, dressed completely in black full-body armor and carrying various gear, arrived and crouched with the others. Each person's eyes were wild with anticipation yet focused on the mission. John Wesley counted them down, and they stormed through the front door— every officer, except the dog.

The dark store was instantly illuminated, and the officers quickly cleared the front room. Staging beside the partly opened door to the back room, they went on a rehearsed silent count and then burst into the back room. Three quick shots were fired.

Radios erupted with chatter as the captain and his men frantically ran to the building. "I need info!" the captain yelled as he charged to the shop's outside door. "I need intel!"

Radio silence fell for ten seconds as the men sorted out what had happened.

"I need info! What's happening!" the captain barked.

"It's okay, Captain. We're all clear," a voice on the radio reported.

"What about the shots!"

"We shot a lion!"

"What?" he asked as he started inside.

"It's a life-size mounted lion!"

"You're shittin' me."

"I swear, it looks alive, sir."

CHAPTER 75

M ONDAY MORNING WHEN SHE DROPPED KATY AT OAK
Hill Academy, Morgan went inside to advise the office
staff and headmaster of what had happened in Tupelo. She
wanted them to be on high alert. Her worst fear was that Katy
would be kidnapped for revenge for Jake's actions that night
in the swamp, and Katy's school was one place where Morgan
couldn't directly protect her. She did have faith in the staff, and
she noticed a police cruiser sitting in the parking lot when she
left. The young officer waved, and she realized why he was there.
She pulled up beside the patrol car.

"Thank you."

"No problem, ma'am."

"Are you here all day?" she asked.

"For as much of it as I can, unless I'm needed somewhere
else. We're rotating so somebody's around here during the day
until this thing dies down."

Morgan was almost moved to tears. "Thank you. Can I get
you something? Are you hungry?"

"No ma'am. My wife cooks me breakfast every mornin'."

"That's sweet. How long have you been married?" Morgan
wondered.

261

"Four months, yesterday," the officer admitted proudly.

"Oh, so you're still honeymoonin'!"

The officer blushed. "Yes ma'am."

"I really do appreciate y'all doing this. Thanks again," she said as she drove off and mumbled to herself, "Hot breakfast will probably last two more months, at most."

CHAPTER 76

ᶜ

T HE POLICE SWARMED MOON PIE'S HOME SO FAST THAT HE didn't have time to get out of his La-Z-Boy. He had been watching ESPN analysts debate which teams would be paired in the upcoming college football national championship game. One minute he was pumped that an SEC team might be in the top two, and the next minute he had his hands up like he was signaling a touchdown—a beer in one, the TV remote in the other.

"What's your name! Are you Ethan Daniels! Is there any-body else in the trailer!" an older officer asked as he holstered his weapon.

Ethan looked around at four pistols and two AR15s pointed at his head. "Yeah, you got me. I'm Ethan Daniels. What'd I do now?"

Two more officers entered the trailer and began searching it. Moon Pie watched them disappear down the small hallway.

"Shitter's the second door on the left!"

"Okay, wiseass, where's Tam Nguyen?" John Wesley asked him.

"Who?" Moon Pie acted surprised.

"Don't play stupid with me, shit-for-brains. I ain't got the time."

"I don't know nobody named Tam. Who is she?"

"Get up. We're goin' downtown to talk about it and refresh your memory."

The two officers returned. "It's clear, sir," said the younger of them.

Moon Pie now was beginning to feel a bit cocky. "Why do you think I know this person?"

"Because his vehicle is parked behind your business."

Moon Pie smiled. "People park back there all the time. That ain't a crime, and it don't mean that I know shit about it."

"Nope, but harboring a fugitive is, as is aiding, abetting, and accessory after the fact. Plus, anything else we can dig up when we get a warrant and bring in the drug dog."

"Look, I don't need any trouble. I'm clean. I'm trying to be respectable. If I knew anything, I'd tell y'all."

"Where's Levi Jenkins?"

"He's in love or heat or somethin'. He ain't here."

"Where is he?"

"I don't know."

"You don't know much of anything, do ya, shitbird?"

"Naw, I don't. I do know that I was just sittin' here, mindin' my own business, watchin' television, and y'all done come bustin' up in here, treatin' me like I'm some kinda common criminal. I do believe that's po-lice harassment. I guess I'll just have to speak with my attorney about this. He's gonna—"

A local officer who knew Moon Pie interrupted, "Where's your FJ Cruiser?"

The task force officers immediately understood the question. Moon Pie did as well. If he said it was stolen and they caught Tam in it, Tam would have another charge against him. If he said he had loaned it to Tam, it would implicate him as being involved. *Shit! Shit! Shit!*

Moon Pie's bravado was now turned down a couple of notches. "Look, you know...I ain't sure. I usually just leave it at the office. Levi and my other employees use it all the time. I don't ever think about it. I like drivin' that old Bronco out there."

John Wesley said to another officer, "Cuff him. Let's take him downtown. Maybe his memory will improve with better surroundings."

Moon Pie didn't like this, but there were way too many cops to resist. He couldn't think of anything clever to say to get out of this bind when a muscular officer snatched him out of the chair and pulled his arms behind him, applying the cuffs. The officer began to frisk him and uncovered a Mercedes smart key. The officer tossed it to John Wesley.

"Well, this is interestin'" he said, turning it over in his hand. "I bet this doesn't work on that old Bronco. Let's see." John Wesley pointed it out the front door and pushed the button. He pushed it again and then looked at Moon Pie and smiled.

Moon Pie looked down at the dirty shag carpeting.

CHAPTER 77

———— ☾ ————

SEVERAL OF THE TENNESSEE MEXICANS CALLED AN EMER-
gency meeting to discuss recent developments with the Gulf
Coast load. A midlevel manager in the organization was trying
to shield the initial bad news from el Jefe. Managing assets was
a daily task for several of these key employees. The boss gave
them plenty of latitude in managing their respective pieces of the
business. This approach was good in the sense that they could
make decisions on the fly, in the heat of the moment. It was a bad
approach if their decisions were not good ones, which could cost
dearly, in monetary and legal terms.

The normally tough-acting manager was humble and obviously nervous in the presence of his boss, the second in command. "He called about an hour ago. It was Mr. Moon Pie's
brother. He said they had been robbed and the money was gone."

The second in command was very calm as he smoked an
authentic Cohiba he had personally acquired from the Partagas
factory. Rather than looking at the manger, he studied the burning end of the Lancero. "And what did you say?"

"That we will kill him and his brother."

"I hope that's not all."

"No, sir. I said we wanted all of the *dinero*."

"*Bueno.* Who do they think did this thing?"

"Us. They think *we* stole the *moneda.*"

"What made him say such a stupid thing?"

"He claims to have proof because we left a tobacco can with a gold *M* on it. He said the *M* stands for Mexico."

"What could he be speaking of?"

"I have no idea, *señor.* And he says that we put the GPS device on his brother so we would know where he was all the time…to help us steal the money."

"Has anyone been away in the last few days?" The second in command didn't totally trust anyone.

"No, sir. He also said that Señor Moon Pie was just put in jail in Columbus, which is in Mississippi. But our tracking data shows that right now he is at a place called the Macarena Club in Aberdeen, Mississippi."

"Where is the money?"

"A retirement home in West Point called the Henry Clay."

"Is this place in Mississippi?"

"*Sí.*"

"This is not good."

"Can you give me a few days to clean this up before you report it to el Jefe?"

"Do you know anything about this Moon Pie person?"

"*Sí,* he works for the Gulf Coast distributor, who has a very strong reputation, and he is a source that el Jefe wants. He told me to do this, so that's why I took a chance."

"I see."

"I can fix this if you will allow. Trust me, *señor.*"

The second in command was disappointed with his men and the situation. "You have two days. Take Guillermo and the tracking equipment. Do what is necessary to get back our money or the drugs. And Julio?"

"*Sí?*"

"Your quality of life depends on success."

CHAPTER 78

———— ☾ ————

A T EIGHT THIRTY MONDAY MORNING, A FULL HOUR BEFORE
the Gold Mine's scheduled opening, Jake sat in his pickup
truck across the street and down the block from the business.
He looked through hunting binoculars to see if he could get a
glimpse of Moon Pie. He wondered what had happened to cause
there to be yellow police tape across the front door. He wasn't
sure what he would do if he saw Moon Pie. He actually didn't
know what the guy looked like but hoped he'd be able to pick him
out. The police described him as fence-post thin, except he had
a pronounced paunch. He had shoulder-length, stringy brown
hair, and he shaved only once a week.

In the seat beside Jake, in an unzipped canvas case, was a new
Ruger 9 mm semiautomatic pistol. Jake reached over and grabbed
the weapon without pulling it from the case. It felt good in his
hand and gave him a sense of assurance. Jake wanted to walk up
to Moon Pie and settle things. He suspected that Moon Pie would
be equally willing. Jake was tired of wondering and worrying. He
was ready to move on. Jake had yet to hear from R.C. He wanted
him along, but now he was going to have to go it alone.

Jake's BlackBerry was blowing up with interoffice e-mails.
The market was open, and his day was already getting crazy busy.

He dreaded it. He hated talking to customers about domestic and foreign financial markets, the global recession, the disaster that was the European Union, and how the collapse of the euro was going to affect the value of the US dollar and their investments. He hated discussing how the Chinese yuan was being pushed by our own treasury secretary to become a reserve currency in order to stoke inflation in America. And he hated that his clients were never satisfied. They always thought he got them out of a stock either too soon or too late. They all thought they were the only ones missing out on some position or play that would make them wealthy or at least recover some of their portfolio losses. Clients always thought they were just getting the leftovers, the crumbs. They bitched about having to pay commissions on trades, whether it was bought or sold. They all had stories about out-of-town friends whose brokers were making them rich beyond measure. Jake was sick of it.

Jake just wanted to stick the barrel of his pistol in Moon Pie's face and permanently end this game of cat and mouse.

He cranked the truck and slowly pulled away from the curb. On the radio, Mike and Mike were on ESPN, recapping the weekend's college football games, which was a welcome distraction. Jake headed to his office for another day of the grind, although he had no intention of putting in a full day. *I'll come back here later*, he thought, zipping the gun case shut, and then placing the pistol under his seat.

CHAPTER 79

———— ☾ ————

T HE COLUMBUS POLICE DEPARTMENT HAD TO RELEASE Moon Pie. They had exhausted every technicality that would justify keeping him longer. Although his lawyer looked like an idiot, he actually knew what he was doing.

The search of Moon Pie's trailer didn't turn up anything illegal, and there wasn't any contraband or anything suspicious at the Gold Mine, other than the mounted lion. The police suspected that the mount had been stolen from a local doctor who had endured a bloody public divorce, but it was never reported as stolen, since the doctor had much more important things to worry about during that time.

The Mercedes key tied Moon Pie to Tam's car, not to a specific person. It was circumstantial. The police knew Moon Pie's lawyer could argue successfully that Moon Pie simply had a key to a vehicle that was parked in a public area for security purposes, in case a building caught fire and the car needed to be moved. The key did not prove that Moon Pie had ever met, much less worked with, Tam. They knew it was pure bullshit, but it gave him some wiggle room.

"We'll just have to keep an eye on him," the Columbus police captain explained. "I've got men that I can put on him."

"That son of a bitch is slick, now," John Wesley cautioned.

"These fellas are good. Real good."

John Wesley's phone vibrated, signaling receipt of a text. Everybody saw a relieved expression as he read it. "My son found his retainer. Those damn things are expensive," he said with a smile.

Most people don't consider that police officers have normal lives and sometimes kids and wives—lives trudging inexorably forward without regard to ongoing manhunts. The captain knew that an officer away from home needed those tidbits of familial information to keep him grounded and sane.

The captain chuckled as he stood. "Good. Been there, done that. As to Ethan 'Moon Pie' Daniels, I ain't got a choice. I gotta cut him loose in an hour."

"Okay, I get it. I understand. Well, then, I guess we're gonna head back to Jackson and then probably to Biloxi. I'll keep in touch," John Wesley explained.

"Don't ya worry; we got your back up here. We'll keep a sharp eye on your boy. If we get a lead on that FJ Cruiser, you'll be the first to know."

CHAPTER 80

———— ☾ ————

S INCE MOON PIE WASN'T ARRESTED BUT WAS BEING HELD FOR questioning about Tam and other things, he demanded and was granted telephone access. He used it to contact Levi. In code, he carefully instructed Levi to first call the Tennessee Mexicans and plead for time to get him out of jail and then to sort out the other issue. Moon Pie almost retracted that direction, realizing that the safest place for him (due to the pissed-off Mexicans) was locked up. He thought better of it and then told Levi to alert Tam's crew and to make sure no one called Moon Pie's cell phone while the police had it. Finally, Levi was to contact their lawyer cousin.

The task force guys and the local police grilled Moon Pie relentlessly until everybody was exhausted. On the rare occasion when Moon Pie answered their questions, he didn't say anything important or incriminating. When they returned him to the holding cell, he spent the rest of his time there avoiding eye contact with his cellmates, particularly the one Mexican.

On Monday at 10:00 a.m., when the jailer came to let him out, Moon Pie really didn't want to leave. But he knew that the longer he stayed in jail, the better chance they had of digging up something that could actually stick. His instincts were telling him to run—to put as much distance as he could between himself and the police, Tam, and the Mexicans.

Moon Pie's cousin dropped him at the Gold Mine, and by ten thirty, he was at his desk, trying to come up with a plan. His cash was gone, Tam's cash was gone, and, to add insult to injury, the rifle he loved the most was gone too. His world was a disaster, and he knew that he had only a matter of hours, if not minutes, before the Mexicans arrived. Moon Pie had entered the Gold Mine though the back door. He didn't want any customers. At the moment, he only wanted Levi to show up with a fresh change of clothes. He absentmindedly picked up the Copenhagen can as he thought about how quickly his life had gone to shit. The shiny silver lid glinted off the light from his desk lamp. As he turned it, the M became a W and then became an M again.

"Them sons of bitches," he spat angrily. "Damn wetbacks," he said aloud as he thought about how the Tennessee Mexicans had ripped him off. He was trying to figure out how they had learned the safe's combination when his cell phone rang. He recognized the number as his Alabama taxidermist.

"What up?" Moon Pie answered, skipping all pleasantries.

"How many good deer ya killed?" the criminal taxidermist asked as he watched an intern clean the paint overspray from a freshly mounted turkey's eyes.

"Would you believe that I ain't even been but twice since gun season opened?" he said, happy to talk about something other than the stolen money. "And on one of those hunts I had a landowner all over my ass."

"You gotta get with it, man. Early season, you're usually good for five or six. I got orders for about twenty heads I need to get filled."

"I'll get plenty; you know I always do. I got you a couple things you'll like, and I got a nice buck in full velvet I took on Labor Day weekend when everybody was shootin' doves and had the game wardens all tied up. You'll love him. Lately, though,

I've just had too much shit goin' on around here. Really bad shit, man."

"You always do."

"I know, man, but this time it's really heavy-duty." Moon Pie suddenly had an idea. "In fact, I need a place to crash for a while. Can I stay at your place? Just till things cool down some."

"Yeah, sure, come on and bring that deer. We can make some money while you're here, night huntin'."

"Thanks, dude. I can always count on you. I'll see you in a day or two," Moon Pie replied, thinking it might be more trouble than it was worth to take his horses.

"Hang on. I called for a reason."

"What was it?"

"Don't you know where there are some bald eagles?"

"Yeah. I know several."

"I need one. A collector called me."

"Finding one ain't that hard. I know right where a pair is, and they are close to town. But gettin' caught with one is a whole new world of federal shit."

"I understand. I need a mature male, big-ass whitehead."

"So your customer wants what no one's got. We're talkin' serious risk here and big money."

"You're the best, aren't you? Deliver it in good shape and I'll split the money with you. Fifty-fifty."

Moon Pie was desperate for cash. "Okay. I'll see what I can do. I'll really have my ass hanging out big-time on this one."

CHAPTER 81

𝐜

J AKE HAD ENDURED THE MORNING IN HIS CUBICLE AND SEV-
eral times had popped his head up like a meerkat when he
heard a strange voice. He struggled to focus and avoided most
telephone calls and e-mail, while his frazzled mind raced over the
events of the past few days. He constantly checked his silenced
cell phone to see if R.C. had called or texted.

It was the week of Thanksgiving, and his coworkers were
verbally jabbing each other about the upcoming Egg Bowl—the
annual college football game between Mississippi State and Ole
Miss. Like so many rivalries, it divided families, friends, and
coworkers each year. Today these sometimes-heated exchanges
were nothing but a bunch of yammering to Jake.

The more Jake thought about his conversation with the
Tupelo police sergeant, the more confused he became. R.C. had
stated that the Tupelo police knew about his situation, but they
were obviously not watching Moon Pie very closely. They had
allowed the guy to get within a few yards of him. *How and why
would they let that happen?*

What Jake didn't appreciate was that most police departments are short staffed, and budget constraints impede them from
conducting many ancillary investigations. Crime was rampant,

and most departments were stretched thin dealing with actual victims, as opposed to potential ones. The truth was, all things considered, most were doing an exceptional job with dwindling human and financial resources.

The insurance company wasn't inclined to pay Jake's claim for the burned camp house. That old cabin had been a big part of Jake's life, and now it was gone. He knew he could not rebuild it anytime in the foreseeable future. He assumed it was either arson or faulty wiring that had destroyed it. Deep in his gut, though, he was beginning to believe that it was an act of vengeance by Moon Pie. Jake also realized that there wasn't just some random Peeping Tom at his house but that it was most probably Moon Pie.

Jake's life and family had been invaded, violated by Moon Pie, and he hadn't really done anything about it, out of deference to the promise he had made to Morgan after the night of terror in Alabama. He had promised not to put himself or Katy in any type of risky situation.

He studied a framed vacation photo of Morgan and Katy in the big pool at the Marriott Grand Hotel in Point Clear, Alabama. They were his life. He couldn't continue to live in fear. He decided that it was past time to take charge and be proactive, aggressively protecting his family.

Jake watched the clock on his computer inch toward noon. *Morgan's just gonna have to deal with it; this is who I am!*

CHAPTER 82

——— (———

LUCILLE CALLED WALTER AND ASKED HIM TO BRING THE GUYS to her apartment as soon as possible. He detected a bit of trepidation in her voice, but she wouldn't elaborate, even after being asked twice. He said he would be there as soon as he could find them.

It took Walter several minutes to round up the guys. Sebastian had been drinking coffee and eyeing a Wilson Combat CQB .45 ACP at Steve Barnett's Fine Guns, a couple doors down. Bernard had been flirting with the owner of Rose Drugs while she attempted to take inventory.

Lucille opened the door the moment Walter knocked. The old men filed inside. Lucille swiftly looked up and down the hall to ensure no one was snooping. She then quickly shut and locked the door. Sebastian sensed her anxiety and quickly looked at Walter. Lucille was rubbing her hands as she started to pace when Walter said, "Lucille, talk to us—tell us what's going on."

"It's gone," she blurted.

"What's gone?" Bernard asked as Walter rushed to where the bags had been.

"The money," Walter said, looking at the empty floor where over a million dollars in cash had very recently been sitting.

"That's right," Lucille said with a deep exhale. "It's all gone."

"How? What? What happened to it?" Sebastian asked.

Walter watched Lucille's eyes, and she prepared to answer Sebastian's question. Bernard scratched his head in confusion. Sebastian wondered if someone in the room had betrayed everyone's trust. He looked at Walter.

Lucille said, "I ran some errands, like I always do on Mondays, and when I got back it was gone."

"When is the last time you saw it?"

"Before I went to the store."

"Even the Kroger money?"

Lucille was about to cry. "Yes. It was all here to count and organize."

Sebastian rubbed his head in frustration. He wanted to scream. Bernard was still confused. Walter studied Lucille, who was now sitting at the kitchen table.

"Where's Bailey?" Walter firmly asked, biting hard on a cigar.

"I don't know. She left early this morning."

"Have you tried to call her cell?"

"Yes."

"And?"

"She doesn't answer."

"Did anyone else know about the money?"

"No."

"Could she be at the Gold Mine?"

"She doesn't work on Mondays."

"Where does she usually go on Mondays?"

"She's been goin' over to the W."

"What's that?" Walter asked, still unfamiliar with much of the area.

"The Mississippi University for Women. It's in Columbus."

"It was the first university for women in the United States," Sebastian added.

"She's takin' a course?"

"I'm not sure."

"Only once a week seems odd for a schedule," Walter stated.

"I don't know," Lucille replied weakly. She feared Bailey had the money but also wondered if one of the guys had broken into her room and taken it.

"Can't we call the police?" Bernard asked.

Everybody glared at Bernard.

"No, Bernard. We can't call the police. We stole the money first!" Walter said loudly.

"Shhhhh, my neighbors will hear us."

"They can't hear it thunder."

"We need to stay calm and figure this out," Walter said.

"I've figured it out," Sebastian said. "Haven't y'all ever heard that the second mouse gets the cheese?"

Bernard's eyes lit up. "'Cause the first mouse gets whacked by the trap, so the second mouse is safe to take the cheese."

"Exactly. With no worries of gettin' caught," Sebastian replied.

"You're saying we're the first mouse," Walter said as he tossed his chewed-up cigar into the trash.

"Yep, I'm saying not only do we not have the cheese, but we don't have any legal options."

Walter sighed as he looked around at everyone. Lucille was crying. There was a mixture of confusion, anger, and distrust. He said, "We need to talk to Bailey. I hate to jump to any conclusions."

CHAPTER 83

———— ☾ ————

LEVI QUIETLY WALKED THROUGH THE BACK DOOR INTO THE Gold Mine and immediately heard Moon Pie talking to himself. All the lights were off except in Moon Pie's office, where he was rummaging through desk drawers. Levi knew that he was troubled when he saw the pistol lying on the desk and Moon Pie looking like he hadn't slept in days.

"You okay, Moon?" Levi asked.

"What the hell do ya think?"

"I'm just askin'. Here's your clothes."

"Wadda them damn Mexicans say?"

"That they're gonna kill us if we don't come up with the money, but he didn't freak out or anything like I expected. He was actually calm, and it kinda spooked me."

"That's cuz they stole it and they got somethin' up their sleeve."

"How do you think they got the safe combination?"

"No clue. Hand me those bullets."

Levi handed him a half-empty box of 9 mm rounds. "I just don't see how they coulda figured it out."

"Those high-tech bastards probably got some kinda computer they hooked up to it and it went through the possible combinations. It don't matter how they got the money," he said as he tightly packed a bag with gear. "The point is, they got it."

"Hey, did you notice the plainclothes cop across the street, watching the building?"

"You sure it's a cop and not a freakin' Mexican hit man?"

"The car has a municipal tag."

"Dammit. I don't need their shit right now! I gotta lose him. He probably followed me from the jail and saw me get dropped off."

"How ya gonna shake him?"

Moon Pie stopped packing and then went to look out the front door. "We'll switch clothes, and I'll wear that cap you got on. Since we're about the same size, and he woulda seen you come in too, he'll think it's you leaving and that I'm still here."

"What about me? They'll be on me, and I need to get gone too."

"Let me think about it. I'll figure out something."

"You still goin' up north?"

"Nope, change of plans. Since Tam's got my good truck, I'm goin' to 'Bama to stay awhile with my taxidermist buddy."

"That's better. You'll be a lot closer if I need you."

"True. Here, we'll use these prepaid phones. I expect they're listenin' to mine." Moon Pie handed Levi a throw-down.

"I'm sure glad you're stayin' kinda close. Maybe we can talk our way outta this mess with the Mexicans or Tam might help us."

"Tam might...I've already thought about that. He owes me a favor now; I just don't know if he'd consider it a million-dollar favor. I just need to buy a little time until I can get him involved. I think he might stick up for me."

"Hard to put a price on freedom," Levi said as he sat down in a chair. "I'm serious. Maybe Tam would take us on full-time instead of this once-a-month shit and help us outta this bind."

"It's possible. I just gotta talk to him. We may have to start over—you know, reinvent ourselves. It's better than being dead. I'll call Mike on my way outta town and see if he'll talk to Tam."

"So whatcha need me to do?"

"Let's switch clothes. Can you get someone to come by and pick you up later?"

"Yeah, sure," Levi replied.

"Good. I'll leave your truck at the trailer. So when are you gonna skip town?"

"I don't know. I got this new girlfriend I really like, and I'm thinkin' she may be the one. I may just get on the houseboat and move up and down the river until things quiet down. That way I can still see my girl," Levi said as he pulled off his ball cap and shirt.

Moon Pie looked at him with disgust to mask his jealousy. He had always wanted a serious relationship but never seemed to find the right girl. His lifestyle seemed to attract ones that couldn't be trusted. "So who is it?"

"Bailey."

"You're shitting me."

"Nope."

"That little uppity bitch wouldn't give me the time of day."

"We've kinda hit it off."

Moon Pie was now standing in Levi's clothes, and from a distance, he could probably pass for him.

Moon Pie said, "Whatever. I'm goin' to the trailer to pick up some things, and then I have a few business deals before I leave. Watch the cop and call if he's followin' me. And if he don't follow me, I need you to stay here until I'm outta town. I'll call you."

"I got it."

"Good deal. I'll see ya, little brother."

"Good luck, Memphis."

Moon Pie stopped and turned. "This could get crazy. You up for it?"

"Oh yeah."

"You better watch out for Woody too."

"I got it."

"Okay. You take care of yourself, now." Moon Pie smiled and walked out the back door.

CHAPTER 84

━━━ ☾ ━━━

J ULIO AND GUILLERMO GOOGLED *WEST POINT, MISSISSIPPI*, before leaving Tennessee and quickly determined that the nicest place to stay was the Old Waverly Golf Club. Julio called and made reservations for them in a lake-view cottage. They had long since realized that they attracted much less attention staying in finer accommodations than they did in budget hotels. They needed to get in and out of town without rousing any suspicions, so for the next few days, he and Guillermo became Mexican cheese importers looking for new outlets in the Golden Triangle. Everybody knew there had been a recent sharp rise in the Hispanic population in the area.

Several hours later, once they checked in, they paid the lodging attendant with a black American Express card. The attendant later asked her boss if he had ever seen one. His eyes lit up in anticipation, and he nodded. He knew that these men could charge anything they wanted, even a house, a lot, or a lifetime club membership. The word quickly spread through the staff that high rollers were staying in cottage number three.

Guillermo used the Wi-Fi to check the location of the money. The locator hidden inside the bag placed it at the local police station. Guillermo switched the tracking device's identification

283

numbers to find the ankle unit on the redneck. It appeared to be in the parking lot of a government housing project in Aberdeen.

"What do you want to do, Julio?"

Julio was looking out the window at several mallard ducks swimming on Lake Waverly. He said, "The clubhouse is closed today, so let's first go into town to eat. Then we ride by the address to confirm the money is at a police station, and then we go find Mr. Pie. *Me gustaría mucho que hablar con él.*"

Guillermo drilled down further into both addresses and wondered if Bing maps had any bird's-eye views. While he was searching, he heard Julio work the tight action of his small pistol.

"*¿Guillermo, si le robaron nueve mil millones de dólares, qué haría?*" Julio asked.

Guillermo leaned back in his chair. He sat silent for a long moment, thinking. Finally he said, "If I had stolen the money, I would leave town quietly, never to be seen again. If I could not run—if I had to stay—I would claim someone else stole it."

"*Lo que causaría que usted permanezca?*"

"Children, wife, parents, maybe even a girlfriend, would cause me to stay."

"*Sí*, these things are important to you. But most drug runners are cold-blooded. They know the risks. They don't get attached to any place or person. You can't."

Julio paused for a long while and then said, "This behavior doesn't make sense."

CHAPTER 85

———— ☾ ————

TAM ARRIVED AT HIS GATED HIDEOUT IN BAYOU LA BATRE, Alabama, exhausted from the stress of being hunted. Alexa had attempted to call him several times, but he didn't trust her any longer. In his gut, he had known that the trip to Tupelo would be a mistake, but because Alexa was so crazy about Rascal Flatts and this was going to be her best bet to meet the band, he gave in. He should have trusted his instincts. He didn't believe she had knowingly participated in the sting, but she was now a substantial liability. Tam spread the word within his organization that no one was to have any form of communication with her. No text. No e-mail. No phone calls. Nothing. *She's on her own, at least until I can order a hit on her. It will have to be up close and personal, preferably to appear natural—possibly a slip and fall in a hotel shower. I can't risk what she might divulge under pressure.*

Moon Pie had been picked up for questioning, since he was in possession of the Mercedes's ignition key and because of his now clearly established association with an alleged drug dealer and escaped prisoner. Through the jailhouse grapevine, Tam had learned already that Moon Pie had kept his mouth shut about even knowing Tam. He realized that he had probably lost the Benz but wrote it off as a cost of doing business, albeit a very expensive one. Tam had never been a big fan of Moon Pie because he seemed to fly by the seat of his pants, and he used him for the one trade route only because he didn't have an alternative. Although Moon Pie had come through for Tam today, he had also lost the client's money. This had to be resolved before he would continue using Moon Pie. Tam respected loyalty, but he also demanded dependability. *About the only thing that didn't go to shit this weekend is that I still got my load of drugs*, Tam thought.

Tam needed to relax, to think through his next moves, but first, he had one piece of important unfinished business. He placed a hand on a black monitor outside a heavy metal door. Once the pad read his palm print, the door unlocked with a click and a hissing sound. Tam walked into the vault room, put on a pair of white cotton gloves, opened one of several large safes, and withdrew four stacks of bundled hundred-dollar bills. He closed and locked the safe and then walked over to a metal table in the center of the room. He removed an appropriately sized Tiffany box from the shelf under the table, placed the cash inside the box, and taped it closed.

After closing and locking the vault-room door, he called one of his most trusted associates. When he arrived, Tam gave him the box and a slip of paper with the name and address of a Vietnamese family in Biloxi.

Tam handed him the box and instructed, "Take this box and give it to the family tonight. Do not say anything else. Do not tell them where it came from."

The courier nodded his understanding and bowed slightly, leaving Tam alone.

Tam removed the gloves as he walked over to a bottle of Macallan eighteen-year-old single malt sitting on the bar.

CHAPTER 86

SEBASTIAN AND WALTER LEANED AGAINST THE RENTAL VAN and looked up at the old Henry Clay hotel. Only one other building in town even came close to it in terms of height. The hotel had changed names and ownership several times since being constructed in the mid-1840s. Walter chewed his cigar and imagined that this old building had seen countless interesting events. But none could rival someone walking through that front door carrying over a million dollars in cash. Both the old men were unsure what to do about the missing money or the missing Bailey.

"Bailey hasn't answered her phone all day," Walter finally said.

"Would you?"

"We should drive by her place. Maybe she told a neighbor where she was goin'."

"I'm ready when you are."

"What are we gonna do if we find her? Pull a pistol and rob her?"

"Yeah!" Sebastian said immediately, and then thought better of it. He continued, "I mean...maybe. Hell, I don't know."

They heard a car stop behind them and turned around at the same time. A police cruiser had stopped. The same officer they had bumped into Saturday night was smiling at them. Walter waved awkwardly.

"How y'all doin' today?"

"We're doin' just fine, Officer," Walter replied somewhat sarcastically, but the officer didn't pick up on it.

The cop, obviously happy to see them, said, "Big football game this weekend in Starkville. You guys goin'?"

"Nah, we'll probably just watch it on TV," Walter said, looking at Sebastian. "We don't really like crowds."

"Or long walks," Sebastian added.

"Yeah, I know. I gotta work the game. At any rate, I just wanted to stop by and thank y'all for the bag."

Walter and Sebastian traded looks of confusion.

"Y'all didn't have to do that. But I gotta tell ya, I really do appreciate it. It's perfect for my gear," he said.

Walter struggled for what to say or ask. He wanted to learn more but feared asking many questions. All he could come up with was, "I hope we got all the magazines out."

"Yes, sir. It was empty and laying on my desk. Thanks again. Gotta jump," the officer said. Then, with a salute, he drove off.

Sebastian and Walter looked at each other. They knew who it had to be. Only one other person was there Saturday night. At the same time they said, "Bernard!"

CHAPTER 87

———— ☾ ————

L EVI DIDN'T LIKE THE IDEA OF BEING ALONE IN THE GOLD
Mine, thinking about the Tennessee Mexicans that he
assumed were lurking somewhere in the shadows. Anticipating
that encounter was killing him. He used binoculars to make
sure that the police officer watching the Gold Mine was still
inside the unmarked car. Knowing that a cop was keeping an
eye on him was comforting, in a weird, ironic sort of way,
since he typically spent most of his time eluding the police.
Now that he knew they were actively watching, he appreciated
them.

He chuckled to himself as he dialed Moon Pie's cell phone.
"It worked. He's still out here," Levi said, adjusting the pistol
tucked into the waistband at his back. "And I'm kinda glad."

"As soon as I get my shit loaded and cross the state line, I'll
call ya."

"About how long you think?"

"Maybe an hour and a half. No more than two."

Levi was now sitting on the floor at the back of the lobby
in the dark, watching the police officer. "Sounds good. *Adiós,
amigo,*" he said, chuckling mockingly, and then flipped shut the
cell phone and exhaled. He was bait, and it wasn't a good feeling.

He leaned his head back and tried to think of Bailey. He wondered what she was doing. He couldn't take her earlier call, and he was considering whether he should try to reach her. She was everything he wanted in a partner and was different from other girls he had dated. She was smart and hardworking, went to church, and was a stunning natural beauty with a giant, caring heart. Levi knew that he was smitten. He also knew to have any hopes of a meaningful relationship with her, he was going to have to get a real job. Love is a powerful incentive, and Levi was suddenly feeling motivated.

After he had been sitting on the floor for about twenty minutes, a mud-covered Chevrolet pickup truck parked in front of the Gold Mine. Levi pulled himself deeper into the shadows as he watched the driver open his door and step out. Levi instantly recognized Jake Crosby, and a smile formed on his lips. Levi flipped open his cell and hit the redial key.

Moon Pie's patience had run thin with interruptions of his packing, but he resisted the urge to snap at Levi. He assumed the call was important. He answered, "Yeah?"

"You'll never guess who just drove up and is standing outside the Gold Mine," Levi said in a whisper.

"Who?"

"I wouldn't believe it if I wasn't seein' him right now with my own eyes."

"Dammit, Levi! I ain't got time for this shit. Just tell me who it is!"

Jake had walked to the front door and put his face and hands against the glass to look inside. Levi was invisible in the shadows behind a table, less than ten feet away.

"Jake Crosby."

"Well, hell fire. I'll be damned."

"Live and in person," Levi continued in a whisper.

"Is the cop still there?"

"Oh yeah. He's still sittin' across the street, pro'ly tryin' to figure out what the hell's goin' on."

"What's our boy Jake doing right now?"

"Tryin' real hard to see in…he's lookin' for something."

"That crazy bastard's lookin' for me!"

"You think he's got some gold he wants to sell?" Levi asked sarcastically.

"I think that note you handed him pushed him over the freakin' edge."

"He does kinda look nervous."

"Damn! I wish I was there. Shit! Look, I gotta go. Call me if he does anythin'," Moon Pie directed and then hung up.

CHAPTER 88

———— ☾ ————

W HEN BAILEY GLANCED OUT THE WINDOW AND SAW
Woody aggressively walking toward the old hotel, she
knew it meant trouble. He had been to her grandmother's apartment, and locked doors had never slowed him down. He would
pick the lock, or more times than not, he would just kick the door
in.

The old men and her grandmother were not around. As she
looked for something to use to defend herself, she saw the cash-
filled luggage and knew Woody would assume the bags were hers
and that she was leaving. He wouldn't hesitate to dump out the
contents to make a point that she wasn't going anywhere.

In that moment, Bailey devised a plan. She grabbed her purse
and the luggage and took off for the stairwell next to the elevator.
She dashed down the stairs one floor and waited on the landing
until she heard the elevator pass. She opened the stairwell door
and quickly punched the down button. Then she retrieved the
suitcases as she nervously waited on the elevator. She held her
breath when the door slowly opened. It was empty. She quickly
pulled the bags inside and punched the button for the lobby.

Bailey hurried to her car, loaded it, and pulled away from
the hotel and Woody as fast as she dared. She knew that he was

inside her grandmother's apartment at that moment, searching for her or any sign of where she was. If she hadn't fled with the money, neither she nor it would have survived.

She said a quick prayer of thanksgiving as she tried to think of a place to hide—someplace where no one would think to look. Places like the Best Western in Columbus or the Holiday Inn Express in Starkville would not work; they were too obvious and too close to home. She needed privacy, a quiet place to sort out what she had done and what she would do. The first place that popped into her mind was the Golden Moon hotel at the Pearl River Resort in Philadelphia, Mississippi. It was only about an hour's drive. With its luxury rooms, great restaurants, and a spa, she could be pampered while making plans.

Not fully thinking through the ramifications, she decided not to tell the others for a day or so to protect them, and the money, from Woody. She feared that if he threatened or hurt one of them, they might reveal her location.

She concocted her cover story on the way. She transformed herself into a country-music songwriter who needed extreme privacy to finish several songs...and she said that she might have a guest joining her later. The Golden Moon's front desk understood Bailey's need for discretion and allowed her to pay cash without asking for identification.

Bailey lay on the king-size bed in one of the hotel's VIP suites. Her luggage was stacked neatly in the far corner. She sat up to take a drink of bottled water. She rationalized what she had done; she knew that the group would be proud of her for protecting their money. She had identified a threat and reacted.

Her whole life, she hadn't had many material things or even time to herself. She had placed all of her dreams on hold while she worked to take care of her mother and pay all of her medical and then funeral bills. Bailey was beginning to see the money as a chance to escape her past and start fresh. But she also was beginning to hear disapproving voices, clear as day, of all those people who had been instrumental in raising her. She heard her mother, her grandmother, and one of her Sunday-school teachers she had long ago forgotten.

She lay back on the bed and wrestled with right and wrong, marveling at the amount of money in the room with her. She desperately wanted to recapture some of the time she had missed while taking care of others.

Out of the blue, she began thinking of Levi. There was something attractive about him—the person. It was something you wouldn't notice necessarily if you only briefly talked to him. *You gotta get to really know him before it's noticeable. I guess it's not so much noticed really as it is revealed,* she thought.

Levi made her smile, and he made her belly-laugh—something she hadn't done in the last five years. She looked at her phone, wishing he would call or text. She wanted to talk to him. Thanksgiving was in a few days. She had never been with a boyfriend for whom she was thankful. As Bailey grappled with new emotions and old thoughts, she drifted off to sleep.

CHAPTER 89

———— ↄ ————

S EBASTIAN AND WALTER ASKED LUCILLE AND BERNARD TO
meet in the library of the old hotel. Outside the big windows, Bernard stared at the traffic on Commerce Street. It was as though he were in a trance. This meeting demanded privacy, so Walter asked the two other residents, playing cards, if they would leave. Once they did, Walter shut the door, turned to Lucille, and fired the first question: "Have you heard from Bailey?"

"No. She's not answering her phone."

"Is there some family she could be staying with?"

"Hell, she's got over a million bucks; she could stay anywhere she damn well wants," Sebastian aggressively chimed in.

"We don't *know* that she took it," Lucille said defensively.

Walter took a deep breath and held his hand up, indicating Sebastian needed to remain calm. Walter prodded, "Do you have *any* idea where she might be?"

"Why? What are y'all gonna do?"

"We just wanna *talk* to her," Sebastian offered.

"Y'all sound like the cops on them TV shows."

"Lucille, don't you want to know what happened?" Walter asked. "This isn't like Bailey...but the truth is, for this much money, people will do crazy things."

Lucille remained quiet but fidgeted in her chair.

Walter tried to read her body language and get her to talk instead of shutting down. "What we did was wrong, and now somebody's wronged us. We just wanna know who."

"And why," Sebastian said. Then he added. "Although...I suppose we know *why*."

Lucille glared at Sebastian.

Walter knew that he needed to defuse the situation. "Okay, everybody, let's just stay calm and focus."

Walter shifted his attention to Bernard, who was still staring out the window. He was watching two Mexican men standing on the sidewalk. They were looking at the hotel building as though they were considering buying it. They made eye contact with him and then walked away.

"Do you know them, Bernard?" Walter asked, taking a hard look at the men walking down the sidewalk. "Bernard!" Walter said loudly enough that Bernard jumped. "Do you know them?"

"Who? Those two? Naw, I've never seen 'em before in my life," Bernard answered.

"That was odd. Kinda creepy," Walter said as he realized everyone could see them. "It's like we're in an aquarium and those guys were just watching."

"Or a zoo," Sebastian offered.

"Bernard, did you take that big bag to the police station?" Walter asked.

"Yeah, after Bailey and I bought some luggage for the money...I knew the police officer really wanted it."

"Okay, just checking. We ran into him earlier and didn't know how it got to him."

Bernard looked at everyone at the table. "What? Did I do somethin' wrong?"

"No, that's fine."

"So what are we gonna do now that we've lost all our money?" Sebastian asked. Then he added, more to himself than the group, "I don't think my heart can take any more breakin' and enterin'."

"I don't know. I sure would like to talk to Bailey. Anybody got any ideas?" Walter asked, looking at Lucille, who was waving at a guy standing on the sidewalk who was staring at them. He looked like he had just stepped out of an Abercrombie & Fitch catalog, except nothing was pressed.

"Who the hell is that?" Sebastian asked suspiciously.

"That's Levi. Bailey works with him at the Gold Mine," Lucille said.

Walter smiled. "Really? Invite him in. I'd like to meet him. We can finish this discussion later."

CHAPTER 90

———— ☾ ————

S AMANTHA SAT QUIETLY AT HER DESK IN A STATE OF MILD shock after the three old men explained the current situation. She would not have believed them if she hadn't been in the Kroger meetings. After a long silence, she stood when there was a knock at her outer-office door. She walked to her coffeepot and filled a Styrofoam cup on her way to answer the door. The three men watched.

When she opened it, a middle-aged man gawked back, nervously asking, "Where'd the marriage counselor move to?"

"Are you really having marriage problems?"

"She was good to…you know…talk to."

Sam handed him the cup of coffee, saying, "It's black, just like your eyes will be when your wife finds out what you're doing. Go down to the lobby and drink it, and think about what you'll lose if your wife finds out that you've been cheating on her." Samantha slammed the door and marched back into her office, where the old men were wild-eyed. "Men," she said in disgust.

"Half," Bernard said.

"Excuse me?"

"You lose half of everything in a divorce…I've lost half of everything three times. That's why I'm so broke I can't pay attention."

Sebastian snickered, and everyone shifted in their chairs while Sam coldly looked them each in the eyes. When she got to Walter, she said, "Just so I understand, the money we were gonna give back to Kroger is gone?"

Walter, knowing his tail could be in a crack, sighed and said, "Yes."

"And yet somehow, the three of you managed to lay your hands on nearly a million more dollars without getting caught or killed."

Bernard smiled proudly and answered while Walter and Sebastian groaned. "That's why we're here. We want you to do some investigatin' to see if you can find where Bailey Worden is. We know she's got it."

"You've been watching too many *Perry Mason* reruns. I'm not an investigator," she informed them.

"Can't you hire one?" Bernard asked.

"And pay him with what?"

"When we find the money, there will be plenty," Sebastian said hopefully.

"Guys, I'm afraid y'all may be close to getting in some serious trouble."

Nobody said a word. They all looked at the floor. To Sam they looked like three grade-schoolers in the principal's office.

"Where on earth did y'all steal the money, and who's Bailey Worden?"

"Is this…what's the word?" Sebastian asked.

"*Privileged*," Sam almost screamed. "And whether I like it or not, I'm your attorney. So, yes, sir, what you tell me is privileged and will remain confidential. Now, tell me everything. Start at the beginning."

CHAPTER 91

———— ☾ ————

From where Jake was parked near the entrance to the mobile-home park, he could see Moon Pie's trailer—the third single-wide on the left. A restored Bronco with the back open was parked next to it. The trailer park had been around since the mid-sixties, and several of the homes appeared to be that old. About half of the trailers had old tires on their roofs. Next to an overflowing green Dumpster was the frame of a swing set from which a small skinned deer carcass was hanging by its legs in a gambrel.

Jake had called in a favor from a Rotary Club friend who worked for the police department to get Moon Pie's address. He still couldn't believe that no one in law enforcement had warned him that this guy was living less than twenty miles away. Jake had also learned that Moon Pie drove a tricked-out late-model FJ Cruiser, which he couldn't see parked anywhere.

Since Moon Pie's vehicle wasn't around, Jake decided to sneak a look in the windows. He pulled down his Mossy Oak fleece jacket to cover his pistol, which was jutting out of his back pocket. He then eased the pickup door shut. His heart was racing. He took a long, deep breath and slowly let it out through his nose in an effort to calm his nerves. Although he couldn't see anyone, Jake assumed that someone was probably watching out for anything suspicious.

The windows at the rear of the first trailer were all covered in aluminum foil. Next to it was a sporty new orange Camaro that undoubtedly cost more than the trailer. The second trailer appeared to be unoccupied. Tall grass grew all around, and all of the window curtains were closed. Jake hugged the edge of the aluminum house as he peeked around the rear corner at Moon Pie's trailer. From this vantage, he could see several bags were being packed into the back of the Bronco.

Jake's cell phone rang, causing him to jump. He quickly disconnected the call from his office and placed the phone on silent. He didn't move for several minutes in case Moon Pie or whoever was loading the Bronco had heard it. Jake said a silent prayer of thanks when there was no reaction to his turkey-gobbling ringtone.

Moon Pie's trailer appeared to be deserted. Jake tried to listen for any sounds coming from inside, but he couldn't distinguish any noise because of the constant drone of training flights overhead from the nearby Columbus Air Force Base. He had to look in the open window. Jake hurried across the dirt patch between the trailers and pressed flat against Moon Pie's. Instinctively, Jake touched the pistol in his back pocket. It comforted him. Jake looked at the trailers on the opposite side of the park but couldn't see anyone, so he turned to look in the window.

The inside of the trailer was a mess. Jake didn't notice anything of importance. He really didn't know what he was expecting to see, but he wanted a closer look. He eased to the next window. It too was open. He peered in and didn't see or hear anyone or anything. The trailer appeared to be empty. Jake knew that if someone were walking around, he'd hear footsteps.

Jake slid down the side of the trailer. His heart raced. After quickly looking around to see if anyone was watching, he tried the handle. It was unlocked. He quickly drew his pistol, slowly opened the door, and quietly stepped inside. His body raced with a mixture of fear and the dump of adrenaline. *How in the hell do the police do this shit every day?* he wondered.

The trailer looked as if it had just been ransacked. It smelled of stale beer and cigarettes. Jake couldn't hear anyone or anything. The place looked like it had never been cleaned. Hunting magazines, beer cans, and empty ammo boxes were strewn about. There were several antlers on the walls and the worst flying-turkey mount Jake had ever seen. As he looked around the living room, the smell of cigarette smoke was almost overwhelming, and then he realized that there was a cloud of smoke in the room. He wheeled around toward the kitchen and saw an almost completely burned cigarette, long with ashes, resting in a clear ashtray. He instantly knew that Moon Pie was in the trailer. His hands were shaking as he quietly eased the pistol's safety into the off position. Jake's logical, rational side was being blocked by a primitive emotion—the one that desired to kill the person haunting and tormenting his family.

As Jake started across the tiny den, he caught a blur out of the corner of his eye and spun around just in time to face his attacker. The adrenaline coursing through him significantly impaired his fine motor skills, causing his attempted shot to be off its mark. The attacker pistol-whipped him before he could squeeze the trigger again. Jake's gun hit the floor an instant before he did.

Moon Pie kicked Jake's pistol out of reach and then stood over him. The acrid smell of gunpowder filled the room. Moon Pie put his free hand on his burning side. His fingers were wet and warm. He knew he had been hit but felt no pain. That would come later, when the adrenaline subsided. He pulled up his shirt and saw where the bullet had struck him. Another two inches and it would have missed. *Dammit*, Moon Pie thought as he lightly touched the wound.

He walked over to the front door to see if anyone was coming after hearing the gunshot. When he was satisfied that no one either had heard the shot or cared enough to investigate, he closed the door and locked it. He walked over to Jake's gun, picked it up, and then put it into the back waistband of his pants. Moon Pie, breathing heavily, had a wild look in his eyes as he stood over Jake, trying to decide what he would do next. He looked again at his wound and knew that he would live but that Jake Crosby wouldn't.

CHAPTER 92

———— (————

A FTER DRIVING BY THE POLICE STATION FOUR TIMES, THE Tennessee Mexicans were convinced that the money bag was inside. The GPS tracking program installed on the laptop showed the bag's location in the middle of the municipal police station. The Mexicans were pissed. They turned their attention to the ankle bracelet on Moon Pie.

According to the tracking program, the Chocolate City Club was their next stop. They closed the computer when they pulled through the packed parking lot of the juke joint. By the types of vehicles in the lot, they knew that they would not be welcome. Neither one wanted to go inside to look for Moon Pie, so they quickly decided to wait and follow Moon Pie to a more private location. No matter how well armed they were, this was not the place to make a scene. The Mexicans drove back to West Point and parked downtown by the granite memorial to Delta-blues legend Howlin' Wolf.

"Why he was named Howlin' Wolf?" Guillermo asked in broken English, shutting his car door.

"Who knows? Why would somebody be named Moon Pie? This Southern rural culture fascinates me," Julio said, as he lit a long cigar.

"Americanos locos."

Julio walked closer to the monument and carefully read the inscription. "Guillermo, take my picture. Señor Wolf is famous."

Guillermo snapped a quick picture of his boss with his camera phone. He marveled at how Julio acclimated himself to the area before a confrontation. Guillermo knew this wisdom was the result of years working the streets. It provided Julio with the confidence to move slowly and precisely when the situation warranted. Julio made it a point to understand his quarry.

"What now, *señor*?" Guillermo asked, anxious to do something of value.

"I want to go back by the old hotel where the money bag stayed for a day and see what we can learn. We may have missed something," Julio said, pointing with his cigar.

"Tengo hambre. ¿Desea comer?"

"We will eat soon. *Paciencia*," Julio replied, checking his holstered weapon hidden under his camel-hair jacket.

CHAPTER 93

———— ☾ ————

ITHAD BEEN A LONG SUNDAY FOR LEVI, HANGING OUT AT THE
Gold Mine, waiting. Since he and Moon Pie had exchanged
clothes, the local cop watching the store had him pinned down
until Levi was sure that Moon Pie was safely out of the state.
He was growing more concerned about the Tennessee Mexicans
finding him or mistaking him for Moon Pie. Levi finally called
a friend to give him a ride to Moon Pie's trailer. As expected, the
police officer followed, and when Levi got out at the trailer park,
he waved the police car over.

When the police officer pulled up and rolled down his window, Levi leaned in and asked, "Afternoon, Officer. Is there anythin' I can do for ya?"

The confused policeman stared at Levi for a few seconds,
processing the incongruity of the person asking the question
wearing Moon Pie's clothes. He grunted and drove off.

Once inside Moon Pie's trailer, Levi grabbed a cold beer from
the refrigerator and started to look around. The place appeared
to be messier than when he had left. The first thing Levi thought
was that the Mexicans had found the place and trashed it, looking for their money. Levi quickly glanced into his small bedroom.
Since it looked exactly as he had left it, he assumed that Moon Pie

must have left in a hurry. Levi changed out of Moon Pie's clothes into his own, packed a bag, and left to go find Bailey, driving an old, uninsured pickup truck that Levi hated.

When Bailey wasn't at her apartment, Levi went straight to the Henry Clay Hotel and found himself standing out front, waving at her grandmother inside.

Lucille didn't really like that Walter and Sebastian were so anxious to talk to Levi, but she too wanted to know about Bailey, so she motioned for him to come inside.

After Lucille made the initial introductions, she offered Levi a seat at the table. She smiled at him as he sat down. "Levi, have you heard from Bailey?"

"No, ma'am. That's why I came by here. I was hopin' to find her."

"When's the last time you talked to her?" Sebastian asked.

"Late Saturday night, or actually Sunday morning when I dropped her off here. Wait a minute—so y'all don't know where she's at either?" Levi asked.

"No, we don't. We thought you might."

Levi quickly stood, almost knocking over his chair. The expression on his face was one of anger mixed with concern. He yelled, "Woody!"

Lucille quickly glanced at the old men, who shrugged, and then at Levi and said, "I doubt it. She hasn't mentioned him in a few days."

"We have to find out. He ain't no good, Miss Lucille."

Walter looked at Sebastian. They hadn't considered Woody, since they assumed that they had scared him sufficiently enough to stay clear of Bailey. It was possible that she had reached out to him; if so, that would be enough encouragement for him to ignore Sebastian's .357 Magnum warning. They now had to consider that Bailey, with or without help from Woody, had stolen the money and that they had run off together.

Bernard noticed the silent exchange between Walter and Sebastian, and wanting to participate, he said, "Never trust a guy who has a monogrammed can of tobacco."

Sebastian and Walter looked nervously at each other. They did not want Bernard talking.

Levi didn't respond. *Yes! That's it. It was a* W *and not an* M. *Woody stole the money,* he thought.

Everyone noticed Levi's eyes light up. Walter asked, "Levi? Levi? Levi, what's wrong? What are you thinkin'?"

Levi didn't respond. He quickly pulled out his cell phone as he headed for the door. The third "Levi" finally broke through, and he said, "I gotta find Woody."

"I'm goin' with ya," Sebastian said as he began to rise from his chair.

"No, sir! I gotta do this alone."

Levi was out the door and in his truck before Sebastian was fully standing.

CHAPTER 94

———— ☾ ————

I T WAS 8:00 P.M. MORGAN WAS IN HER BEDROOM PACING, WOR-
ried about Jake. Since the Dummy Line incident, it was
extremely unusual, even when he was hunting, for him not to
respond to calls or texts. Jake never went anywhere—not even
the toilet—without his BlackBerry. If he couldn't take a call, he
would at least text a reply. Morgan always received some type of
response within a few minutes. She sensed that something was
very wrong.

Katy was sitting at the kitchen table, diagramming sentences
for her English class, but she couldn't concentrate. Plus, she could
hear her mom on the telephone in the bedroom, calling people,
looking for her dad. The more people Morgan talked to, the more
upset Katy became.

As she walked back into the kitchen, Morgan saw Katy quietly crying. She realized that Katy had heard her frantic conversations. "Katy, honey, don't cry. Dad's probably at a meeting and
forgot to tell me about it, that's all."

"Why won't he answer his phone?"

Morgan squatted in front of Katy and put her hands on her
arms. "Maybe he forgot to charge the battery. You know how for-
getful Dad is. Everything's gonna be okay."

Katy wanted to believe what Morgan was saying. She took several deep breaths and began to calm. Morgan knew too well that the last several days had taken a toll on Katy and brought up all of the memories of the killings a year and a half earlier.

"Momma, kids at school are saying that there's a man tryin' to kill us."

"Who's saying that?"

"Jenna said it, and so has Haley."

"Honey, that's just talk. Ya know, sometimes people like to say things...even when they don't know what they're talkin' about."

"Jenna said her uncle told her, Momma."

Morgan tried to think who that might be and didn't know. In a small town like West Point, it was difficult, if not impossible, to keep anything secret. She wondered just how much to tell Katy. "Honey, there's this one man from that gang that night in the woods who the police are watching. They promised that they would keep an eye on him."

"There was a policeman at school today, and Jenna said he was there to watch over me to make sure nobody got me."

Morgan had been to countless counseling sessions for her own issues, so the first thing that popped out of her mouth was the ambiguous "How does that make you feel?"

"Safe. Someone, besides you and Dad, is concerned about me," Katy replied.

"Honey, we wanna make sure you're safe...always. And having that policeman there—well, that's good. Isn't it?"

"I guess so."

"Katy, honey, everything's gonna be okay. Please finish your homework. I have to make a few more phone calls, okay?"

"Okay, Mom. Thanks."

Morgan gave Katy a hug, kissed her forehead, and headed toward her bedroom.

"Mom?"

Morgan turned around and said, "Yes, dear?"

"Where's Scout?"

"I don't know, sweetheart. We'll find her," Morgan replied, trying to hide her own escalating emotions.

Scout was part of the family. She had been Jake's puppy when Morgan and Jake had gotten married. Now Morgan had to find their dog and her husband. She walked into their bedroom and pulled out the local phone book. She leafed through it until she found the chief of police's home phone number. She knew his wife from Junior Auxiliary. She exhaled deeply and dialed. A tear dropped onto the open book.

CHAPTER 95

———— ☾ ————

HAVING JAKE WALK INTO HIS TRAILER WAS A POORLY TIMED but pleasant surprise for Moon Pie, and he planned to take full advantage of the situation. For a long moment, he watched Jake's heavy breathing as he lay on the floor, blood from his head slowly soaking an old canvas decoy bag. He had decided to haul Jake into the woods and kill him slowly before heading to Alabama to hide from the cops and the Mexicans.

With Jake still unconscious, Moon Pie quickly looked through drawers until he found a bag of large, thick, black zip ties. He bound Jake's hands and tightly secured his ankles. Moon Pie was confident that the heavy-duty plastic ties would hold.

Moon Pie found several white socks that he duct taped over his bullet wounds in hopes that the pressure would stop the bleeding. He then washed up and changed into clean clothes.

He located his stun gun and did a battery test with a quick press of the trigger. The blue electrical arc between the metal posts reminded Moon Pie of a tiny, personal bolt of lightning. The first thing he had done after buying the device was to test it on a neighbor's cat that always sat on the hood of his Bronco. He never saw the cat again. The thought brought a sinister smile to his face as he looked down at Jake. *This oughta keep that son of a bitch in line.*

Moon Pie placed the stun gun in a coat pocket as he thought about what to do with Jake's truck. It was much newer than the Bronco and would be significantly more comfortable to drive. And with thousands of Z-71 Chevy trucks in the South, he would be able to blend in, more so than in a restored old Bronco. Plus, it would only be a matter of time before the Mexicans learned that he owned the Bronco, and they would be looking for it. Moon Pie found Jake's truck keys in his front left pocket and then went to look for the truck.

Moon Pie quickly found it and backed the truck next to his Bronco. He then swapped everything from it to Jake's truck. Jake was still unconscious when he finished loading everything, including the frozen head and cape of the big full-velvet whitetail he had told the taxidermist about. Moon Pie knew his buddy would pay top dollar for it.

Moon Pie splashed cold water on Jake's face, waking him abruptly. The outlaw squatted down next to Jake's face and said in a menacing tone, "Hey, sunshine, you comfy?"

Jake's head pounded, and even as he struggled to free his arms and legs, he realized it was useless. His breathing was labored. Jake watched the wild eyes of his captor as he finally asked, "Are you Moon Pie?"

Moon Pie laughed out loud and then said, "Yep. That's what they used to call me. But I go by Memphis now." He watched Jake's reaction. He liked that Jake had never known what he looked like. Now it didn't really matter.

"And you're the guy who killed Johnny Lee and Reese," he said, shaking his head disapprovingly. Then he added, "You musta caught 'em by surprise—too much of a chickenshit to take 'em on face-to-face, I guess."

Jake struggled to sit up but couldn't. He asked, "So...is that why you been followin' my family?"

"I don't know what you're talkin' about. Look, *you* broke into my house. Guess you ain't ever heard of the Castle Doctrine. You stupid shit! I got every right to shoot and kill your ass right now in the name of self-defense. There ain't a jury in the great state of Mississippi that'd convict me. Hell, I doubt that I'd even get arrested."

Jake realized he had been an idiot to come after Moon Pie. He had let his anger get the better of him. No one, not one soul, knew where he was. He wanted to keep Moon Pie talking, to buy some time to devise a plan to get out of this mess. He asked, "What about last night?"

"What about it? I watched a football game, bro. Right here. Got two neighbors that'll alibi me."

"You weren't at the Rascal Flatts concert last night?"

Moon Pie was enjoying Jake's confusion. He said, "Hell no. Sat right here and watched a good ol' slobber-knocker on TV and drank some beers."

Jake didn't believe a word of what Moon Pie was saying. He'd been a stockbroker long enough to recognize a lie when he heard one. He looked around for his gun.

Moon Pie knew what he was looking for and pulled it out of his waistband, waving it in front of Jake. "This what you're looking for? Sweet piece. I always wanted a Ruger. Guess what? Now I got me one." He aimed it at Jake's forehead, closing one eye to look down the sights.

Jake knew that he was toying with him, and from the look in Moon Pie's eyes, it was clear that he was capable of anything and everything.

"What now?" Jake asked.

"You and I are gonna take a little ride to a very remote swamp, and we'll see how long you can hold your breath," Moon Pie said with an evil smile.

"I'm not goin'."

Moon Pie pulled out the stun gun and squeezed the trigger, letting the electricity pulse for a long moment, and then calmly replied, "It don't look to me like you gotta choice." He chuckled as he brought the bright blue current so close to Jake's eyes that for a moment Jake believed Moon Pie was going to blind him.

Jake was angry with himself and furious at Moon Pie. In an attempt to mask his fear, he yelled, "I want you to leave my family alone or I'm gonna kill you!"

"I want you to shut the hell up!" Moon Pie said and then touched the two metal probes into Jake's neck and squeezed the trigger, instantly sending 4.5 million volts through him. Jake began flopping convulsively as Moon Pie counted to four.

Jake lay still. His eyes rolled back in his head. The smell of burning flesh made Moon Pie laugh. He carried Jake to his truck and folded him into the backseat. Moon Pie went back inside to clean up the blood on the floor. When he finished, he picked up an old decoy bag, thinking it was perfect for hiding a dead bald eagle.

CHAPTER 96

———— ☾ ————

LEVI PARKED IN FRONT OF WOODY'S PARENTS' HOUSE. WOODY still lived with his folks and bullied both. Levi had heard Bailey talk about how Woody's mother cooked whatever he wanted to eat, made his bed every morning, did his laundry, and ironed his dark-blue pants and work shirts, with his name embroidered above the left chest pocket. Woody treated his mother like crap, and that was reason enough for Levi to despise him. Levi loved his momma.

Twenty seconds after Levi knocked on the door, the porch light came on and a woman's soft voice asked, "Who is it?"

"My name's Levi. I'm a friend of Woody's."

"Who?"

Levi smiled and then said, "My name's Levi. I'm a friend of Woody's. Is he home?"

"No. He's not here."

Levi expected that the couple were probably scared to open the door because of Woody's lowlife friends.

"Ma'am, do you know where he is?"

"He's at work."

Levi could confirm that easily with a drive-by of the steel mill's parking lot. If Woody's car was there, it would greatly reduce the likelihood that Woody had stolen the money. Levi knew that if Woody had come into a large sum of money, he would never weld again.

"Thank you. I'm sorry to have bothered you. Have a good night," Levi said and then walked off the porch to his car.

When he got behind the wheel, he could see Woody's parents looking through a window at him. As he backed out of the driveway, the porch light darkened. He thought about the old couple and was glad they had each other. That made him think of Bailey, and he wondered why she hadn't called. He tried to think of reasons he hadn't heard from her. She had had fun at the concert, he could tell. His thoughts quickly went to the far edge, and he wondered if the Tennessee Mexicans somehow knew about her and had kidnapped her for leverage.

Levi grabbed his prepaid cell and dialed Moon Pie's number. Moon Pie, out of breath, answered on the third ring.

"Man, I'm glad you called," Moon Pie said before Levi could say anything.

Levi smiled knowingly. Moon Pie needed something. That's why he answered the phone this time but not the fifteen other times Levi had called today.

"I was just checkin' on you to see if you made it."

"Nah, not yet. I got delayed. I'll tell you about it later. Get me some big bandages and some hydrogen peroxide, and meet me at the Chevron station on 45, where you turn to go to Caledonia, in about an hour or so," Moon Pie demanded.

Levi could hear a different pitch and cadence in his half brother's voice. He sensed excitement and stress. "You okay?"

"Yeah, I just gotta bad wound that won't stop bleeding."

"You get cut?"

"I got shot."

"Shot! What the hell happened?"

"I ain't got time to tell ya. I'm okay. Just meet me there," Moon Pie said and then abruptly hung up.

Levi couldn't believe it. Moon Pie was deep into something bad, something that had gotten him shot. Levi was fairly sure that it wasn't a jealous husband, since Moon Pie had mentioned on their return trip from picking up the Mexicans' cash that he hadn't been with a woman in several weeks. *That's it! It's them damn Mexicans*, he thought as he drove Military Road back into town.

As Levi passed the Columbus Country Club, his phone rang. When he looked down and saw the number calling, he immediately hit the send button to answer, forgetting everything else. "Hey, babe, I'm glad you called."

"You are?"

"Of course. Are you okay?"

"Yeah, I'm…I'm…I'm just kinda bummed out. I've got a lot on my mind."

"Wanna talk?" Levi asked, turning onto the entrance ramp for Highway 82. He was going to check on Woody at work. He added, "I'm a great listener."

"I need to. I wanna ask you a question."

"Where are you? I'll come to you."

"No. First, I need to ask you a few questions, and I'm scared I'll run you off."

"Run me off?"

"It's possible."

"Not really, so ask away," he said.

Bailey took a deep breath. "Okay, the last few weeks have been really fun, and I feel like we've got somethin' special goin'. I need to know if you feel it too."

Levi smiled, thinking of her struggling to ask this question. "Yes, of course I feel it too, and I don't like bein' away from you or not knowin' where you're at."

Bailey beamed. "That's good. I'm not sayin' it's goin' anywhere serious, but I just know it feels different and that maybe it could."

"I agree. We've got potential."

"Exactly…and, well…I need to know if you'll still be my friend and feel that way if you find out I did something really, really stupid."

"Stupid? Like dyed your hair orange or stupid like made a sex tape?"

Bailey sighed deeply. "You're gonna hate me."

"Bailey, try me."

"I helped steal something."

"Well, can you give it back?"

"It's not that simple. Others are involved, and I'm sure they're pissed at me."

"Bailey, everybody makes mistakes."

"Yeah, I keep tellin' myself that, but it's not helpin'."

"Who are the others?"

"My grandmomma and her friends."

Levi thought about the group at the table and how anxious the men were to find Bailey.

"What did y'all do? Rob a bank?" he asked with a chuckle.

"Kinda."

Levi was stunned and suddenly had an inkling of what may have occurred and why she might be feeling so remorseful. "Bailey, where are you?"

"Are you mad? I'm not a bad person," she said, starting to cry. "At least I didn't use to be."

"No, I'm not mad. I wanna help. I don't want you gettin' hurt. Where are you? I need to see you."

"I'm at the Golden Moon Casino hotel in Philadelphia."

"Don't leave, and don't let anyone into your room. I'm comin' down there right now, and I promise we'll work all this out. Okay?"

"Okay," she said and felt some relief.

"I'll be there in an hour. Promise me you'll be there."

"I will."

"And Bailey, I still feel the same way. Nothing's changed."

Levi stomped on the gas pedal, and the old truck's engine roared.

CHAPTER 97

————— ☾ —————

M OON PIE'S GUNSHOT WOUND WAS BEGINNING TO BURN white-hot. While straining to load Jake into the backseat, he caused the wound to open up. He could now feel blood running down his side from both the entrance and exit wounds, only six inches apart above his hip. With his right hand, he could apply pressure with his middle finger and his thumb, but the pain intensified as he did so. To combat the intense throbbing, he swigged straight Jack Daniels as he drove toward the massive swamp.

In warm weather, the area was home to water moccasins, timber rattlers, wild hogs, alligators, and enough chiggers and mosquitoes to drive the unprepared crazy. In November it was just cold, muddy, and desolate. Migrating waterfowl sought refuge in the shallow sloughs, and white-tailed deer bedded in the river-cane thickets. Beavers flourished, coyotes howled, and mythical black panthers were thought to inhabit the vast oak flats surrounded by half-circle-shaped old river sloughs. This was the ancient hunting ground of the Chickasaw Indians. The Spanish conquistador and explorer Hernando de Soto traveled these same woods on his journey to the Mississippi River. As the crow flies, just a few miles south was an Indian village that had been home to thousands. Now it was at the bottom of Columbus Lake, forever preserved, albeit under silt and river water.

The leafless trees were devoid of color in the truck's headlights as Moon Pie pulled up to a locked gate on a seldom-traveled gravel road. Moon Pie knew this area well. He was familiar with every logging road, and he knew of a forty-acre pond that the Corps of Engineers managed strictly for ducks. On the river side of the pond was a corrugated steel pipe. The pipe was just wide enough to drop a man into it. It went straight down ten or twelve feet and then turned ninety degrees and continued another fifty feet under a manmade levee, discharging into another wetland. This pipe functioned to maintain a maximum water level so ducks could feed on the native plants in the shallow water. If the water level rose above the top of the pipe, it flowed down and out the other side.

This simple, effective water level control worked flawlessly, until beavers packed mud and limbs around the lip of the pipe, causing the lake level to rise several inches. Moon Pie knew the busy beavers had this lake holding at least six inches of water more than normal. He planned to stuff Jake into the pipe and leave him. Moon Pie would tear out some of the beaver construction, allowing the water to slowly drown Jake inside the pipe. Moon Pie relished the idea of Jake's slow death. Even if he didn't drown first, he would die from hypothermia. It didn't matter to Moon Pie what the ultimate cause of death was just so long as it was slow and terrifying. Since the pipe was full of tree limbs and debris, Moon Pie thought Jake's body—whole—would never flow out the other side. Moon Pie smiled at the thought of Jake stuck inside a dark pipe with ice-cold water washing over him, knowing that death was coming and there wasn't a thing he could do to stop it, slow it down, or even speed it up.

Moon Pie realized that, since he was in Jake's truck, he didn't have his universal gate key—a stolen pair of Klein thirty-six-inch bolt cutters. He glanced back at Jake, who had started to come to on the drive, but another jolt from the stun gun knocked him out again. Moon Pie grunted as he opened the door and stepped outside to search Jake's gull-wing toolbox for something he could use to cut off the lock.

"Damn Goody Two-shoes," he muttered, slamming closed the lid after not finding anything helpful.

Moon Pie grabbed his pistol from under the driver's seat and shut the truck door. The third shot disabled the lock.

The gunshots woke Jake. He was extremely disoriented and tried to sit up but couldn't. His body wouldn't respond. Each pistol shot made him flinch. *What's going on? Where the hell am I?* he thought.

When Moon Pie opened the truck door, the dome light illuminated a pink Mississippi State ball cap lying on the floorboard that Jake had bought for Katy but hadn't given to her yet. Jake's mind immediately raced to the thought that he would never see her again. He wouldn't see her first date or her high school and college graduations. He'd miss walking her down the aisle. Grandkids. He would miss sharing all of these things and more with Morgan. *Oh God, Morgan and our baby!*

Adrenaline flooded him, and he fought his restraints, the effects of the electrical disruption of his nervous system, and the confines of the small backseat. He then tried again to sit up, grunting loudly, but couldn't.

"Oh, goody, you're awake," Moon Pie said excitedly. "Got any last requests, asshole?"

The words shocked him. "Let me go! You don't have to do this!"

"I know I don't. I ain't gotta do shit. But you see, I *wanna* do this. Besides, I made a promise. And a promise is a promise, ya know."

"I have a wife and a little girl—please."

Moon Pie slammed the truck door. He pressed his hand against his wound and took a big swig of Jack with the other.

"Oh, I know. Believe me, I know. I've seen 'em, remember? Oh yeah, that little Katy's gonna be a hottie too, and you ain't gonna be here to do anything 'bout all them guys that are gonna come sniffing 'round," he said with a lascivious snicker.

CHAPTER 98

———— ☾ ————

A FTER LEVI HAD DRIVEN THROUGH MILES OF THE PINE plantations and farmland of rural Mississippi, the giant glowing orb that sits high atop the Golden Moon Hotel and Casino in Philadelphia looked peculiar against the night sky. Since it was a Monday night before Thanksgiving, the resort's parking lots seemed surprisingly full. *Must be a big Monday Night Football party*, he thought as he hurriedly parked.

Levi took the elevator to the top floor and walked quickly toward Bailey's room. Before he stopped at her door, he looked both ways down the hallway to see if anyone was following. Bailey opened the door as soon as he knocked. As soon as the door shut, they hugged.

"Never open the door without knowing who it is," he said, pulling back to look into her eyes.

"I could see you through the peephole. I've been standing there waiting since we got off the phone," she said, wondering why he was so suspicious.

"Oh, okay. That's good," he said, locking the dead bolt and flipping closed the safety hasp.

When Levi turned around, Bailey pulled him close and said, "It's so good to see you. I've missed you." She kissed him.

Levi leaned into the kiss and pulled her tight. When they stopped, Levi said, "I know. It's only been a coupla days, but I've really missed you too."

"Us missin' each other so early in a relationship...this is bad, isn't it?" she asked.

"Yeah, but in a good way," he replied with a broad smile. "They say the heart knows what it wants."

Bailey led Levi by the hand into the suite. She was wearing black sweatpants and a loose-fitting T-shirt from Reed's bookstore in Tupelo. She looked like she hadn't slept in days. In the center of the main room of the suite was an oversize leather couch. Bailey fell back into it.

"Nice crib. I like the way you roll," Levi said, looking around.

"I could live here. This is the nicest place I've ever been in my life," she said. Then she added, "Which ain't saying much, since except for goin' to Memphis, I haven't been out of the state."

"Girl, we'll have to change that for sure."

Levi sat down on the opposite side of the couch and put his feet on the coffee table. Bailey turned to face him, sitting Indian-style.

Levi noticed that the exhausted look seemed to be fading and was slowly being replaced with relief and happiness. In response he said, "Babe, please tell me everything that's been going on. Start at the beginning. Let me help ya."

Bailey looked him dead in the eye, sighed deeply, and then, after several seconds of silence, started talking. She went into the specifics about her mother's battle with leukemia and the resulting financial hardships, not going to college, her grandmother and her friends; she told about all the meaningful projects the old guys wanted to do and how they just wanted to be helpful to their families. She explained the Kroger situation, including Samantha, and how they now wanted to give the money back.

Levi was dumbfounded as Bailey gave the details of robbing the Gold Mine, counting the money, buying the travel bags to store it in, and how, when she saw Woody approaching the hotel, she grabbed the money and ran. She also explained how she had obsessed about the money all through the night.

It took Bailey twenty minutes to bring Levi up to speed. She circled back at the end to reemphasize Walter's story.

Levi never interrupted. He soaked it all in and marveled at the old folks' ingenuity. He also understood their motives.

Bailey was relieved to have unburdened herself but was on the verge of collapse from carrying such a heavy load. She watched Levi for a response and could ascertain only that he was worried.

"I'm sorry to drop all this on you, and I really want you to know that we didn't steal the money from you…we stole it from Moon Pie," she said as she pushed her hair behind her right ear.

Levi finally asked, "Does your grandmother know that you're okay?" He gently touched her face.

"No. I haven't called. I didn't want Woody to have any leverage."

"They're worried. I saw them earlier."

"I'll call." As she hugged Levi, she asked, "So you're not mad at me?"

He rubbed his face and then ran his fingers through his hair. He broke off the embrace, looked her in the eye, and said, "No, I'm not mad. Look, I ain't gonna judge y'all. I can't. I haven't done right. Moon Pie's as mean as a snake, and I've helped him steal and cheat. And worst of all, I've helped him distribute drugs. I know they're ruining people's lives, and I think about that all the time. I just ain't figured a way out. It's been really botherin' me lately. The only reason I do it is 'cause it's easy money, pure and simple. I'm smart enough not to use drugs…but I'm stupid enough to haul 'em. It's crazy, and I've been tellin' myself that it's all about the money, and what's bad about that is that I don't have anything to really show for it. It's crazy.

"What y'all wanna do has got some meaning and purpose. I'd love to see you have that dress shop. I know you'd be successful if you just had the money to get started. Bailey, I'm very impressed with you and what you did for your momma. You coulda run from those debts and problems, but you didn't. Nobody woulda blamed you. I understand what y'all did and why. But you know that it makes y'all criminals...just like me and Moon Pie."

He stopped talking when he noticed tears welling in Bailey's eyes. She knew what she had done was wrong, and that had been haunting her. Her lip was quivering, and it was hard to speak. She didn't like being called a criminal.

Bailey asked, "What are we gonna do? I don't wanna be a criminal."

"I don't know," he said, looking around the room, his eyes stopping on two rolling suitcases. He pointed at the bags and continued, "That money right there...that is some dangerous shit, bad dangerous. It's gonna get somebody killed. You ain't got a clue who all's involved with that."

Bailey started to tremble. Levi moved next to her and wrapped his arm around her. He noticed the time on a wall clock. It was 8:00 p.m., and he hadn't eaten all day.

"Look, I'm starving. Let's get something to eat and talk this through, see if we can't find a solution."

Bailey seemed to welcome the idea. "There's a ton of restaurants here!" She handed him a brochure from the coffee table.

"Cool. Go get ready. We'll go somewhere nice," Levi said, opening the brochure.

"I'll take a quick shower and be ready in fifteen minutes!"

Bailey jumped up, kissed him on the cheek, and grabbed a small travel bag as she ran into the bedroom and shut the door.

Levi stood, stretched, and walked to face the massive floor-to-ceiling window. Though the night was inky black, he couldn't see any stars because of the giant parking lot's orange lights. The moon also was nowhere to be seen. Levi remembered from the drive that rain clouds had been rolling in fast. The sound of the shower running and Bailey singing "Broken Road" brought his thoughts back to where he was. He turned to look around the room, his gaze falling on the suitcases.

He walked over to the bags and opened one to see the cash wrapped with rubber bands and neatly stacked inside. He smiled, grabbed a bundle, and then zipped the suitcase shut.

Seeing the money jolted Levi back to the fact that Moon Pie needed help. While he was looking at his phone to see if Moon Pie had texted him, the battery died and the screen went dark. An overwhelming sense of urgency hit him. He dropped a thousand dollars onto the coffee table, grabbed the suitcases, and headed for the door.

The last thing Levi heard before closing the suite's heavy door was Bailey's joyful singing in the shower.

CHAPTER 99

———— ☾ ————

THREE HOURS EARLIER, TRANCE MOSER AND YANCEY Fuller, two grave robbers, had been dropped off at the eastern edge of the vast river-bottom swamp by one of their wives. Inside their backpacks were black tarps, small shovels, wire screens to shift the dirt for artifacts, and a variety of other tools and accessories. They carried one loaded AR-15 rifle and two four-foot sections of metal rod that they would push down into the earth until they felt something solid, and then they would dig.

While scouting a few weeks back, they had discovered an Indian mound along the edge of an old river run. The mound was inconspicuous to a layman, but these two easily recognized the slight rise in the terrain. It appeared to them to be unexplored, and they eagerly anticipated digging. This area of Mississippi was known among artifact hunters for the presence of long ceremonial-spear points that brought top dollar.

The grave robbers retrieved the waypoint of the Indian mound from their handheld GPS and started hiking toward it.

These guys had perfected their illegal activities. They dug only at night, arriving after dark and leaving before daylight. They preferred winter, when the soil was moist and easier to work; plus, there were no snakes, and the insects weren't a nightmare. Following their new approach, last year they had sold over $95,000 worth of illegal artifacts to private collectors, mostly from Japan. Lately several law enforcement officers, tasked with protecting sacred Indian artifacts, had come close to catching them. Consequently, they now had to be dropped off and picked up to facilitate their concealment.

When they finally reached the mound, they spread the tarps to build low, tentlike structures over the area they wanted to dig. With this setup, they were able to use small battery-powered floodlights to illuminate their immediate work area. Inside, it was brighter than midday. Unless you were a few yards away and heard the shovels, you would never know that an excavation was occurring, about to unearth a Native American buried deep in the past. The grave robbers could not have cared less about the Indians. They just wanted the cache of beads, arrowheads, spear points, and ceremonial pieces buried with them for use on the other side.

Tonight had been a slow dig, so Trance stood outside the tarp, smoking a cigarette and thinking. His wife had recently left him for the UPS delivery guy, and he was having trouble focusing on the task at hand. He had almost finished the cigarette when he noticed vehicle lights on the other side of the lake. He immediately called to his partner, Yancey, to turn off the lights. Paranoia struck deep, and for a long while, they both stood stock-still but ready to flee, abandoning their project.

"Game warden?" Trance whispered nervously.

"Nah, I don't think so," Yancey responded as he looked through binoculars, watching the vehicle's lights bumping down a logging road several hundred yards away. They could hear the engine rev and mud and water splashing.

"Well, at least they're on the other side of the slough."

His buddy didn't respond as he intently glassed the truck.

"Sheriff?"

"Nah."

"Corps patrol?"

"No."

"Well, who the hell is it, then?"

"I don't know. I can't make it out. Just shut the hell up so I can think!" Yancey shot back.

CHAPTER 100

— ☾ —

THE MEXICAN DRUG DEALERS HAD AN INTERESTING NIGHT. After casing the police station and the Henry Clay Hotel and not learning anything they didn't already know, they decided to eat supper. Julio wanted to experience the local vibe and cuisine. He felt this was the only way to connect, albeit indirectly, with the target. Based upon the almost-unanimous recommendation from everyone in town they asked, they pulled up to the front of Anthony's Market. From the outside, it appeared to be a dive. Once inside, however, Julio loved the atmosphere. He ordered one of every Cajun appetizer on the menu, just to sample it. The men gorged themselves on spicy food and drank nearly a case of Corona while watching Monday Night Football on a huge flat-screen. Guillermo had kept his laptop powered up, monitoring the movements of Moon Pie's ankle bracelet.

Full as ticks, and feeling bulletproof, the Mexicans decided to follow the GPS tracking of the ankle bracelet as it moved from Chocolate City. They asked for the check and then spoke quickly to each other in Spanish so no one would understand. Both watched the red dot on the screen as it traveled closer to them. When it stopped moving three blocks north, Julio dropped three hundred-dollar bills on the table and thanked the waitstaff as they walked out. At the front door, Julio's stomach rumbled once and then again before he got to the car. He paused and considered going back inside to use the restroom, but the anticipation of the chase overpowered his guts.

As the Mexicans approached the location of the tracking device, they noticed that the street was lined with run-down shotgun-style homes. The beer had contributed to Julio's conviction that he understood the dynamics of the neighborhood. He believed that they had the element of surprise on their side and didn't have to worry about a big crowd. They drove by once and saw the purple car pulling into the yard. Only a few lights were on inside the house. Turning around, they turned off their headlights and rolled silently to a stop, putting the purple Cadillac between them and the house. Julio grabbed his pistol and Guillermo his laptop as they silently approached the house.

Julio's stomach rumbled again. Guillermo heard it and looked at him, but Julio was focused on his approach to the dwelling. When they walked past the car, Guillermo noticed that the tracking program indicated that the ankle monitor was inside the car. He gave Julio a quick whistle.

"*Es en el coche.*"

"What?" Julio asked in a loud whisper.

Turning the computer screen toward Julio, Guillermo said in Spanish, "It's in the car, not the house."

Julio shook his head in disbelief and then looked for movement in the old house. Not seeing anything, he walked back to the car and tried looking inside it, but the windows were darkly tinted.

"*Está dentro,*" Guillermo insisted.

Julio knew to trust this technology. Since they had started using this program, it had proven to be accurate to within three feet. He quickly glanced around for anyone watching and saw no one. As he pulled up on the door handle, he was surprised that it was unlocked. He opened the door, pointing his pistol inside.

When he saw no one, he pocketed the pistol and began looking inside the car for the anklet. Guillermo studied the screen and then began helping search the car.

The car reeked of menthol cigarettes. The dashboard was greasy and shiny, as though it had just been wiped down with Armor All. There was a golden crown-shaped air freshener in the back window. Julio didn't see the tracking device.

"Look under seat," Guillermo advised.

Julio felt under the seats until he finally found the ankle monitor.

When he straightened to show Guillermo, he saw a pistol pointed right at his head and one pointed at Guillermo's. A short, fat black man had a gun in each hand.

"You wetbacks ain't taking Heavy G's car! I done told that fool I'd make a payment on my rims next week when I get my check!"

In heavily accented English, Julio said, "We just want this." He held up the anklet.

"That shit ain't Heavy G's!"

"Do you know where Mr. Moon Pie is?"

"What the hell you talking 'bout, fool? I don't know no Moon Pie! All I knows is that you ain't taking Heavy G's car. Now, get yo' jalapeno-eatin' asses outta here 'fo I pop a cap in 'em!"

Julio and Guillermo glanced quickly at each other. Guillermo held his computer with his back turned to Heavy G. Julio had his hands raised, showing he was unarmed.

"I said I'm gonna pop a cap in your ass if y'all don't get the hell away from here!"

"We leave, *señor*. We make mistake."

"You damn right you made a mistake. Don't nobody mess with Heavy G's shit!"

Julio and Guillermo starting to back away. Heavy G continued to hold the pistols sideways, pointed at their faces, until they got into their car.

"Go, Guillermo," Julio said, holstering his gun. He was embarrassed and angry.

Guillermo floored the accelerator, squealing the tires as they sped away.

CHAPTER 101

——— (———

MOON PIE HELD HIS SIDE AS HE DROVE. THE ROAD WAS slick and rutted, causing him to put the truck into four-wheel drive. Despite the pain from the gunshot, he loved being in the swamp at night. It felt like home and was energizing. He was confident that Jake's body would never ever be discovered. There was no reason for that drainpipe to be replaced or inspected before the body decomposed. And if Jake's body somehow washed through the pipe, alligators and turtles would take care of it.

He smiled, held up the whiskey bottle in a toast to his brilliant plan, and took a long drink as he reviewed his plans for Jake. First he'd zap Jake again to knock him out and then drop him into the drainpipe, feetfirst. Then he'd bust the beaver construction and listen to Jake beg for his life as the pipe filled with water, slowly drowning him. The next step would be to get medical attention for his wound. At daylight, he'd kill the bald eagle near Officers Lake Road with his suppressed .22 rifle, and then, finally, he would head to Alabama.

Jake had been in and out of consciousness. He was awake, lying on his side on the small backseat of his truck. He couldn't sit up. Every muscle in his body hurt, and he assumed that the electric shocks had caused it. His hands were bound in front of him, and he tried to force his knee down in between his wrists to break the large black zip ties, but he couldn't get enough leverage, and he only caused the ties to cut deep into his wrists.

Moon Pie punched the CD button on Jake's stereo, and the Conway Twitty song "Hello Darlin'" flowed from the speakers. He shook his head as he punched the stereo's off button.

"Say, Jake, my boy, got any Johnny Cash?"

Jake ignored the question. He was staring at the back of the driver's seat, trying to think of what to do. He had found a small flashlight in the cup holder and held it like a weapon. He was thinking that if he could stall long enough, he might be able to regain control over his muscles, throw his bound arms over Moon Pie's neck, and strangle him with his own zip ties.

Jake finally said, "So what can I do to make you change your mind and not do this? Money? I can get you cash. I've got several gold coins and some silver too. Name it. Just tell me what you want. I'm willin' to do whatever you ask."

"This ain't about money," Moon Pie said, growing agitated as he took a pull of whiskey. "It's an eye-for-an-eye thing. You know that."

"There's gotta be—"

Jake didn't get to finish the sentence because Moon Pie erupted in anger, slamming on the brakes, throwing Jake into the floorboard. And before Jake could say or do anything, Moon Pie zapped him in the back of the head with the stun gun. Jake's eyes rolled back in pain.

CHAPTER 102

———— ☾ ————

B AILEY FINISHED HER SHOWER, DRIED HER HAIR, AND PUT
on a strapless dress that she had designed and sewn. She
hoped Levi loved it as much as she did. It had taken her only
twenty-eight minutes to get ready.

As she stepped out of the bedroom into the suite, she said,
"I'm ready, Levi."

Levi's jacket lay across the back of an armchair, but he was
gone, and so were the two suitcases.

She ran to the window overlooking the parking lot, hoping to
see him. When she didn't, she ran out of the suite into the empty
hallway and looked both ways. It was empty. She dashed to the
elevators and noticed that the indicators showed both elevators
were between the lobby and the mezzanine level. Bailey slowly
walked back to her room and discovered the door was locked.
She hit the door with the palm of her hand and cursed. Turning
slowly, she put her back to the door and slid to the hall floor.

The man she thought loved her had just abandoned her. She was
crushed. She didn't care as much about the money as she did about
the man, problems and all. He was to be her fixer-upper project,
with lots of upside potential. Bailey felt she had hit rock bottom. She
began sobbing uncontrollably at the realization that Levi had chosen
the money over her.

CHAPTER 103

———— ☾ ————

NOT WANTING TO SEARCH FOR AN OPEN STORE IN THE middle of the night to buy a cell-phone car charger, Levi drove straight to Columbus from Philadelphia. He had to talk to Moon Pie face-to-face. He had to find him before the Mexicans did.

As Levi approached the mobile-home park, he could see two police cars parked close to Moon Pie's trailer. All the lights in the trailer were on, and he could see Moon Pie's Bronco right where it had been earlier. Levi didn't think Moon Pie was in custody, based on his earlier phone call. He suspected that he was on foot. *I gotta get a damn phone charger and call him.* Levi kept driving past the trailer park and straight to the Columbus Walmart Supercenter.

When Levi's cell phone powered up, he searched his sent calls and found the Mexicans' number. He hit send.

Julio, recognizing the number, answered, "*¡Hola!*"

"Julio?"

"*Sí, quién es este?*" Julio asked, anxious to talk.

"It's Levi. I called you a few days ago…to tell you about our problem."

"*Sí, sí.* We need to talk. We have bad situation."

"I understand, and I have what you want. Do you have Moon Pie?"

"No we don't, but we want to talk to him. Where are you? I'll come to you right now."

"What? So you're here? Close? No. No. No. We do this on my terms, my choice of turf. Where are you staying?"

Julio did not want to tell him. As he was thinking what to do, Levi asked again, "Where are you staying? I just need to know what city so I can set up the meet. Believe me, I don't want any trouble from y'all."

"We are in West Point."

Levi instantly knew a spot; just east of them was a landmark windmill. It sat on the edge of a huge field, with excellent visibility. He said, "I'll call you in the mornin' to tell you where to meet me at. It'll only take about fifteen minutes from the middle of West Point."

"You will have my money?" Julio said.

"*Sí, señor*," Levi said in his Southern-accented Spanish, and hit end.

CHAPTER 104

M OON PIE RECKLESSLY BOUNCED JAKE'S TRUCK THROUGH the rutted road. Rooster tails of mud flew from the tires as he mashed the gas pedal to the floor whenever the truck lost traction. Moon Pie couldn't believe that Jake Crosby had just walked into his trailer and presented such a fine opportunity to make things right with Reese, Johnny Lee, and the universe.

As he approached the duck-pond levee, Moon Pie clicked the headlights on bright. Since the levee was higher ground, he had better traction and slowed down. He glanced back at Jake on the floor before looking out the passenger-side window for the drainpipe.

The pipe was right where Moon Pie remembered it, and he turned Jake's truck at an angle so the headlights cast beams of light across the slough, fully illuminating the pipe.

"Honey, we're home!" he yelled. Then he took another swig of Tennessee whiskey and laughed. He added, "Man, this is great. Looks like the beavers have been busy trying to clog it up. That looks to be 'bout six inches over the lip. Whoa, there's gotta be several million gallons of water being held back by just some sticks and mud. Hot damn, this is gonna be fun!"

Jake tried to raise his head to see what Moon Pie was talking about, but he couldn't see past the dash. He did manage to force the small flashlight down into his pants pocket and wished that he had any type of weapon. Being careful not to be seen, he checked his cell phone but had no service. *Jesus, just like at the Dummy Line*, he thought.

"Please don't shock me again, and please listen to me," Jake pleaded. "The past is past. We can't do shit about it. I didn't kill *your* friends in cold blood. They were gonna kill my little girl. Don't ya get it?"

Moon Pie slammed on the brakes and put the truck into park before it quit moving. He turned to face Jake. "Let me ask you one question. Did you kill them?" Moon Pie was now slurring his words.

Jake didn't want to answer. Moon Pie was drunk and irrational. Jake exhaled deeply and said a silent prayer. Jake assumed that Moon Pie was slurring from the liquor. He wasn't aware that he'd been shot and was losing blood also.

"I said: Did. You. Kill. Them? It's a pretty simple question. Answer me, or I swear to God I'll shoot you in the face and then put your head in bed with your daughter! Do you hear me?"

Jake was determined to keep him talking. "You know I did. But it was purely self-defense. The cops said so, and so did the DA. Did you know that?"

"I'll tell you what I do know...I know they're dead and you're responsible, asshole."

"Why is it so hard for you to understand that I was only protecting myself and my little girl?" Jake asked.

"Yeah, yeah, yeah. You're some kinda of hotshot, ain't ya? The newspapers made you out to be a hero, and my friends, they were just low-life white trash...like they had it comin' or sump'n. Hell, you even made national news. CNN! I can't believe that shit!"

"I wasn't a hero."

"Oh, but they was white trash, huh?"

"I never said that."

"I'm tired of this bullshit. It's over. I'm gonna keep my word. At the end of the day, I just might be some sorry white trash myself...but I keep my promises. Say your prayers Mr. Jake Crosby," he said and then opened the truck door and stepped out. When the dome light illuminated the inside of the cab, Jake frantically looked for anything he could use. Then he saw the truck keys.

Moon Pie stood at the door as if he had just remembered something, and he smiled when he saw Jake looking at the truck keys. He reached in, turned off the ignition, and took the keys. Holding the keys and shaking them in one hand and Jake's pistol in the other, he said, "Just In case you got any bright ideas, I think I'll keep these."

Moon Pie then flipped the headlights back on and shut the door. The swamp was still, except for the fog floating slowly over the water through the lights.

Jake's adrenaline was flowing, so he was finally able to pull himself off the floor and onto the seat. He struggled until he could see clearly out the front windshield. He could smell the unique scent of the Tombigbee River, so he knew it was close. He saw Moon Pie wading out to a big pipe that had tree limbs and mud piled all around it. Clearly it had been that way for a while, because there were remains of various plants that had been growing on top of it. When Moon Pie bent to look down into the pipe, Jake could see a large bloodstain on his right side. The side of his shirt was slick with it.

Jake figured that Moon Pie would open the small passenger-side door to pull him out. This would be his only chance. Jake lay back across the seat and kicked the dome light as hard as he could. He then pushed himself to that side of the truck and pulled his knees into his chest. His legs were cocked like a spring trap. As soon as Moon Pie opened the door, he was going to kick the crap out of him, preferably where he was bleeding. The force would knock Moon Pie down, giving Jake a chance to get out of the truck and try to break the zip ties on the trailer hitch. He couldn't run, but he could drive if he could get the keys.

Jake smiled at the thought of turning the tables on Moon Pie and drowning that evil son of a bitch. He had to kill Moon Pie— right now. Jake took a quick look to see what he was doing and saw him struggling in the deep mud surrounding the pipe. Then it occurred to him that Moon Pie's plan was to stuff him into that drain. Jake said a silent prayer for himself and for Morgan, Katy, and his baby on the way.

Moon Pie was climbing the levee bank when an air-force jet passed overhead much lower than normal. Planes were such a common occurrence in the area that he barely glanced up to see it. He leaned forward to grab the brush guard on the front of the truck for purchase. Moon Pie's wound burned, and he was beginning to feel a little weak. *That son of a bitch shootin' me's reason enough to kill him...very slowly.*

Moon Pie yelled, "Hey, pretty boy, did you know you shot me?"

Jake heard what Moon Pie said, but he didn't remember it. All that he could recall was being attacked from behind and hit over the head.

"There's my very own personal reason for killin' you right there. So quit your bitchin' and moanin' about shit and beggin' for your life. You're as good as dead!"

When Moon Pie stood at the front of the truck, Jake could see the vapor of his labored breath in the cold night air. It was a brief moment of satisfaction, knowing that he had inflicted some pain on the psychopath.

"I'm glad I shot you...you worthless piece of shit!" Jake screamed back at him. "I only wish I'da killed ya!"

Moon Pie blew out a deep breath and forced a smile. "Oh, you're gonna wish you'd killed me when you see what kind of slow death I got planned for you!" Reenergized with desire for personal vengeance, Moon Pie flung open the passenger door and then the small half door of the extended cab.

Instantly, Jake kicked Moon Pie with all his might. His boots hit Moon Pie square in the chest, knocking him back to the water's edge, where he landed on his right side.

Struggling to get out of the truck, Jake wiggled quickly to the edge of the seat and tried to stand up. He had no balance, and when his feet wouldn't move, his forward motion propelled him face-first down onto the levee. The steep sides caused him to roll to the bottom. He stopped with his face only a few inches from the cold water. Jake lay still, trying to catch his breath and cussing the zip ties that bound him so tightly.

Moon Pie fought to get up. Jake's kick had knocked the breath out of him, and he had landed on his injured side. The pain was almost unbearable. When he finally got to his knees, he almost blacked out.

Jake tried using his arms to push himself into a seated position, but his muscles still weren't as responsive as his mind. He was struggling to get out of an awkward position when suddenly Moon Pie grabbed his head and started screaming. Moon Pie dragged Jake by the hair two feet and dropped his head into the cold water. Jake's mind raced, trying to find an out, but all he could do was hold what little was left of his breath. Moon Pie's knees were in his back, pinning him to the muddy bottom. He was under the control of a merciless man.

After about forty seconds, Moon Pie slid off of Jake, grabbed him by the hair again, and pulled him out of the water. Jake gasped for air. His lungs burned, and he threw up cold swamp water.

"Not yet," Moon Pie said, struggling also to breathe. "It ain't gonna be that easy or that fast."

Jake couldn't speak. He lay there, struggling just to breathe. Moon Pie pulled the stun gun from his back pocket and zapped Jake's exposed back for about three seconds. Jake flopped briefly and then passed out. *That oughta give me enough time to stuff him in the pipe*, Moon Pie thought.

When Moon Pie realized that he was wet from the waist down, he began to get cold. He grabbed Jake under the shoulders and started dragging him to the drainpipe. The deep mud made it very difficult to get Jake to the pipe. When Moon Pie finally got Jake on top of the circular beaver dam, he stopped to rest and lit a cigarette, inhaling a long drag. The nicotine calmed him a bit.

Moon Pie lit some thatch from the dam and dropped it into the pipe. It was relatively clean deep down to just about where it made its bend. He held the cigarette in his lips as he stuffed Jake's feet into the pipe. He then grabbed him under the arms and strained to lift him to the edge of the metal pipe.

Moon Pie, his side burning from the strain, held Jake above the narrow abyss and in a singsong voice said, "One is for Johnny Lee, two is for Reese, and three is for me...asshole!" Then he let go.

The grotesque sound Jake made when he hit the mud and debris at the bottom made Moon Pie double over laughing. He then started pulling mud and sticks from around the pipe, allowing water to start flowing in. The more he tore out, the more the water helped as the cold swamp sought to level itself through the pipe. Moon Pie stopped to watch the water flowing and realized that he was hurt much worse than he had originally thought. As badly as Moon Pie wanted to stay to hear Jake's dying screams, he realized that he needed medical attention or he was going to die too.

Moon Pie leaned over the pipe and yelled, "See ya in hell, Jake Crosby."

He chuckled as he sloshed toward the truck.

CHAPTER 105

————— ☾ —————

ORGAN WATCHED THE WEST POINT POLICE CHIEF AND two uniformed officers walk to their patrol cars. They had been at her house for almost two hours. She had given them all the information about Jake she could think of. One of the officers said he was going to spend the night parked in front of her house. Morgan was very grateful. The police chief put out a statewide alert for Jake Crosby and his vehicle.

The officer who was going to pull guard duty turned around and said, "Mrs. Crosby, please leave all of your outside lights on." He said something to the two officers she couldn't understand and then turned back to her and said, "I promise I'll call if I see or hear anything. Go ahead and lock up now."

As soon as Morgan closed the door, the house telephone rang. It was one of Jake's coworkers. He was just one of several who had called. Jake's boss had called twice to check on her and Katy and to see if Jake had made it home. Their friends and family were concerned because it was very uncharacteristic of Jake to leave without telling Morgan or someone else. Every law enforcement agency in the Golden Triangle area was looking for Jake and his truck.

When Morgan hung up the call, she could hear Katy crying. She went straight to her and tried to console her. Katy had heard everything she and the police had discussed. Katy's memories of that terrifying night in the swamp came flooding back. The fear. The screams. The gunshots. Katy Crosby was scared for her daddy, and nothing her mother said or did could help that.

When Katy had finally cried herself to sleep, Morgan quietly left her side. It was heartbreaking to see her little girl so upset. Morgan knew she had to be strong for Katy and that if she also cried, Katy would fall to pieces. Morgan shut Katy's bedroom door and then walked to the front of the house and stood with her arms folded, staring out at the dark, cold night. She could feel in her bones that something bad had happened to Jake. He would never leave work without telling her, and he most certainly would never stay out this late without calling. *He'd call if he could. If he could.* The thought of it sent a chill down her spine.

Morgan touched her belly and wished she could feel the tiny baby inside—Jake's baby. Her lip trembled at the notion of raising the baby without him. *Lord, I want my baby to know its father. It's a simple request.*

She was frightened but was also getting angry—at everybody, including Jake. This was not the life she had envisioned. She wanted normal.

The headlights of the approaching car gave her a flash of hope, but when she saw that it was the police chief, her chest tightened. She just knew it had to be bad news. She could not fight back the tears anymore. The chief parked his sedan and gave a quick wave to the young officer in the patrol car. He trotted toward the house. Morgan felt like she was living a movie, watching herself on-screen—like it wasn't really happening to her. She saw herself open the front door.

"Morgan, you heard anything?" he asked.

Thank God—he's not here to tell me Jake's dead, she thought, but she just said, "No, nothing. Have y'all?"

"No ma'am, not yet, but I've got everybody lookin'."

Morgan smiled weakly to show her thanks and folded her arms again. The police chief could see she'd been crying, but he needed to clarify some things. People under stress often forgot the simplest things, and talking could jog their memories.

"May I trouble you for a cup of coffee?" he asked.

Morgan looked at him gratefully. She really liked him. He was a pillar in the community, a deacon in their church, and a friend of Jake's. She could see that he, too, was upset. He just hid his feelings better than she did.

"Yeah, sure, come on in, please," she said, realizing she was glad to have something to do.

"Thank you, Morgan, have you thought of anything else since I left that might help us? Anything?"

"No, and he still isn't answering his cell."

"We've still not been able to locate Ethan Daniels."

Morgan stopped pouring the coffee when she heard that. It sounded serious to her that they couldn't find him.

"Do you actually know this guy?"

"I arrested him once…years ago. He's probably the best poacher around. He's gotten into drug running for the money. Kinda took over the business, so to speak, from that first guy Jake had to kill over in Alabama."

Morgan finished pouring the coffee and handed the cup to the chief.

"Thank you. He was picked up over the weekend on an unrelated charge but got out Monday morning. The Columbus PD is all over his lawyer and his known associates right now. We'll find him."

"I feel like I need to be out lookin' for Jake—that I need to be doin' something to help." Morgan bit her bottom lip to keep from crying.

"Morgan, listen to me. You're doin' exactly what you need to be doin'. I need you here, by the phone; and Katy needs you to be here with her."

"I know, but—"

"Listen, we have every available officer riding roads right now. We're tryin' to cover as much ground as possible because the weather's about to get really bad. They're callin' for several inches of rain."

"That's not good."

"No, it's not. It's gonna hinder the off-road searches when it gets daylight. I need to go back and help the boys." The chief stood, looked directly into Morgan's eyes, and said, "Please, Morgan, just stay here…and call me if anything happens. Okay?"

"I will."

The chief took a big sip of coffee and then gently set down the mug.

"We're gonna have another baby," she blurted, smiling tearfully.

"I didn't know that. Congratulations."

"We haven't told anyone, and I…I just thought you ought to know. Jake wouldn't just leave me."

"I know that, Morgan, and we're gonna find him. I promise you."

CHAPTER 106

———— ☾ ————

T HE FRIGID WATER POURING OVER JAKE WOKE HIM. BOTH his legs were burning, as if they were on fire. Dazed from the electrical shocks and disorientated by the circumstances, he took a few moments to realize what had happened to him. It was inky black around him; but, when he looked up, he could distinguish the night sky.

Though the pipe wasn't flooding yet, Jake could not move his legs. Pain shot through them when he tried to stand. He surmised they must be broken. He could tell that his ankles were still zip-tied.

The air reeked of rotten bottomland mud. The top of the pipe appeared to be about six or seven feet away, and the walls were slick with algae. It was the flowing water that really concerned him. He had no way out, and stifling his growing panic was his most immediate challenge. His face was against the pipe wall, and his shoulders had only a few inches of room. with: He considered bouncing, to force his way out though the lower end of the pipe, but he was stuck too deep in the mud, and there wasn't enough water flowing though to break the below obstruction of silt and beaver limbs.

Jake's coffin was to be long, cylindrical, and rusty.

After several deep breaths, Jake remembered his cell phone. His wrists were still zip-tied together, but painfully and slowly, he contorted his arms until he pulled it from his pocket. He mashed the center key, and the screen glowed. It showed forty-one missed calls and eleven texts. He smiled as he recalled putting it on silent before he slipped up on Moon Pie's trailer. Most of the missed calls and texts were from Morgan. His hands shook as he tried to click on her name to redial. On the third try, the phone dialed, but the call immediately failed. Jake noticed that he didn't have service.

The phone started getting wet from the water splashing down around it, so he leaned forward a few inches to shield it so he could read Morgan's first text, at 4:43: "Can u get some bread on the way home?"

"I wish I could, babe," he said out loud and then smiled.

He read the rest of his messages.

5:35: "Where are you?"

6:01: "Did you go hunting?"

6:20: "Jake I'm worried Call me."

6:33: "Richard Pharr at ur office said u never came back from lunch Where r u?"

6:51: "I called the police Please call or text!!"

7:02: "Jake I love u! Call me"

7:07: "Dad when r u coming home ☺"

Jake choked up. His missed his family. The more texts he read, the more upset he became. The water falling over him was relentless. He couldn't imagine that waterboarding was worse than what he was experiencing. He would confess to anything to get out of this pipe. Jake did his best to wipe the moisture from the phone, and with great effort, he placed it into his right pocket. He felt it hit something and remembered the flashlight. As Jake pushed himself against the left side of the pipe, intense, fiery pain shot from his left leg, almost making him black out.

What the hell happened? Somethin' ain't right, he thought as he struggled to catch his breath.

Careful not to apply pressure on his left leg, he reached slowly down into his pocket for the flashlight. His mind was working faster than his muscles, and he assumed that was caused by all the electrical jolts. He was shaking from the cold and the pain, but the flashlight in his hands was comforting...until he clicked it on and could now clearly see that he was in a death trap.

The steady flow of cold swamp water was growing stronger. Vapor from his heaving breathing filled the pipe. The outside temperature was in the low forties. That and the cold water were taking their toll on Jake's body. He considered that hypothermia might kill him before drowning did.

Jake knew that he had to get the water flowing out of the pipe so the rising level didn't overtake him. His right leg would barely move but it didn't hurt like his left. He tried to push down with his legs to clear some of the mud and limbs, but it was no use. At least the water backing up was beginning to numb the pain in his legs. He tried to see his left leg with the flashlight, but the beam couldn't penetrate the muddy water. He noticed that every movement he made stirred more silt, so he remained still to let the dirt settle enough so he could see.

Standing motionless and looking up, Jake tried not to think that this would be how and where he died, never to be found. *Moon Pie—that son of a bitch—is gonna win.* Jake shook his head, trying to clear his mind, but he was beginning to feel claustrophobic.

The water in the bottom of the pipe had cleared somewhat. With his left hand, Jake lowered the flashlight, shining it down into the water. He could see his blood flowing like spilled red ink. Apparently a bark-skinned stick had impaled his leg. Jake looked up, took a deep breath, exhaled, and contemplated trying to pull it out. He looked down, shined the light again to get a better assessment and then realized that it was not a limb sticking into his leg but his exposed bone protruding through his pants.

Jake's head fell forward, hitting the pipe with a thud, as everything went dark.

CHAPTER 107

———— ☾ ————

S HAKING HIS HEAD, MOON PIE WAS HAVING DIFFICULTY focusing his eyes as he drove. Blurred vision and bouts of confusion were making the drive out of the dark woods even extremely difficult. Grimacing in pain, he touched his side and saw that his hand was covered in blood. He knew that he needed to get to the ER, but being gunshot was going to necessitate police involvement, and that would be a problem he didn't know how to solve. He sped up, grabbed his cell phone, and tried to remember Levi's number, but his mind went blank. As he began searching his cell phone's address book, he glanced up to see that he was running off the side of the old dirt road. His instinctive reaction was to punch the gas. The truck dug down in the mud and slung rooster tails. The limbs from an oak tree scratched down the side of Jake's truck, causing Moon Pie to laugh deliriously, missing the turn that led to the highway.

After another mile, the river cane became more prevalent, and Moon Pie realized that he had missed his turn. He was now closer to the river and deeper into the swamp. The road had become muddier, and Moon Pie was in danger of getting stuck. He stopped on a dry spot and turned on the windshield wipers, smearing mud. "Son of a bitch!"

Moon Pie looked around inside the truck for something to wipe the windshield. The only thing he found was Jake's corduroy sport coat. He smiled at that and enjoyed the thought of Jake struggling inside the muddy drainpipe, waiting to die.

While Moon Pie was wiping the mud-spattered windshield, his knees buckled, and he barely caught himself before hitting the ground. *Shit! I gotta get the hell outta here!*

He climbed back into the truck and looked for a place to turn around but didn't find one. Beginning to panic, Moon Pie reversed the truck, plowing through bushes and small trees. He dropped the gearshift into drive and stood on the accelerator, causing the truck to fishtail out of the muddy ditch.

As he raced down the muddy road, he tried to think of something to tell the hospital that wouldn't raise too many suspicions. He knew that going to the hospital was a huge risk, but he couldn't think of an alternative. He was about to bleed out, and he knew it. He drove faster, screaming, cussing, and pounding the steering wheel. This was not how he wanted to die...or get caught.

CHAPTER 108

———— ☾ ————

T HE COUNTY GAME WARDEN WAS PATROLLING THE BACK roads that night, looking for spotlighters. He had received a tip that some Louisiana boys, staying near Columbus, planned to poach wherever they could jump a fence or find a clean stretch of road. The warden was by himself, as usual. His wife had reminded him for the millionth time to be careful. Everyone he ran across, particularly at night, was armed and potentially involved in some illegal activity. As he drove, he monitored the various law enforcement agencies' frequencies, in case he needed to help. His friendship with one of the locally stationed Mississippi troopers had really been helpful in covering his own back and backyard and was much appreciated. As a game warden, he encountered all sorts of riffraff these days, especially with meth labs popping up in old barns and outbuildings everywhere. Plus, the newest "shake and bake" method of manufacturing methamphetamine in a two-liter plastic bottle was a constant physical and psychological drain, since any seemingly benign situation could turn deadly in a breath.

He had listened to all of the radio reports regarding Jake Crosby's disappearance. He had first met Jake at a National Wild Turkey Federation banquet a few years back and had since checked him on a few dove shoots. Jake was a good guy, always polite and always legal. He wrote down the description and tag of Jake's pickup, just in case.

When his cell phone rang, he checked the caller ID and saw that it was the general from the Columbus Air Force Base. This guy was the most rabid duck hunter he had ever known. He'd lived on base for longer than the warden could remember, and the general considered the public hunting areas along the river to be his personal domain. During duck season, the general had his pilots buzz certain areas for daily duck reports. The warden was happy to answer the call.

"Hello, General."

"Hey there, Warden. Sorry to be callin' so late."

"Not a problem. What can I do for ya?"

"At nineteen hundred I was bein' flown back from a meeting. Our approach was low due to the ceilin'. At any rate, I clearly saw a truck with its lights on inside the Buttahatchee area."

The warden knew that no vehicles should be inside those locked gates. It was strictly a walk-in area. He also knew that the general was extremely concerned that poachers were wreaking havoc all over the area.

"Are you sure the lights were on the inside of the gates? I mean…it's dark and y'all woulda been flying pretty fast."

"Hell yes, they were inside. You know that pond that I call the Honey Hole, where I always kill so many pintails? That's where the vehicle was. It wasn't a four-wheeler either. The lights were too far apart and too bright. It was parked on the levee, pointing out on the water."

"It coulda been some Corps of Engineer boys workin' late."

"No way. It was a civilian's truck," the general replied bluntly.

"Okay, I'll check it out."

"Duck season's close, and I bet it was somebody baitin' my hole."

The warden smiled. They were picking right up where they had left off last January.

"You know that I don't see much baitin' on public areas, sir."

"They're tryin' to set me up."

The warden smiled, knowing that the general worried more about ducks than anything else. "I tell you what, I'll call a Corps buddy of mine and find out if they are workin' around there, and if not, I'll drive by and take a look."

"Please let me know what you find out."

The warden was amazed at how clearly the general could see at night while riding in a Lear. *Good military training*, he thought.

"Will do, General."

CHAPTER 109

———— ☾ ————

WHEN JAKE REGAINED CONSCIOUSNESS, HE COULDN'T feel his broken leg and he was shivering uncontrollably. The water inside the tube was now around his waist. He desperately tried kicking with his right leg, to force mud and debris down the pipe, and then, realizing that his body was also blocking the flow of water, he strained to wiggle and twist. Jake fought through the pain, knowing that his life depended on it. For the moment, the water level appeared to recede.

Jake quit moving when he realized that he wasn't holding the flashlight. He had dropped it when he passed out. Rocking back and forth as he squatted into the water, he was able to reach the light, but doing so was costly.

He was completely soaked and knew that his core body temperature would be dropping like a stone. The higher cost, however, was that all his movements jarred the pipe, causing mud from the beaver dam to loosen and erode, allowing more water to rush into the pipe. The greater the water flow into the pipe, the farther down it sucked Jake. It was a vicious and rapidly escalating circle.

"Shit! I gotta fight this. I gotta figure a way out for my girls," he said aloud.

Jake looked up and shined the light out of the pipe into the misty fog and in desperation screamed, "Help me! Can anybody hear me! Help!"

Jake Crosby was exhausted and growing drowsy from the onset of hypothermia and, unbeknownst to him, blood being forced into his legs by the suction of the current. He'd been defeated, and the realization was settling in. He leaned his head back against the pipe and slowly closed his eyes in silent prayer.

CHAPTER 110

—————— (——————

T HE MYSTERIOUS TRUCK DRIVING BY THEIR DIG UNNERVED
the grave robbers. They discussed options for a few minutes
and decided that one of them would resume work while the other
stood guard, listening and watching for anything else unusual.

Several minutes passed, when Trance heard unintelligible
shouting. He listened intently but could not figure out where it
was coming from. He called for his partner to discuss the situation. But because sound travels great distances over water and
through winter woods—coupled with their promising site and
impending bad weather—they decided to resume digging.

The same truck sped back by twenty minutes later. The robbers again discussed what to do. They were in the middle of several thousands of acres of public-hunting property owned by the
US Army Corps of Engineers. Every access point had large metal
gates to prevent vehicle entry, as the area was to be strictly walk-
in. A pickup truck racing up and down a logging road was puz-
zling but possibly explainable as joyriding teenagers, something
they both had done as kids. They wrote off the strange events and
went back to work.

An hour later, while taking a smoke break, Yancey heard a
man's scream in the distance. A chill went down his spine. When

he clearly heard the scream for help, he tossed his cigarette and called to his partner.

"Shhhh. Listen!" Yancey said.

Silence filled the swamp until the distant sound of a barred owl interrupted the eerie quiet.

"I don't hear shit…'sides that owl. And there's that campground just down the river. If someone was callin' for help, it coulda been someone down there."

"I don't think so."

"Man, we don't need this shit," Trance said nervously.

"We gotta go check it out."

"Are you a hundred percent sure you heard, 'Help me'?"

"Absolutely," Yancey said, obviously unnerved.

"Man, I don't know. We'll be in serious shit for being here. It's federal property."

"Look, I know, but somebody needs help. It came from that direction," Yancey explained, pointing northwest. "But I couldn't judge how far."

The two men weren't known for making good decisions, and for obvious reasons they didn't want anyone to know about their activities; but the thought that somebody needed help stirred something in both of them.

After a long moment, Trance spoke. "Shit! Okay, iffin' somebody's in trouble, they can't be too far away. Mark the direction on your GPS, and we'll ease that way and see what's goin' on."

CHAPTER 111

————— ☾ —————

T HE OLD MEN SAT IN THE HENRY CLAY'S LIBRARY LOOKING despondent—gloom and despair written all over their faces. They had managed to steal over a million dollars and had effectively gotten away with it until Bailey took it. Now they had less than zero, and Walter was facing another meeting with Kroger's security team, at which, Samantha had warned, he might be arrested.

"I'm not gonna let you take the rap for the Kroger deal," Sebastian said, discreetly sipping an adult beverage.

"Me neither," Bernard added.

"I 'preciate it, guys. But maybe Sam will think of something."

"How we gonna pay her?"

Walter sighed and then said, "I'm hoping we haven't used up the retainer yet."

"You better ask."

"Walter, you got any other ideas?" Bernard asked.

"I don't have the heart to do another job. I'm not cut out for this. This was all just a crazy dream of some crazy old men. Not to mention it was illegal," Walter said, stirring the ice in his drink.

Bernard and Sebastian looked at each other. A big question hadn't been answered yet. "Walter, what about your plan...you know...to get even with your ex-son-in-law?"

Walter took a big swig of his drink and then leaned his head back. He noticed the wall clock showed 10:32 p.m. The halls of the retirement home were quiet. His gaze moved to the big windows and out onto Commerce Street. No one was moving outside either. He smiled and said, "There's one thing I'm certain of: I have been so vocal about wantin' revenge that if anything ever happens to that guy, I'll be the first one they come looking for. That's why I wanted the money to hire a pro. I'd have a solid alibi, and there'd be no financial records tying me to it."

"What about me?" Sebastian offered.

"No, Sebastian. Thank you, but it's over. We've pushed our luck...past the edge. I'm thinkin' that I should focus my energy into doing somethin' good. We, as a group, oughta look at helpin' folks some other way."

"Legally?" Bernard asked.

"Yes, legally."

The three old men sat quietly drinking, staring out the windows, thinking about all that had happened and what the future might bring.

"Well, I'll be damned," Sebastian said.

"What?" Walter asked.

"Bailey just drove up."

CHAPTER 112

————— ☾ —————

B AILEY PARKED IN FRONT OF THE OLD HOTEL AND ALMOST started crying when she saw the old men in the library looking out at her. She dreaded having to face them. She hadn't slept much during the last few days, and she had lost over a million dollars of their money to a guy who she had thought loved her. Most of the stolen money had been Moon Pie's. But, since he treated Levi like shit, she hadn't thought they were close enough for Levi to choose a hateful half-blood over her. Obviously she had misread both relationships, so she never attempted to call Levi. Bailey figured that he would just lie, and she was tired of being lied to and tired of lying herself. It was time to face what she had done. Her main motivation in taking the money had been to protect it, but it was now painfully obvious that she should not have told Levi. Her next move was to tell her grandmother and her friends the truth and pray that they would one day forgive her.

On the drive home, she had decided to commit herself to achieving her dream of designing dresses, knowing that it might take several years to legally earn the needed start-up money. She was ready to make a fresh start, and she desperately wanted her grandmother in her life. Family is everything. Bailey supposed she would also have to pay back the money from Kroger that she had lost...though she had no idea how. That notion was almost too overwhelming to contemplate.

Bailey—embarrassed, confused, and praying for no small amount of forgiveness—walked inside to face the four old folks whose dreams she had destroyed.

CHAPTER 113

———— ☾ ————

As MOON PIE FINALLY MADE IT BACK TO THE ROAD THAT exited the Corps of Engineers property, his cell phone rang. When he saw that it was Levi calling, he was relieved. He wiped sweat off his face and answered, "Hey, man, where the hell are you!"

Levi could hear Moon Pie's voice, but the connection was poor. "Listen, I've got the money."

Moon Pie couldn't hear Levi. He said, "Levi, I can't hear you, so shut the hell up and listen to me. I'm bad hurt. Where are you?"

"I'm near the Holiday Inn. The cops are all over your trailer. Don't go there!"

Moon Pie was still driving and hadn't turned the radio down. He only heard something about cops at his trailer. What he said was, "I've lost a lot of blood, I...I need a...I'm goin' to the hospital!"

"I can barely hear you! Where are you? How bad are you hurt?"

Moon Pie was getting weaker and having great difficulty focusing on anything. Everything seemed to confuse him more the harder he tried to concentrate.

"I'll call you when I got better service!" Moon Pie yelled in frustration and hung up.

Moon Pie was now taking short, quick breaths and was getting colder. He turned the heater and blower to high. He rounded a bend, and through the dim fog, he saw the gate about two hundred yards ahead. Once his tires finally hit pavement, he knew that he'd make it to the hospital.

His glance down to check his injury was not quick. His mental acuity and reflexes were sluggish due to blood loss. The problem, besides the obvious, was that he couldn't recognize it.

When he finally looked back to the road, he saw a vehicle pulling up to the gate facing him. By the time he stopped, he was about eighty yards away.

He was trapped because the only other way out that he knew was several miles down the road he had just traveled and most likely impassable beyond where he had turned around. For what seemed like a long time, Moon Pie just stared straight ahead at the bright headlights. He couldn't make out any details of the vehicle.

At the gate, the game warden was surprised to see a vehicle coming out of the public hunting area, especially at ten thirty at night. *Damn spotlighters!* he thought, flipping on his dash-mounted blue light. He radioed the county dispatch his location and that he was approaching a suspicious vehicle.

The game warden assumed that it was meat hunters. Because the economy had gotten so bad, a fresh-killed deer would bring fifty dollars cash in some communities. A good group of night hunters, under the right conditions, could kill five to ten deer each night. If it was just a couple of teenage boys, he usually could put the fear of God in them. He hoped for that.

He took a deep breath. He knew he was in a position of strength. Not only did he have the authority of the state behind him, but he also had the training and the experience, and his truck was blocking the only exit of the property for miles. He noticed that the gate chain was hanging loose. *That asshole cut it*, he thought.

Moon Pie could see only the bright headlights in front of him. He wanted to continue forward. He could tell he didn't have the time or the strength for a chase. He pulled his pistol with the intention of shooting his way out if necessary, but he was too weak to hold it, so he rested the weapon on the side mirror with his left hand and eased his foot off the brake pedal, slowly rolling forward.

The game warden smelled trouble. He grabbed his binoculars, but the lights were so bright that through the fog everything was magnified and it looked as if it were snowing. *Dammit!*

He used the push bar on the front of his truck to bump the gate open, then slowly eased toward the suspicious vehicle. He stopped his truck just inside the gate so that the metal posts on either side provided an even wider barricade. The trucks were now only forty yards apart. The warden used his binoculars again.

"Shit! That looks like Jake Crosby's truck," he said aloud.

Moon Pie was eyeing what appeared to be an open spot to the right of the gate. He revved the engine and grinned deliriously. Either he was going to shoot the gap or he was going out in a hail of gunfire.

The warden flipped on the mounted spotlight, and Jake's truck was completely illuminated. He hoped that it would blind or disorient the driver. He slipped out of his truck, ran behind it, and then ran into the woods on his right side so he could identify the driver of the other truck and better assess the situation. Once he was into the woods, he saw the pistol resting on the mirror. He pulled his weapon and trained it on the driver as he crept toward the truck. The driver had been revving the engine, but now the truck was idling, stopped in a mud hole. The warden took three cautious steps toward the truck and noticed that the driver's head was slumped forward, leaning on the steering wheel. *What the hell?* he thought.

At twenty yards, the warden trained his pistol on the slumped head and gripped the pistol tightly enough to activate the laser sight. A small, bouncing red dot appeared on the side of the driver's head. He yelled, "Drop the gun and get out of the vehicle!"

There was no response and no movement. Again he yelled, "Drop the pistol! Get out of the vehicle right now!"

Still there was no movement in the truck or by the driver, which was very disconcerting.

The game warden had decided that he would give one more verbal warning and then he would approach the vehicle, ready to shoot the driver in the head if he moved a muscle. At that moment, a state trooper pulled up behind his truck, and more blue lights popped on. Their bright, fast, erratic pattern reflected off everything.

The warden, still sighting on the driver's head, eased closer to Jake's truck. At ten yards, he loudly ordered the driver out of the vehicle. There was still no movement. At this distance, he could tell that the driver was not Jake Crosby. This guy had long, stringy hair. Keeping his pistol trained on the driver's head, he quietly slipped up to the driver's side of the truck, and with snake-fast reflexes he grabbed the pistol free. The slumped driver never twitched. Upon securing the pistol, the warden once again ordered the driver out, and when he didn't respond, he snatched open the door, and Moon Pie, along with two additional handguns, fell out onto the muddy road.

As the state trooper approached, weapon drawn, the warden kicked the two guns out of reach and did a quick look inside Jake's truck to ensure there was no one else there.

The warden recognized Moon Pie, but his ashen color was shocking. When he saw his bloodstained shirt, he knelt down to feel for a pulse. He used the barrel of his weapon to push the bloody shirt back to reveal the wound.

"Gunshot! Call an ambulance! We got a gunshot victim."

The trooper called it in using his shoulder mic while the warden handcuffed Moon Pie. He knew better than to trust a dead snake. Administering first aid never crossed the mind of either officer. With Moon Pie secure, the warden quickly searched the vehicle and checked its tag.

"This is Jake Crosby's truck," he said excitedly and then stood over Moon Pie. He shook him while yelling, "Moon Pie! Wake up! Wake up, you sumbitch! Where's Jake Crosby! Where's Jake!"

Not getting any response, he left Moon Pie lying handcuffed, facedown, on the cold, muddy ground and ran to his truck to radio in the details and request assistance.

CHAPTER 114

A FTER TRAVELING LESS THAN A QUARTER MILE, THE GRAVE robbers checked the GPS to make certain they hadn't gotten off track. They could hear a tugboat pushing a barge down the river. Since the constant drone of the diesel engines was going to make it difficult for them to hear anything for several minutes, they decided to sit on a log and wait.

Although these men were not easily spooked, the presence of the vehicle and the screams had them very much on edge. At times, the searchlight of the tugboat reflected off the water into the air, briefly creating the appearance of an aurora. Each time the captain panned the several-million-candlepower light on their side of the river, it created hundreds of eerie, quickly moving shadows though the woods.

"It seems extra dark out here tonight, don't it?" Trance observed.

"Moon's underfoot; that's why. Darkest nights are when the moon's underfoot."

The men simultaneously pondered the idea of chasing a screaming sound in a river swamp on a dark night. "It's gonna take at least ten more minutes for that damn boat to get by us," Yancey said, watching how deeply the light penetrated the woods.

"I know, I know, but I swear I heard somethin'."

"I believe you heard something; we just don't know what."

"Maybe it was that campground."

"Coulda been anything, the way sound travels over water." Yancey paused and added, "Well, you 'bout ready? Your ex-wife will be pissed if we don't find some artifacts to sell."

"Look at that!"

"What? Where?"

"Right there. Almost at the far edge of the water. It looks like a light shining straight out of the water into the fog."

"Well, I'll be damned."

They watched in amazement as a narrow column of light went straight up out of the water into the fog and then disappeared. The light returned in a few moments and then went out again.

"What the hell is it? That's just too freakin' weird," Trance said, trying to focus his binoculars on the light beam.

"It ain't the tugboat. He's searching past us now."

"I'll tell you what…if I was out here by myself, I'd be running like crazy to get as far away from whatever in the hell that is."

"There's gotta be an explanation. Come on."

"Are you out of your freakin' mind?"

"Oh, hell, come on. After years of digging in graves, you ain't gone and got scared of haints on me now, have ya?"

CHAPTER 115

———— ☾ ————

T HE WEST POINT POLICE CHIEF WAS WITH MORGAN WHEN he received the call on his cell phone. He listened intently as Morgan tried unsuccessfully to read his facial expressions in response to the one-sided conversation that seemed to last forever. Morgan had a hand over her mouth and closed her eyes, saying a quick prayer. When the chief finally ended the call, she begged him to tell her what it was about.

"Okay, that was the sheriff. The game warden found Jake's truck over in a big swampy area along the river."

"Was he in the truck!" she interrupted.

"No. No, he wasn't…" he said and then paused, trying to find the best words to articulate the rest of the story.

"Why would…I don't understand. He'd tell me if he was going huntin', and I checked, his rifle is in the gun safe, and his hunting clothes are in the garage."

The police chief exhaled deeply. "Morgan, there's more."

Morgan collapsed into a chair, awaiting the news.

"Moon Pie Daniels was driving Jake's truck. He was coming outta the swamp when the warden stopped him."

Morgan's heart nearly stopped. It was her worst fear—the devil himself. That evil man who had been tormenting them had done something horrible to Jake. "So they have him in custody? Is he talkin'? Let me talk to him. Come on, let's go now!" Morgan jumped up.

"He's in bad shape. He'd been shot and basically had all but bled out before the game warden got there. He's barely alive, and the officers on scene don't think he's gonna make it."

Morgan fell back into the chair and blinked several times as she tried to understand what could have happened. "Jake musta shot him! Jake's still out there somewhere. We gotta go look!" Morgan jumped up again.

"They are...we're moving everybody we've got to that area to search. It's muddy, so they can follow the truck's tire tracks. We just seriously narrowed the search area, so we'll find Jake, okay?"

"I'm going!"

"No. You need to stay here with Katy," he said, immediately noticing Katy standing at the bottom of the stairs.

Apparently, Katy had been listening. She had tears rolling down her face, and when she saw Morgan stand up and head toward her, she started shaking.

Morgan picked Katy up and hugged her tightly. She surreptitiously wiped her own tears with her sleeve and then brushed back Katy's blonde hair from her face and said, "Katy, honey, they're real close to findin' Daddy. Okay? They think he's in the woods, and you and I know that's the best place he could be," Morgan lied.

The police chief needed to leave to help search, but he didn't want Morgan following, so he walked to the door and waved at the officer across the street to come inside.

"Katy, honey, look at me. Katy? Say something. Please," Morgan begged. Then she turned to look at the chief.

The police chief looked Katy in the eye and said, "Katy, you know better than anyone that your dad is a brave man and that he'd do anything for you. Right? Well, right now, he needs something from you. He needs you to help your mom. You gotta be strong for her. Okay? Can you do that for your dad?"

Katy nodded but didn't say anything. The tears were now pouring down both Katy's and Morgan's face. They didn't realize they were squeezing each other.

"Morgan, I gotta go. I promise to call the second I know anything. When they find him, the officer outside will take you wherever you need to go. In the meantime, stay here. Katy, you take care of your mom. Okay? As soon as I see your dad, I'll tell him what a big help you've been."

Morgan was now sitting on the stairs, holding Katy. They were both shaking. Morgan also finally nodded her head.

As soon as the police chief shut the door, he whispered to the young officer now standing on the front porch, "Do *not* let her leave without talking to me. This doesn't look good at all right now, and it's liable to get much worse."

CHAPTER 116

———— ☽ ————

As THE GRAVE ROBBERS APPROACHED THE LEVEE, THEY COULD now determine that the source of the light they had been following was coming from inside a mound of debris.

"This is crazy," Yancey said in a whisper. "How can that light just come out of the ground like that?"

"I think that's the drainpipe for the impoundment. It's got a bunch of limbs and shit piled around it, probably from beavers."

The two men were now just ten yards from the pipe. They could hear water flowing down it but nothing else. The light hadn't flashed in several minutes. They looked at each other, hoping the other had an idea that didn't include wading.

Finally, Trance yelled, "Hello, can you hear me? Is there anybody out there?"

The only sound was water spilling over the top of the pipe, and it seemed to be getting louder.

This time he screamed, "Hello!"

Not getting any response, Trance shrugged his shoulders and then said, "Well, I guess we should head back."

Jake couldn't hear anything but the sound of water rushing into the pipe. He was freezing and becoming disoriented. He was exhausted and thought that if he could sleep for a few hours, he'd be stronger and would be able to get free. He wasn't aware that his heart was straining to pump blood to his brain. His condition was deteriorating rapidly. Before he went to sleep, he wanted to see if the water volume was increasing or if it was just his imagination. He clicked on the flashlight.

"There! There it is!" Trance yelled. He stripped off his jacket and tossed his cell phone onto it. He immediately waded out into the water.

Yancey, the older of the two, didn't want to get wet, since their ride wouldn't arrive for another five hours.

He asked, "How deep in it?"

"I don't know yet!"

When he reached the pipe, the waves created from his wading splashed more water down the pipe, and the light went out. He climbed up onto the beaver debris, peered over the edge into the darkness, and yelled, "Hey! Can you hear me?" He then turned to his buddy and yelled, "Quick, bring me your flashlight!"

"Here, catch," Yancey said, still not wanting to plunge into the cold water unless and until he absolutely had to do it. He clicked on the flashlight and tossed it underhand.

Jake thought that he could hear voices, but he couldn't recognize the words. He thought he might be dreaming.

The grave robber didn't really know what to expect when he shined the flashlight into the drain. He was shocked to actually see a man in the bottom of the pipe.

"Holy shit! Get over here, quick! There's a guy trapped in the pipe!" Trance screamed toward Yancey. He turned his head back to the pipe and stuck his head into it. "Hey, man, can you hear me?"

Jake thought he was hearing voices again but opened his eyes and saw light. He initially thought it was coming from his flashlight, but when he realized that he could see his flashlight and it was turned off, he jerked his head back to look up.

Trance turned again to his partner and yelled, "He's alive! Get your ass over here! We gotta hurry!" He could see the water was almost to the man's neck. He yelled at Jake, "Hang on, mister! We're gonna get you out!"

Trance realized he couldn't reach the man. When Yancey arrived and looked down, he said, "Oh my God, we need ropes. I'll run back and get ours!"

"No! There's not enough time. He's about to drown. We gotta think of another way. Come on, let's start pushing mud up around the top of this pipe, and maybe we can slow the water down."

After several minutes, most of the water flowing in had slowed to a trickle. The two guys' hearts were racing. They were terrified that the man was going to drown and they couldn't stop it. One of the men shined the flashlight down to survey the situation. The water was at the man's chin, but it was swirling, so he assumed it was draining. He yelled, "Hang on! We're gonna get you out!"

Breathing heavily, the men looked at each other and they knew they didn't have much time.

Trance said, "You're gonna have to hold my legs, and I'll go down and grab him and you pull us up."

Yancey, who was not as physically fit, groaned. He didn't like that idea because he didn't think he could pull them both up. In fact, he knew he couldn't. He said, "If I drop ya, there won't be any way you can get out, and you'll drown too!"

"It's our only chance."

"I don't like it. I can't let you risk your life."

"It ain't your choice, it's mine," Trance said as he shined the light on Jake. As a former marine, he still believed in the code of not leaving a man behind. He said, "Look, we ain't got time to waste. I'm goin' down; grab my legs. You can do this!"

The younger guy knelt over the pipe and yelled, "I'm coming down. Hang in there, buddy."

The man slowly crawled over the edge, and he could feel his friend holding his legs tightly. He yelled to let him down some more. Water sloshed over the sides, hitting Jake in the face.

"Grab my hands!" Trance yelled and then placed the flashlight in his mouth and reached for Jake, who looked to the rescuer as though he had resigned himself to death. It was sickening to see an expression of complete hopelessness. If Jake didn't raise his arms, the rescuer wouldn't have anything to grab.

"Come on, man, don't give up on me," Trance screamed. He didn't have any other way to get the man out. He yelled again, "Grab my hands!"

After what seemed like several minutes to Trance, Jake raised his hands out of the water, but they still couldn't touch. To Trance's shock, he noticed that the man's wrists were bound and realized that he hadn't fallen in this pipe by accident; someone had dumped him here.

"Hey, we got a vehicle comin'!" Yancey screamed when he saw lights flashing through the trees in the distance.

"What?"

"Here comes a vehicle!"

Trance realized it could be the people who dropped the man into the pipe—probably coming back to admire their handiwork and to see if their victim was dead yet.

"Quick, pull me up!"

"I'm trying!"

CHAPTER 117

———— ☾ ————

T HE GAME WARDEN HAD BEEN BRIEFED ON THE HISTORY
between Jake and Moon Pie when he radioed in what had
happened in the swamp, so he had the trooper stay with Moon
Pie until the ambulance arrived while he went in search of Jake.

Reinforcements were en route, but the warden needed to get
started. It was easy for him to backtrack Moon Pie until he got
to the crossroads. He studied the different directions the tracks
went and chose to follow the freshest.

Moon Pie's driving was all over the road and off in the ditch,
causing the warden to wonder if Jake and Moon Pie had been
struggling during the drive. When he reached the end of the
tracks, he could see where Moon Pie had turned around. He
shut off his truck and got out so he could listen for anything that
might give him an idea of where Jake was. Not hearing anything,
he clicked on his large flashlight to look for footprints.

He immediately saw a brown coat lying in the ditch and
walked over and picked it up. The outside was covered in fresh
mud, and there appeared to be smeared blood on the inside lin-
ing. *I can't see Moon Pie wearing something this nice*, he thought.
There were footprints all around, but they didn't lead anywhere.

"Dammit!" he said aloud as rain began to fall. He started yelling Jake's name several times.

"I'm the game warden, and I'm here to help you!" he then screamed. He stood still, listening and praying for a response.

The warden knew that if he could find footprints, they would lead him to Jake, but the few here didn't leave the road. He doubted that in Moon Pie's condition he would have been able to cover his tracks. He wished that he had paid attention to what type of shoes or boots Moon Pie was wearing.

As the trained observer stood in the rain, studying the tire tracks, the few footprints, and the muddy coat, and thinking of Moon Pie's condition, it occurred to him what had happened. "He went the wrong way. He missed the turn because of a muddy windshield. Shit!"

The warden jumped into his truck, cranked the engine, and punched the gas.

CHAPTER 118

———— ☾ ————

"**A**RE HIS HANDS TIED?" YANCEY YELLED.

"Yeah, with plastic zip ties, and I'm guessin' whoever you just heard drivin' is the same asshole that dropped him in this pipe."

"Shit, they'll kill us too if they find us!"

They could hear a truck coming closer fast. They had less than thirty seconds.

"Man, I can't leave him."

"Listen to me—they'll kill us. It's probably the Dixie Mafia or some drug thing!" Yancey yelled with great urgency.

"We gotta get some help. Do you got cell service?"

"No, I already looked. Come on, we gotta get the hell outta here. We're freakin' sittin' ducks if they drive up!"

"I can't leave this poor bastard," Trance said.

"You ain't no good to him or your kids dead! Now come on!"

The truck's engine revved as it went through a mud hole, and it was definitely getting closer. "Dammit to hell."

"We gotta hide on the other side of the levee!"

The two men quickly sloshed back to the levee, grabbed their coats, and crawled into the button brush as the truck's headlights flashed through the trees above them. They were out of breath and running on adrenaline, not realizing just how cold they were.

"Get down, here they come," Yancey whispered.

The would-be rescuers turned their heads from the approaching truck and pushed their white faces down into the mud so they wouldn't be seen in the headlights. Doing so, however, prevented them from seeing the small, flashing blue light on the truck.

The warden followed Moon Pie's tire tracks right to the middle of the levee and turned off his truck so he could listen for clues. He quickly got out and didn't hear anything. He immediately shouted, "Jake Crosby!"

The rescuers looked up slightly and saw the small blue lights flashing on the dark truck.

"It's the law," Yancey whispered.

"Do you think he dumped him?"

"How do I know? But why would he be yelling some guy's name?"

"Jake! It's the game warden! Can you hear me!" the warden yelled as he walked down to the water's edge. *This has to be the location*, he thought. With his flashlight, he could see plumes of muddy water, indicating that something or someone had recently been in it.

"Maybe he's tryin' to see if he's still alive," Yancey whispered.

The warden walked closer to the edge of the muddy water. When he saw two sets of fresh footprints leading over the levee, he quietly removed his Smith & Wesson service revolver from his holster, then shined his flashlight down at the tracks.

The grave robbers turned rescuers were too committed to hiding to run, so they lay facedown in the wet leaves and hoped the warden wouldn't spot them. They prayed they weren't about to be executed, since they didn't know if the officer was crooked and responsible for the guy in the pipe.

The warden followed the tracks over the levee and down to the woods' edge, where he saw the two men. He trained his pistol on them and shouted, "You there, in the woods, put your hands where I can see them. Now!"

The rescuers complied.

"Stand up and walk to me!"

They did as directed, shaking from a combination of fear, cold, and adrenaline. They slowly walked up the levee bank, hands in the air, straight at the man who was shining a bright flashlight in their faces. They noticed a red laser moving between them, and it made their legs feel like jelly.

"Who are you, and what the hell are y'all doing here?" the warden asked when they got close.

"We're lost. Who the hell are you?" Yancey asked.

He realized that in all the excitement, he hadn't identified himself. "I'm the game warden. Tell me the real reason that you're here!" he said, keeping the light in their faces.

The men sighed from relief. Trance started to explain as he took a few steps closer, "This is gonna sound crazy—"

"Stay right there. Don't move any closer," the game warden interrupted.

"Listen to me—there's a guy trapped in the bottom of that drainpipe. We heard him screaming for help and were trying to pull him out when you drove up. His hands are tied, and we heard you comin', so we just freaked out and hid. We thought you were gonna try to kill us too!"

The warden quickly processed what they were saying. They looked normal enough, aside from being soaking wet. He quickly glanced over his shoulder at the drainpipe without taking his weapon off the two men.

"I swear, Officer. I'm tellin' the truth. That guy's in bad shape, and we're wasting time!"

Trance bolted down the levee, yelling, "Come on, we need your help!"

All three men quickly sloshed out to the pipe and peered in. The water had receded some, but Jake's head was slumped back, facing up, and his eyes were closed. The game warden instantly recognized the man as Jake Crosby.

"Jake! Jake! Can you hear me? Jake! We're here to rescue you! Hang on!" the warden yelled rapidly. He could see the vapor from Jake's breath, and he knew that he was alive.

"I went in upside down, but he couldn't reach up to me. It's a long way down."

"It'll take all of us to pull him out, if we can," Yancey said.

The warden did a quick announcement and said, "I got an idea. We'll use my winch!"

As the warden ran through the water to his truck, he yelled, "One of y'all come help me."

The warden flipped his Warn winch to free spool and said, "Start pulling this to the pipe while I radio in where we're at and what's goin' on."

He grabbed his radio mic and keyed it. "This is unit Twenty-Two for county dispatch. Do you read me? Over."

There was about a five-second pause, and a young female voice said, "Go ahead, Twenty-Two."

"I got an urgent situation. I located the missing person, Jake Crosby. He's trapped in a drainpipe, but I think I can get him out. But he's gonna be hypothermic for sure. Have an ambulance meet Trooper Wallace at his twenty. It's too muddy for the van to get back to where I'm at. I'll meet 'em at the gate. Make sure they got warm blankets. Over."

After several long seconds, she responded, "Ten-four, unit Twenty-Two. Copy that. Will advise."

The warden had another idea. He quickly searched through his hunting gear until he found his tree stand safety harness. When he looked up, they had the winch cable pulled almost all the way out. He inserted the remote control and laid it on the hood, and when he saw they had enough cable, he flipped it from free spool to lock and took off running for the water.

"Okay, look, you're the thinnest and you look plenty strong," the warden said to Trance as he took off his belt. "There's barely enough room in the pipe for him and no way both of you can fit down there at the same time, so I need you to let me lower you down into the pipe by my belt, and then you wrap this safety harness under Jake's arms, leaving a loop, and we'll winch you out. Then we'll drop the cable hook down and catch the loop on the vest so we can slowly winch Jake out. Got it?"

"Got it. I'll do whatever," Trance said, shivering.

The warden then turned to the older man. "Ever run a winch?"

Yancey nodded. "I can handle it."

"The control's on my hood. Go! When I holler, give me some slack. Okay?"

Yancey started running to the truck. "You got it!"

The warden shined his light into the pipe to analyze the situation one more time. "All right, Jake. Hang on, buddy. We're comin' to get you!"

He then turned to Trance and said, "I wish I could see his legs. He could be wedged in some debris down there. I can't tell anything with that muddy water. The winch is gonna pull him in half if he's stuck on something down there. So when you get down there, look closely to see if you can tell anything."

"I understand," Trance said as he put the belt around his chest and they tightened the winch cable.

"Be careful and hurry up," the warden said, as they lowered him headfirst into the drainpipe.

CHAPTER 119

———— ͡ ————

T HE RAIN ON THE WINDOWS WAS THE ONLY SOUND IN THE
house, and the aroma of coffee filled the air. Morgan and
Katy had been sitting together in silence on the couch for almost
an hour. Since Katy had not answered any of Morgan's questions,
Morgan decided to just sit beside her and hold her. She knew
Katy was strong and that she would talk or ask questions on her
own terms.

When the phone rang, Morgan jumped and screamed, but
before the second ring, she answered it. It was the police chief.

"Morgan, they found Jake. He's alive, but he needs medical
attention."

"Where is he!"

"They haven't gotten him out of the woods yet. I called as
soon as I heard. I can have the officer outside take you to where
the ambulance is waiting, or he can take you straight to Baptist
Hospital in Columbus. That's where they're gonna take Jake."

"I wanna go right now! Thank you!"

"Morgan, listen to me—I don't know anything yet. Keep
your cell with you."

Morgan turned away from Katy and asked in a whisper, "Has
he been shot?"

"I honestly don't know. We only know at this point that he needs medical attention. That's all I've got, but I promise I'll call you when I know more."

CHAPTER 120

———— ☾ ————

A S TRANCE WAS SLOWLY WINCHED DOWN INTO THE PIPE, HE yelled, "Hey, do you know this guy?"

"Yeah, sorta. His name's Jake Crosby," the warden yelled back.

"How the hell he get in this pipe?"

"It's a long story, but this really badass dude has wanted him dead for over a year."

Once the rescuer got near Jake, he was shocked at how pale he was. His head was still leaned back against the pipe, but the water was now below his shoulders. With both hands shaking, the rescuer held his flashlight in his mouth as he tried to stretch the vest around Jake's arm. He took the flashlight out of his mouth and with his free hand slapped Jake's face. His eyes slowly opened.

"Jake, I'm here to get you out. Can you hear me?"

Jake's eyes were not focusing, and he slowly closed them. His body shivered. The water pouring down around them was increasing.

The warden couldn't see anything but the rescuer's back. "How's he doing?"

"We gotta get him outta here quick! He's out. His breathing's real shallow, and he's shaking. He's dying. And it's real tight in here."

"Hurry up!"

Trance was straining. The belt around his chest constricted his breathing, and blood was rushing to his head. His hands shook as he tried to attach the vest around Jake.

Having seen Jake's face several minutes earlier, the warden also knew that they didn't have much time. He had dealt with hypothermia before; Jake's core body temperature would be dangerously low. He hoped that Jake was still just pale, not yet blue and puffy. If they didn't get his core temperature up, he'd die.

Finally, Trance secured the vest around Jake, but the loop the winch cable needed to hook on kept dropping into the water. It wasn't visible.

"Jake, can you hold this loop up?" he struggled to ask, trying to put the loop in Jake's hand. Jake's eyes cracked open but quickly shut.

"Is it on him!"

"Yeah!" Trance answered with a groan.

The warden rose and yelled at Yancey, by the truck, "Okay… slowly start tightenin' up! When I drop my hand, that means stop!"

The eight-thousand-pound winch kicked in, and the cable slowly pulled Trance up. The warden dropped his raised arm and assisted the shaking rescuer out of the pipe. Trance quickly unfastened the belt around his chest and looked the warden in the eye as he pulled slack. Even in the pitch-blackness, the warden could tell from his face that he was worried. The warden screamed for slack, and it came to him slowly.

"He looks like he's given up," Trance whispered.

"Shit! I was afraid of that!" The warden dropped the winch cable hook into the pipe and started trying to catch the safety vest.

"Dammit! Come on. Come on. Don't give up on me, Jake! I'm trying!"

The hook hovered in the muddy water where the loop should have been, but after three unsuccessful attempts to hook the loop, the warden was getting frustrated. He heard the radio in his truck announcing that the ambulance had just arrived at the gate.

"Try to the left a bit!" Trance offered. "There! Right there!"

Tightening the cable by hand, the warden felt the hook catch and the weight of Jake's body.

"I got it! Take up the slack!" the warden screamed, not letting go of the cable. "Okay! Slowly, in short bursts! Start pulling him up!" he screamed.

All three men said silent prayers that Jake's legs weren't held too tightly on anything. The winch would easily pull off his legs if they were hung, and they wouldn't know it until it was too late.

Jake rose out of the water a few inches at a time. His head slumped forward, and it rubbed against the pipe as he was pulled up. As Jake's waist cleared the water, they could see his wrists zip-tied together.

"Come on, take in more cable!" the warden yelled as Jake's knees cleared the water, which started draining faster.

The warden was now trying to guide the winch cable, but it was too much to hold. The cable had already cut his hands. They were so cold that he couldn't feel it.

"Grab him!" the warden yelled to Trance, who had already reached down for the safety vest and started pulling.

"Whoa! Stop the cable!" the warden screamed. Jake was near the top, and the cable was burying into the side of the pipe, threatening to cut into Jake's shoulder.

"We gotta pull him out from here," the warden explained to Trance.

They both pulled with all their strength. Jake's dead weight, coupled with the awkwardness of kneeling on the muddy beaver dam, made the task all the more difficult. Slowly they freed Jake from the pipe and laid him on his back.

"Oh God!" Trance exclaimed when he saw Jake's lower leg.
"What!"

The rescuer pointed at the leg bone protruding through Jake's pants.

The warden saw it and grimaced. Jake's body was limp—lifeless.

"We gotta get him outta here," he said, unhooking the winch cable from the vest. "Wind it in!" he yelled to Yancey. "Here, get under one arm. Help me carry him to the truck," the warden said.

Both men wrapped Jake's arms around their necks, praying they weren't carrying a dead man.

"Come on, Jake! Hang in there!"

They slipped a few times in the mud but were almost walking on water by the time they got to the levee and laid Jake down on his back. They were breathing heavily, and giant plumes of vapor could be seen in the truck's headlights, along with the rain.

The warden pointed at Yancey, who was almost finished rewinding the winch cable. "Turn the heater in my truck on high! Let's get these wet clothes off him fast."

They started pulling off Jake's jacket and shirt. He had no color, and the warden touched his neck to feel for a pulse. When he couldn't find one, he almost panicked, but he caught himself.

"Here, use this knife to cut his pants off," the warden said, handing the knife to Trance before running to his truck. He had an emergency blanket in his tool box. When he returned, he was dismayed to see Jake's legs. They were black, and his calves and ankles were swollen so badly they couldn't see the zip ties buried in his pants and flesh. He noticed something appeared odd but didn't take the time to look closely. He had to get Jake to the ambulance.

"What's caused this?" Trance asked in shock.

The warden started wrapping Jake's wet, nude body in the blanket. Then he took the knife and carefully cut off the zip ties binding Jake's wrists.

"I'm guessing that the suction in the pipe has sucked all the blood in his body down into his legs. That's a really bad thing. Open that truck door!" he said as he picked Jake up without hesitation.

After laying Jake down on the passenger's side, he instructed the others to climb into the bed. The truck had only a single bench seat.

"An ambulance is on the way. It oughta be at the gate when we get there. We'll get y'all dry blankets there. Hang on!" he said as he jumped in and punched the gas, spinning the truck around

Once he was pointed out, he stood on the gas pedal and picked up his radio's microphone "This is unit Twenty-Two to county dispatch, come in!"

"Go ahead, Twenty-Two," she immediately responded.

"I got Jake Crosby in my truck! Advise medics he's unconscious and severely hypothermic, and he's got an open, compound fracture of his left leg! My ETA is five minutes! Out!"

"Ten-four, Twenty-Two. Copy that."

The game warden threw the microphone down, reached across, and put his hand on Jake's chest as the truck bounced in the ruts, saying, "Hang on, brother! I'm gettin' you outta here!"

CHAPTER 121

———— ☾ ————

T HE STATE TROOPER ASSISTED THE TWO MEDICS IN LOADING Moon Pie into the ambulance. They were rushing to get their patient to the hospital. One asked if the handcuffs were necessary.

"I ain't taking 'em off," the state trooper explained.

Moon Pie was a bloody mess lying on the white sheets of the gurney. It was obvious he had lost a great deal of blood, and nobody thought much of his survival chances.

"What's he done?" the female medic asked as she stowed some gear.

The state trooper nodded toward their new patient. "That's Ethan 'Moon Pie' Daniels. He's violent, a world-class poacher, a con man, we suspect he's beginning to dabble in Internet scams, we know that he's a drug runner, and he's basically just a worthless piece of crap who would do anything for easy money…and sometimes just for the hell of it. You should consider him very dangerous."

Suddenly the paramedics seemed to have lost their urgency.

"Well, we'll keep him cuffed even though the hospital hates having their patients handcuffed. We'll tell 'em about this dude."

"I promise you, cuffed is the only way to travel with this guy."

"Gotcha. You're comin' with us, aren't you?" she asked, feeling uncomfortable about being in the back with such a notorious criminal.

"Yeah, I guess so. I sure hate leaving my buddy out there, but I gotta follow protocol," the trooper answered.

The trooper explained the situation to a young deputy who had just arrived and then asked him to keep an eye on his cruiser until he returned.

Before loading Moon Pie into the ambulance, the state trooper bent to his face and said, "Hey, Moon Pie? Can you hear me? Can you open your eyes?"

Moon Pie didn't move. The two medics and the deputy watched curiously.

"Moon? Open your eyes!"

Moon Pie barely opened them, and the state trooper leaned in until the front brim of his hat almost touched Moon Pie's face. He said, "I got your sorry, gutshot ass, and I'm gonna stay right beside you."

As the trooper stood, blocking the view of the medics, he put his hand on Moon Pie's wound and squeezed. "Is that where it hurts?"

Moon Pie let out a quick whimper and then passed out.

"We really should go," the female medic said awkwardly.

She and her partner loaded the gurney into the ambulance, and the decorated Mississippi state trooper climbed in too.

The trooper had a deep satisfaction, knowing that, most likely, the last thing the racist, white-trash thug would ever see was a black state trooper smiling down at him.

CHAPTER 122

———— ☾ ————

ORGAN AND KATY RODE IN THE BACKSEAT OF A BLACK-
and-white West Point police cruiser, its blue lights flashing as they sped east on Highway 50. Morgan held Katy's hand.
Katy still hadn't uttered a word for the last two hours. Tears were
steadily pouring down their cheeks.

When they heard the game warden alerting county dispatch
that he had Jake, Morgan's heart jumped for joy, but then hearing that Jake was unconscious scared her. She cradled Katy and
prayed for Jake.

Morgan noticed that the young officer driving had both
hands on the steering wheel, so she raised her head enough to
see the speedometer read eighty. On the bridge, high over the
Tombigbee River, she glanced out the window to see a barge
pushing downriver with its powerful spotlight like a giant white
laser cutting the fog over the black water.

The young officer nervously cleared his throat. "They found
your husband up the river…a few miles that way," he said with a
tilt of his head to the left, never taking his hands from the steering wheel or his eyes from the road.

Morgan looked into the gloomy, drizzly darkness. She could
see the outline of the wilderness—giant skeletons of dead trees

standing in the flooded sloughs like huge, silent witnesses to hundreds of years of life and death in the swamp.

"How long until we get there?"

"Ten, maybe twelve minutes at the outside. I'm drivin' as fast as I can. The roads are really slick."

Morgan considered what she was about to see. She wondered what Jake had been through and about its toll on him. She considered how to protect Katy from seeing her dad, if his injuries were visible. Morgan tried to be strong as she tightly squeezed Katy and again silently prayed for their small but growing family.

CHAPTER 123

———— ☾ ————

THE GAME WARDEN DROVE LIKE A BAT OUT OF HELL DOWN the muddy road. The truck's heater was blasting on high, and the windows were fogging quicker than he could wipe them off.

"Hang in there, Jake…you oughta be feeling warmer soon!" he commented as he wiped the windshield.

"Unit Twenty-Two to base. What's the ETA of my ambulance?"

"Stand by, Twenty-Two," she responded immediately. "Unit Twenty-Two, they report four minutes."

"Roger that."

He could not imagine what Jake had been through tonight. Jake's legs scared him. He had never seen skin so dark from blood and wondered how any could have been left for his brain to function. He feared the worst.

When his truck rounded the last curve on the remote property before the gate, he could see Jake's truck's lights and several other vehicles. Knowing there were others to help was a huge relief. He passed Jake's truck in the road and slid to a stop just outside the gate, where multiple police cars were parked, with lights flashing. Before he could open his door, five officers were there to help.

"The ambulance will be here any minute!" one shouted.

"What can we do?" another asked.

He looked at Jake, still unconscious, and said, "I need dry blankets!"

The two deputies immediately sprinted to their cars.

The warden wiped sweat from his face and then turned to look in the back of his truck at the two wet rescuers, who were now trying to stand. He could see them shivering.

The warden got out of his truck and yelled, "I need to get these guys warm and dry too!" He heard the ambulance. It cut its siren when it got close. He grabbed a deputy and said, "Get those guys warmed up, but don't let 'em out of your sight. I've got a lot of questions for them, and I don't want to lose 'em."

"Do I need to cuff 'em?" asked the deputy.

The warden looked at the two men who had just risked their own lives to save Jake. They were hiding something, but he didn't think they were a threat at this point. They were sitting opposite one another on the wheel wells, their heads in their hands, shaking.

"No. But watch 'em," he said, only loud enough for the deputy to hear.

The warden turned to Trance and Yancey. "Look, guys, I don't know who y'all are yet, or even why you were back there in the first place, but I wanna thank you for what y'all did. You saved that man's life, and that means a lot to me."

Being around so many cops terrified the two grave robbers, and they were nearly frozen, so all they could muster were slight nods.

"One of these deputies will take y'all to the hospital. We'll talk there."

"Oh, that's okay. We're fine, Officer. We can walk from here," Trance instantly replied and stood. Yancey nodded his agreement.

The warden, expecting something like this, said, "I'm sorry, fellas, but y'all don't have a choice."

When the warden turned around, the gurney was quickly being unloaded from the ambulance. He climbed inside his truck to help.

"Watch his legs. They're bluish black with blood, and the left one's broken."

The medics looked up, wanting a further explanation as they opened the blanket to examine Jake's legs.

"He's been stuck in a pipe full of running water. I think it sucked all the blood down into them."

The medics carefully laid Jake on the gurney. They did a quick assessment. His pulse and respiration were extremely low; the color of his face was pale, verging on blue and puffy. The biggest concerns were his legs and that he was unconscious.

"His legs can't get above his heart. We gotta move, stat!" one medic said to the other. "Let's roll!"

As they loaded Jake into the back of the ambulance, the warden heard one say that the electric blanket was already warm.

"You riding?" a paramedic asked the warden.

It would be just as easy to follow in his truck, but the warden really wanted to stay with Jake. An older deputy understood immediately and spoke up, "Go. I'll bring your truck."

The game warden, dripping wet, climbed into the back of the ambulance, the doors slamming shut behind him. Through the windows, the ominous blue lights filling the cold night air contrasted with the stark white, warm, sterile inside of the ambulance. He looked down at Jake's colorless face. His head rocked in rhythm to the swaying of the big van as the driver sped to the hospital.

The warden tried to warm his hands as he watched the young medic, who looked barely old enough to shave, deftly start an IV in Jake's left arm.

"Hang in there, Jake!" was all that the warden could think to say.

CHAPTER 124

———— ☾ ————

L EVI WAS WAITING FOR MOON PIE OUTSIDE THE BAPTIST
Hospital Emergency Department in Columbus when an
ambulance rolled in. He never heard a siren, but the flashing red
lights set the stage for bad news for someone. Two orderlies hurried out to help. Levi overheard one of them say that it was a
DOA, a gunshot victim from a swampy area north of town.

That got Levi's attention. He was expecting Moon Pie to
drive up, not ride up in the back of an ambulance. He asked,
"Huntin' accident?"

The orderlies didn't realize anyone could overhear them.
They exchanged glances, wondering who this guy was.

"I'm just wondering if it was a hunting accident."

Levi was dressed respectably and looked like any normal
citizen who might be anxiously waiting in the ER.

"I don't think so," one replied slowly.

The other orderly crossed his forearms, making an X, signaling the driver to stop backing up.

Levi said thanks and then stood silently as the orderly opened
the back doors. The first thing Levi saw was a state trooper sitting inside. No one seemed to be in a rush, and when the gurney and the patient were pulled out, he immediately understood.

Whoever was on the gurney was completely covered in blood, as was the formerly white sheet covering the person's head.

Levi sensed that it was Moon Pie, which wasn't a surprise. He had always lived on the edge, cheating death more times than Levi could count, but he needed to know for certain that this was his half brother.

Levi exhaled deeply and then approached the medics as they wheeled the body inside. At the last moment, he decided not to ask any more questions that could raise suspicions about him.

"Car accident?" he asked the trooper instead.

"I'm sorry, sir. We can't give out any information," the state trooper replied politely.

Levi trailed several feet behind the covered gurney. He watched a young doctor in scrubs hurry to the side of the deceased. He raised the sheet, did a quick examination of the body, and pronounced the victim dead at 11:23 p.m. He pulled the sheet back over the body and pointed down the hall.

From Levi's vantage point, he clearly saw Moon Pie's face. His half brother was dead. He looked around the empty ER and then slowly, calmly stepped though the exit next to the automated doors.

As Levi walked to his truck, he realized that he didn't feel anguish or sorrow. Moon Pie had tormented him all of his life. Ethan "Moon Pie" Daniels was not a good person, and Levi had allowed Moon Pie to lead him down many a wrong road from an early age.

Levi experienced something liberating from Moon Pie's death, and it occurred with perfect timing. Levi had been at a crossroads and needed guidance or a sign. Moon Pie's death was one or both. He needed to find out who had killed him.

He glanced back at the hospital. The state trooper was staring at him through the glass door.

CHAPTER 125

c

M ORGAN, KATY, AND THEIR POLICE ESCORT HEADED
straight to the hospital after listening to the radio chatter that Jake was in an ambulance, en route to the ER.

When Morgan saw an ambulance parked at the hospital emergency department's door, she swallowed hard even though she knew from the radio that Jake had not yet arrived. The police car parked as close as possible to the entrance. The officer quickly got out to open the back door for Morgan and Katy. Morgan jumped out and was pulling Katy by the arm as she hurried inside.

It was late, almost Tuesday morning, and there were no patients around, but she immediately garnered the head nurse's attention when she rushed inside.

"Is Jake Crosby here yet?" she asked, thinking that she might have missed something.

"No, ma'am," she replied, looking over her bifocals.

Before the nurse could expound, the policeman said, "He's not here yet, Mrs. Crosby. I just heard on the radio that the ambulance is just a few minutes away."

Morgan squeezed Katy's hand.

The nurse was looking at Katy but asked the policeman, "Is he the hypothermic patient en route?"

"Yes, ma'am. This is his wife and daughter."

The nurse walked over and put her arm around Morgan and smiled down at Katy. "We're ready for him. We've been warming blankets and IVs. We'll take good care of him. I promise."

Morgan tried to smile.

"Do you know what happened?" the nurse asked.

Morgan sighed deeply. "No, no, we don't."

The nurse glanced down at Katy and was about to suggest that Morgan and Katy see a doctor, when the policeman ran to the back door.

"They're here!"

The ER nurse called back to someone, and the ER suddenly came to life. Orderlies and nurses ran through the common area to help. A doctor stood ready, and a state trooper emerged from a back room with a cup of coffee in hand.

Morgan picked up Katy, and they pushed their way outside to get as close as possible to the ambulance. The red lights made Morgan squint, and she could see people in the back of the ambulance before the doors opened.

When the doors opened, Morgan could see Jake's colorless face. His eyes were barely open.

Morgan gasped, "Oh my God!" She squeezed Katy and turned her so she couldn't see Jake.

The medics were explaining Jake's condition to the nurses. At the top of the list were his swollen legs and ankles. The color had started coming back to his legs, but his ankles and calves were still grossly enlarged. During the drive, the medics had determined that Jake's ankles were zip-tied together and, although it was difficult, had managed to cut off the ties. They relayed his last vitals. Jake's temperature had improved considerably, but it was still dangerously low.

With everything quickly explained, the hospital crew was wheeling Jake inside. Everyone followed into the main ER. Morgan touched Jake's face when he rolled by. She knew he wasn't recognizing anything because of his blank stare. She sat Katy down but kept holding her hand as she tried to follow the mass of people.

The nurse stopped Morgan as Jake entered the trauma area. "Mrs. Crosby, you must stay out here. As soon as I know something, I'll come and tell you." And with that, she disappeared behind an automatic door. As the door closed, Morgan could hear several frantic voices discussing Jake's condition, and she caught a glimpse of Jake naked. His legs were dark blue, almost black, from the thighs down. They quickly covered him with a blanket.

"Why is he naked?" she muttered to no one.

"His clothes were wet, and we cut 'em off to help warm him up," the game warden said, standing behind Morgan. He was dripping wet too.

She jumped. She had not heard him approach. When Morgan turned to face him, he introduced himself. "Mrs. Crosby, I'm Banks Gran. I helped pull your husband outta the pipe tonight."

"Pipe? What? What pipe?" Morgan asked slowly. Then she continued, "I don't know about any of this."

Two blanket-wrapped men walked into the ER with two deputies escorting them. When Morgan saw them, she pulled Katy behind her, thinking these men were responsible for what had happened to Jake. She stared at them, trying to fit the puzzle together in her mind.

"Will you please tell me what the hell happened?" she asked. Then, pointing to the men, she said, "Did they do this to Jake?"

The West Point police chief arrived in time to hear Banks beginning to talk to Morgan and interrupted, suggesting that they all sit down in the lobby. Morgan reluctantly walked away from where she had last seen Jake. She picked up Katy again, walked to the lobby, and then sat down with the warden and the chief.

Everyone listened intently as the warden shared his story about where, when, and how he found Jake and the rescue. Morgan kept looking back and forth between the warden and the ER, watching for a doctor or the head nurse to appear. She was stunned to learn that Jake had been tied up and left to die inside a drainpipe. The warden explained that he knew only what happened to him after Jake arrived at the Corps of Engineers property. He didn't have any idea how Jake and Moon Pie had crossed paths. The police chief admitted that he didn't either but that they would piece it together soon.

Morgan dropped her face into her left hand and kept her right on Katy. She asked, "What about Moon Pie? Has that bastard been arrested?"

The warden looked at the police chief, who nodded his assent. He then scooted closer to Morgan so that not everyone could hear. He had just been briefed about the terror that Moon Pie had wrought on this family.

"I left out one piece of the story."

Morgan looked straight up at the warden and then at the police chief. The warden placed his hand on her knee for reassurance. "Moon Pie's dead. He didn't even make it to the hospital. We're pretty sure that Jake shot him."

Morgan was absolutely stunned.

Katy lifted her head and blinked her eyes, a huge sense of relief sweeping over her. She asked enthusiastically, "So Dad shot the bad guy?"

The chief didn't really know what to say. He looked at Morgan and then back at Katy and said, "Yes, Katy, that's what it looks like."

Katy exhaled deeply and said, "Way to go, Dad!"

The chief and warden exchanged quick, uncomfortable looks and then smiled knowingly at Katy. Katy smiled back.

Katy was finally free to be a kid again. Just a kid. Not one that was constantly being watched and talked about. A normal, regular kid, finally.

Morgan leaned down and kissed Katy on the head. Katy hugged her back. Time seemed to slow as Morgan savored the first expressive hug from Katy in quite some time.

The ER door pushed open, and a nurse called, "Mrs. Crosby, you and your daughter can come back now."

Morgan stood and wiped the tears from her eyes and then wiped Katy's. Katy pulled free from her mom's hand and then walked over to the warden and police chief.

Katy hugged the chief and said, "Thanks for helping my dad." Then she went to the warden, hugged his neck, and said, "And thank you for saving my daddy's life."

Katy turned around and then ran toward the nurse. Over her shoulder, she yelled, "I love y'all!"

Morgan, tears streaming down her face, was right behind her. As they passed the nurse, she handed them towels, since they were now wet from hugging the officers. The Crosby girls quietly walked into the stark white room. Jake was covered in several blankets and some odd-looking electrical cover. Only his neck and face were visible. He had a fleece toboggan on his head. His eyes were closed, and his facial features displayed exhaustion, but his skin color had improved greatly since they first saw him. Morgan hurried over and touched Jake's face. Katy, afraid that she might hurt him, lightly touched his shoulder. Morgan's bottom lip started quivering when Katy squeezed her hand.

The doctor, who had been entering information on a handheld electronic tablet when they entered, looked up and smiled at Morgan and Katy, looking each in the eyes. He had bifocals on top of his totally bald head. Katy smiled. She thought he looked funny.

"Mrs. Crosby, your husband's had quite a night. He was in pretty bad shape when they first loaded him in the ambulance. We think his core temperature had dropped into the upper seventies, but he's responding nicely. I'm sure you know it needs to be around ninety-nine degrees. Typically, major organs start shutting down when the core temp drops, but all indicators are that didn't happen.

"I have two concerns. During his time in the drainpipe, the suction of the water pulled a substantial amount of blood from his upper body down into his legs. If he had stayed there much longer, it would have been fatal. Very, very fortunately, when he was pulled out, they laid him on the ground with his head higher than his legs and transported him that way to the ambulance. By doing that they kept the blood circulating at a controlled pace. He also sustained an open fracture of his left fibula, and I am deeply concerned about infection at that site. As soon as he's stabilized, he'll need surgery."

Morgan was trying to take it all in, but she was just listening for the words *He's going to be all right*. That's what she needed to know.

The doctor pressed on. "Primarily, at this moment, however, we are worried about blood clots. He's not in the clear yet. His blood was violently reorganized inside his body, and when this happens, the red blood cells can get crushed. We have to closely monitor his progress. We'll be giving him blood thinners to help dissipate any clots. In a nutshell, he needs rest. A lot of it. We will have to take all of these things in stages. Do you have any questions?"

"When can I take him home?"

The doctor smiled. "We'll know more tomorrow."

"Can I try to talk to him?"

"Sure. He was awake a few minutes ago, but he's very groggy. Mr. Crosby, if you can hear me, open your eyes. Your family is here."

Jake cracked open one eye. He could see Morgan tightly holding Katy against her side. He could only move his lips to form a fraction of a smile.

The doctor stepped away, saying, "I'll be right over here if you need me."

Morgan bent over, kissed him, and straightened a few strands of hair that were escaping from the tight toboggan. She said, "I've been so worried about you."

"Me too, Dad," Katy chimed in.

"It's been a long night," he slurred.

"I love you," Morgan said, fighting back tears.

"I know, and I love you too. Both of you. All three of you!" Jake said with as much emphasis as he could muster.

"It's over, Jake. Moon Pie's dead," Morgan said.

Jake closed his eyes, and it felt good. He would learn the details later, but for now, that's all he needed to know.

Katy said, "Good job, Dad! I'm so proud of you."

Jake smiled, and a tear began to roll down his cheek.

Morgan sat Katy down, leaned into his ear, and said, "I'm glad that son of a bitch is dead too."

Katy said, "Hey, Dad, Scout came home! Guess what? She hadn't run away. The neighbors went outta town, and she got locked in their garage! The whole time we were calling for her, she was trapped and couldn't get out!"

Jake smiled deliriously and managed, "That's good, kiddo." He was thinking back to his near death inside the drainpipe and that same feeling of helplessness. With tears again in his eyes, he added, "Give her a big hug for me. It's really scary to be trapped like that."

"Hey, Dad, can I have a Kindle Fire?"

Jake turned to Morgan and smiled. They both knew that the Crosby family was going to be fine.

CHAPTER 126

———— ☾ ————

B AILEY HAD NOT HEARD FROM LEVI SINCE HE WALKED OUT of her hotel room four nights earlier with over a million dollars. Then he unexpectedly called and asked her to get the old folks together so he could talk to everyone. She was astonished at how nonchalant he was on the phone, offering no explanations or apologies.

The old-timers had already made peace with their lost fortune and understood Bailey's intentions. Now they all were worried about Walter. A police detective had been asking serious questions, and Sam was certain an arrest was imminent, regardless of what anyone said or did. Had the events of two days ago with Moon Pie not distracted the police force, it probably would have occurred already.

Mostly out of curiosity, they all gathered at the long table in the Henry Clay library, sitting patiently while they awaited Levi's arrival. Walter was secretly planning to flee, though he hadn't quite figured out all the details, since he lived month to month on his social security check. Sebastian didn't think Levi would show and was very vocal about it. Bernard didn't care. He was more interested in watching *Dancing with the Stars* than in anything Levi might have to say.

Moon Pie's death had been a shock because they felt they had set in motion the events that contributed to it. The more details they read in the newspaper about Jake Crosby and Moon Pie, the more shaken they became, especially Walter. They had been playing with more than they could have imagined. They also learned that Levi was Moon Pie's half brother. While Bailey assured them that Levi wasn't capable of Moon Pie's violence, they couldn't ignore that Levi had taken the money and that he was a blood relation to Moon Pie. His wanting to meet with them in public, however, helped to calm everyone's nerves a bit. Sebastian wasn't taking any chances. He had a pistol in his pocket.

When Levi walked into the library, the room fell silent. Bailey folded her arms defensively. All were curious as to what was in the travel bag he carried.

Levi stood at the end of the table and smiled at everyone before placing the bag on the floor. Everyone's eyes followed his movements. The bag was expensive looking. Only Bailey recognized it as hers, which really pissed her off.

"Thank you all for comin'," he said awkwardly and then took a seat. He quickly looked around to ensure no one else was in the room. He then smiled at Bailey, who wanted to smile back but didn't.

"It's been a rough few days. I suppose y'all heard about my brother?" he asked.

Everyone simply nodded, since no one knew what to say and they were all glad that Moon Pie was dead.

Levi sensed this, quickly saying, "Look, I know that Moon Pie was nothing but a criminal. I also know that I was headed down that same road. All my life, I really wanted his approval... which I could never get. And now I know that was a good thing. Just before he died, I really had a change of heart, and that was mostly due to Bailey. She showed me a better way...a way to be better. That's it. That's what I'm tryin' to do, and now I'm here for you, if you wanna give me a chance. Bailey, I'm...I'm like that

Rascal Flatts song you like so much, 'Changed.' I'm changed." He looked at Bailey and blushed slightly.

The group nodded in response, and each made encouraging comments or remarks, except Bailey.

Levi exhaled deeply and continued, "Bailey told me about why y'all took the money. I know each of your stories and your reasons. I'm not mad about any of that. But I couldn't let y'all keep that nine hundred thousand dollars. That money woulda gotten me killed...and probably y'all too. It belongs to some seriously mean Mexican drug dealers. It's a long story, but I've already given them their money back."

Walter jumped in, "Levi, we didn't know. I mean, we knew we were stealing...but we didn't know what we were stealin' and what the blowback from it was gonna be."

"I understand." Levi looked around again to confirm that no one had walked into the big room.

Bailey studied him. She saw a man trying to make things right, not a man trying to con a bunch of old folks into or out of something. She sensed his sincerity, and she liked it.

"Okay, I've got a proposal for y'all," he said, scanning their faces. Each one either leaned in or sat up straight, indicating he had their full attention. He pressed on: "Inside this bag is a box with the exact amount of money that y'all...let's say, acquired from Kroger. Let's get the attorney Bailey told me about to return it and get Mr. Walter out of hot water." Levi noticed the relief on Walter's face, and the rest wholeheartedly nodded their agreement.

"After the smoke clears, that leaves a little over three hundred thousand dollars in cash that was Moon Pie's. So here's my idea. Each of you four, plus me, gets forty grand apiece—free and clear—to do with whatever we want. Spend it on yourselves, help out a family member, pay for someone's school—whatever. It's up to you."

Bailey realized she was being left out. Watching the others' reactions, she remembered how the money had made her crazy. *Maybe Levi knows*, she thought.

Levi continued, "And," he looked at Bailey, "I propose that we take the balance—one hundred grand—and invest it in Bailey and her clothing designs. Let's put her in business, and we'll all own a piece. I checked, and there's a small vacant store right down the street. We can work outta there. We can get her a website built, and she can be right here, designin', makin', and sellin' dresses all over the world! It'll give each of y'all something to do every day, and, well, I just think after all Bailey's been through, she deserves a shot and we can give it to her!"

Bailey was shocked and almost in tears. She looked around, and everybody seemed to think it was a great idea. She ran around the table and hugged Levi. Even if nobody else wanted to invest in her dream, she was impressed with the gesture and Levi's sincerity. All she really wanted was Levi. After what he had done, she knew she could be happy with him.

"I thought you stole the money and left for good."

"No way! I knew that I needed to make things right before one of us got killed. I got really busy and focused trying to get things settled with the Mexicans. They had come to town lookin' for me. But that's done. They're gone, and now I'm here for you, if you wanna give me a chance."

"Ya know," Bernard interrupted eagerly, "I bet we could get a whole bunch of women from all over the city to sew for us!"

"I've heard there's a lot of markup in clothing. We could make a killin'," Sebastian added.

Lucille watched Bailey's obvious excitement and feelings toward Levi. She stood, touching him on the arm. "I think it's a wonderful idea, Levi. I'm so proud of you."

Walter stood and said, "I love Southern styles. Mississippi dresses will be a hit. We've got a whole lot to do!"

Levi smiled at everyone's enthusiasm. He leaned into Walter's ear and whispered, "Mr. Walter...you can't leave town for the next several days. In fact, you need to make sure that you're seen every day."

Walter cocked his head suspiciously. "Why?"

"I made a deal with those Mexican drug dealers that I would return all of the money on the condition that a certain someone's ex-son-in-law receives a little of what he's been dishing out…and if something permanent happened, then that would be fine. It's goin' down this week."

Walter looked up at Levi, remembering why he had started the whole project. He thought of all the wrongs he had done. He thought of his daughter's suffering and life cut painfully short. He smiled thinking of his wife and what she would want—of her strong moral compass even in their darkest hours.

He placed a fresh, unlit cigar in the corner of his mouth and said assertively, "Thanks, but call it off, son. He'll get what's comin' to him."

ONE YEAR LATER

———— ☾ ————

J AKE CROSBY SLOWLY RECUPERATED FROM HIS NIGHTMARE IN the pipe. There were some complications with his fractured leg, but after three surgeries, it finally healed. He and Morgan welcomed Kendall, another beautiful daughter, into the world. With Morgan's blessing, Jake started searching for a career that interested him. With legal assistance from Sam, the insurance company finally paid the Crosbys' claim for the fire-destroyed river cabin, and they plan to rebuild with an extra bedroom.

Katy Crosby won the Mississippi Spelling Bee for her age, correctly spelling *catamaran*. She was so relieved and proud that her dad had killed Moon Pie that she never again spoke to another counselor.

R. C. Smithson finally replied to Jake's calls and e-mails. He claimed to have been beaten up by three different jealous boyfriends at the same time. He wished he had been there for Jake.

Moon Pie was buried next to his momma in a tiny cemetery outside Noxapater, Mississippi. Levi had him dressed in his autographed Peyton Manning jersey. Levi was the only person at the funeral.

One day after returning from Tupelo, Tam was arrested when his car was broadsided by an elderly couple going to swing-dancing lessons. Tam was pinned and couldn't escape. An observant Biloxi police officer got the glory. The Mississippi Drug Task Force happily moved on to their next target.

Alexa became a bikini model for a start-up swimwear company based in Pensacola, Florida. She still hasn't missed a Rascal Flatts concert anywhere within three states.

Bailey continued her college education at the W, making the dean's list the last two semesters. The dress shop has been an Internet success. Her Mississippi-made dresses have become fashionable with college girls around the country. Projected sales for next year are just over $800,000. Watch any SEC football game, and you'll probably see a host of smiling sorority girls wearing her designs.

Lucille, Walter, Sebastian, and Bernard are at the shop every day. Lucille deals with all the orders. Walter manages the money. Sebastian stays busy managing operations, and Bernard manages the six ladies who sew for them. He takes them all to lunch every day at the Ritz and tries to expense it. He also started a scholarship fund in his dad's name at his high school.

Samantha's legal career spiraled up when Kroger decided to put her on retainer. She recently moved into nicer offices. Her totally refurbished antebellum home is now on the Columbus Spring Pilgrimage, and Tom the cat sometimes tolerates the sightseers.

The First Baptist Church and First Methodist Church in West Point received significant donations earmarked to help the poor. Nobody ever determined where the money came from.

The two grave robbers finally explained their true reason for being in the woods that night. Although they were in serious trouble, the judge took into consideration their heroics in saving Jake's life. They received lifetime prohibition from all Corps of Engineers properties, and Warden Gran demanded that each man spend three weeks working with the community liaisons from two Indian nations. They continued to volunteer beyond their mandated service, working with the tribes to identify potential archaeological sites for preservation.

The Tennessee Mexicans, relieved to have their money returned, sent Levi a $25,000 cashier's check as a finder's fee. Julio joined Old Waverly Golf Club and spends many weekends relaxing by the pool and in the clubhouse.

Levi used the cashier's check for a down payment on an A-frame cabin on the Tombigbee River. He proposed to Bailey, and they are planning a small wedding as soon as she graduates. In the meantime, Levi works as a groundskeeper at the historic Waverley Mansion, an antebellum showplace, and he is taking care of Mississippi's oldest magnolia tree. He's also carrying a full load at Mississippi State.

Moon Pie's taxidermist buddy was arrested during a raid. He was charged with possession of illegally taken animals. He was subsequently charged with sixty-one violations of the Lacey Act after agreeing to mount a spotted owl for an undercover officer.

The mounted African lion from the Gold Mine was returned to its owner just in time for his wife to demand it in the divorce.

Sebastian had his prostate removed and takes his medicine religiously. He's looking forward to his son's arrival home after serving his country in Iraq and Afghanistan.

Two months after Walter asked Levi to call off the Mexicans, he received news that his former son-in-law had been run over and killed by his current wife in their driveway. She was wearing giant sunglasses to hide a black eye as she explained to the police that her car had a mysterious acceleration problem.

ACKNOWLEDGMENTS

———— ☾ ————

THERE ARE SO MANY PEOPLE TO WHOM I OWE A HUGE DEBT of gratitude.

Kyle Jennings and his wife, Jill Conner Browne, have personally made my books possible. A simple thank-you doesn't seem enough for all they have done.

I offer special thanks to all the folks at Amazon Publishing, particularly Terry Goodman for believing in and supporting my stories, and the various Author Teams, editors, and supporting staff—consisting of Sarah Tomashek, Katie Finch Rinella, Jessica Poore, Jacque Ben-Zekry, Rory Connell, Danielle Marshall, Reema Al-Zaben, Kaila Lightner, Justin Golenbock, Kathryn Rogers, Amanda Price, and Alan Turkus—who have worked tirelessly on and for my books. I really appreciate their efforts. And to Sarah Burningham at Little Bird Publicity, who did a wonderful job garnering press and exposure for *The Dummy Line*.

My wife, Melissa, is nothing short of a saint for putting up with me. I know it's not easy. She also struggles to keep me from dangling my participles. I love her more than I can say with words.

My beautiful daughter seems to enjoy the "Dad writes books" experience. She has traveled with me to select book signings and somehow manages to make the torturous experience of being an unknown author trying to sell a book fun. Also, I'll never forget her enthusiastic telephone call to a radio show that I was on, promoting my first book. It was the only call we received, and it made my day. Thanks, Jessi, for the great memories. I love you!

I thank and deeply appreciate my mother, Peggy Cole, for all her love and support. She deserves a medal. (Mom, I apologize for my characters' profanity.)

My sisters, Barbara Bryan and Deborah Speigner, are the best sisters a brother could expect. Maybe one day I'll write a story that doesn't prompt their friends to ask, "Was Bobby a normal child?"

I am profoundly appreciative of my family at Mossy Oak, who have been incredibly supportive of my storytelling attempts. I especially wish to thank Toxey Haas, who has always been there for me. I also want to thank Mr. Fox Haas, Bill Sugg, Ronnie Strickland, Lannie Wallace, Chris Hawley, Ben Maki, Chris Paradise, Asif Sakhawat, Rob Barefield, Cindy Cliett, Larry Moore, Pat Epling, Neill Haas, Daniel Haas, Vandy Stubbs, Jordan LaSuzzo, Blake Hamilton, Jesse Raley, Norman Sneed, Jason Cleveland, Austin Delano, Dudley Phelps, Todd Amenrud, Phil Barker, Carey Sizemore, Bob Turner, Greg Tinsley, Joedee Henry, Jacopo Re, Tim Anderson, Greg Briggs, Patricia Fulgham, Lynne Schubert, Resa Vickers, Erin Molino, Joe Bush, Mark Drury, Terry Drury, Matt Drury, the entire Drury team, and Mossy Oak's newest family member, Gary Levox.

Roger Pangle, Tommy Paulk, James Fudge, Al Cheatham, Jim Allen, Tim Wood, John Curtis, Russell Gibbs, Doug Dean, David Westmoreland, John Gilbert, Sonny Jameson, Connie Hudson, Lucille Armstrong, David Westmoreland, Bruce Hudalla, Eddie Gran, Brett Bainter, Mary Ella Marshall, and Clay Worden also deserve thanks for their support.

Mick Plummer and Roger West hosted my first book signing, at a *tiny* country store in Mountain Grove, Missouri. We sold out of books and had loads of fun doing it. Thanks for that and for your continued support.

Justin "Moon Pie" Davis deserves thanks for allowing me to borrow his nickname. He's a great guy, nothing like the Moon Pie in my stories.

Special thanks goes to the countless readers of *The Dummy Line* who took time to find my e-mail address and contact me. Now you can reach me on Facebook, at Bobby Cole Books.

My writing efforts have forced several friends to suffer—not always quietly—through reading rough drafts. Thanks to Traci LaChance, Carsie Young, Jon Sverson, Ladonna Helveston, Tim Brooks, Dr. Bill Billington, Scott Ross, Robbie Upright, and Art Shirley for your time and helpful comments.

Danny Young, Rusty Faulk, Todd Smith, Russell Thornberry, John Staff, Bill Miller, and David Maas went out of their way to spread the word about *The Dummy Line*. Thanks, guys.

There are many independent booksellers still "hand-selling" *The Dummy Line* to their clientele. I *really* appreciate your efforts!

Finally, a big thank-you to all of you who told friends and family about my writings, e-mailed links, gave books as gifts, invited me to book clubs, and encouraged me at every opportunity. I could never name everyone, but you know who you are. It's my sincere hope that you enjoy this story too.

ABOUT THE AUTHOR

Bobby Cole is a native of Montgomery, Alabama, and president of Mossy Oak® Biologic®. Additionally, he is an avid wildlife manager, hunter, and active supporter of the Catch-A-Dream™ Foundation. He lives with his wife and daughter in West Point, Mississippi. Bobby is also the author of the novel *The Dummy Line.*